Wayne Williams has been writing, editing and publishing magazines for over 23 years. Until September 2005 he was the co-owner and Editorial Director of Live Publishing, an independent magazine publisher based in South Manchester. He is now a full-time freelance writer, focusing on his twin passions of technology and travel.

Darren Allan studied history and philosophy at York University, before joining a popular home computing magazine, eventually becoming an editor. In 1999, he left to pursue a career as a full-time freelance journalist writing for an array of technology and video-game-related publications, also taking a year out to travel the world.

They have collaborated on two previous non-fiction books. This is their first novel.

I KNOW WHAT YOU DID LAST SUPPER

WAYNE WILLIAMS & DARREN ALLAN

To Romay

Hope you enjoy the book !

D Allen

piatkus

PIATKUS

First published in Great Britain as a paperback original in 2013 by Piatkus

Copyright © 2012 by Wayne Williams and Darren Allan

The moral right of the author has been asserted.

A CIP catalogue record for this book
is available from the British Library.

ISBN 978-0-7499-5887-9

Typeset in Caslon by M Rules
Printed and bound in Great Britain by
Clays Ltd, St Ives plc

Papers used by Piatkus are from well-managed forests
and other responsible sources.

MIX
Paper from
responsible sources
FSC® C104740

Piatkus
An imprint of
Little, Brown Book Group
100 Victoria Embankment
London EC4Y 0DY

An Hachette UK Company
www.hachette.co.uk

www.piatkus.co.uk

I

GENESIS

Chapter 1

Caiaphas pulled out a chair and sat down heavily. He stared across at Judas Iscariot for a while, eyes unblinking, before leaning forward and placing his elbows on the table.

'You are willing to go through with this?' the fat high priest asked.

Judas nodded. The hour was late, the room lit by a solitary oil lamp which struggled to cast his shadow on the wall.

'Good. We will only have one chance to arrest him. One chance. You must not fail the Sanhedrin. You understand this?'

Judas nodded again, his locks bobbing as he did so. His medium-length hair was the darkest of blacks, thick and tightly curled. It spilled out onto the side of his cheeks, where it tumbled down like an inky waterfall into an equally dense beard.

'When the time comes, you will identify him to us with a single kiss.'

'A kiss?'

'Yes.'

'Is that not rather –'

'Not rather what?'

'Unnecessary?'

Caiaphas sat back, the chair cracking under his bulk as he did so. The darkness seemed to eat at his face as he leaned away, leaving just the hooked nose and two beady, hawk-like eyes visible. Eyes which now burned with annoyance.

'You will greet him as I have indicated,' the priest said. 'We need it to be a kiss.' He leaned forward. 'You understand?'

Judas didn't understand. At all. He was fairly sure most members of the Sanhedrin council would recognise Jesus anyway. It's not as if he wasn't well known to them. The theatrics of the betrayal seemed designed just to make an unpleasant situation even more hurtful. But there was nothing to be gained from arguing. He needed the money desperately. So if the Sanhedrin wanted a kiss, then a kiss it would have to be.

'Very well,' he said, and waited for the high priest to continue.

The two men sat in silence for a while. Judas's forefinger traced the outline of the crescent moon-shaped birthmark on his neck, around and around.

'The money?' he asked eventually.

'You will get your twenty pieces of silver once the act is complete. Now if that is all?'

'I think we agreed thirty?' Judas said, his voice wavering a little.

'We agreed twenty.'

'I think thirty is fairer. You're asking me to betray my teacher and friend. Thirty for a kiss. It's fair.'

The priest shook his head slowly.

'This man, this Nazarene, is dangerous, Judas. He has delusions. I hear he proclaims himself to be the son of God. The son of God! He must answer for this blasphemy and with your help, he will. Do this and you will forever be regarded as a hero.

Knowing you have helped us to … deal with the problem should be reward enough, but yes, you shall have your thirty pieces of silver, Judas Iscariot. Just make sure you earn them.'

The fat priest leaned back, indicating the conversation was over. His wooden chair creaked and popped in the darkness. Judas prayed hard that one of the legs would snap and send the pompous fool crashing to the ground, but nothing happened. God, it seemed, was not listening to him.

Chapter 2

She stumbled forward, her hand flailing out towards the chair she knew to be there. Grasping its arm, she collapsed into the seat, her head spinning.

Her world, normally one of darkness, had sprung alive with a giddying array of visions, knowings, voices.

Fierce orange flames burned against the black canvas.

A single word came from beyond the void, each syllable choked with rage.

'Suffering.'

A limb appeared in the blazing tendrils of flame. She could smell the air thick with the stench of burning flesh, hear the skin as it slowly split, the crackle of the fat underneath as it oozed forth and spat under the searing heat.

The vision faded, the fire dimmed, but the spitting and hissing of flesh remained, slowly morphing into a whistling noise which grew stronger, louder. It became a screaming which tore against her eardrums. The sobbing shrieks of a young woman violated in the most horrific manner.

An underlying sound was now audible. The rhythmical rasp of metal sawing through bone. Another image formed, a man being cleaved down his ...

The old crone gasped in a breath as the brutal cacophony ceased, the visions of death finally relenting. There would be many of them. Each more terrible than the last.

So many victims. Such pain and torment. She could sense it was close at hand ...

Chapter 3

Jesus raised the polished wooden grail and drank deeply from it. His face remained, as always, a mask of quiet serenity.

Judas had always thought it was his master's skin which gave his countenance such a peaceful appearance. Jesus spent many, many hours outdoors – travelling, teaching, counselling and healing – yet despite the light golden tan he bore, his skin wasn't weathered by the sun as it should have been. There wasn't a single line upon it, his complexion fresh and untroubled by the tracks of worry which life normally etched across the adult face.

Jesus supped from the grail once again. When he lowered the cup Judas could see the wine had stained his master's top lip ruby red. A flick of the tongue and the colour was gone. Nothing about the action was unusual. Everyone else was partaking of wine in the same manner. To his right, Judas could see Thomas raising his cup and drinking exactly as Jesus had seconds before.

And yet . . .

Miracles like walking on water and raising the dead were awe-inspiring and breathtaking, but watching Jesus perform everyday actions – eating, drinking, sleeping – had always seemed just as profound to Judas.

That had been the case ever since he'd met his master. He was passing through the village of Emmaus, around ten miles west of Jerusalem, when he first encountered Jesus. There had been a landslide, and a huge boulder had tumbled down a slope, smashing into some poor fellow's house and crushing half of it. Judas tried to help Jacob, the owner, and his friends lever the rock out of his home, but it was so massive that this had proved an impossible task.

Then they noticed a man approaching the dwelling, his stride long and purposeful. He held himself noticeably upright, a bearing that made him seem taller than his already above-average height. Russet brown, shoulder-length hair framed his face, which tapered down to a pointed chin neatly outlined with trimmed bristles.

Jacob's friends had looked bemused when Jesus said he could help, and asked them to stand back. They motioned him through, sniggering as he passed them. Judas, however, wasn't laughing.

Jesus approached the boulder, and stood directly behind it.

'Would you help me push, friend?' he asked, motioning Judas to come over.

'I don't know what on Earth you're thinking, but there's no way we can move that rock,' Judas had replied.

'Please. Indulge me.'

Judas did as he was bid, placed his hands on the boulder, and began to exert himself. The stone was so heavy, he might as well have been pushing against a mountain. Then Jesus laid his palms on it. The boulder jolted, and began to roll slowly forwards.

The other men stood mesmerised.

The rock seemed to have lost all its weight, and while it still looked perfectly solid, Judas could feel the stone vibrating wildly beneath his hands. Judders ran up his arms, through his chest, into his skull, yet the tremors didn't grate in his bones, they seemed to resonate throughout his body like the most delicately plucked harp chord.

They pushed the rock onwards. Through joyously teary eyes, Judas looked across and saw that Jesus's hands weren't even touching the boulder. They hovered a short distance away from it.

When the stone was clear of the dwelling, the vibrations ceased as Jesus lowered his hands. The massive rock reverted to its previous density, solid and immovable.

Jesus then promised to help rebuild the house, and Jacob prostrated himself at his saviour's feet in thanks. The men gathered materials, cypress wood beams, tools and ladders, and set about repairing the broken walls and roof.

Judas worked on the ladder next to Jesus, hammering nail after nail into the wood. The other folks dared not speak to him, merely whispering among themselves about the man who had worked a miracle, but after a while, Judas had to ask what they were all thinking.

'Why don't you use your powers to fix this beam into place?'

'The rock, I could not move with my bare hands alone,' Jesus had replied. 'But the nails, I can hammer. As can Jacob.' He turned to face Judas directly. 'As can you. There is a lesson to be learned in the nails.'

In the presence of Jesus, Judas found his work seemed to gain clarity, a focus, as if he was fully and completely dissolved into the action of driving each nail home. As if that was all there was in the world. Judas felt different inside – calmer, more relaxed. His everyday cares and worries ebbing away to nothing.

It was a sublime release. He worked harder still, beads of sweat clustered on his face, but a joyful feeling bloomed deep in his gut.

When they were done, Judas lay down, exhausted and spent, yet numb with a kind of ... ecstasy. He'd never forgotten the words Jesus had spoken as he'd placed one hand on Judas's aching shoulder.

'Whether a nail is hammered, or a king is crowned, everything is just an experience. This is the true path of life. It is not what you do, but how you do it that matters.'

And so it was with Jesus. It wasn't just the miracles, but also the nails.

Each simple breath, word, movement of his master all carried an equal significance. Every moment of his life shone with an empyreal vitality. When Jesus ate lamb and washed it down with wine, he wasn't merely feeding his own body; he was nourishing the whole of humanity.

Judas left the village of Emmaus with Jesus, and had been a steadfast follower ever since. The potent memory of his experience at Jacob's house had always remained with him, but this evening, it seemed much weaker and more distant.

'Are you not eating?' Thomas said.

The question jolted Judas from his introspection. He stared over at his fellow apostle, and then let his gaze wander across the considerable feast laid out on the table in front of him. Jugs of dark red wine stood alongside loaves of flatbread, roasted lamb and scatterings of greenery; lettuce, watercress and parsley. The enticing smell of lamb intermingled with freshly baked bread hung in the air, but food was not on his mind. Tonight was not about enjoying himself. Tonight was about betrayal, and Judas felt sick to his stomach.

By way of an answer, and to placate his friend, he reached

over and gathered some parsley, which he dipped in a bowl of salt water before chewing slowly. Judas turned back to Thomas, but he was now talking to John.

All twelve apostles had been gathered together for this meal in a sparsely furnished room on the upper floor of a house in Jerusalem. Its stark white walls were punctuated by hanging green tapestries, woven with simple patterns in gold thread. The apostles sat around a low table, reclining on cushions or perched on short stools, gathered either side of Jesus.

Throughout the evening Judas had found himself feigning laughter at Philip's attempts at humour, listening to Thomas bickering with Bartholomew, and just generally trying to behave as if everything was normal. As if this was just another ordinary day. When it was manifestly anything but.

Jesus stood, drawing the gaze of every single apostle as he did so. Quiet descended on the room, the only audible noise coming from the large bowl-shaped lamp which was suspended on a long chain from the high ceiling. Twin flames wavered on opposite sides of the vessel, whispering to each other in brittle crackles.

Jesus shed his robe down to his waist, the doubled-up folds of the mauve-coloured material rustling against his legs as he walked a couple of paces to pick up a nearby bowl of water.

He took a white linen towel, tied it around his midriff, and then one by one he thoroughly washed the feet of each apostle, carefully dabbing them dry with the towel afterwards. Judas said nothing when it came to his turn, he simply willed it to be over quickly. What he had to do later tonight would be difficult enough without additional kindnesses such as this.

Of all the apostles, only one spoke when Jesus kneeled in front of him with the bowl.

'I refuse to let you wash my feet, master,' Peter said, crossing his legs underneath him.

'I do this with good reason, I assure you. You must let me cleanse you, Peter.'

After a few moments of hesitation, the apostle acquiesced.

When he had finished, Jesus sat back down and said, 'Do you understand why I have done this?' He paused, but no answer was forthcoming. 'I have washed your feet, even though you consider me your master, because every man should selflessly serve others. You should wash each other's feet. That stranger, that beggar in the street – you should wash his feet, or her feet.'

'Everyone is equal,' Bartholomew said.

'Exactly. Nobody, not even me, is master over anyone.'

Down the row of apostles Judas could see Matthew diligently recording everything Jesus said, scribbling on a piece of parchment with his inky quill.

'But you're the son of God, aren't you?' Thomas said. 'I think that makes you rather special.'

'We all carry the light of creation, Thomas. We all carry the light of God within us at a fundamental level, whether it is awakened, or not.'

Thomas nodded, a slight and not entirely convincing tilt of the head.

Judas let the to and fro of the conversation that followed wash over him. The gathered apostles were questioning, debating and philosophising as always and it was strange to watch them carrying on as normal, so blissfully unaware of the actions that he was about to set in motion. Jesus seemed no different in this respect. Like those around him he had absolutely no idea of what was to come. Perhaps he wasn't quite so sagacious after all.

Judas cast a glance in his master's direction and watched as Jesus stood again and cleared his throat. All talking respectfully ceased. 'This meal with you tonight,' he began, 'will be our last supper together.'

13

'Last?' Peter said.

Judas felt his body stiffen, his breath caught in his throat.

'Yes. For one of you, sat at this very table now, is going to betray me.'

'Surely not!' Peter cried out.

The room burst into life as every apostle began speaking at once. Heat spread across Judas's cheeks, his mind a whirlpool of questions. How could Jesus know? Had someone told him? Who ... ? He pushed those thoughts away, momentarily, to concentrate on muttering his own protestations, looking around the table as if trying to identify the would-be betrayer. Thomas reached over and grabbed his arm with long, bony fingers. A gesture intended to reassure himself as much as his friend.

'Enough,' Jesus said, his voice cutting the chatter dead. 'I am to suffer. But he who brings this betrayal will suffer far, far more. He will wish that he had never been born.'

There was a period of uneasy quiet as the apostles tried to absorb what their teacher was saying. Judas's heart was beating so loudly he was convinced that everyone in the room could hear it. He pulled his arm away from Thomas so the apostle wouldn't feel the rush of blood thundering through his veins.

He felt sick, but he had to hide it. If anything, the necessity to conceal it made the nausea worse. Could he still go through with all of this, with Jesus somehow knowing, or having been warned, a betrayal was coming? Did that make any difference? He couldn't think straight. He needed some air.

Still the question persisted ... could he do this?

Could he betray his teacher, his master, his friend?

A simple image flashed into his mind in reply. His uncle's face. Streaked with blood.

He didn't have a choice.

His eyes were drawn to a pair of nails, the heads of which

were visible on the corner of the table. Was it a sign? A timely reminder to focus on the task at hand, one nail at a time. One step at a time.

It is not what you do – but how you do it that matters.

And sometimes, why you do it.

Judas looked up as his master leaned forward and took a hunk of bread from the table. Blessing it in the name of the Lord, Jesus broke the bread and passed it around to the apostles, saying, 'This bread represents my body, which I give to you. And when you eat it, remember me.'

He then took a cup, filled it with wine, and passed that around saying, 'This wine represents my blood, of which you must take your fill. And when you drink it, remember me.'

The meal continued in a very subdued mood. Judas, heart still racing, excused himself as quickly as he felt prudent, saying that he had some urgent business to attend to. No one questioned his departure. As he was leaving he heard Jesus say to Peter, 'When we have finished eating we must take a stroll. First to the Mount of Olives, then afterwards to the garden at Gethsemane.'

Chapter 4

As the stone wall surrounding the garden came into view, Judas Iscariot began to reflect on the path that had led him here. Not the long and winding one, strewn with occasional rocks that had conspired to trip him up along the way, but rather the path he had most recently chosen through life.

Jesus was a good man. No, he was a great man. He was the man Judas would like to have been, if things had been different. If he'd been born to a virgin mother, a deity father, and blessed with a divinity that shone from within, for example. Jesus made him aspire to be a better man, and here he was about to betray him. To give up the son of God for thirty pieces of silver.

Judas shook his head. This was all his Uncle Daniel's fault. Daniel and his stupid gambling habit. His uncle had always suffered from a weakness for the dice, an addiction that was never going to end well, but the trouble he'd managed to get himself into this time around went beyond belief.

The grey-haired man carrying a burning torch out in front of Judas stopped and turned, wheezing lightly, and momentarily unable to speak. The uphill walk hadn't caused Judas to break so much as a sweat. He was fit, even for a man still in his late twenties, his lean legs well used to walking long distances when following the ministry of Jesus, and spreading his word.

'We're here,' the man eventually managed to gasp. Judas was well aware of that fact. The apostles visited Gethsemane regularly – sometimes individually, often as a group – to pray or just to enjoy the peacefulness among the whispering leaves.

Judas looked back at the group of followers behind him. The mob, bearing torches and weapons, was made up of Roman soldiers, Sanhedrin temple guards, and various servants of the priests armed with makeshift staves.

They had all stopped, every one of them now staring at him expectantly. Judas turned his attention back to the garden, and scanned the familiar lines of olive trees which were intersected by narrow dirt paths marked out using small rocks. He could see well enough, just about, by the light of Thursday night's full moon, coupled with the glow from the many torches carried by the crowd.

It wasn't long before he spotted what he thought was his master, standing along with several others to the side of the shed which housed the olive press, underneath one of the older olive trees with its impossibly thick and gnarled grey trunk. He moved a little closer, until he could be certain it was Jesus. The messiah appeared to be animatedly imparting wisdom to Peter, John, and James the Greater. Or berating them for something, perhaps . . .

'That's him,' Judas said, pointing. No one moved. 'In the middle there, that's him. The one holding up his hands.'

Malchus, the bull-necked right-hand man of the high priest Caiaphas, took a step closer to Judas, faint traces of sweat glistening on his bald head. 'Identify him as agreed,' he growled.

The menace in his voice was as unmistakeable as the madness in his eyes.

Judas took a slow, measured breath, trying to calm his thudding heart. He could do this. Jesus knew this moment was coming. He had said that one of his apostles was about to betray him, and if he knew that then maybe he even knew it would be Judas.

'All right, let's go,' he said, and set off towards Jesus, his band of followers trailing a short distance behind.

The chain of events that had led to this moment had begun last week when Daniel had come to see him. Judas had been with Jesus and the apostles at a gathering to celebrate Lazarus's return from the dead. Desperate and in tears, his uncle had confessed to owing a small fortune to a fierce war veteran known as 'the Butcher', a grizzled ex-gladiator renowned for his short temper and fast blade. What the hell Daniel had been thinking gambling with such a man, Judas didn't know, but the Butcher had a unique – and persuasive – method of dealing with debtors.

He'd promised Daniel that if he didn't receive the money he was owed by the end of Passover, he would chop off both of the unfortunate gambler's arms. And then his legs, and finally his head. Those body parts would then be delivered to his close family, the likes of his wife, daughter, and his brother Simon, Judas's father.

Daniel, not wishing to worry his immediate family, had begged his nephew for help, but of course Judas didn't have anywhere near enough coins. He didn't even have anything to sell, or anything of value for that matter. Except Jesus's friendship. Which, as it happened, was something Caiaphas and the Sanhedrin were prepared to pay handsomely for.

As they drew near, Jesus looked up and said something to

the apostles. They all turned to see Judas and his crowd approaching.

When they were just feet away, Judas stopped and looked at his teacher. While Jesus appeared calm on the outside, his eyes told a different story. Their usual piercing powder-blue clarity was enervated by a dreadful knowing sadness that seemed to encompass all of the grief and misery in the world. Doubt tore through Judas and for a second he contemplated pointing out Peter instead, but he knew the deception would be short-lived.

He tried to tell himself that betraying Jesus wasn't a big deal. He'd sought assurances from the Sanhedrin regarding his master's treatment, and was told he was to be arrested and then questioned. That was all. What Caiaphas's word was actually worth was another entirely different matter. There were darker motives at work, no doubt. Yet whatever the Sanhedrin had planned, they'd clearly underestimated Jesus and the extent of his powers. He could conjure miracles. What sort of jail could hold his master, when he was capable of collapsing the four walls around him by his very will? Jesus would surely escape, and life would continue as always.

It would be the Sanhedrin who were betrayed then. The council would look like fools, having paid him thirty pieces of silver for nothing. When it was all over and the dust had settled, Judas was sure his friend would forgive him. Forgiveness was his thing, after all.

Even if he didn't, even if Jesus cast Judas out of the apostles and the group turned their backs on him forever, he still had to do this for Daniel. He couldn't let his uncle die. He couldn't bear the thought of his father opening the front door one morning, and seeing his brother's bloodied, severed head staring up at him.

Those thirty pieces of silver would prevent all that. They'd save a life, and immeasurable heartache. Surely that was something his master would understand.

'Friend, do what you are here to do,' Jesus said. The sadness in his eyes vanished as he spoke, replaced by a steely resolve.

'I ...' Judas wanted to speak, wanted to explain, but the words turned to ashes on his tongue. He felt worthless and ashamed, but grateful too. Jesus had been expecting this. Unless Judas was mistaken he even seemed to be willing him on. Perhaps he knew why Judas was doing this. Perhaps he did understand.

A hard shove came from behind, Malchus no doubt, and he stumbled forward. Jesus put out a hand to stop him falling and overwhelmed with gratitude – *Friend, do what you are here to do* – Judas embraced and kissed him hard.

The kiss felt right and natural. He stepped back, his part in this complicit act of betrayal complete. Jesus looked a little surprised.

'Judas, are you betraying the son of man with a kiss?' he asked.

Then total chaos erupted around them.

'That's him!' a voice shouted from somewhere to the right of Judas.

'Arrest him!' another voice shouted, or it might have been the same one.

The temple guards surged forward and grabbed Jesus. Judas was pushed out of the way, and through a gap between the backs of two soldiers he saw Peter leap into the fray, a sword in his hand. He watched the blade flash in the moonlight and heard someone yell in pain. The soldiers fell back briefly to reveal Malchus clutching at one side of his head with a crimson hand.

20

'Stop,' Jesus commanded. It wasn't immediately clear who he was addressing, but the effect was electric. Everyone froze and fell silent. 'All who live by the sword shall die by the sword,' Jesus said to Peter. 'Put down your weapon and cease your resistance.'

Peter lowered his head and his sword. Jesus placed one tender hand on Malchus's wound and at once the bleeding stopped. The man's ear, which Judas could have sworn had been hacked clean off, was whole again.

After a little awkward shuffling and some muted apologies, the band of soldiers led Jesus away, with the three apostles following a short distance behind. Malchus kept touching his ear as they walked, almost as if expecting it to fall off again at any moment.

When they had left Judas looked around the now empty garden. The shadows looming from the walls and ancient trees seemed somehow darker, more dense. He pulled his robe tightly around him to ward off the chill that had arrived out of nowhere, and began the slow, lonely walk back the way he had come.

Chapter 5

They called the hill Golgotha; the place of the skull.

When the steep face of the mount was viewed head-on, two large sunken holes formed what looked like the dark eyes of a jagged skull, staring across at the west wall of Jerusalem as if in constant brooding judgement of the people within.

Golgotha's name was also partially derived from its role as a place of execution.

Three crosses were atop the summit today. Hiding in a copse partway up the gently sloping side of the hill, Judas stared up at the wooden constructions and tried to work out which of the figures being crucified was Jesus. The angle of the nearest cross pretty much obscured the view of the other two and the distance added a further layer of uncertainty, making identifying his master all but impossible from here.

It was hard to know exactly how long the trio of unfortunates had been nailed to their wooden torture posts, but two or three hours seemed a reasonable guess. Hours that must have dragged past like days.

A sizeable crowd of spectators had gathered around the

crosses and their shouts carried to Judas on the wind. Some questioned the messiah's powers. Others bellowed outright taunts, every word of which dragged like barbs through Judas, cutting him to the core.

How had it come to this?

Following Jesus's arrest the previous evening, events had unfurled at a sickening pace. To begin with, his master had been interrogated by Caiaphas's father-in-law Annas, a former high priest who still held much sway in Jerusalem, and then afterwards by Caiaphas himself.

The high priest had paid people to come forward with stories that he could use to prove Jesus's guilt. Some of the tales were patently absurd. One person said the fish that Jesus had given him after the Sermon on the Mount wasn't properly filleted, and he'd nearly choked to death when a bone had become lodged in his windpipe. Someone else claimed he'd heard Jesus threaten to tear down the temple and rebuild it in three days.

The lack of any credible evidence had enraged Caiaphas, and he'd shouted and ranted at his prisoner for hours, trying to goad him into saying something to incriminate himself. Eventually the fat priest had succeeded in getting an admission from Jesus that, yes, he was the son of God, and on the basis of that blasphemy they'd handed him over to be dealt with by the Romans.

Pontius Pilate had sentenced him to death, but reluctantly by all accounts. The governor even offered the crowd that had gathered for the feast a chance to free Jesus, but in an unlikely turn of events, they had comprehensively opted to release Barabbas instead. Barabbas the mad thug. It didn't take a genius to work out that Caiaphas was behind the notorious thief's sudden rise in popularity. They might just as well have released a rabid wolf back into the community.

Judas had heard, from two gossiping centurions, that after he was condemned, Jesus had been dressed up like a king and mocked. A crown of thorns had been placed upon his head, and he'd been brutally lashed. A scourging, delivered by a multi-stranded whip tied with pieces of bone and metal, in excess of a hundred strokes. An inconceivable amount of suffering.

Judas realised his fists had balled up, and were clenched so tightly it was painful. He made a conscious effort to relax his hands, and noticed several red lines, where the nails had dug into his palm.

He stared at the thin slivers of blood peeping through the broken skin. It should have been him who had been whipped. Flogged until he could barely stand. Mocked mercilessly. Judas felt the bile rise within him ... how could they have done that to Jesus? To him, of all people. The most gentle soul ever to have ...

His thought process trailed off as he noticed something strange happening to the light. One moment everything on the mount was bathed in bright sunshine, and the next a subtle dullness seemed to have crept over the land.

He looked up in time to see the sun's outline disappearing beneath a layer of feathery white cloud. As he stood there transfixed, more clouds began to arrive. Ash-grey in colour, these were thicker and more opaque. They were followed a short while later by heavy storm clouds which rolled in and swallowed the last of the light.

A shiver coursed the length of Judas's back and took up residency in the nape of his neck. A deluge of rain looked imminent, and the thin black robe he'd donned that morning would offer scant protection against light drizzle, let alone a serious downpour.

Fortunately, despite the thunderous nature of the clouds, it remained dry and after another hour had passed Judas made a decision. He needed to get closer. While he didn't relish the prospect of being recognised by anyone, it wasn't likely that any of Jesus's many disciples would be here. They all seemed to be keeping a low profile just as he was, albeit for entirely different reasons. No one wanted to find themselves in the same position as Jesus.

He had to get nearer and see his master on the cross, to witness for himself the extent of the horror that Jesus had been forced to endure. And he needed to be with him because ... because of the unthinkable. Because this could be the last time Judas might ever see his friend alive.

He gathered his robe around him and, keeping his head down, made his way towards the crosses, quickly blending in with the crowd of subdued onlookers that seemed to have grown tenfold since the skies had darkened.

Picking his way carefully through the mob, he caught his first glimpse of Jesus. The messiah was naked save for a white loin-cloth, and suspended from a cross twice his height. The horizontal piece of wood was so close to the top, it made the construction almost T-shaped.

A sign which read 'King of the Jews' had been affixed to the cross. Nails had been driven through Jesus's wrists, and his feet were nailed one atop the other to the upright piece of wood. Tens upon tens of deep red lines had been lashed into his blood-splattered torso and down his legs, the savage streaks peppered with torn flesh and angry welts.

His head was slumped forward and although his matted hair and a circlet of thorns partially obscured his face, Judas could see his master's eyes were tightly closed and his mouth locked in an agonised grimace.

Judas had never seen Jesus look so ... broken. Crushed. It

was a truly pitiful sight. While his own hands hadn't bloodied his friend's body raw with a flail, and he hadn't cracked through the messiah's wrists with hammered nails himself, he may as well have done. Ultimately, he was the architect of all this suffering.

True, if he hadn't betrayed Jesus the Sanhedrin might have found someone else willing to, but somehow he doubted that. Everyone close to Jesus was fiercely loyal, willing to lay down their lives for their master, and he'd given him up to pay off his uncle's stupid gambling debt. In trying to save a foolish man's life, he had condemned a great man to death and that, in turn, would doubtless cause many others anguish as a direct result. Lepers and cripples that Jesus would have otherwise healed, starving children he might have fed, the lost and the misguided he would have set back on the right path ... all now condemned to suffer.

Judas took a couple more steps forward, but could barely move, his legs leaden. The irremediable guilt which had settled on his shoulders now felt bone-crushingly heavy.

Why was his master not doing something to help himself? Why was he not using his powers?

'Where is your God now?' someone shouted at Jesus, almost echoing the same sentiments.

'Have you looked up lately?' someone else answered. The clouds above them continued to boil in a loosely checked fury.

It was hard to keep track of time without the sun's passage as a guide, but a couple more hours must have passed before Jesus finally said something. He lifted his weary head, gazed up at the heavens and cried out in anguish, 'My father, my father, why have you forsaken me?'

His words cut the chatter dead. Someone a few feet away

laughed; a short barking burst of nervousness that ended almost as quickly as it began. It was clear to all watching that the end for Jesus was nigh.

'Give him a drink,' one woman pleaded, a lone voice in the darkness.

Judas watched a man dart forward and soak a sponge in wine vinegar. He skewered it on a stick and hefted it up towards the cross.

Jesus, his breathing heavy and rasping, ignored the sponge dancing next to his face and continued to search the heavens with his eyes as if looking for a sign. Then, in a voice as commanding as it was final, he said, 'Father, into your hands I commit my spirit!'

His body slumped forward as far as the nails and restraints would allow, and his head lolled to one side.

The watching crowd remained deathly silent as Judas sank to his knees, a single, piercing sob escaping his lips in a half-stifled spasm which seemed deafeningly loud against the blanket of quiet. Judas turned his head away. He couldn't bear to look upon the lifeless body which had once been his friend and teacher.

And then, it began.

First there was an ominous, deep rumbling which came from the clouds above. A couple of seconds later a similar sound answered it from below. Judas felt it in his legs first, but the vibration soon spread to the rest of his body. The crowd started to panic, scrambling to get away but the ground began shaking so wildly that any attempt to run was immediately denied. Judas also tried to stand and run, but the force of the quake threw him to the floor, subjugating him.

The sky replied now, unleashing its own unfettered display of power and glory. White lightning arced all around, lighting up

Jesus's body and blinding Judas with every coruscating flash. Again, he tried to stand, but it was impossible. Everywhere people were being tossed around like fragile boats caught in the waves of a deadly storm.

The wind came next, bringing with it dust that flagellated any exposed skin, preparing it for the freezing rain that followed. All the while the ground continued to roar in terrible, tortured agony. Judas curled up into a ball and tried to protect himself from the ferocity of the elements, pushing down into a sodden patch of hillside that was doing its best to shake him off.

He cried out in terror, but his words were lost to the wind. His prayers, uttered in vain, were similarly whipped away. And then, just as it seemed as if the very earth was going to be torn asunder, a loud crack sounded in the distance. Judas had long since lost his bearings but he knew instinctively it had come from the direction of the temple.

The rain slowed, and with a final series of judders, like the death throes of a giant, the shaking subsided too. Judas opened his eyes. Up above the clouds were thinning rapidly. All around him people began staggering to their feet. One by one their faces, caked with mud, turned to face the cross.

A centurion, standing a few feet away, his red cape in disarray, bowed his head and whispered, 'Surely he was the son of God.' His voice was choked with wonder.

Judas nodded as tears streamed freely down his cheeks. There was nothing he could say to that.

He had betrayed the son of God.

And now the son of God was dead.

What did that mean for mankind?

What had he done?

From out of nowhere, the voice of Jesus echoed back to him.

I am to suffer. But he who brings this betrayal will suffer far, far more. He will wish that he had never been born.

They had sounded like hollow words when Jesus had spoken them at the meal last night. An empty threat.

Now they circled inside Judas's head like vultures.

He felt wretched, worthless and utterly, utterly terrified.

Chapter 6

The old hag caught a fleeting glimpse of a brown robe splattered with blood floating, disembodied, in the dark depths of her unseeing eyes.

Then a bone-handled dagger flashed in the blackness, its blade grinding on a sharpening stone, the sound of a demon's fingernails scraping on the underside of the Earth's crust.

A stout length of rope.

A dark forest. The trees began to fade.

'It begins,' she whispered quietly to herself.

II
NUMBERS

Chapter 7

Gideon poked the fire with a thick charred stick. It crackled and dispensed hundreds of miniature orange fireflies into the cool twilight air. He cracked another walnut open and popped it in his mouth, crunching noisily, then glanced down the hill at his flock. One of the sheep walked into the backside of another and they baa'ed at each other. He shook his head.

It was a well-known fact in the shepherding trade that sheep were the dumbest animals in the world. When it snowed, which fortunately wasn't many winters, the sheep would huddle against a wall. Which might sound sensible, but they'd huddle against the wrong side of the wall, where the snowdrift was building up. And they wouldn't attempt to move while being buried alive and freezing to death. Gideon had found himself digging out several sheep during past snowstorms. Quite frankly, he found it something of a miracle that they could remember to breathe on a regular basis.

He prodded the fire again, and went through the hourly ritual of counting his sheep. He tallied fourteen. Fourteen stupid white fluffy irritating stool-encrusted animals. The problem being there should have been fifteen stupid white fluffy irritating stool-encrusted animals. He stood, went up on his toes and gazed down, trying to see if he'd missed one. Another count still produced the number fourteen. He sighed, picked up his crook, shouldered his sling and bag of shot, and strode down the hill to investigate.

He reasoned that one of them must have somehow managed to jump the wall at the foot of the slope, escaping into the woods beyond. Gideon vaulted the wall himself and made his way cautiously through the trees. It would be too dark to see soon enough, so he'd have to find the missing animal as quickly as he could.

He heard a bleating at a distance directly to his right and changed course. He moved faster now, swiftly weaving between tree trunks, before ducking under a low branch into a clearing. The dumb animal was there. Staring at him. Tied to a wooden stake embedded in the ground. Who the blazes had tied it up? He peered around the clearing and down through the woods ahead, but couldn't see anyone.

He took a couple of slow steps towards the sheep, then stopped and listened. Nothing. Maybe it was a practical joke? Yes, one of Baruch's asinine jokes, that made sense. Better untie the thing and get it back to the field. Gideon continued forward, but as his hand reached to undo the rope around the sheep's neck, his perspective changed in an instant. There was a rustling of leaves and a blur of movement before he found himself looking at the sheep's nonplussed face upside down. Something had encircled his legs and whipped them up in the air, leaving him dangling off a tree branch.

He craned his head to look up and saw he was suspended from a length of rope. It was tight and painful around his ankles, and he could feel the blood beginning the slow march to his brain.

34

'Hey,' Gideon shouted. 'This isn't funny. Not funny.'

He heard scraping noises, something moving against the bark of the tree, and the rope was pulled up a little higher.

'Who's there? I can hear you behind that tree.'

A man emerged from the rear of the trunk. He was wearing a brown robe, topped by a deep cowl which hid his face completely.

'Who are you? What are you doing out here?'

The man didn't reply; just stood there silently, facing Gideon.

'Look, just let me down now and we'll say no more about this.'

The robed stranger began to circle around the suspended shepherd, his footsteps slow and deliberate.

Gideon fumbled for his sling but then realised all of the shot had dropped on the floor when he'd been hoisted in the air. It lay on the ground, scattered like rabbit droppings around his crook.

'Who are you?' Gideon asked again. 'If this is a joke, it's gone too far.'

The man, now behind him, sprang forward quickly and seized Gideon's right arm, then the left, and pushed them up behind his back, holding and binding them together.

'Please . . .' the shepherd's voice cracked with fear. 'What are you doing? What have I done? What –'

The man stepped around and stood right in front of him now, but Gideon still couldn't make out his features. Partly because they were hidden within the hood, and partly because it was nearly dark. And partly because Gideon was too busy focusing on the viciously sharp-looking dagger that had appeared in front of his face, silencing him. The man moved the knife forward, slowly, until the point hovered at Gideon's right eyeball. The shepherd closed his eyes reflexively.

As the finely honed edge of the blade touched his skin, Gideon tried to jerk away, but the man's other hand had moved behind his head, holding it steady with an iron grip. The knife carved around his eye; first over, then underneath. A single teardrop rolled down Gideon's forehead as the hooded man began to peel his eyelids away.

'Please –'

The shepherd was interrupted as a kaleidoscope of colours exploded in his eyeball. The blade was driven down into the back of the socket, and a squidgy popping sound followed as the knife was levered up. Gideon's brain struggled to comprehend why he could now see the leaves on the ground and the tree in front of him simultaneously.

Then the knife arced, zipping through the air, almost nicking his forehead. The attacker released his grip on the shepherd's head, and reached down to catch something, bringing it up to Gideon's stunned face. With his one remaining good eye he stared into the dead pupil of the other, suspended as it was from some manner of fleshy thread.

The man moved behind him again, grabbed his long hair and yanked it upwards with great and sustained force, as if trying to press the back of Gideon's head flat to his spine. Or as close as it would feasibly go without actually snapping. Gideon cried out in pain. The attacker held the knife tightly in his fist, and pointing it upwards, placed the tip inside the shepherd's gaping socket, allowing it to lightly touch the back of the concave hollow recently vacated by his eye.

With a light grunt, the man let go of Gideon's hair. The shepherd's muscles strained intensely and he managed to hold his head where it was for a few fleeting moments. Then his neck started to spasm in pain – a brief hold was all he was ever going to muster in that unnaturally awkward position. A split-second later, gravity fully had its way, and the shepherd's head sagged swiftly downwards. The knife pierced his brain as the man held the weapon unyieldingly steady.

Gideon's consciousness ebbed from the world as the blade twisted savagely inside his skull.

Chapter 8

The heat coming off the roof of his house was palpable, even though the sun was now sinking towards the horizon. Judas looked up at the sky. There wasn't a single cloud to be seen, which was the only reason he had spent this Saturday afternoon up on the terrace, sitting in the shade underneath a taut sheet of yellow material attached to poles at each corner. Since yesterday, glimpsing even the remotest wisp of white in the sky had caused him to be gripped by a profound sense of unease.

A low rumble startled Judas, provoking another flashback to Golgotha. It took him a few seconds to realise what it was. Teams of oxen some distance up the road were hauling huge chunks of limestone for some construction project or other. Building work was a part of everyday life in Jerusalem, as much as haggling in the markets, or donations to the temple.

Even here in the lower city, which lay in the shadow of the grandness of Herod's palace, the magnificent Temple Mount, and the towering viaduct which ran between the Mount and the upper city, hammers and chisels provided the constant heartbeat of Jerusalem by day.

The rumbling continued, noisier still. Perhaps it was time to go back inside. He made his way over to the opening in the roof and descended the narrow wooden ladder. A stone bench ran along one wall of his front room, the far end piled with matting and blankets for sleeping. A large piece of blue and yellow striped cloth was hung above the bench, to add a little colour against the dull brown soil and chalk mixture which served to plaster the interior. Shelves were built into the opposite wall, but they were mostly empty, with just the odd wineskin and sheaf of parchments here and there.

Several oil lamps fashioned from black clay were dotted around the room on tall iron lamp stands. There was one next to the wooden table and chairs that would usually be the room's focal point. Today, however, it was the items on the table's smooth sycamore surface that had Judas's attention. He pulled out a chair, sat down, and just stared at them.

The day had not begun well. Following a restless night's sleep in which the events of the crucifixion had played over and over in his mind, matters had gone from bad to worse.

After getting up and dressing, he had pulled the silver out from its hiding place, tucked away in a pouch underneath some old, worn blankets, and looked at it properly for the first time, scattering the payment over the threadbare rug that covered part of the floor. Laid out like this, it seemed like nothing. The price of a great man's life was thirty shiny pieces of metal. He picked up one of the silver staters, turning it over in his hand and gazing at the coin, before returning it to the pouch. He picked up another piece and did the same.

As he counted the last of the coins he knew something was amiss. There should have been thirty, but there were only twenty-nine. He'd lost one piece. Had it rolled away somewhere? He checked all around, including under the blankets, but it was nowhere to be seen. Had he dropped it elsewhere? How could he have been so careless?

He carefully examined the pouch, to see if there were any holes or tears in the material. There were none, it was in good condition.

He'd double-checked the money when they'd given it to him at the temple and there had definitely been thirty coins then.

It was just as well his uncle only owed twenty-five pieces, so the payment would still cover the debt, and that was all Judas had ever set out to do anyway. Saving his uncle's life would be scant consolation for the loss of Jesus, but at least it would bring some degree of meaning to the betrayal.

Keen to get the task over with, Judas had left shortly afterwards and walked the twenty-minute journey to his uncle's home with his head down, lost in his thoughts. He was greeted at the door by a surprisingly buoyant Daniel. A marked contrast from the last time they had met.

'Not here,' his uncle had said as Judas opened his mouth to speak. 'Abigail and her mother are inside. Let's go round the back. I trust you haven't told anyone about my little problem?'

'Of course I haven't,' Judas said. 'You made me promise not to, remember?' He followed Daniel around the outside of the building to the yard where his uncle worked. The bag of silver pieces was tucked away inside his robe, and he could feel the heaviness of the metal bouncing against his hip with every step.

When they reached the shed, Daniel had turned to Judas and shot him that familiar smile. The one in which his uncle's green eyes and tightly pursed lips collaborated in an impish piece of facial mischief which left his fellow man with the distinct impression that Daniel knew something that he didn't. Or in the case of his fellow woman, that Daniel knew of a hundred different ways to give her pleasure, and all she needed to do was succumb to his undeniable charms to experience them all.

'What is it?' Judas asked, his curiosity piqued.

'I've got the money!' Daniel said.

'What?'

'The money I owe. Well, it would have been a crime to let the Butcher mess up this face,' he said, jutting his square jaw forward. 'Or this body, for that matter. And now that won't happen, because I can pay him back.'

The silver resting against Judas's hip felt somehow heavier.

'I don't understand. What do you mean, you've got the money? How?'

'I sold my tools.'

'Your woodworking tools? But they're your livelihood.'

'They are, or rather they were. But I figured, what good are tools to a dead man? It's not like anyone in my family would use them after my death, so I sold them.'

'To who?'

'Another carpenter. He was happy to pay over the odds too.'

This all sounded like another one of Daniel's tall tales. 'He gave you twenty-five silver pieces in exchange for your old tools?'

'Hardly. He gave me three silver, and I used it to win the rest.'

'You wagered it?'

'Of course. How else was I going to get the money? I went from three pieces to twenty-five in little over an hour. I couldn't stop winning. In fact the only reason I did stop winning was because the other players ran out of money. Look,' he said, pulling out a small money bag and showing Judas its silvery contents.

The sight of the pouch, so similar to the one he carried, made Judas feel faint. He staggered a couple of steps to one side, white lights darting about in front of his eyes as the realisation hit home. He had betrayed his friend and master for no reason. Sold him out for silver he didn't even need.

'Are you all right?' Daniel asked as he reached out a hand to steady his nephew.

Judas tried to nod, but his head felt too heavy to respond. His mind was full of images of Jesus on the cross, of Jesus dying.

For no reason.

A wave of nausea surged through him, and he turned and vomited on the ground. His legs gave way and he grabbed onto the side of the shed, then threw up some more.

'Someone's had a little too much wine,' Daniel said. His voice sounded muffled and far away. 'Here, let me get you a chair. I've got a nearly finished one that should be fine.'

It had taken Judas a long time to recover from the news. He had sat in Daniel's roughly hewn chair for close to half an hour, not speaking, not even thinking. Just staring blankly down at the ground. Once, when he had been younger, he had contracted some dreadful disease that had kept him in bed for a fortnight, and prevented him from eating and drinking almost the entire time. Everything he swallowed came back up instantly. Sitting in his uncle's yard he had felt like that again. Except, it wasn't just his stomach that was sick, it was his heart too.

Throughout the entire betrayal process, from agreeing the money with Caiaphas to leading the Sanhedrin to Jesus, and watching his master die on the cross, the one thing – the only thing – that had made his actions justifiable was the knowledge that he was doing it to save his uncle. And it had turned out his uncle didn't need saving.

'Feeling better?' Daniel asked with impeccable timing, just as fresh tears had begun to well in Judas's eyes. 'Only I've got to get going.'

'Going?'

'Yes, there's a new game starting, and I want to be there from the off.'

'Game? What game?' Judas rubbed at his red eyes with the sleeve of his robe and tried to focus his attention.

'Dice! Are you all right? Have you had a bang on the head or something?'

'You've won all the money back – you don't need to gamble any more.'

'I won the twenty-five I owe, yes, but I still need to win a little more. To buy back my tools. Don't look at me like that. It's fine. I'm on a serious winning streak so it shouldn't take me long. Although, it might be nice to win enough to buy all new tools. My paring chisel was getting rather blunt.'

The lunacy of what his uncle was proposing had given Judas the impetus he needed. He had pulled himself together and dragged Daniel to the Butcher's house in a particularly shady area of the lower city. He'd paid off the debt with his uncle's winnings, and then they had gone to the other carpenter's place of business where Judas had bought back the old tools for the slightly inflated price of four silver pieces, using his own money.

After eventually leaving his uncle, for reasons he now found almost impossible to fathom – save for the fact that he was likely driven by guilt – Judas had decided to rid himself of the remaining silver by going on a spending spree. His first, and thankfully only purchase had been so crazy, so out of character that he could hardly believe he'd spent seven silver pieces on it. A moment of pure folly.

43

He shook his head, bringing his thoughts back to the present. On the table in front of him were two stacks of nine shiny silver staters. What remained of his payment. It was still a substantial sum and the coins had great worth, but a far greater cost. That was abundantly clear now. He thumped the table hard. The coins toppled and scattered across its surface, as if running to hide from his wrath.

Judas pushed the chair away from the table, stood up, and took a deep breath. Why had Jesus allowed himself to die? Why hadn't he saved himself?

He was going round in mental circles and his thoughts were starting to feel claustrophobic. He had to get out and do something. He needed to talk to someone. His father. He'd pay a visit to his father.

Judas swept the coins into the pouch, stashed them back in their hiding place, and then went outside. He mounted the imposing black stallion tethered out front, lashed the horse once and went thundering off down the road, as all heads turned to watch.

Chapter 9

Judas hadn't seen his father in months. That wasn't unusual, as they'd never been particularly close. Still, Simon Iscariot was one of the few people in the world who Judas could always turn to when things got tough. It didn't matter how long he'd been away, every time he came home his father would greet him with a hug and a few kind words.

'What in the name of the great salt sea is that bloody thing?' Simon said, eschewing the usual greeting conventions.

'It's a horse,' Judas said.

'I know that. I'm just wondering what my son is doing with one.'

'Do you like it?'

Simon studied the black beast with its shiny coat, examined its teeth carefully, and finally gave its ears a cursory once-over.

'It's certainly healthy enough,' Simon said. 'A fine specimen, if a little old, and that's quite a collection of war scars on the flanks. Let's get it in the barn. Stop anyone ... stealing it.'

Judas knew exactly what his father meant. Stop anyone seeing it, more like. Simon Iscariot lived in Ishmael's Rest, a way along the road to Bethany and not too far from the Jerusalem city walls. Like most small hamlets, the locals had tongues which were quick to wag and a towering black horse like this was sure to attract attention.

They took the stallion round the back and went inside. Whereas Judas's house was sparse in its content, his father's was the exact opposite. Bundles of cloth were stacked on top of each other, next to a low bench littered with miscellaneous cooking utensils, up against which was propped a broom. The two shelves that ran around the walls were haphazardly jammed with an assortment of jugs, pots, bowls, goatskin bottles, basketwork trays and ornaments, not to mention hammered-in nails from which hung strings of onions.

Judas sat down at the table, and watched his father begin to prepare a small meal. He still moved with considerable vigour for an old man, but nonetheless, he looked every single one of his advanced years; if not more.

His cheeks were marred by tangles of thin, broken red veins, and there were several large brown spots on the top of his head. Judas had always thought the latter marks underlined the uncanny likeness of his father's bald crown to that of a giant eagle's egg, mottled and poking out of a thatch of scruffy grey nest which was thick around the sides and back of his head.

'You must be doing well for yourself,' Simon said as he sliced some bread which had been baked the day before. 'To afford a beast like that. The last time I saw you, you were living the life of a pauper and following that Joseph around.'

'Jesus. Joseph was his father.'

'Jesus, yes, that's his name. Are you two still friends?'

'No.'

'No?' Simon stirred a pot of stew which hung above the

46

glowing embers of the firepit that was dug into the floor. 'Have you had a falling out?'

'No.'

'Well, that's good to know. I've never met him but from what you've said he sounds like a decent man.'

'They crucified him. Yesterday.'

Simon stopped stirring the stew and looked over at Judas.

'Oh, I'm sorry, I didn't know. Ah well, you're probably better off without him. You don't want to get mixed up with that sort. Talking of crucifixions, did you hear they freed Barabbas? Everyone at the feast started shouting his name and Pilate let him go.'

'Yes, I know.'

'I have to admit it felt strange to be shouting for Barabbas. I mean he's never done us any wrong, but –'

'*You* were shouting for Barabbas?' Judas couldn't believe what he was hearing.

'We all were. Me, Gilead, Ugly Saul, Eleazar the grape picker, your friend Ethan ...'

'Why were you shouting for Barabbas?'

'I don't know really. Everyone else was and to be honest I didn't hear who the other person up for release was.'

Judas sat in stunned silence. Not only had he betrayed Jesus, but his father had helped condemn him in his own small way, too.

Simon Iscariot located a dirty clay plate, scraped off the dried leftovers, dumped it in a bucket of filthy water and shook it dry. He wiped his sleeve over it for good measure and then began ladling out the lukewarm stew.

'Are you keeping that horse then?' Simon asked as he placed the food on the table and sat down next to his son.

'Not sure to be honest,' Judas replied. He broke off a piece of bread and prodded at the plate's contents. It looked like there was meat in it – suspiciously pinkish-looking meat. It was probably lamb, but it could just as easily have been donkey. Or rat.

'It's lamb,' Simon said, as if reading his son's thoughts. 'I purchased it from Gideon last week. It was born dead so I got it cheap.'

Judas pushed the meat aside and scooped up some vegetables on his bread instead. It was quite hard to work out what they were. He didn't want to ask just in case his father revealed something revolting about their origin too. Every time he ate here Judas left hungry. He could count the number of good meals his father had cooked for him in recent years on the fingers of one foot. Still, there was always the bread. That at least was fresh.

'What made you buy a beast like that anyway?' Simon asked.

'I don't know. I bought it on a whim. I haven't really got anywhere to keep it.'

'Well you can't keep it here, if that's what you were thinking. A horse that big would eat me out of house and home. I can barely afford to feed my remaining livestock as it is. And what are you going to do with it come winter? Throw a blanket over it and hope for the best?'

'I could rent a stable maybe?'

'Rent a stable? For a horse you don't even need?'

Judas swirled a chunk of bread around in the meaty juice on the plate to soften it, then took a bite. It tasted disgusting. He swallowed the piece whole.

'You have a job now I guess?' Simon asked, changing the subject. Judas stared across the table. This was one of his father's famous casual questions. A polite inquiry designed to

lull the unwary. It was what followed that you had to watch out
for.

'Actually, I don't. I've come into a little money so . . . are you
all right?'

Judas watched his father wrestle with a particularly tough
piece of lamb for several seconds, pulling at the meat with his
fingers while trying to grind it down with his teeth. Eventually
he gave up, fished out the whole lump and placed it on the side
of the table.

'That bit was quite tough,' he said. 'Disappointing. How's
yours?'

'It's . . . why are you asking about work?' It was better to fall
into his father's poorly disguised conversational trap than to get
into a discussion about the leathery and potentially diseased
meat.

'Oh yes. Well I don't know if you're interested, although I
can't see why you wouldn't be, but Gideon's flock's up for sale.
You could probably trade your horse for it. Well, not trade it. No
one would swap a flock of sheep for an impractical stallion, but
if you could get your money back you could probably afford to
buy them. You'll have to act quickly though. Other people are
bound to be interested.'

Judas sat back. A mouthful of mushy vegetables and some
nauseating bread and he was done. He'd go to bed with his stomach growling, but that was preferable to eating anything more.

'I can't really see myself tending a flock of sheep. It's not
exactly my thing. Why's Gideon selling them? Is he finally
going travelling?'

'You haven't heard then?'

'Heard what?'

'He's not likely to be travelling, given that he's dead.' Simon
stuffed another lump of meat into his mouth.

'Dead?'

'Jose found him this morning. Stabbed in the head and dangling upside down in the forest.'

'He was murdered?'

'Apparently.'

'That's just ... horrible.'

'Yes, it is. I know you used to be good friends, and it is a terrible shame, but there is another side to this. You could look at it as a business opportunity. If you bought those sheep it would give you something to do.'

Judas shook his head in disbelief. His father had never been a compassionate man, but this was a new low even by his rather callous standards.

'Do they know who did it?'

'Not yet. Early days though. So are you interested in those sheep? We could take a walk round to Jose's now and let him know before he sells them to someone else. He'll be thrilled that a friend of his son's wants to take them on. We'll probably be able to get a good price. He might even throw in some of his son's clothes for free too. It's not like they'll have any use for them any more. Jose certainly wouldn't fit into them.'

Simon continued to eat and prattle on about sheep and Gideon's father, but Judas was no longer listening. He hadn't seen or spoken to his old friend since around the time Jesus had come into his life, which was a shame. When they were little they had spent almost every waking hour in each other's company, pretending to people who didn't know better that they were brothers. But like so many friends, they'd become divided by circumstance as they'd grown older.

'Why would anyone want to kill Gideon? It doesn't make any sense.'

'Gilead reckons Gideon disturbed someone trying to steal

one of his sheep. He challenged the thief and was strung up and killed.'

'Sorry?' Yet again Judas couldn't believe what he was hearing. 'There's a lunatic shepherd murderer on the loose, and you think now is a good time for your son to get into the sheep business?'

'We don't know for certain that's why Gideon was killed. It's only Gilead's theory. And anyway, even if he's right, you know what they say – lightning never strikes twice. The killer is probably on the other side of Judea by now. I know Gilead will be thinking of buying the flock for his son, but Baruch's the last person Jose would want taking control of Gideon's sheep. I bet that lummox can't even count – he won't know how many sheep he has!'

'He might seem it, but Baruch's not that stupid. He can count. He can read and write, actually. But anyway, I'm still not buying any sheep.' Based on what Judas had seen yesterday, he knew for a fact that lightning could easily strike the same spot twice. Considerably more than twice, actually. 'I don't like sheep, and being murdered for owning sheep just doesn't appeal.'

'I think you're overestimating the risk.'

'Maybe, but I don't want to buy any sheep. Can we drop the subject now?'

Simon stood up, sighing. The plate was nearly empty, but he tipped the remaining contents back into the pot. If Judas stayed here overnight he could expect to see a remarkably similar snack for his breakfast.

'I'm going to go,' Judas said.

'Go where?' Simon sounded genuinely put out. 'I thought you were staying the night. Look – it's getting dark,' he said, gesturing towards the window. 'It's too late to go out. Stay here.

51

One night won't hurt surely? I've got some goat's milk I can warm up later, to help you sleep.'

It was Judas's turn to sigh. He didn't want to stay, but then he didn't want to leave either. The news of Gideon's death, coming so soon after the crucifixion, had really shaken him, and he didn't fancy being alone tonight.

'All right. I'll stay. But on one condition. You have to promise me you won't mention sheep again. Do we have a deal?'

'You drive a hard baa-gain,' Simon said, grinning.

Judas smiled back. Despite their history they were bound by blood, and it seemed they both needed company tonight. For all the man's talk of friends like Jose, Gilead and Ugly Saul, it was clear he missed having someone to share his life with.

'If you like,' Judas said, 'we could go for a ride tomorrow. Take the horse to Amasa.'

'Is that where you got it from?'

'No, in Jerusalem. The Christopher Street market.'

'Let's go there then. We can walk back.'

Chapter 10

Ethan lay flat on his back on a long, raised wooden table. Its brown surface was stained with ominous red patches. He hated this place. The air hung heavy with an awful cloying stench. It was a combination of the sweet scent of olive oil from the lamps that cast their flickering light across the room, the unearthly stink of a multitude of jars of rare herbs, and the sweat and blood of many previous patients. Ethan so hated this place.

But he had been forced to come here now he'd been cursed. He didn't know what he'd done wrong to deserve it, but they had come and infected his mouth. One of his back teeth had been burrowed into, and burrowed deep, by tooth worms. The infernal creatures wriggled inside, causing a stabbing pain in his lower jaw that was almost intolerable at times.

Praying to be rid of them hadn't worked, so now it seemed more drastic measures would be necessary. He heard the footsteps of the physician approaching behind him, and tried to steel himself mentally for the upcoming ordeal. It would be worth it, he told himself. When it was done, he would be able to live his life again. Free from constant grimacing; well, his own anyway, if not his wife's. He'd be able to eat meat again, too. Stewed vegetables were fine, but a constant diet of them had led to his bottom griping as much as his face.

The footsteps stopped directly behind his head and the physician's shadow fell across his body.

'Maybe you could coax the worms out with some honey?' Ethan said.

The physician was silent.

'I mean, it would be a shame to lose the tooth. I'm sure you have lots of methods for dealing with a problem like this that don't involve extraction.'

The physician held out a pair of tongs above Ethan's face and snapped them together, twice. That was his answer then.

'Have you got something for pain?' Ethan asked.

The physician grunted in a presumably affirmative gesture.

'Aagggghhhhhh!' Ethan cried out as something plunged into his right arm. He stared in shock at the bone handle of the knife that protruded from his limb. It had gone right through and pinned his arm to the table. A few heartbeats later, the wound began to colour with blood.

'What in ... Beelzebub's ... name,' Ethan gasped, reeling – but then a realisation snapped to the fore of his mind. Perhaps the physician needed to bleed him in order to release the evil spirits trapped inside his body? It certainly seemed to be working. The pain in his tooth didn't hurt all that much now, and although his arm was on fire, a sort of calm had come across him.

'The bleeding is working,' Ethan said.

The physician nodded. Or shrugged, possibly. It was difficult to tell, with him standing directly behind and in the dim light. Ethan felt his head being guided back down onto the wooden surface, and then the cold tongs were inserted into his mouth, probing and prodding one tooth after another. They secured themselves around a tooth. The physician took grip with both hands – it was the tooth in front of the bad one. The wrong one.

'Ith thuh hwong whooth,' Ethan said. 'Hwong whooth!'

The physician brought his foot up on the back of the table behind Ethan's head and yanked as hard as he could. He yanked, and yanked again. The tooth loosened in its socket, Ethan's back arching with each savage pull. He waved his free left arm around madly and tried to push the physician away, but the man was too strong, and too fiercely engaged in his task. And then, with a crack that reverberated down Ethan's jawline, the tooth came free. Blood began to run into his mouth.

'Ahhhhhh! That was the wrong damn tooth,' Ethan spat. 'It's the one behind it.'

Before he could say or do anything else, the tongs went back into his mouth, but this time they clamped around the correct offending molar. Ethan braced himself. The physician didn't pull this time, but simply squeezed the tongs as hard as he could with both hands, grunting with exertion. The tooth cracked. Pain exploded in Ethan's head the like of which he'd never known before. Then the tooth shattered under the pressure, and that new record pain level was broken as quickly as it had arrived; his nerves screamed as if molten lava had been injected directly into them.

The tongs were removed and Ethan squirmed sideways, spitting blood. He felt his head being forced back down flat on the table, and looked up at the new tool the physician had grabbed and was now holding aloft. A hammer.

Before he could react, it came down with huge force and impacted into his front teeth with a sickening thud. Ethan felt one of his incisors stick in his throat. The hammer came down again and again, the vibrations jarring through his skull. Dazed

55

and light-headed, it seemed to Ethan as if he was watching this happen to someone else, from outside his body.

Again and again and again the hammer struck. The front of his mouth felt like mush, with loose fleshy strips hanging down over his tongue, blood gushing now, the taste of iron thick, filling his throat. He could no longer breathe. Ethan tried to say some last words, but all that came out was a series of gurgles, and a bubble of red saliva that briefly formed on his smashed lips.

Chapter 11

As the last of the rocks slotted into position Simon Iscariot stepped back and admired his handiwork. The white marker stone gleamed brightly in the sunshine.

'That's better,' he said quietly. 'It should hold for a while now. I'll try not to leave it so long between visits next time, my love.'

Judas, standing a respectful distance behind as he always did on these trips out to the desert north of Jerusalem, stretched his arms back in a grand yawn. His father had awoken him first thing and insisted they go straight to the Christopher Street market to get a refund on the horse. After a protracted bout of haggling the trader had agreed to give Judas three silver pieces and a mule in exchange. They'd left the market on the sturdy beast's back and decided to come out to Amasa after all. Plodding at a deathly slow pace, they'd arrived here an hour or so ago.

Simon, head bowed, began speaking to the pile of stones again. Judas could make out the occasional word, but nothing that made much sense. He waited for his father to go quiet and then said, 'You know we really should be thinking about –'

Simon's head whipped round and the look on his face silenced Judas instantly. Clearly, his father would be the judge of when it was time to leave.

Judas shrugged his shoulders and resumed waiting. There was nothing to do up here in the hills above the town, and nothing much to see apart from the settlement itself a distance below, surrounded by the desolate and undulating desert. There weren't even any other graves to look at. The sky, which seemed to stretch on forever, was a cloudless blue wash that rippled in the perpetual heat haze but failed to offer any kind of distraction.

The yellow orb above beat down mercilessly. Judas had worn a cream-coloured robe, one of his thinnest garments, knowing he was coming out here. But even so, he was still getting uncomfortably sweaty. He could feel the heat prickle atop his crown, despite the white cloth covering over his head, which most men donned to protect them from the sun on warmer days. And all women, of course, for whom a headdress was compulsory, at least when out in public.

Judas yawned again and shuffled his feet impatiently in the sand. It wasn't that he hated coming here; he just hated not being allowed to do more than stand in the background and watch his father converse with a pile of crumbling rocks for hours on end. It had been tedious enough when he was a boy.

The boredom was unexpectedly broken not by an external stimulus, but an internal one – the image of a pile of silver manifesting itself in Judas's thoughts. The considerable sum of money he now possessed had been playing on his mind ever since he'd found out that his uncle didn't need it.

He figured he had to put the ill-gotten coins to good use, somehow. Giving the silver to the poor seemed an obvious solution, but perhaps there was a better, more fitting option.

Building some kind of permanent ministry for Jesus had occurred to him, but who would teach there? Judas no longer felt qualified, and he doubted he would be able to persuade any of the apostles. Also, a physical place of worship centred around the lessons and wisdom of the messiah wouldn't be tolerated by the Sanhedrin, no matter where it was located.

Besides, people didn't need a building to help remember Jesus. He had touched so many lives through his great deeds, you could travel to any of the towns around Jerusalem and hear some tale which involved him.

Judas's eyes alighted on the distant blob that was Amasa. Jesus had performed several miracles there alone. The most memorable incident for Judas, though, hadn't been a 'miracle' at all.

He'd been with his master, along with the apostles Thomas, Philip, Peter and Andrew, in a small olive grove just outside the town's east gate. Sitting in the shade of a particularly large and imposing tree, they'd just begun a meal of fish soup, seasoned with onions, garlic and cumin, when Judas had noticed Jesus staring at a group of men talking nearby.

'That man is in pain. Ask him to come to me,' Jesus had said, motioning to Andrew, who was seated next to him.

Andrew finished the last of the barley cake he was eating and stood, without question. He made his way over to the three men, and then spent a long number of seconds, glancing up and down at the trio, trying to decide which man Jesus had meant. Finally he pointed at one of them, a fellow whose skin looked like a dried, cracked riverbed, with many warts clustered about his face.

'I think you are in pain,' Andrew said to him.

'No,' the man replied. 'But you will be in a minute, if you don't clear off.'

His friends had laughed and Andrew had looked back towards the apostles, uncertain how to proceed.

Staring at the group, Judas could tell which of them was in pain. It wasn't the wart-ridden person Andrew had spoken to, but rather the man on his right. There was nothing physically wrong with him, but his shoulders told the story of a burden, and his eyes a tale of sleepless nights.

Judas had stood and pointed: 'The man with the green cloak, Andrew. Invite him over.'

Peter had shot Judas a swift sideways glance; Andrew was his brother, and he was quite protective of him. But then Jesus had nodded, indicating that Judas had chosen correctly.

The man wearing lime green proved less reticent than his friend, and came over with Andrew to the apostles.

'What is your name?' Jesus asked, as he motioned for the stranger to join them.

'Samuel.'

'You are in pain, Samuel.'

'No,' the man replied. 'I'm fit and healthy, I assure you.'

'That may be so, but your hurt is inside. In here.' Jesus pointed at his chest.

The man's eyes flicked downwards, and he said nothing.

'What ails you, friend?' Judas asked.

'It's a woman, isn't it?' Thomas said before the newcomer had a chance to answer.

Samuel dipped his head forward in a brief nod.

'Your lady has left you?' Judas said.

'Yes.'

'When did this happen?' Peter asked.

'She ran away with somebody else, three years past.'

'Three years?'

'Yes.'

60

'Find another woman.' Philip waved a chunk of fish at the man as he spoke.

'I can't go through all that again,' Samuel said. 'I can't put myself through it.'

'You are fearful,' Jesus said. 'But you must not fear. Fear can prevent you from living.'

'That's easy for you to say.'

Jesus stood and looked Samuel in the eyes. 'The next woman you meet,' he began. 'Do you believe she will always be true and faithful of heart, ever by your side?'

'No. Why on Earth would I believe that?'

'Why on Earth would you not believe it?'

'That's a ridiculous thing to say.'

'Is that so? If you're going to carry the notion that she will be unfaithful, why not the notion that she will be perfectly faithful?'

'I . . . ' Samuel trailed off as the point started to sink in. 'So, what . . . '

'Carry neither notion,' Jesus said. 'Accept that you do not know – that you cannot know – and that the future holds any possibility. Leave your pain in the past, where it belongs. Let it scar the present, and the future, no longer.'

Judas had seen the spark those words had caused in Samuel's eyes, the difference they would make.

Jesus could move gigantic boulders, calm a frothing, stormy sea, and heal the terminally sick with a single touch. But sometimes, he didn't need to do anything like that. Sometimes, his words alone were enough, and every bit as transformative as his miracles. Maybe even more powerful.

Words that would never be heard again.

A noise brought Judas abruptly back to the real world. He watched as Simon bowed to the pile of stones and then backed slowly away until he was level with his son. As was the family tradition, the two Iscariot men stood side by side and stared at the rocks for a while longer. Then, without saying a word, Simon began to walk back towards the mule.

'You know you could always come here without me,' Judas said as he hurried to catch up. 'When I'm not around.'

Simon nodded. 'I could. But she wouldn't like that. She likes to see her two men together.'

'Don't get me wrong, I like coming here with you,' Judas lied. 'I'm just saying there may be times when I can't always make it as often as you'd like. And rather than leaving it so long that the stones collapse, you could always just stop by on your own – in between our proper visits – or I could come here. On my own.'

'No. You know I don't want you coming here without me.'

'I still don't understand why. She was my mother, why can't I mourn her?'

'Because you never knew her, that's why. She's always just been a pile of rocks to you. She was a living, breathing, loving person to me.'

'That doesn't mean I can't lament her loss.'

'And I said no.'

'I wasn't to blame for her death. No matter what you might think.'

'I never said you were. Come on, let's go.'

The mule looked up as they approached.

'That's a good beast you've got there,' Simon said. 'I'll buy it off you if you like.'

'I always assumed you would.'

'It makes sense. You've got nowhere to keep it. I've got a barn. I can feed and water it.'

'Which is why you suggested taking it in part exchange in the first place. You can have it. For two silver.'

'Two? You'd cheat your own father?'

'Fine, I'll keep him then.'

'Her.'

'I'll keep her, then.'

'If you can't even tell a mule's sex you'll be in trouble. I'll give you one silver piece. She's not worth two. We're family, Judas. You can't cheat family. You shouldn't even try.'

'I'm not cheating you. She's worth more than one, that's for sure.'

'All right. I'll give you your asking price.'

'You will?'

'Yes. Minus a discount for being your father. And taking her off your hands. It's going to cost me to look after her you know.'

'Then don't buy her.'

'One silver piece. Then you'll only be down three pieces on the original deal. And you'll have enough money to buy a flock of sheep. Well, half a flock.'

'Fine,' Judas said. There was no point in even attempting to argue with his father.

'Fine? You'll buy Gideon's flock?'

'No, I'll let you have the mule for one piece of silver. I'm not buying any sheep.'

'Deal,' Simon said. He spat on his hand and offered it to Judas.

'I'm not shaking your hand. You can have the animal, but I want the silver when we get back.'

Simon wiped his spit-covered palm on his robe and mounted the mule.

'Of course,' he said. 'Provided she makes it back. To be honest, it would be better if you walked alongside us. You don't want her keeling over before we get there. She's still your property right now, after all.'

*

Judas snapped back into consciousness with a start, blurry-eyed and blinking in the afternoon light. The early start to the day had taken its toll, coupled with the trip to Amasa, and when he'd arrived home he'd double-checked his money – counting twenty-two silver now – then lain down to rest his eyes for a moment or two.

He'd awoken with a strong feeling that something wasn't right. Still blinking, he slowly scanned the room, dogged by an unshakeable sense of unease. The table. There was something unfamiliar to him on the table. He approached it slowly, and as his eyes fully adjusted, he saw that it was a small bundle of white linen cloth. A shiver ran through his body. Someone had been in his home, while he was asleep, and left ... left what exactly?

Judas tentatively took hold of a corner of the cloth, which was rather dirt-stained, and began to unfold it. His hand jumped away, involuntarily, as his unravelling revealed a different-coloured stain. A red smear. His heart instantly began to beat faster. He sat looking at the bundle for a brief period, then steeled himself, and as quickly as he could, unfurled the cloth so it was fully spread on the table.

He stared at its contents dumbfounded. And they stared back at him. Or the human eye, blue with a short stringy thread attached to its rear, seemed to at least. There was a bloody tooth inside the package as well. And a note. Judas's stomach turned as he picked it up, and read it. Five short scrawled words said: 'I know what you did.'

Chapter 12

The four men sat upon a rocky outcrop on the outskirts of the city. They'd put down several multi-coloured blankets to lounge on, and a few wineskins lay on the ground in between.

A deep valley stretched out in front of them, plunging downwards steeply and rising up with more grace on the other side. The glow of the disappearing sun played faintly across the ridges which snaked along the more gentle slope opposite. A bird screeched, somewhere in the distance, probably in one of the clumps of green trees and bushes that added spots of colour to the otherwise dusty, barren landscape.

Judas took a gulp from a wineskin, passed it to Jonathan, and wiped his mouth across his forearm. The alcohol was inducing a touch of numbness, a most welcome effect after the terrible cloth-wrapped discovery he'd made that afternoon.

'Well this is nice,' Jonathan said. 'Any time you feel like gathering together all your old friends and rushing up to the hills, on an urgent matter of looking at some trees in the distance –'

'Or listening to a bird,' Aaron chimed in.

'Absolutely. Any time at all that these matters of the utmost importance have to be attended to, feel free to invite us.'

Judas continued to sit in silence.

'Yeah. We'll rush around and look at woods with you, day or night. Just fine with us,' Aaron added, as he adjusted his belt. The five-inch wide leather strip hugged his dark red robe rather too tightly these days.

'It's not fine with me,' Baruch said, his voice gruff, each word as blunt as a hammer. 'I had other plans for my Sunday evening.'

'And I think we can all guess what they were, Baruch,' Jonathan said.

'How's that?'

'Because your plans are always the same.'

Baruch thought for a moment, turning his hands over and gazing at his fingernails as if trying to remember something. The backs of his hands were well calloused, a patchwork of scars from where dropped bricks had impacted on them.

'So are yours,' he said at last.

'What do you mean?' Jonathan asked.

'Your plans are always the same. Collect a message, deliver a message.'

'That's not a plan ... That's my job. I am a messenger after all. It's what I do.'

'Exactly. That's what I mean.'

'What are you on about?'

'You know.'

'I beg to differ.'

'It's not a proper job, anyway, is it? It's not man's work. Boy's work, more like.'

'Oh really, Baruch. You try telling Aretas the Fourth that his daughter was last seen in Lydda and has gone missing. See how long you live with that diplomatic tongue of yours.'

'Just walking and talking. A baby can do that.'

'Baruch,' Jonathan said, holding his hand up in front of his face and staring at his palm, 'I think there's a message for you here.'

'What?'

'It says . . .'

Jonathan dived across towards Baruch, but the intended open-handed slap failed to connect as the larger man instinctively dodged out of the way.

'Hah, missed!'

'All right, you two, that's enough,' Aaron said. 'Much as I'm enjoying this lively debate, I'd rather hear what Judas has to say. So come on, why have you brought us up here?'

'Yes, we hardly ever see you these days,' Jonathan said, 'you're always off gallivanting with that lot, the . . . erm . . .'

'The apostles,' Judas said, finally breaking his silence.

'Yeah. Them. Then, all of a sudden, you drag us all out here tonight, just to sit around drinking in silence. Ethan had the right idea. I should have made sure I was "out" as well.'

Baruch fixed Judas with a stern look, his thick black eyebrows coming together to meet over his broad, flat nose. 'It's not about the sheep, is it? Father's got this idea about me giving up labouring to become a shepherd. Said you were interested in Gideon's flock too. I don't want to fight with you over sheep.'

'No, nothing to do with sheep. It's . . . difficult to explain.'

'Try,' Jonathan said, lying back and looking up at the sky. He stretched out his legs, flexing sinewy muscles.

Judas shifted uncomfortably. 'Well, all right, but I warn you, it's not pleasant. This afternoon, while I was napping, someone sneaked into my home and left something for me.'

'What?' Aaron said.

'A note.'

'Nothing to do with me,' Jonathan said. 'I haven't delivered anything in your area for months.'

'It wasn't the actual note that bothered me, so much as what it came with.'

'Ooh, mysterious.'

'Really, it's not funny,' Judas said, mustering his most serious tone. He was silent for a moment. The others stared at him, except Jonathan who continued his cloud gazing.

'So, what did the note say?' Aaron asked.

'It said – *I know what you did.*'

'What you did? What did you do?' Aaron looked confused.

'Something really bad. I let a friend down a few days ago. Got him in trouble with the Romans.'

'On purpose?' Jonathan said, turning his head languidly to look at Judas.

'No, of course not. Not really. It's a long story – it was something I said, that I, well, I didn't mean to say. And then it went from bad to worse.'

'Is he in jail now then?'

'No. He was executed.'

'Ouch,' Jonathan said, sitting up.

'Like I said, it's what came with the note that's the really disturbing thing.'

'What?'

Judas reached into his robe, pulled out a dirty folded piece of cloth, and placed it on the ground. They all gathered around the bundle as he began to unwrap it. 'Brace yourselves,' he warned, as he pulled the final fold of cloth away.

Everyone stared at the two items.

'Well I'll be the son of a harlot,' Aaron said. 'Is that a tooth?'

'And an eye.'

'Looks like someone's got it in for you then,' Jonathan said.

Judas nodded.

'What do you mean?' Baruch asked.

'There's a saying – an eye for an eye, a tooth for a tooth,' Jonathan said, his finger tracing down his long, narrow face, pointing first to his eye, and then his mouth as he said the words. 'Seems like that's what this refers to. The eye and the tooth together, in with the message, means that whoever sent this is seeking revenge on Judas.'

'Either that, or they've got a really bad case of leprosy.' Aaron's joke was greeted with silence. He coughed nervously and picked up the wineskin.

Baruch's weather-beaten face clouded over. 'That eye could be poor Gideon's.'

'What?' Judas turned to stare at his friend.

'It could be,' Baruch insisted. 'One of his eyes was gone.'

'Gone? I heard he was stabbed in the head. My father didn't say anything about eyes.'

'I knew he was stabbed through the eye. It's news to me that it was actually taken though,' Jonathan said.

'He was stabbed in the eye *socket*,' Baruch explained. 'The eye itself was missing. Cut out. So that, there, could be Gideon's.'

Judas shifted himself backwards a foot or so, away from the bundle.

'Urggh,' Jonathan said.

Aaron craned over and peered closer at the offending object. 'What colour were Gideon's eyes?'

Judas shook his head. 'I'm not sure. I haven't seen him in quite some time. Anyone else remember?'

'He was more your friend than ours,' Jonathan said. 'And anyway when I did see him, I can't say I spent much time gazing into his eyes.'

'No,' Judas said. 'I guess not.'

'This is either a spooky coincidence, or just . . . awful.'

Judas nodded. 'So what should I do?'

Jonathan took a swig of wine. 'The man you crossed is definitely dead, right?'

'Definitely.'

'Then whoever sent the note must be a friend or a family member, I would think. Do you know his friends, or any relatives?'

'I do, yes. He has – or rather had – quite a large, close-knit extended family.'

'It's likely to be one of them, then.'

'Or all of them,' Aaron added.

'Hmm,' Judas murmured. He couldn't imagine the apostles banding together to do something like this.

'But what about the tooth?' Jonathan asked. 'Did Gideon have any teeth missing, Baruch?'

'I've no idea. My father just said about the eye.'

'So if it's not Gideon's tooth, whose is it?'

'I don't know,' Judas said. 'Maybe it's no one's in particular. Maybe whoever sent the note found it somewhere, on the floor perhaps.'

'Maybe it's his own tooth. Or her own,' Jonathan offered.

Judas wasn't sure he wanted that to be the case. Receiving a message from someone mad enough to punctuate it with their own body parts didn't bear thinking about.

'Or it could be some sort of practical joke, ever think of that?' Aaron stroked his long brown beard as he spoke.

'It's one hell of a joke,' Judas said.

'Still, it might be a mistake. It might not be anything to do with what you did. Does it say anything about Romans, or being arrested or executed? Or mention any names? No.'

Judas grunted a vague approval of that sentiment.

'Or look at it this way,' Aaron continued. 'They snuck into your house while you were asleep, correct? If they'd wanted to harm you, they could have killed you there and then. Dead,' he finished, slapping one hand hard into the other.

'That's true,' Judas said. 'That is true.'

'Look, until you're in possession of the full facts about the tooth and the eye, there's no point worrying about it too much for now.'

'Yeah, nothing to worry about,' Jonathan said. 'Just an eye, a tooth, and a scrawled note. It was probably for next door, anyway.'

They all laughed. Judas took at least some consolation from his friends' platitudes, and indeed the simple comfort of talking about it all. And the wine. Yes. The wine was helping, too.

'To wine,' Judas said, and raised the skin in the air so a little of the liquid sloshed onto his sleeve. They drank to his toast.

Baruch stood and beckoned Judas to join him, as he said, 'I know what will cheer you up.'

'You do?'

'Yeah,' his friend grinned broadly. 'I do.'

Chapter 13

The lower city was a mass of thickly clustered houses, huddled around and across the slopes of a steep valley. Most homes were compact, squat, single-storey affairs and many were in a state of disrepair with cracks across their limestone walls, stones missing from corners, and doors that were rather bowed and rotten around the edges.

A multitude of alleyways snaked across this cluttered landscape, and it was through one of these that the two men wove, Baruch leading with Judas trailing a little way behind. The alley sloped upwards at quite an incline, which wasn't made any easier to negotiate due to the fact that the thoroughfare was bustling with people. Jerusalem was always packed with pilgrims around Passover, stomping along in clouds of dust.

Except they didn't appear to be stomping anywhere thanks to the group of Roman soldiers standing shoulder-to-shoulder at the top of the alley, blocking the way. People were being diverted down another pathway to the right. Baruch pushed his way up to the soldiers, with Judas following.

'You can't go down there, scruffy,' one Roman barked.

'Who you calling scruffy? This is my best robe,' Baruch said as he smoothed down the deep-blue material.

The solider snorted. It was Baruch's best robe, and had been for many years. However, he'd now worn it that much, the hem and sleeves were tattered around the edges, and the cloth bore many jagged scars of thread from repairs, each a different colour to the next.

'Why can't we go that way, anyway?' Baruch asked.

'They're fighting over there,' the Roman spat. 'A dispute over a chicken.'

'A dove,' a bald and scarred veteran corrected him.

'Some stupid bird anyway. Go that way,' the soldier pointed behind them, then put a hand on his sword when Baruch didn't move.

Judas tugged his friend's sleeve and pulled him away into the nearby ginnel, which was an even steeper slope. So much so that it turned into stairs midway up. 'Come on, I've just had a thought. While we're headed this way, let's nip up and visit the pool.'

'Ahh horse testicles,' Baruch said. 'You're not wimping out as well, are you? It's bad enough that Jon and Aaron have gone home to their wives.'

'I just want to see if Jeb is around.'

'What d'ya want that miserable little weasel for? No, don't answer that, come on, we'll look for him after.'

'It won't take long –'

'I'm in the mood now, right now,' Baruch protested. 'It won't take long afterwards, either.'

He pulled Judas along and they turned left onto a mercifully wider and more spacious street. The strong smell of fish drifted over from a shop on the corner, which was apparently also selling two sparrows for a copper, according to the booming voice of the owner.

'All right, all right, you don't have to drag me,' Judas said as he wriggled free of his friend's grasp. 'Anyhow, we're going the wrong way, you dolt.'

'Nope.'

'Yes. Trust me.'

'No, Judas, I've been going to a new place this last month.'

'A new place?'

'Yeah. It's a bit more private. Not that I'm bothered about that much. It's just nice to have a change, more than anything. Getting a bit bored of the same old faces. And the same old –'

'Funnily enough,' Judas interrupted, 'I recognise this area. We used to play there as children.' He pointed at a yard which was stacked with broken and half-repaired barrels. 'Gideon, too.'

'It's just behind there, two streets over,' Baruch said, ignoring Judas's nostalgic interlude.

Their destination was a two-storey building in relatively good repair with a doorway covered by a yellow curtain. Judas was about to brush it aside and walk straight in when his friend stopped him.

'Wait a second.' Baruch reached inside his robe and produced a pouch on a thin cord that was tied around his neck. He grinned like an over-excited child.

'What's that?'

'Har-har!' Baruch said, opening up the pouch. He leaned in closer and offered its contents up for inspection. Judas sniffed suspiciously at the mossy yellow-brown herb, then wrinkled up his nose as if he'd submerged his entire head in a bucket of lemon juice.

'What is that? Tufts of the devil's armpit hair?'

'I got it from Blind Mary.' Baruch took a large pinch of the stuff between his thumb and forefinger. 'You want some?'

'Not a chance. You're actually going to eat it?'

His friend nodded enthusiastically.

'And why, exactly?'

'It's for downstairs, you know.' Baruch crammed the herb into his mouth and swallowed. The smell, and presumably the taste, didn't seem to bother him. 'For little Baruch. Blind Mary swears it will put a spring in his step. All night long.'

Judas rolled his eyes. Blind Mary, the old seer woman, was always selling Baruch expensive wards or potions that doubtless didn't work, but still he kept going back for more. Not that he needed any help in the downstairs department. 'Little' Baruch was famously anything but small and it was safe to say if he did have any more spring put in his step, he could end up causing a girl some serious internal injuries.

'You sure you don't want some?'

'No, I think I'll pass, thanks.'

They entered the building and were greeted by a woman with intricately plaited hair, who was wearing an outfit that consisted of a number of skimpy white strips of material that just about succeeded in preserving her modesty.

'Hello, Priscilla,' Baruch said. 'Two of us? Just the basics, please.'

The girl nodded. Her expression was unreadable due to the veil that covered the lower half of her face. She consulted a parchment on the desk in front of her, presumably to find a room that was free, nodded once more and then held out her hand.

'I'll get this.' Baruch ferreted for the money. 'You can owe me.'

He counted six copper coins into Priscilla's palm. She nodded again and then pointed to a bench. They both sat down as she turned and, hips swaying hypnotically, sashayed towards a corridor that led to the back of the building.

'Talkative sort,' Judas said.

'Yeah. She can't talk – can only make noises. The way a woman should be.'

'What do you mean she can only make noises?'

'The owner of this place, Caleb, he keeps these girls strict,' Baruch said in hushed tones. 'He ripped her tongue out.'

Judas was speechless himself for a few moments. 'Why?'

'She blabbed something about a customer. Got them in trouble. So Caleb cut out her tongue. The whole thing, to the root. None of the girls gossip any more.'

'Lovely. I bet they don't. Maybe this isn't such a good idea.'

'Not a good idea? How can going whoring not be a good idea? What is wrong with you?'

'I'm not really in the mood.'

'How can you not be in the mood?' Baruch seemed genuinely confused by the notion. 'You know your problem? You think.'

Judas expected his friend to add 'too much' to the end of his statement, but he didn't.

'I'm just not ... I don't ... can't we just leave?'

'Of course we can't. I've paid, for starters. This will be good for you anyway. Help take your mind off things.' Baruch scratched his head. 'Look, try thinking about the best sex you ever had. Or maybe your first time, with Atarah? Those amazing breasts, that long dark hair down to her slim waist ... that should be enough to get you in the mood. Picture the scene, you and your cousin, the dead of night, sneaking into your uncle's den –'

'Don't mention that place,' Judas hissed. 'Daniel would go mad if his private hideaway was made public. I was sworn to secrecy – I shouldn't even have told you. And I did ask you never to say anything about it again, remember?'

'I know that, but there's no one around, just us two.'

'You never know when someone might be listening.'

Baruch looked pointedly around the room. 'The only person anywhere near doesn't have a tongue to blab with.'

'Be that as it may, I'd still prefer it if that place was never mentioned again.'

'I understand. My lips are sealed.'

'Good.'

'She's coming back,' Baruch said. 'You ready? No backing out? It's not too late to have some of my herbs, if you want?'

'No thanks. I'll be fine.'

Priscilla re-entered the room and beckoned them to follow her. As Baruch stood, Judas couldn't help but notice that his friend's robe was rapidly turning into a tent around the midriff area. He turned his head away as Baruch strode out in front, apparently oblivious to the fact that the covering around his lower regions now resembled the home of a small desert-dwelling tribe. Maybe Blind Mary's herbs weren't a con, after all.

They were shown through to a large, dimly lit room which was divided into a series of areas, each separated off by thick sheets of material hanging from the rafters. The air was tinged with the faint odour of sweat and hormones, which even the strong incense burning in the corner couldn't entirely succeed in masking. Grunting and squelching noises carried from the far side of the room somewhere.

Priscilla showed Judas to a makeshift compartment in the corner of the room and Baruch to the one next to it. Judas approached the mattress, the only object inside the space, and greeted the naked woman reclining on top of it with a smile.

'Hello. I'm . . . Peter,' he lied unnecessarily.

The girl smiled, but didn't offer her own name. She had small but firm-looking breasts and a narrow frame which filled out more at the hips, but was still pleasantly shapely. Toned legs, smooth white skin, pretty face – a number of boxes were being ticked here. Yet little Judas stirred not. Apparently little Baruch was already in action, if the high-pitched squeak of shock from next door was anything to go by.

Judas sat down next to the girl and placed his hand gently on her right breast. Her soft nipple stiffened slightly under his touch. An image of an eyeball and a tooth appeared in his mind, which meant Judas's stiffening was equally slight.

'Do you like that?' she whispered.

'Yes,' Judas replied. The wine seemed to be wearing off a bit.

'What do you want me to do?' the prostitute said as she sat up. 'Would you like me to lick you up and down, before taking you in my mouth?'

'Uhh . . .'

She turned around, kneeling forward on the mattress, so her rounded buttocks were fully on display; two touching crescents of pert flesh. 'Or do you want to enter me like this?'

The whore in the next cubicle began to gasp rhythmically and with increasing speed; a noise more pain than pleasure.

'Or maybe . . .' the prostitute teased as she shifted back down next to Judas, undid the white cloth belt around his waist, and opened his cream-coloured robe. Her hand rustled under the folds of the garment.

'I'm sorry.' Judas felt his face flush red as he pushed her away. 'I can't do this.'

He got up and made swiftly for the exit. What had he been thinking? Why had he allowed himself to be pressured into this? To take his mind off things? How could he possibly take his mind off all this; Jesus, Gideon, the note, the eye, the tooth . . .

Preoccupied with this whirling maelstrom of recrimination, Judas completely failed to notice that he'd taken a wrong turn. He headed further into the back of the building, walked around the corner of an L-shaped corridor and froze. There, in a doorway about ten feet in front of him, was someone he'd hoped to never again see in his life.

Chapter 14

The man was facing away from Judas, but he recognised the back of that bald head immediately. The red and yellow silk cloak, the sword sheathed within its ornate scabbard, broad shoulders, and the throaty voice as he spoke to someone inside the room ... it was unmistakably Malchus, the high priest's right-hand man. The evil bastard he'd led straight to Jesus on that fateful night.

'I trust I've made myself clear?' Malchus said to his unseen companion.

Judas took a swift step back, flattening himself against the wall. He was sure he hadn't been spotted. Part of him wanted to get straight out of there, but another part of him was keen to listen in on what Caiaphas's lapdog was saying. He strained to hear, leaning slightly around the corner again.

'That's why you get paid so much, isn't it?' Malchus took a full step back into the corridor, forcing Judas to withdraw quickly, or as quickly as he could on tiptoes, hurrying back up the passage towards the central area of the brothel. Glancing behind him, he was grateful to see that Malchus wasn't following.

He reached the curtained compartments where Baruch, and others, were still satiating their lust, and headed directly into the front room. He didn't say anything to Priscilla, just gave her a quick wave and was out the door and into the cool, welcome evening air.

Sitting on a nearby wall, Judas took a moment to gather his thoughts. What was Malchus doing in a house of ill repute? And more to the point, in the lower city? Surely if he wanted a whore he could afford the finest. The ones who bedecked themselves with diamond necklaces, emerald brooches and gold earrings. The ones who walked like they owned the Earth and looked down their noses at scum like Judas. Something very odd was going on. He couldn't have been there purely for sex, surely? But then what other reason would he have for going to a brothel? Unless he was the part-owner or related to someone who worked there. Maybe he had a sister who was a whore? It seemed unlikely.

Having composed himself somewhat, he recalled his previous intention to pay a quick visit to Jeb. Baruch was probably going to be a while and there was no point hanging around waiting when he could make better use of his time.

Still ruminating on what reasons Malchus might have for frequenting a brothel, Judas made his way across town. He hurried down Herodian street, the vast ten-metre wide thoroughfare that led up to the Temple Mount, before striking out east on a narrower lane towards the pool. Walking quickly, he reached the place in around fifteen minutes.

Nestled in the shadow of the main city walls, the pool was rectangular in shape, around three times as long as it was wide. It was a popular destination, thanks to its rumoured curative powers, and predictably busy. Stone steps on three sides led down into the water and groups of people were clustered around, some in the pool, others perched on the steps, washing themselves as best they could. Many were unable to get anywhere near, so simply sat on the floor chatting.

He scanned the crowd as he weaved through it, looking for Jebediah. The remaining daylight was now fading rapidly, but Judas still managed to spot the distinctive figure, eventually, sitting with his back to the city wall.

'Jeb,' he said, crouching down next to the thin, very slightly built beggar. 'How are things with you?'

The man sighed. 'Not so good.'

'No luck yet, then?'

The cripple looked down pointedly at his withered and useless damp left leg, which was half the size of his right, and then back up at Judas.

'Sorry. Not thinking,' Judas said. 'Had a bit to drink earlier. Still, I'm sure the waters will come good for you some day. Keep positive.'

'Right ... maybe I would have had more luck with that Jesus fellow.'

'I did arrange for you to meet him, Jeb.'

'I know, I know. And I appreciate you getting me that chance. But you know my father, he said your friend was a fraud, a waste of time.'

'Why didn't you just go? I don't understand why you even told your father in the first place.'

'I don't know,' Jeb shrugged his shoulders. 'I guess I thought he'd be happy for me. But he wasn't. Of course he wasn't. Why would he have been?'

They sat in quiet contemplation for several seconds, the beggar staring down at the ground, his lank, greasy hair hanging forward so it partially obscured his face. Eventually, Judas broke the silence. 'I've got to ask you something. Have you heard anything about Gideon? Jose's son, the shepherd?'

'Gideon,' Jebediah repeated. 'Jose. Sheep. Hmm. Strange. I'm having this problem concentrating. I feel a bit light-headed. I think it might be because my belly's empty. Can't think on an empty –'

'All right,' Judas said, flicking the man a copper coin.

'Yeah, Gideon. He was killed. Strung up, stabbed and they carved his eye out.'

Judas nodded. It was a good job he already knew all this. Jeb didn't so much break news as smash it over your head.

'Any whispers as to who did it?'

'Nope. Not a one.'

'Did they take any other bits of him?'

'Like what?'

'Like, say, teeth.'

'Teeth? What makes you say teeth?' The cripple eyed him suspiciously.

Judas inched closer to Jeb and whispered, 'A friend of my father's found this tooth in the woods where the killing happened and I just wondered whether it might have been . . . '

'Gideon's,' Jebediah finished his sentence for him.

'Yes.'

'I expect I'd have heard about it, if he'd been mutilated with lots of bits and pieces of him hacked off.'

'It's just one tooth. He didn't find a bag of earlobes, nostrils and eyebrows.'

'Right. Well, I don't think it's Gideon's. I just heard about his eye. That's all.'

'So whose is the tooth, then?' Judas mused aloud.

'Is it an old tooth?'

'No, it was pretty fresh. Still bloody, in fact.'

'I see. Hmm. It's funny you should mention it, as there is something I've heard about teeth . . . '

'What?'

'That tooth of yours was found in the woods, though. Whereas this happened in the city. So I doubt there's any connection –'

'What happened in the city?'

'Those hunger pangs are coming back again.'

'Jeb, Jeb, Jeb. One visit, one coin, that's the way it works. Don't be bleeding me dry, or I won't come back.'

The beggar tutted and was silent for a moment. 'Go see Isaac the physician,' he said, eventually.

'Isaac? What does he know? Just tell me what happened in the city.'

'If you want to know the details, Judas, it'll cost you one more copper. And that's that.'

'Gah,' Judas said, but his curiosity had already been stoked to a blazing fire. He slapped another copper coin down on the ground. Jebediah's hand shot out, grabbed it and deposited it somewhere on his person in a blur of movement.

'There was another savage killing last night. At Isaac's practice, apparently,' Jebediah said. 'A man who had his teeth smashed right in. Good and proper by all accounts. But like I said, I can't see there'd be any connection with your tooth, not if it was found all the way out –'

'Do you know who it was?'

'The man who had his mouth smashed in?'

'Yes. Or the person who did it.'

'I've no idea who killed him, but the victim was someone called Ethan.'

The blood drained from Judas's face. His friend Ethan had been complaining about tooth worm the last time he saw him, a few weeks back. Isaac was his doctor. And Ethan hadn't been around today . . .

'You all right?' Jebediah asked, but Judas was already too far away, pelting down the street as fast as he could push past and shove people out of the way. Isaac ran his surgery in the evenings so there was a chance he might still be there, even though it was getting late.

Fuelled by fear, he reached the physician's just in time to see Isaac dousing his oil lamps and preparing to leave.

'I'm not seeing anyone today,' the man snapped as Judas burst into the room. 'You'll have to come back another time.'

Judas tried to speak but between the stitch in his side and his heaving lungs, all he could manage was a couple of incoherent syllables punctuated by a great deal of wheezing.

'It sounds like a lung condition,' Isaac said, 'but whatever it is, it will have to wait until I start seeing patients again.' He doused the final lamp and pushed past Judas, or would have done if he hadn't been grabbed by the shoulder in the doorway.

'Get your hands off me,' Isaac bellowed. 'What is your problem?'

'I just ... ' Judas gasped, 'just want to ... ask you ... one ... question.'

'And that'll take all night at this rate.'

'Sorry ... I've been ... running.'

'Get on with it.'

Judas took a long, slow breath. 'It's about a patient ... of yours ... Ethan, son of Enoch.'

Isaac's face took a dark turn. 'What about him? That was nothing to do with me.'

'So it's true ... he was murdered?'

'He certainly was, but not by me. He arrived early and I let him in, told him I'd just be away for ten minutes to eat my supper. When I got back, someone had taken a hammer to him. Quite, quite brutal.'

Judas felt sick. 'You didn't see who did it?'

'No. There was no one here when I got back. Just the body.'

'Were his teeth missing?'

'What? Yes. Most of them. His mouth was totally caved in. The whole place was a mess. I've spent all today getting it cleaned up.'

'That's awful,' Judas muttered, numbly.

'If he was a friend of yours, I'm sorry for your loss,' Isaac said, patting Judas on the arm. 'But I'm afraid I have to go now. I don't really want to be here any later than I have to, I'm sure you understand.'

Judas nodded and stumbled out of the surgery. Gideon and Ethan, both of them dead. His old friends, murdered in the most brutal-sounding fashion. Gouged, stabbed, bludgeoned ... blood-soaked images assailed his mind. Reaching out, he grasped for the nearby wall and leaned against the cool stone to steady himself.

Why was this happening? Why?

The words of the note seemed to provide a pretty clear answer.

I know what you did.

Chapter 15

Trudging down dark alleyways, among unfamiliar buildings, Judas realised he had absolutely no idea where he was. He had wandered aimlessly for a while now, lost in his thoughts. Or rather, trying to lose his thoughts; images of some lunatic smashing in Ethan's face with a hammer just so he could get a tooth to go with Gideon's eye.

He looked up and saw a roughly woven striped blanket over one of the windows in a building up ahead. The colours had been bleached away by the moonlight but he was sure he'd seen it before. This neighbourhood was familiar to him. In the daylight he'd no doubt recognise it, and the houses all around, in a heartbeat. At night everything looked different. Like an old friend wearing a disguise.

Judas paused and tried to get his bearings yet again. Why couldn't he find his home? He knew it was close at hand – definitely near here somewhere. This was stupid, stupid, stupid. He could have sworn on his father's life that he knew every inch of the lower city. That he could have found his way from Dung Gate to Sheep Gate, blindfolded and drunk, so where the hell . . . ?

He resumed walking and turned a corner. There was the building with the striped blanket again. The building he'd passed minutes ago. He must have doubled back on himself. Or maybe it was just a similar blanket in a similar window.

A large black bird, a raven possibly, alighted on a ledge nearby, ruffled its midnight feathers and let out a loud, sharp 'kraak'.

'Do you know where I am?' Judas asked. His voice sounded strangely hollow. 'Because I don't.'

The raven regarded him inquisitively, but said nothing.

'I'm lost,' Judas continued. 'Do you know where I am?'

The raven seemed to shake its head.

'Can you understand me?'

The bird paused, as if thinking of a suitable reply, then launched itself up and over the rooftops, kraak-ing as it went. A single black feather see-sawed downwards and vanished as if dissolved by the darkness all around.

Judas laughed at his own foolishness. Talking to birds. Whatever next?

He needed to get a grip. If he just kept walking then eventually, inevitably, he'd find somewhere familiar. A landmark that would help him to finally make his way back home.

Judas strode off with renewed purpose. He was just nearing the end of another street when he heard a noise behind him. A sort of scratching sound. Subtle, but just audible enough to pull him up short. He held his breath and listened intently.

Nothing. Then … something. Scraping. Like someone pulling a cart? No, it was more like someone dragging a sheet of metal.

It was getting louder. Nearer. Curious, he waited for the source of the rasping to reveal itself. The raven from earlier, or a different one perhaps, called out from somewhere high up above.

A lone figure came into view from around the corner of a building. He – for it was unmistakably a man – was a tall fellow dressed from head to toe in white, although his clothes seemed an off-grey in the murkiness of the night. He had something in his hand. Something he was running against the stonework of the houses as he passed.

Judas couldn't see what the man was holding but he knew instinctively it was a blade. He felt his mouth go dry and his stomach tighten.

The figure stopped, still some way off, and stared. It was hard to tell if he was surprised to see anyone out here, or was simply sizing up the situation.

Judas turned and began to walk in the opposite direction. Quickly, but with what he hoped was an air of nonchalance. As if he was just out for an evening stroll, taking in the sights and admiring the buildings. He was half-tempted to start whistling, but that would appear desperately contrived. Maybe he could pretend to be drunk? No, that would just make him seem like an easy target.

He came to a half-built house, turned out of sight and quickened his pace. By the time he'd reached the end of this street all was silent again. He sighed with relief. What had that been about?

To the left was a path he thought he recognised. He began to head towards it when the scraping noise started up again. It sounded very near.

Judas froze, unsure what to do or exactly where the sound was coming from. How the hell had the man with the blade got here so quickly?

He didn't know or care. As the figure from before appeared

around a barn in front of him, the knife in his hand continuing to gouge the stonework, Judas turned on his heels and fled.

He heard an echoing set of rapid footfalls behind him. The man with the weapon was giving chase. All pretence gone now, Judas put his head down and sprinted as if his life depended on outdistancing this stone-scoring stranger. Which it probably did. Judas was in no doubt that this was the madman who had killed Gideon and Ethan. The lunatic who had sent him that note.

He reached a wooden gate and vaulted over it effortlessly, continuing to run. Strangely he didn't feel at all out of breath. Not like earlier at the physician's.

The footsteps behind him sounded incredibly close now. He wanted to sneak a glance, to see exactly where his pursuer was, but that was clearly a bad idea. He reached another low gate and went to clear it like the one before, but then damned curiosity got the better of him as he did so. Turning his head slightly to look behind, his foot snagged the top part of the bar and sent him sprawling. He hit the ground with his shoulder, sending up a shower of sand, but somehow managed to scramble to his feet and keep running. His stupidity had cost him less than a second but it was all the time his assailant needed.

Judas felt a sharp pain between his shoulder blades. He staggered forward, sank to his knees and collapsed face-first onto the path. Lying there, exhausted and spent, he watched helplessly as a pair of sandalled feet approached. This was it, then.

The feet stopped just inches away from him. Judas tried to roll over, to see what his attacker looked like, and the man duly assisted him with a swift kick to the ribs that carried him over onto his back.

He gasped in pain and then, as his attacker looked down at him, in shock.

It couldn't be.

He was dead.

Judas had watched him die with his own eyes.

Jesus of Nazareth, clad in a blaze of white, plunged the blade deep into his betrayer's ribcage with bone-splintering force.

Chapter 16

Judas awoke to the sound of screaming. His own. Instinctively he put both hands to his chest to try to stem the flow of blood. But there wasn't any. He looked at his hands, clean but damp with perspiration, and then down at his nightwear. There was no sign of a wound. The pain he'd felt when the knife had sliced into him had all but faded away. He looked at the blanket beneath him. No blood there either.

It had been a dream. A silly, but utterly terrifying nightmare. Maybe he should have drunk some more wine when he'd got back last night. That might have blotted out his night terror. He'd been having bad dreams lately, which was hardly surprising, but this one had been the most real yet. And the most ridiculous.

Monday had scarcely begun, indeed it was so early dawn's light was only just beginning to leak into the sky, but Judas got up and washed himself, scrubbing hard to remove the sweat and memory of the previous night from his body. Then he got dressed, took some of the silver out of his secret stash, weighed it in his hand briefly and then popped a single piece into his money pouch. Just in case.

By the time he left the house, the sun was just peeking over the rooftops. He set off at a brisk pace, passing lots of streets and buildings, all of which he recognised. One or two had striped blankets up at the windows. As he walked he watched the skies, half expecting a large raven to appear at any moment. He didn't understand the significance of the bird in his dream, but it was commonly recognised as a harbinger of death, so that hardly boded well.

Kicking a stone along the street, Judas looked up and was surprised to see the tiny village his father called home just up ahead. How had he ended up at Ishmael's Rest? He certainly hadn't intended to walk this far, or in this direction when he first set off. His stomach growled to inform him he was hungry. It perhaps wouldn't have bothered if it had realised where the nearest food was located.

He knocked on the door to his father's home. After a few seconds he heard footsteps. 'Who's there?' Simon asked.

'It's me.'

'Esme? Do I know you?'

'It's your son.'

'Judas?'

'You have another son I'm not aware of?'

'Unfortunately not,' Simon replied, although his answer was largely drowned out by a grinding sound as he began pulling the hefty boulder away from the inside of the door.

'Hold on,' Simon's voice echoed through the woodwork. More grating. 'Nearly there,' he panted.

'Why don't you just use the bolt I bought you?' Judas said to the door.

'I gave it to Gilead,' the door grunted back. 'For his goat shed. But this works better. No one can break in once it's in place.'

Eventually a gap opened up that was just wide enough for Judas to squeeze through. His father greeted him on the other side, adding, 'And it doubles as a terrific doorstop.' Judas took the ropes from the older man's hands and pulled the large lump of sandstone fully clear. It had once formed part of a Pharaoh's head, but time and Simon's daily exertions had long since rubbed its noble features clean away.

'It's hugely impractical,' Judas said. 'And you're too old to be lugging it about all the time. Look at you, you're exhausted.'

'I'm fine,' Simon said, looking anything but. 'Anyway, what can I do for you? Second time in a week. That has to be some sort of record.'

'I happened to be passing and thought I'd drop in and say hello.'

'Happened to be passing? From where?'

'From home.'

'You came all the way out here, where there's nothing as far as the eye can see, apart from a small ramshackle collection of buildings, ringed by a pathetic crumbling wall that the elders pretend isn't a problem, and thought you'd drop by to say hello?'

'Yes.'

'So who are you on your way to see?'

'What?'

'Well, maybe you were passing here on your way to Bethany to see Clopas?'

'I'm not going to see anyone.'

'You can't have been passing then can you? Unless you've got a new job as a stonemason. Which I doubt with those lady hands. Breakfast?'

If he ever felt guilty about not seeing much of his father, five minutes in the man's company was usually enough to assuage the feeling.

'Breakfast would be ...' Judas sought the right word. Revolting, chewy, stringy, indigestible – there were so many possible choices – 'welcome.'

'Sit down then.'

Judas pulled up a chair and watched as Simon busied himself starting a fire and throwing some leftovers into a battered old iron pot which he filled with murky water, before adding a long meaty bone which looked suspiciously mule-like.

'Changed your mind about those sheep yet?'

'No.'

'That's a shame. I mentioned your interest in them to Jose and he said he'd do you a deal. Said it's what Gideon would have wanted. I swear there were tears in his eyes at the thought of you taking over his son's flock.'

'You mentioned "my interest" in them? What interest would that be exactly? I have no interest in sheep. I have less than no interest in sheep.'

Simon continued to tend the dubious concoction in the pot.

'What about if the price was right?'

Judas sighed.

'I figured that might make a difference.'

'The answer would still be no.'

Simon made a half stifled grunting noise, but said no more. In fact he was silent for so long that Judas began to hope that was the end of the matter. Right up to the point when his father cleared his throat.

'He's desperate to sell, we're keen to buy. A strong bargaining position. We'd be fools to pass up the chance.'

'We? I've told you a hundred times I'm not interested in buying bloody sheep. Buy sheep for yourself if you want the bloody things. I'm not a shepherd.'

For a moment or two Simon said nothing, just poked the vegetables in the pot with a bent skewer and stirred them around in the simmering water. Then without warning he straightened up, turned to Judas and hurled the metal rod across the room. It missed his son by inches and struck the collection of pots on the shelf behind. Fragments of clay shot off in all directions.

'So what are you then, exactly?' Simon roared, his face red, and not just from the heat of the fire. 'You're not a shepherd, you're not a stonemason, you're not a priest, you're not anything. You're not married, or even seeing anyone, well not anyone female.'

'Hey, I –'

'Shut up.'

Judas did as he was told. He hadn't seen his father this angry in a very long time.

'You're my son, but I don't understand you. Forget the sheep. You don't want to look after sheep. Fine. You don't want a family. Fine. There's probably not a woman around who'd have you anyway. But you're not a child any more. You're a grown man. It's about time you acted like one.' Simon kicked the pot. Hot water splashed out over the edge and doused the fire. Some splashed on his leg as well, but he was too irate, or too proud to acknowledge its scalding touch.

'What's this about?'

Simon stalked over to retrieve his skewer from the floor. 'Where were you yesterday?'

'At Amasa. With you, remember?'

'No, I mean after we got back.'

'I went out with some friends.'

'All day and night?'

'Pretty much. We met up in the afternoon, then started drinking into the evening. Why?'

96

'You had a visitor come here. Said you weren't around at your place, and a neighbour pointed him in my direction. He arrived about four in the afternoon, some man called Thomas. He said you'd know him. He asked me to tell you he was travelling alone and he'd be staying at the Sheep Gate Inn in the city, if I saw you before he did. He wouldn't say what it was about.'

Thomas was in Jerusalem! That was unexpected news. Judas had assumed he was the only apostle still in the city. He was certainly the only one the high priest didn't want to have arrested on sight anyway – for now at least. It was a big risk for Thomas being here. Maybe his friend was the one behind the note. Although out of all of the apostles, he seemed the least likely.

'Now a strange man, on his own, inviting you to his room is one thing, but then you had another caller late on. Just as I was getting my head down for the night.' He nodded in the direction of the boulder.

'Who?' Judas asked.

'Some soldier type. Works for the high priest apparently. Kept touching his ear like a madman. Said the priest wants to see you. As soon as possible. He said he'd be at the women's hall in the temple, all day today. And to come and find him.' Simon shook his head. 'Bloody hell, Judas, you upset the Sanhedrin and they'll crucify you like your teacher friend. I don't know what you're tangled up in, and I really don't want to know. But get yourself untangled, quick.'

97

Chapter 17

'His name is Thomas,' Judas said. 'He told me he rented a room here.'

The innkeeper just stared at him.

Judas reached into his money pouch, his fingers circling the piece of silver briefly. No, he wasn't going to trade that much for information.

'I'm supposed to meet him at this inn. Is there a Thomas staying here?' Judas slapped down a couple of copper pieces and some accidental fluff on the counter in front of him.

The man looked down at them, then up at Judas. He swept the coins into his pocket and grunted, 'He's upstairs. Red door.'

Judas nodded his thanks and made his way towards the stairs on the far side of the courtyard.

The Sheep Gate Inn was a large rectangular building, with a central inner square open to the elements. The poorly cobbled floor was strewn with straw for the guests' animals. Several tethered donkeys regarded him suspiciously as he made his way around the feed bags and up the narrow stone stairs to the balcony of the upper level. He almost tripped twice on the poorly carved blocks of stone, which were of varying height. He'd been here once before, years ago, and remembered the stairs being wooden. But then the rest of the place had changed considerably since then, too.

The walls were mostly sandstone, although some attempt had been made to beautify the main entrance hall. While other establishments used colourful drapes or carved ornaments to liven things up, the Sheep Gate Inn's owner had opted to get someone to decorate the place with an oasis scene. Unfortunately, the artist clearly wasn't a particularly gifted man and his palette appeared to be limited to shades of brown, with no green or blue to be seen. The result looked as if a madman had chosen to brownwash the walls with his own excrement. It was no accident that the place was known locally as the Sheep Shit Inn.

Judas knocked on the peeling red door. It opened slowly, as a face framed by neatly trimmed sandy brown hair appeared in the crack. Thomas smiled as he recognised his visitor.

'Come in,' he said, stepping backwards to allow Judas into the room.

The inn's accommodation wasn't especially accommodating. It contained a small uncomfortable-looking bed and a cracked, sloping wooden shelf.

'Come in,' Thomas said again. 'Sit.' He gestured at the bed. Judas did as he was told, and Thomas sat next to him.

'You found me then?'

'Yes, my father said you were looking for me and staying here so . . .'

Thomas nodded. 'Quite so. Well thanks for coming, I wasn't sure you would. It's not a good time for any of us to be in Jerusalem really. Risky. But I wanted to see you. To see if what the others have been saying about you is true.'

'What have the others been saying?'

'That you gave Jesus up to the Sanhedrin. Identified him with a kiss.'

Judas looked away. How could he answer that?

'They all say it's true,' Thomas continued. 'And Jesus did say one of us would betray him, but I don't know. I just can't believe that you would do something like that. You were as shocked as any of us at that last supper, I recall.'

Out of all the apostles, Judas had been closest to Thomas. They had a bond, an understanding, but if he admitted the truth here, now, that would be the end of their friendship. Thomas would probably understand, maybe even be able to see things from Judas's point of view, but he would never, ever forgive him.

'It's not that cut and dry. Yes, I identified him with a kiss, I don't deny that. But I didn't betray him. Not intentionally. The people I was with wanted to meet Jesus, said they'd heard about all the good things he'd done, and I thought I'd help. I didn't know they were Sanhedrin.'

'You just thought they could be new followers?'

'Yes. Exactly. I loved Jesus, Thomas, you know I did. Do you honestly think I would betray him if I thought it would lead to his death?'

'I'd like to trust you.'

'How can I prove it? If Jesus was alive you could ask him but –'

'Yes, that's not a bad idea.'

'What?'

'It's a possibility, certainly. Maybe we could ask Jesus. He'd clear up any misunderstanding, I'm sure.'

'He's dead, Thomas. Crucified, remember? That tends to put an end to most people's conversational skills.'

Thomas smiled. 'But Jesus isn't most people. That's the other reason I wanted to meet with you. To see if you knew.'

100

'Knew what?'

'Jesus isn't dead.'

'What?' Judas stared blankly.

'He's risen again.'

'Risen?' He was having a hard time following the conversation.

'Yes. The other apostles saw him.'

'Who saw him, exactly?'

'They all did.'

'Everyone? And you?'

'Not me, unfortunately. It all started yesterday when the two Marys, Magdalene and the other one, went to anoint Jesus in his tomb and discovered the stone rolled back and his body gone.'

'Gone where?'

'No idea. Anyway, then he appeared to both Marys, they told the apostles about it, and later on, Jesus visited the apostles themselves. I mean they seemed genuine about it. All really awestruck. You know me, I'm as open-minded as the next man, but until I see Jesus myself, and see the nail marks with my own eyes, slide my fingers in and out of the holes even, I'm not sure I can totally believe it's true.'

Judas wasn't sure what to think about all this, let alone what to say to Thomas. He should have been elated; thrilled to hear that his master had managed to overcome death and return to continue his good work. But the truth was he found the revelation terrifying. Maybe it was just the guilt he'd been carrying around for days now, laced with the haunting remnants of last night's unshakeable dream, but the idea of a resurrected Jesus scared the living daylights out of him.

It also introduced an unthinkable possibility.

Someone who knew what Judas had done had brutally killed two of his oldest friends. The idea that particular someone might be Jesus was utterly ridiculous. Retribution wasn't his style, for starters. Yet, at that last fateful meal his master had calmly and matter-of-factly prophesied that his betrayer would come to suffer greatly as a consequence.

Could this be what he had meant? Could Jesus be the person responsible for the deaths of Gideon and Ethan? It was absurd. Laughable. The Jesus he knew would never do such a thing. Yet, maybe this wasn't the Jesus he knew. Maybe this was a brand new and terrible incarnation returned to right the wrongs he'd suffered here on Earth. God had wiped out whole nations in the past for their wickedness, perhaps Jesus was back to do a similar thing, but on a more intimate, personal level.

'Wouldn't it be wonderful if it was true?' Thomas was saying. 'If Jesus really was back from the dead?'

'Yes,' Judas found himself replying. 'Wonderful.'

Chapter 18

He paused to catch his breath. After leaving the inn and Thomas – who had assured him that if he did encounter Jesus, the first question he'd ask would be about the intention of that fateful kiss – Judas had known exactly what he had to do. He'd gone straight back to his house, grabbed what he needed, and then come directly here to the Temple Mount.

Stopping only to cleanse and purify himself in a ritual bath, many of which were dotted around the base of the steps to the Mount, he'd bounded up the wide stone stairs, and made his way through the massive gates, onto the walled plateau at a swift pace.

The temple complex was a grand affair, to say the least. The outer wall, which defined the edge of the vast plateau, was ringed on the inside with a double layer of elaborately worked Greek-style pillars some thirty feet in height. Indeed, on the south side, these columns were four layers deep. They supported a porch structure that was a popular and well-shaded place for people to meet and chat. As impressive as this was, it paled in comparison to the temple building itself.

Judas adjusted his white headdress, which had slipped slightly to one side while he'd been running, and as he did so took a brief moment to survey the structure towering above him. The temple never failed to impress, especially from this close. Huge white marble stones gleamed in the midday sun; a pair of vast pillars, clad in glinting gold, flanked its grandly recessed entrance, and the edge of the roof was lined with gold spikes. These served to deter birds from landing on top of, and subsequently soiling, the holy sanctuary. Say what you like about old Herod, but the recently departed ruler could most certainly build. It had been one of the arts he was most skilled at, right up there along with butchering and slaughtering.

However, Herod's masterpiece now bore a startling imperfection: a crude dark scar that ran along the front of the temple building and snaked over forty feet across it. Hastily erected wooden supports and platforms had been put in place to stop any further movement following the everyday, totally-unrelated-to-the-crucifixion earthquake that was the officially recognised cause of the damage.

Judas picked his way through the outer court of the temple complex, weaving in between stalls and silently cursing the massed pilgrims who bustled around and about. The sounds of haggling assailed his ears – despite his master's best efforts, this remained the domain of the merchants and money changers. Their driving forth from the Mount had been but a temporary setback.

Vendors and pilgrims bartered over foods and trinkets, money changers tried to shout their rates louder than the others, and there were animals in pens, or being dragged around by their owners, crying out plaintively as if aware of their soon-upcoming fate.

The whole time Judas made sure he had one hand on the

money pouch inside his robe, lest one of the thieves who worked these crowds should have it away. It was crammed with all his silver pieces and he had a purpose for them which didn't involve feeding the family of some light-fingered toe-rag.

As if on cue a man tugged Judas's sleeve and loomed in close.

'Whatever you're selling, I don't want any,' Judas shouted.

'It's genuine high priest spittle,' the merchant beamed proudly, holding up a small, sealed jar. 'I scraped it off my robe just this morning.'

'What would I want with that?' Judas tightened the left-hand grip he had on his pouch.

'It's like holy water, only thicker. Which makes it holier.'

Judas shook his head and pushed on through the crowd. He managed to make his way across the entire outer court without any further major incident. By the time he reached the wall of partition he'd only been hassled to buy a lamb, two doves, a kilo of salt, a sheep's head, and a carved wooden miniature replica of the temple, complete with a hastily drawn crack. Which was good going by anyone's reckoning.

The partition was a low stone wall that marked the boundary of the outer court and the inner court complex, where the temple stood. Jews were able to pass it freely, but anyone else was strictly forbidden. As the inscriptions posted on the ornately carved columns along the barrier reminded visitors: 'Whoever is caught will only have himself to blame for his ensuing death.' Any foreigner who accidentally strayed beyond the wall would be marched off for a swift execution.

Judas walked past the partition, up a flight of stairs, then up another short flight and through a gate which led into the court of women. This was so named because it was as far as any females were permitted to go. Only men were allowed into the inner court to the west, and only priests further than that, into the area where the altar, and the actual temple building itself was situated.

Stopping near the middle of the chequered floor of the women's hall, he looked around. With no roof, the place was largely open to the elements, although the colonnade-supported galleries that jutted out from above provided some shade and shelter around the edge of the room.

He scanned these outer areas, where the majority of people were gathered out of the sun, and quickly spotted what he was looking for. That distinctive red and yellow cloak, over in the north-east corner of the hall, just past the long row of brass donation boxes. Judas made his way over, tossing a copper coin into the wide maw of one of the collection pots as he passed. These were trumpet-shaped and narrowed in to prevent people from taking rather than giving. Well, either that or they were trumpet-shaped because the sound of coins rolling down and chinking into them was music to the priests' ears.

Malchus was busy berating a junior priest who was sorting through a pile of altar wood. The fellow must have done something particularly sinful to have been assigned such a menial task.

'This is clearly rotten,' Malchus said, smashing a piece of wood over the poor chap's head. It duly proved his point by splintering into several pieces. The priest mumbled an apology. 'And so is this,' Malchus said, hitting the hapless fellow with another plank. This one proved to be much sturdier as it bounced off the priest's crown with a nasty sounding thwack. 'Oh, my mistake. I think.' Malchus hit the priest with it again. 'Yes. My mistake,' he concluded.

Judas tapped Malchus on the shoulder and the thug turned. 'You,' he said, nodding as he recognised Judas's face. 'Caiaphas has been waiting.' He threw the piece of wood into what Judas guessed must be the 'good' pile, rubbed his ear and said, 'Follow me.'

Malchus led him across the hall, up a flight of curved, semi-circular steps, and through a massive set of open bronze gates; Corinthian bronze, no less, which shone with an almost golden hue. This was the entrance to the court of Israel, and Malchus proceeded to its north side, before rapping on a stout door. It opened and a guard motioned them both through.

They walked down a narrow corridor and into a small chamber which smelt strongly of wood. The ceiling and walls were lined with cedar that appeared to have been polished to an obsessive degree. Caiaphas was sat at an equally polished desk, scribbling on one of the many scrolls which littered its surface. His quill danced across it with practised speed. Malchus indicated that Judas should sit at a chair on the far side of the desk, which he did. Silence reigned, save for the scratching of the quill.

'I'm sure you're wondering,' Caiaphas eventually said, continuing to write as he spoke, 'why I wanted to see you.'

'Yes,' Judas replied.

'It's a small matter,' Caiaphas said, plopping the quill down in its ink pot and deigning to actually look at Judas for the first time, 'of a missing corpse.'

'A missing corpse?'

'Don't play dumb with me, Judas. Or I'll ask Malchus here to use his sword to make you properly dumb.'

'Really, I'm not sure what –'

'Let me give you a clue,' the priest said, his words tumbling out slowly and deliberately.

'Please do.'

'We thought the Romans did a pretty good job of executing him, with our help naturally. But it would appear that, some would say, Jesus has been reborn.' Caiaphas smiled, or at least unleashed his approximation of smiling. His lips peeled back and he bared his stained yellow teeth which contrasted markedly with the black of his beard.

'I wouldn't know about that,' Judas said, unable to stop himself breaking eye contact.

'You wouldn't? Well he's escaped from his tomb, that much is clear. Which is quite a feat for a dead man. Isn't it?'

'Yes, it would be.'

'And you know nothing of this?'

Judas shrugged.

The high priest leaned forward and clasped his hands together. Sunlight streaming through the window glinted off a lavish-looking gem-studded gold ring on his left hand.

'Malchus, our friend says he knows nothing of this. Despite the fact that the other followers of the blasphemer do. He wouldn't dare lie inside the temple, would he?'

'It's not like I'm close to the other apostles any more, is it?' Judas said. 'Not after what I did.'

'So you're saying, here in the house of God, that you haven't seen any of –'

Judas halted the priest mid-sentence by standing and slapping down the pouch of silver coins on his desk. Interrupting Caiaphas so rashly probably wasn't a great idea, but he'd already done it before the thought occurred.

'Look, I came here on a different matter, anyway. I want to return this. It's yours. I want no part of it any more.'

Caiaphas calmly picked up the pouch, loosened its strings and glanced inside. He looked back up at Judas and that ghastly smile split his face again, turning into a laugh which echoed hollowly against the room's wood-clad interior.

'What?' Judas said.

'So . . . you claim not to have heard anything about Jesus once again walking among us. And yet, the very next day after he has "risen" from his tomb, you suddenly decide to bring back the money you received for your master's blood. Because you *just don't want it any more.*'

Judas could feel the palms of his hands becoming moist. 'Well, yes, I have heard a little something about Jesus. But it's all just rumour and hearsay.'

'What have you heard? Who have you spoken with?' The priest fired the two questions out in quick succession.

'Only Thomas. I met with him this morning. Or rather, he called on me. He just said exactly what you did – that Jesus has risen from the grave.'

'And he believes this?'

'No. He's not sure about it. He said the other apostles have seen Jesus. But he hasn't.'

'I'm sure the other "apostles" have seen Jesus,' Caiaphas said, standing. 'When they levered that boulder out of the way and carried his putrefying corpse off out of the tomb,' he finished, bringing his fist crashing down on the desk.

'I don't think ... well, maybe someone ...' Judas stammered.

'We know he hasn't been reborn, do we not?' Caiaphas bellowed, his beady brown eyes seeming to flash orange with fire.

'Yes,' Judas quickly agreed.

'Go to Thomas then, Judas. Go to the apostles. Take them a message. I will not suffer their foolishness gladly. Tell them to return the body, cease their games, or suffer the full weight of my wrath. And believe me, Judas, those who cross me pay a terrible price. Do you understand?'

'Yes,' Judas repeated. Sure. Go to the apostles. He'd get a warm reception there, he was certain. Although he might have some trouble understanding what they were saying by the time Peter had finished with his ears.

'Why are you still here?' the priest said. 'Get out!'

Judas turned and walked towards the door, which Malchus had already opened. He was halfway there when a small dense object, flung with some force, hit him square in the back as Caiaphas yelled, 'And take that with you!'

Judas span round to see the pouch of silver on the floor in front of him.

'The temple treasury will not accept this money, counted out as it was in blood,' Caiaphas said, his voice running as cold as a winter river. 'That silver is tainted. Its weight lies on your soul, Judas, and none else.'

Chapter 19

Before the betrayal, Judas had been seriously devout. He had prayed to God on a twice-daily basis, at the absolute minimum. He'd always felt that praying, in many ways, was like breathing. It was essential to your general well-being and continued existence. He didn't ask for anything for himself – well, rarely anyway – but instead praised God and took the opportunity to remind him about the suffering of others. God already knew everything that he had to say, naturally, but Judas figured there was no harm in offering his own unique, human perspective.

Since the crucifixion he hadn't prayed once. He'd wanted to, but something inside had prevented him from doing so. Partly it was shame. After all, what would he say to God exactly?

Sorry I betrayed your son and got him crucified.

How did you even begin to apologise for something like that? He hoped, eventually, he'd be able to start a dialogue again, but he couldn't see it happening any time soon, and that only added to his sorrow.

He bent down to adjust the sandal strap that was digging into his foot, then continued around the corner and stopped dead. Although it was a distance away, it was clear that the tomb which had once housed Jesus's body was now open, just as Thomas had said. The roughly hewn stone that had blocked the entrance had been rolled away. From its size alone it looked really heavy. To move a boulder like that you'd need a fair few strong men. Or one recently returned son of God.

There was no doubt the evidence for Jesus's resurrection was compelling. If his body had been snatched, as Caiaphas believed, then Judas was sure Thomas would have known about it. Peter wasn't the kind of man who could pull off a stunt like this and keep quiet about it afterwards. Besides, the apostles had all claimed to have met Jesus. It was possible they were all in on the deception, but Judas just couldn't see that being the case. Jesus had taught them all to believe and trust in the power of truth. Some more successfully than others.

There were two men outside the tomb, with short swords in scabbards, wearing orange tunics which were visible underneath their hardened leather armour. The uniform of the temple guard, posted by the Sanhedrin to keep the crowds away, no doubt, and doing a good job of it too. Only a single goat herder was in the vicinity, and when he paused to look over at the tomb, he was immediately struck on the shoulder by a well-aimed rock.

'Nothing to look at 'ere,' the older and brawnier of the two guards shouted.

The herder took the hint and moved his goats on, allowing the pair to go back to policing an empty stone cave and playing dice.

Judas had come here to see the tomb for himself and now he had. So he could go. Except … except he still needed to see inside. To be truly sure. He shook his head at the foolishness of what he was about to attempt, smoothed his hair back, pulled himself up to his full height, and strode towards the guards with what he hoped would be viewed as a sense of purpose. The burlier of the two men spotted him and nudged his companion. The rat-faced man with appalling skin looked up.

'Go away,' he said.

'How dare you address me like that,' Judas thundered in his most authoritative tone.

Rat Face looked taken aback. Burly Man frowned.

'Do you know who I am?' Judas asked.

Rat Face shook his rat head.

That made at least of two of them then. Judas wasn't sure who he was supposed to be either. He perhaps should have given it some thought before beginning this endeavour.

'I work for Caiaphas,' he improvised. 'The high priest asked me to come here, to check on the tomb, to check on you two. And what do I discover? You playing dice. Caiaphas will not be pleased when I report back. I am not pleased!'

'Sorry,' Rat Face said. 'Who are you?'

'Who are you? Give me your name, soldier.'

'I'm not technically a soldier.'

'Right. Well give me your name anyway.'

'Why?'

'So I may report you to Caiaphas.'

'You won't need my name for that. Caiaphas knows who we are. Describe me. That will probably be enough. Tell him the good-looking one, not the fat one, told you to bugger off.'

'I'm not fat,' the heavily built guard spluttered. 'This is pure muscle.' He flexed a large, rather flabby arm. Rat Face smiled.

'I need to look inside the tomb,' Judas said.

'There's nothing inside,' Rat Face replied. 'So there's no need to bother. On your way.'

'How dare you! Do not talk to me like that again or I will have you on sewage duty faster than . . . ' He couldn't think of something fast.

'Faster than what?' Burly Man said.

'It doesn't matter. If you don't want to be working in shit for the rest of your lives, you will treat me with respect, stand aside and let me inspect the tomb.'

'What did you say your name was again?' Rat Face asked.

'I am Malchus, bodyguard and assistant to Caiaphas.'

'No you're not,' Burly Man said.

Judas stood his ground and attempted a menacing stare. Like the real Malchus would.

'Malchus posted us here. He's shorter than you. And balder. Missing an ear.'

'No he isn't,' Rat Face said. 'I mean, he's shorter and balder but he definitely isn't missing an ear.'

The larger man looked confused for a moment and then said, 'No you're right. Wonder why I thought that? Must be confusing him with someone else.' He turned back to face Judas. 'Anyway, you're not him.'

'I'm not that Malchus, no. I'm another Malchus. Malchus son of Philip. And, yes, I'm not really Caiaphas's assistant, but he did ask me to come here, check on you and look inside the tomb. I can't tell you why, but it's a matter of great importance to the high priest. And the Sanhedrin.'

The burly guard rubbed his chin thoughtfully. 'No you're not,' he said, again.

'What?'

'You're not Malchus.'

'No, I explained. I'm not that Malchus.'

'You're not any Malchus. You're Judas Iscariot. I know your father, Simon. A good man. I thought I recognised you when

114

you first approached. You look like him. More hair of course, but the same nose.'

'Yes, fine, you're right, I am Judas. Caiaphas made me promise not to reveal my real identity. He doesn't want anyone knowing I'm working for him.'

'You're on some sort of secret mission?'

'Yes. One of great importance.'

'You believe him?' Rat Face asked his stout friend.

'I trust the word of an Iscariot, yes. So you want to look in the tomb, Judas?'

'I'd rather not,' Judas shrugged as indifferent a gesture as he could muster. 'Not a big fan of tombs, really, but I'm under orders so it's not like I have a choice. Caiaphas would have me gutted if I failed him.'

'Yeah, he's a mean bastard that one. All right, you can go inside. Just don't touch anything. Not that there's anything to touch.'

The two guards resumed their game leaving Judas free to step inside. The interior of the tomb was cool and the air pungent with the oils and spices used to anoint the body. The walls were dusty and the shelf which had briefly served as a resting place for the corpse bore a faint but discernibly man-sized imprint. There were footprints on the floor all around, but nothing that served as a clue to Jesus's disappearance. Judas bent down and touched his fingers to the sandy impression left by his master's body.

'You finished?' Burly Man shouted from outside.

Judas nodded to himself, stood, and went through the doorway, blinking as he stepped back out into the bright sunshine.

'It's empty.'

'It is. I heard they found some cloth, but I don't know where

115

it went.' The big man rolled the dice and squinted at the upward faces. The sides were so worn it was difficult to work out what the numbers were.

'They say he's the son of God and came back from the dead.' Rat Face sounded impressed.

'You believe that?' Burly Man shook his head. 'That a six?'

'Malchus wouldn't have asked us to guard an empty tomb if there wasn't something in the story. My brother says Jesus's death caused the temple to crack.'

'Yeah, I heard that too. That's definitely a six. Or maybe a four?'

'Have you seen anything strange? Out here I mean,' Judas said.

'What? Like a naked, dead man wandering around?' Burly Man laughed. 'All I've seen is an empty tomb. Same one you've seen now.'

'That's not a six, you cheating bastard.'

'I'll leave you to it,' Judas said. 'And thanks. I'll let Caiaphas know you're both doing a great job.'

He started to walk away. This had all been a huge waste of time. The tomb was empty and Jesus, if he truly was back from the dead, would have no reason to return here. After all, upon being brought back to life, one of the first things Lazarus had done was to plant a grove of olive trees around his burial place so he wouldn't ever have to see it again.

Judas stopped dead in his tracks. Lazarus. Of course. If anyone could offer an insight into the mind of a man who'd been dead and returned to life, it was him. Perhaps a trip to Bethany was in order.

As Judas resumed walking he thought he saw something move out of the corner of his eye. An indistinct shape with what looked like a blade in one hand. Filled with trepidation, he spun around to challenge the shadowy figure, but there was no one there, just a raven watching him inquisitively from the side of the road. He picked up a good-sized rock and hurled it in the direction of the spectator, but his missile found only dirt. In the time it had taken him to scoop up the chunk of sandstone the bird had vanished, leaving behind just a single shiny black feather.

Chapter 20

The high priest was at his desk, scribbling furiously. He dipped his quill in the ink and dashed off another sentence. He needed to focus. To concentrate on the task at hand. He gritted his teeth and loaded the quill with more ink. The urge, ever more frequent these days, was bubbling up inside him again. Becoming harder and harder to ignore.

The lamp on his desk began to flicker, but he barely noticed the dimming of the light. His hands gripped the quill tighter. Its nib scored the parchment as he wrote, pushing down on it firmly, trying to channel the unwanted desire into something pure and worthwhile.

He knew it was just a matter of time.

The wicked yearning was inexorably transforming into something that demanded to be satisfied.

He threw the quill across his desk. Ink sprayed over the parchment, totally ruining the past hour's work. He grabbed the paper with both hands and shredded it angrily.

He had to fight it.

Caiaphas put his head in his hands and tried to think of the things that made him happy. His possessions. His riches. His palatial home. It was no good. His mind continued to wander down that vile, insistent path. He switched tack to matters that made him angry. The so-called son of God, risen from the dead. Ridiculous. For a brief second this fresh anger managed to divert the boiling craving, but then it was back, and more insistent than ever.

There was only one way to end this. He had to act. Had to sate the dreadful desire.

'Malchus!' he roared, standing. 'Prepare my disguise. We're going out.'

Chapter 21

Of all the miracles Judas had witnessed his master perform during their time together, the one involving Lazarus was the most memorable, and not just because it involved a man coming back from the dead. Something equally incredible, but far more personal to Judas had also happened on that day.

As he walked the well-travelled route to Bethany, he tired of gazing at the many tents pitched along the roadside which acted as temporary homes for pilgrims, and found his mind settling among recollections of the days leading up to the miracle. Better, happier days.

Jesus and the apostles had been staying by the river Jordan, close to the spot where John the Baptist had preached in the early days. It was here, the others said, that Jesus himself had been baptised, but if that was true his teacher had never spoken of it to Judas.

Jesus had just returned from the waters when a messenger rode up to their makeshift camp. At first Judas had thought it was his friend Jonathan on horseback, but this messenger was younger, and darker, with a long scar running from his left eye all the way down his cheek. He handed a scroll to Jesus but didn't dismount or wait for a reply, simply turned his horse around and headed back the way he had come.

The news he'd delivered had not been good. Lazarus was seriously ill and, according to the note from his sisters, Mary and Martha, was unlikely to last more than another couple of days at most. If they left immediately they might just make it to Bethany in time, but it would be tight, not to mention very risky. The last time Jesus had been in Judea, the Jews had tried to stone him. Judas, like the others, had expected Jesus to make the journey anyway – Lazarus was a dear friend after all – and was more than a little surprised, not to mention somewhat relieved, when his teacher elected to stay put.

Two days later though, everything changed.

'We must pack, today, for Bethany,' Jesus announced as they were finishing breakfast, a simple meal of bread and honey.

'But why?' Judas had asked. 'It's too late now surely. It will take us days to get there, and Lazarus will be dead by the time we arrive, if he isn't already.'

Jesus simply smiled, acknowledged his concerns, and later that day they started for Judea. By the time they arrived in the town of Bethany they already knew their journey had been in vain. Everyone they'd met along the way had told them the same thing: Lazarus had died four days ago, shortly after the message had been sent.

'If you had been here my brother would not have died,' Martha had said when they met up with her a short while later. Her words had been sad rather than accusatory.

Jesus took her hands, and massaged them gently.

'Don't worry,' he said. 'Your brother will rise again.'

'I know,' Martha said. 'On the final day, but ...'

'But you miss him and want him back.'

She nodded, the folds of her green robe rustling with the movement. The emerald-coloured material was gathered and bunched up around her shoulders, held together by a silver clasp shaped like a butterfly in the centre of her chest. She wore a headscarf, striped with narrow bands of lighter greens and gold, underneath which her hair was gathered. But her fine clothes were nothing compared to her beauty.

If there was a more wondrous example of God's creative skills on the planet, Judas had yet to encounter her. And he'd travelled far and cast his gaze wide. Martha's round face had a striking symmetry, and her skin was white as the moon, but she wasn't entirely perfect. The dimples produced when she smiled weren't quite level with each other, and there was a mole near her ear which was visible when her hair was swept back, as it was now. But if anything those flaws – those infinitesimally small defects – only managed to further enhance her allure. She was a lot younger than Lazarus, and his fiercely protective nature was the reason that neither she nor her sister Mary were yet married. In many ways he was more like a father than a brother to them. But if Lazarus wasn't around, Judas had thought to himself, then maybe she'd find a suitor soon. There would certainly be no shortage of men keen to win her heart.

Jesus stared into Martha's hazel eyes and said, 'I am the resurrection and the life. Whosoever believes in me will live, even if they die; and whoever lives by believing in me will never die. Do you understand this?'

'Of course,' Martha nodded. 'You are the messiah, the son of God.'

'Good. Now go fetch Mary, she must be here to witness this with you.'

Martha left and returned ten minutes later with her sister.

Mary's face was red and scored with tears. It was hard to believe the two were related, let alone siblings. Mary was smaller than Martha's average height, and her face, while not unattractive, bordered on the plain side, even more so when standing next to her beautiful sister.

Like Martha before her, Mary pointed out – somewhat less politely – that her brother might still be alive if Jesus hadn't dallied.

'Where have you laid him?' Jesus asked the sisters.

They led him to Lazarus's tomb, a short walk away. A group of friends, family and villagers had gathered nearby to mourn, perhaps drawn there because they knew Jesus was close by, and as he walked past they whispered among themselves, expressing the same belief that he could have saved Lazarus if he'd wanted to. If Jesus heard these barbed rebukes and criticisms he did not show it, but the sight of his friend's tomb caused him to shed a tear. Judas watched as it rolled slowly down his lightly tanned skin, glistening in the afternoon sunlight.

'Move the stone away', Jesus said.

Without querying the request, several stocky villagers did as Jesus bid. The stone took a while to move clear, and Judas couldn't help but wonder why Jesus hadn't helped, as he'd done with the boulder in the village of Emmaus.

When the stone was fully removed, Jesus stared up at the sky for a long few moments, and then said, 'Father, I thank you that you have heard me. I know that you always hear me, but I say this for the benefit of the people standing here, that they may believe that you sent me.' Turning to face the entrance of the tomb, he said in a loud voice, 'Lazarus, come out!'

There was silence. The crowd gathered around them looked at one another with bemusement. Several even rolled their eyes. Then a sound came from within the tomb. A gentle scuffing noise. Slowly, a figure appeared in the mouth of the chamber and shuffled towards them, its limbs jerking like a puppet's, the feet dragging painfully over the stony ground. The mob of onlookers drew back, afraid. The short, stocky figure was unmistakably Lazarus, swaddled in strips of linen and with a cloth covering part of his face, and yet at the same time it wasn't him. The man's skin was grey and sallow, and his one visible eye closed, dark ringed and hollow. Lazarus's hair, once black and curly, was now as white as sun-bleached sand.

As he stared transfixed at the shuffling figure, Judas felt a hand reach for his and grip it tightly. He cast a quick glance to his right and saw Martha next to him, her eyes locked unwaveringly on her brother as he made his way slowly towards them.

'A chair,' Jesus said. Someone fetched a wooden seat and Jesus guided Lazarus into it. He placed one hand on the grey man's chest and the other on his forehead and said something so quietly that no one could hear. Lazarus jerked as if he had been stung by hornets and gave a grunt. His body arced, then flopped forwards, his chin bouncing off his chest. The cloth that had covered his face fell to the ground.

Jesus pushed him back into the chair, and pressed again on the man's heart and forehead. Lazarus gasped as if he'd been pulled from an icy lake. He coughed and spluttered, but instead of water being expelled from his lungs a wisp of an evanescent black shadow escaped his lips, becoming paler and curling away into nothingness in the time it took to even acknowledge its existence.

'Awake, Lazarus,' Jesus commanded.

Lazarus opened his eyes and there was a collective gasp. His pupils were dark and unseeing. He turned his head like a blind man, first one way and then the other as if trying to identify the direction of the command. It was a disturbing, sorry, and terrifying scene to behold. But as Judas watched, the dark pupils sparked and flickered. Bursts of colour ignited in the centre of each one like twin flames catching hold, and began to spread rapidly. The colouration engulfed Lazarus's eyes and began to haemorrhage out into his skin, becoming pink as it did so. In seconds the complexion of his face had lost its greyness. His cheeks became flushed and ruddy; his nose reddened as if he had consumed too much wine.

As the spread of colour reached his torso, Lazarus's chest began to rise and fall rapidly, accompanied by a gasping sound as if he was trying to catch up on four days of lost air. His tongue slipped out of his mouth and ran across cracked parched lips, but failed to produce any moisture.

'Water,' Jesus said.

Someone fetched a cup and held it to the gasping man's lips. Lazarus's mouth opened and he tried to drink, but most of the liquid just spilled down his chin and dripped onto his chest. He coughed and some water came up, along with another diminutive cloud of dark air that vanished as quickly as before.

'That is enough,' Jesus said, and moved the cup away.

Strands of white hair started to darken on Lazarus's head, twisting and turning like a nest of agitated vipers. His hands began to twitch as the tributaries of pink colour reached them; seconds later his feet began to dance wildly as if they were resting on hot coals.

Judas squeezed Martha's hand, an act of gentle reassurance, but she didn't squeeze back. He looked over and saw her face had turned an icy white, her eyes unblinking. He wanted to tell her it would be all right, but as the words began to form Lazarus suddenly bucked violently in the chair. His body arched, and twitched, and then with an anguished cry that was like nothing

125

Judas had ever heard before, he slumped down and lay deathly still.

'No!' Martha screamed, and her hand went limp as if all the tendons had been cut. Someone to the left of them stepped forward, but faltered almost immediately. No one else moved.

The man in the chair looked at peace now. So peaceful in fact it was almost as if he was –

Lazarus made a noise, coming from deep down in his belly, which sounded almost like a long, drawn out snore.

A ripple of nervous laughter from the crowd caused the sleeping figure to stir a little, and he shifted in the chair as if trying to get comfortable.

'Awake, old friend,' Jesus said, as he shook Lazarus's shoulder. Lazarus opened one eye and squinted up at Jesus. Recognising him, he sat up sharply.

'I'm so sorry, my friend, I must have dozed off,' he said in a croaky tone. He coughed as if trying to dislodge something. 'What's happened to my voice?' He looked at Jesus. 'How long was I asleep?'

'A while.'

'I'm sorry. I didn't know you were here. I'll – would you like – Martha, Mary?'

Without waiting for a response, Lazarus began to rise. The confusion on his face was clear. Jesus put one hand on his shoulder and pushed him gently back down into the chair. At once, Lazarus fell back asleep.

The crowd erupted in delight as one. Mary fell to her knees and began to openly weep. Martha, eyes shining, turned to Judas, freed her hand from his and threw her arms around his neck with such force that they nearly overbalanced. He managed to right himself just as she pulled her head to face him, and kissed him hard on the lips. It was a kiss filled with relief, but with an undercurrent of passion that took Judas's breath away. Martha stepped back, embarrassed, and began to rush around the other apostles, thanking each one effusively in turn. She saved her final thanks for Jesus, sinking to her knees and clutching his hands in reverence. But, Judas noticed, she didn't kiss anyone else during her rounds.

There were many reasons why Martha might have chosen to show him such affection. Perhaps because he had been there for her, held her hand when she had needed support. Or because he was the first person she had turned to when she realised her brother was truly alive once more.

The kiss had ignited feelings inside Judas he had tried to put aside since leaving his old life and following Jesus. His heart felt light, and there was a giddiness he knew was misplaced. Martha had kissed him because she was grateful and he was there. It was stupid to read more into it than that. At least that was what he had told himself at the time.

But as she was leaving with Mary, to prepare the house for the still-sleeping Lazarus's return, Martha had sought out Judas and thanked him once again. Not with a kiss this time, but with a look that told him there was more to their shared moment than just circumstance.

Chapter 22

Judas had seen Martha twice after the miracle. Once they'd gone for a long walk in the woods near her home to pick berries, and although they hadn't kissed then, they had held hands, and talked with an easiness about anything and everything. He told her the story of how he'd come to follow Jesus, and she told him about life with her siblings. They'd listened attentively to each other's anecdotes, shared some laughter, and even fed each other some of the fruit they'd picked. She had told him that his eyes were so deep brown, they almost matched the colour of his black hair. He had succumbed to a heady mix of feelings which melted together as she'd stared into them.

The second meeting hadn't gone as smoothly, however, and threatened to bring their early blossoming relationship to a juddering halt.

Judas shook his head at the memory. The last time he'd seen Martha had been at her home, six days before Passover. A meal had been prepared to honour and thank Jesus for bringing Lazarus back from the dead. The food, succulent beef and mustard, followed by bowls of camel's milk and curds, had been tasty enough, but Judas had found the possibility of spending more time with Martha a far more appetising prospect. He'd devoted much of the evening to admiring her from afar, so much as gaps in the conversation would allow, and every time their eyes met she'd smiled at him. It had all felt so promising.

After they'd eaten, Mary, Lazarus's less alluring sister, had poured a whole pint of pure nard on Jesus's feet and then wiped them with her hair. Nard was a very expensive perfume, an extracted oil from a rare plant, and that quantity would have cost a labourer like Baruch the best part of an entire year's wages. Not that Baruch would ever have dreamed of buying perfume.

At any rate, it had seemed a very wasteful thing to do and Judas had said as much. Even going as far as to suggest that it might have been better to sell the perfume and give the money to the needy.

He hadn't meant to offend poor, plain Mary in her own home. If anything he'd simply been showing off to Martha. It was a seriously ill-judged remark though, and Jesus had rebuked him for it. Made him feel small, foolish even. Embarrassed him in front of Martha.

He'd left the house without saying goodbye and walked back alone, berating himself for the words he'd spoken in haste. He had wanted to go back and apologise, even planned to do exactly that in the morning, but Daniel's visit later that night had thrown his plans into disarray. After hearing about his uncle's gambling woes, Judas had spent the next day agonising over his options instead, and had gone to see Caiaphas in the evening, setting the wheels in motion for what was to follow.

Judas rounded the bend, looked up and saw Lazarus's home just ahead, lit by the orangey-red tendrils of the late afternoon sun which was just dipping behind it. The house was a large stone building with a long wall that snaked around the courtyard and garden to the rear. At the front, the windows were all above head height and designed to let in light rather than afford a view. The front door was a polished oak slab with a sycamore frame. Judas knocked on it, and waited. A few seconds later he heard the sound of someone moving around inside. A bolt slid back and the door opened to reveal Martha. Without her head-scarf covering it, her long dark hair tumbled down over her shoulders, exquisitely framing her delicate white face.

She looked at him long and hard for several seconds, then stepped forward and delivered a stinging slap to the side of his face. Judas staggered back under the force of the blow, his cheek on fire.

'Bastard,' Martha shouted through the sound of ringing in his left ear. Her hazel eyes were flecked with tiny shards of ire. 'How dare you come here?'

She knew then. Knew about the betrayal, knew about every-thing. Except why he'd done it.

'You've got to let me explain,' he began, then ducked as Martha swung at him a second time.

'Explain?' she shrieked the word out. 'Explain what? Peter came to see us. We know what you did!'

'But Jesus isn't dead,' Judas shouted as he grabbed both of Martha's wrists and tried to hold her at bay. It was like wrestling a wild animal. 'He's back.'

'I know. We heard that too.' Unable to do anything other than struggle in Judas's firm grip, Martha just glared at him with undisguised hatred. The fury now colouring her cheeks made her seem even more beautiful, and Judas was gripped by a sudden irrational urge to kiss her. Martha leaned forward, like she was feeling the same conflicting emotion, but then spat in his eyes, temporarily blinding him. He tried to blink away the spittle without releasing his grip on the enraged woman's wrists.

'That's enough, Martha,' a voice from inside the house commanded.

Judas recognised Lazarus's deep tone immediately. As his vision cleared, he watched the man appear out of the shadows behind her.

'Let him go,' Lazarus said.

Martha shot her brother a look of anger. 'He's got me.'

'He hardly has a choice now, does he?'

Judas let go of Martha's wrists and she withdrew reluctantly, still glaring at him as he stepped inside. He allowed Lazarus to usher him through the house, out into a stone-paved courtyard. It was tidy, well swept, and surprisingly free of any livestock. There was a small garden of lush bushes set off to one side. Several padded wooden benches were arranged around the middle of the space, where a large bronze pot hung over a dormant firepit. Judas sat on one bench. Lazarus, clad in a purple silken robe, with a pattern of yellow triangles sewn into the chest, sat opposite him.

'I wasn't sure you'd still be here,' Judas said.

'I shouldn't be. Not really. I love Bethany but the Sanhedrin would quite like me dead again. They wanted to kill me before the crucifixion, and now they just want to tie up any loose ends. So I guess we'll have to leave soon. Water?'

Lazarus indicated the earthenware jug and a single glazed black cup on the bench beside him. Judas nodded and watched as Lazarus poured some water and passed over the cup.

'Thank you,' Judas said, and drank deeply from it. The liquid was cool and refreshing, pulled recently from Lazarus's own well no doubt. He placed the vessel against his cheek and felt it draw out some of the sting from Martha's slap.

'You're the last person I expected to see here, Judas,' Lazarus said. 'Martha won't ever forgive you, you know.'

'I know. I can't blame her.'

'No, I don't suppose you can.' Lazarus gave a simple shrug. Judas looked into his eyes and they seemed as empty as that gesture. Lifeless, blank, but for a tinge of knowing sadness that reminded him of the look Jesus had given him shortly before the betrayal in the Garden of Gethsemane. It made him shudder.

Prior to his death, Lazarus had been jolly and, for want of a better phrase, full of life. After he'd come back, it was as if he'd forgotten how to smile. His mouth was turned down at both corners, he had a permanent frown, and his hair, although still mostly dark in colour, was now scarred with white streaks. Whatever he'd seen during the four days he'd been dead had clearly left him a very changed man.

And Judas had come all this way to ask him about it.

'Actually, it wasn't Martha I came to see, Lazarus, it was you.'

'Me?'

'I wanted to ask you a question.'

'Go on.'

'I just wondered ...' Judas shifted uneasily, 'what it was like?'

'What, what was like?'

'Dying. Well, not dying as such. I just wondered what it was like being dead. What you saw?'

Lazarus rubbed a stubby finger up and down his nose thoughtfully for several seconds, as if searching for the right words.

'I saw nothing,' he said, eventually.

'Nothing?'

'Nothing.'

'At all?'

'Nothing at all, Judas. Just blackness.'

'No light?'

'No light.'

132

'Angels?'

Lazarus glared at him.

'No angels. I saw nothing. At all.'

He seemed very insistent. And his haunted eyes darted around the courtyard as he spoke. Looking everywhere but at Judas.

'Are you sure?'

'I am.'

Lazarus was evidently hiding something, but he clearly wasn't about to reveal whatever it was to Judas. Unless . . .

'I saw Jesus, after he came back,' Judas said. 'He appeared to me.'

'He came to you as well?' Lazarus asked, making solid eye contact.

'He did. I mean, he came to me in a dream, but I know it was real.'

Lazarus nodded. 'Peter said he appeared to him, and the others. This dream, what happened in it?'

Judas paused for a second. He could hardly tell Lazarus that Jesus had stabbed him to death. Instead he needed to improvise something that would get the man opposite him to open up.

'I asked Jesus about dying,' he said. 'And he told me it was nothing to be afraid of. He said he was at peace and that heaven was a place of myriad wonders. He said dying was something that happens to us all. Even to him, and that it was a good thing.'

'A good thing?' Lazarus snorted dismissively. 'Well I saw nothing, Judas. No angels. No myriad wonders.'

Why would Lazarus lie? It didn't make sense, unless he'd seen something truly dreadful. Something he couldn't bring himself to speak about.

'So when you came back from the dead – what did you feel then?'

Lazarus took the cup from Judas, threw the remaining water on the ground, refilled it and downed the cool liquid. 'I was tired at first,' he admitted. 'Just overwhelmingly tired. Food and drink held no appeal to me. A tender breast of roasted chicken tasted like burnt earth, the finest Roman wines were sour and unpalatable. I didn't, if I'm honest, know what to make of it all. And that, after a while, made me feel angry.'

'Angry?'

'Oh yes. Sounds ridiculous, doesn't it? I should have been happy, delighted to be back with my family and my friends and yet I had all this . . . inside, I was . . . ' Lazarus trailed off. 'Don't get me wrong, I'm very grateful for what Jesus did for me, but some days – some dark days – I feel I don't belong here, I shouldn't be here, that the world has moved on, mourned me and forgotten me, and now I'm a ghost person flitting through . . . not connected somehow. Almost like the anger, the rage I have, is the only thing binding me to existence.' Lazarus's face contorted as he spoke, and he choked out the last sentence through gritted teeth.

'But Martha and Mary have been my angels,' he continued, his expression swiftly softening. 'They make it all worthwhile.' He sighed deeply. 'I think being dead, it's an experience that just, I don't know . . . it affects you, Judas. In ways the living can't begin to imagine.'

Chapter 23

It was getting even warmer. Jose shifted his position on the stone bench, wiping beads of perspiration from his brow. He was naked, save for a pair of leather sandals on his feet, as were the other two men in the caldarium.

The caldarium was the hot room in the bathhouse, where water sluicing onto the mosaic-tiled floor rapidly turned to steam due to the high temperature. The walls were hollow and the floor raised on supports to allow hot air from the furnace in the neighbouring room to course underneath, heating the tiles. That's why the sandals were necessary. The heat also rose up through the cavity in the walls. Basically, the caldarium was like a small oven, where people came to sweat out the grime and sins of the day.

Jose turned to Daniel, who was sat next to him on the bench, and asked, 'How's the wife?'

'She's fine. I wish I could say the same about her mother.'

Jose nodded.

Ugly Saul, who was in the plunge bath over on the far side of the room, chuckled as he said, 'Made good your escape tonight, Daniel?'

'I did. I told the wizened old crone I had to go round to Philip's to fix a table.'

'Shame you can't fix her,' Saul said, as he hauled himself out of the ten-foot deep pool of water. Jose found an interesting coloured tile to gaze at on the floor as Saul padded over to join them on the U-shaped stone bench. He was ugly enough when fully clothed, but naked he was spectacularly revolting to behold. From his huge hooked nose, through his slightly hunched spine, to his spindly, bow legs, he appeared to be entirely constructed of angles.

'Getting way too hot in the pool,' Ugly remarked as he sat down. 'Throw some veg in there and we could stir up a nice big soup for supper.'

'Hmm,' Jose said. It did seem unusually warm, but he was actually quite glad of it. At least the temperature had fuddled his mind a little, and muted the anguish of the last three days in a way that copious amounts of wine had so far failed to do. He didn't understand, and probably never would, what had driven someone to brutally butcher his son like that. Rumour had it that Gideon might have lost his life due to an argument over sheep, but that made no sense to Jose.

'You all right?' Ugly said.

'Yeah,' Jose replied. Although he was aware that both his friends knew he wasn't. It was late at night, they had the place to themselves, and normally he'd have been gossiping with abandon like an old wife, not mumbling the odd word.

'Have you found a buyer for the sheep yet?' Ugly asked.

Daniel shot Saul a dirty look.

'Sorry,' Ugly said, 'I'm just trying to make conversation.'

'It's fine,' Jose said. 'Death comes to us all, eventually. And Gideon's flock – both Simon and Gilead have been asking about them.'

'Gilead?'

'Yes, for Baruch.'

'Baruch couldn't look after a herd of rocks,' Ugly snorted.

'Quite.'

'And Simon was asking on behalf of Judas presumably?' Daniel said.

'Yes.'

'I don't think Judas will be too keen on the idea of shepherding, to be honest.'

Jose nodded, going quiet again.

'How is Simon? I don't see my brother as much as I should, these days,' Daniel said.

'He's Simon.'

'Yes. He is. Always was.'

'Is it me, or is it getting a bit much in here?' Ugly asked. 'The last time I sweated like this, I was in the middle of the desert.'

'When were you in the middle of the desert?' Daniel said. 'I didn't think you'd ever left Jerusalem.'

'I travelled with a spice caravan once.'

'What did they want you along for – to scare off the vultures?' Daniel was pleased to see Jose break into a half-smile at his joke.

Saul noticed it too and added, 'No, it was all a mistake.' He paused for a few moments, before continuing, 'They thought I was a camel.'

Jose let out a light chuckle, which the pair joined in with.

'Actually, I was the cook,' Ugly said. They seemed to find that even more amusing and for a brief period laughter mingled with the steam.

'Seriously, what's with it in here tonight?' Daniel ran his hands through his lank hair and examined his glistening palms. 'I swear my feet are starting to get hot even through my sandals.'

'Yeah. I know.' Ugly lowered his hand, palm facing downwards, to hover just above the surface of the floor. 'Ezekiel's donkey! That's really, really warm.' He touched the floor with a finger, which was quickly retracted. 'Shit,' he hissed, 'ouch, ouch, ouch.'

All three men were starting to drip with sweat like hogs on a spit.

'That's enough for me,' Daniel said, standing. He began to make his way over to the door.

'Agreed,' Jose said, wiping down the sweat from his chest and the small pot belly which protruded below it. His flushed face was now the same colour as his ruddy nose, itself a product of far too much wine over the years.

Ugly also stood up. Daniel reached the door and pushed it open. Or at least tried to. He pushed it a bit harder, then shoved it again.

'Er, it won't open,' he said.

'Let me see.' Ugly motioned Daniel aside. He placed both his hands on the door, planted his feet, and shoved as hard as he could, several times. It didn't budge. 'What the hell ...'

It was Jose's turn next. Slightly stockier than Daniel – and much wider than lanky Saul – he took a short run at the door and shoulder-charged it. It rattled on its hinges, but remained steadfast. He tried again, twice more, and still it didn't yield. Jose then had to stop. He bent over, hands on his knees, to recover for a moment, his breathing heavy.

The heat in the room was stifling now, the air thicker still, weighing down on them and exerting an uncomfortable pressure.

'What do we do?' Ugly asked, looking around, then up at the ceiling. 'Is there any other way out?'

'No,' Daniel said. 'No other way. But there's got to be

someone around who'll hear us.' He stepped back up to the door and banged his fist on it multiple times. 'Help!' he bellowed, over and over. Ugly joined in, hammering on the wood alongside him. After a minute or so they stopped and listened.

'It's late. I'm not sure there's anyone about,' Jose said.

'Of course there's bloody someone about,' Daniel snapped. 'There has to be. If only the fellow tending the furnace.'

'Good point.' Ugly banged on the door a few more times. 'Hey,' he shouted at the top of his voice. 'Hey!'

'What is that son of a whore playing at?' Daniel said.

'I'm trying to get us out of here,' Ugly hissed back.

'Not you, I mean the fool working the furnace. Why's it getting so ridiculously hot in here?'

'I don't know,' Jose replied, 'but I don't like it. Let me have another go at that door. You two check around the room and see if you can find anything to batter it with.'

The pair scouted about the place, as Jose launched his foot at the door, sole first, exerting all the effort he could. Five hefty kicks later, it remained firmly closed and Jose had to rest again.

'Find anything?' he asked, when he finally got his breath back.

'No,' came twin replies. The room contained nothing, save for the plunge pool and the stone benches which were built into the floor.

'The pool, though,' Ugly said. 'The thing's almost bubbling over here. Practically boiling now.'

'You're kidding.'

'Do I sound like I'm kidding?'

Jose kicked out at the door, twice more. The only result was a slight creaking. And he suspected that was his knee. His head was starting to feel light with the effort and he had to lean up against the door momentarily. Even the thick wood was hot to the touch.

'I've got to sit down,' Jose said, making his way back to the stone bench.

Daniel continued to pound away with his fists and holler, before he too had to sit, along with Ugly, as the heat started to become insufferable. A few highly uncomfortable minutes passed.

'What ... do we ... do?' Daniel gasped out the words with some difficulty, rivulets of sweat pouring down his back.

Jose shook his head, although he realised as he did so, he'd forgotten what question Daniel had asked. His mind was fuzzy, his eyelids sticking on his eyes when he blinked. He turned his head to look at Daniel and saw his friend had perspiration dripping off his chin in thin salty waterfalls.

They were going to melt to death. Could human beings melt? It felt like it. He moved his arm up to mop his brow and it seemed like there were weights attached to it.

The silence was broken as the door flung open, banging against the wall.

A figure entered the room. Dressed in a brown robe, cowl pulled up over his head, he made his way over to the trio on the bench. They all turned to look at him. Matching smiles crept across their faces.

'Praise be!' Daniel managed to say.

The stranger altered his course and made straight for Daniel, yanking him up off the bench. The other two watched, stunned, as the next few seconds played out in some manner of slow-motion.

The man dragged Daniel across the room, half-running, and hurled him head-first into the plunge pool. There was a splash, which the man leapt backwards to avoid, accompanied by an awful fizzing sound.

Daniel bobbed up and broke the surface of the boiling hot water, his face a patchwork of bewilderment and shock. As some measure of realisation sank in, he let out a crescendoing, inhuman howling noise. His hands grasped for the edge of the pool, trying to get a grip on the floor to pull himself out.

The man stood on one of Daniel's hands, and with his other foot, kicked him viciously in the head. Daniel disappeared back beneath the bubbling water, as Jose stood up, and despite being wobbly on his feet, rushed at the man in the cowl. Ugly Saul followed.

The man moved quickly and smashed an elbow square into Jose's face before he even knew what had happened. Already drained and weakened near to the point of exhaustion, Jose was sent reeling, hitting the wall and slumping to the floor. Saul, disoriented and dizzy from the sudden motion of standing and attempting to run, didn't even make it to the man; instead he veered wildly sideways and also crashed to the ground. The attacker stalked towards him.

Jose tried to stand, to drag himself up off the hot floor which was starting to burn his legs and buttocks, but everything seemed blurry and unreal. It took him some time to get his bearings and haul himself upright. As he refocused on the room, the first thing he saw was Daniel's limbs thrashing as he surfaced once more, his hands scrabbling to get a hold on the floor. Jose looked in horror at his friend's swelling, blistered face and milky white unseeing eyes. Daniel's head started to whip involuntarily from side to side, and his arms began to spasm, his red raw hands now flopping uselessly on the floor they were attempting to grip. He was choking, his mouth opening and closing rapidly, a man trying to scream a soundless scream, his lungs scalded into incapacity by the boiling water he'd gulped down.

With a great effort, Jose propelled himself away from the wall he'd staggered against and went to help his friend. He grabbed Daniel's arm just before he went back under, and tried to pull him out with what strength he could muster. However, the limb was covered with fresh blisters and several of the fluid-filled lumps burst under the pressure of Jose's grasp. Daniel's arm slowly slipped away, Jose losing his grip as ribbons of slick skin sloughed off in his hand. His friend sank beneath the bubbling waters again.

Jose span around as he heard a muffled cry from Saul.

Ugly had managed to crawl back onto the bench and the man was now sitting on his back, straddling him. Jose watched as the attacker took Saul's head in his hands and twisted it left, then swiftly to the right, and then yanked it backwards with a brutal degree of force. Each movement was accompanied by a series of sharp crunches and cracks as the vertebrae in Ugly's neck fractured and splintered.

Jose turned and stumbled towards the open door, praying that his legs would hold. He made it through the opening – into the clean air, the cool, beautiful air – and ran unsteadily for the exit, as fast as he could manage. Through the men's changing room, he hurled himself around the narrow corridor, bouncing off the walls twice, through a door ...

His escape seemed all but assured, when something lying on the floor caught his foot and sent him sprawling.

He was aware of the sensation of heat again. He pulled himself up groggily and saw the furnace in front of him. Effectively a huge open fireplace, it had been built up and stoked voraciously so it raged with flames that crackled like hellfire. No wonder it had been so damn hot in the caldarium. He spotted what he'd tripped over on the floor – the prone body of the man who was supposed to keep watch over the furnace.

He'd taken a wrong turn. The exit was to the right, the furnace room to the left. Jose staggered back to the doorway, but as he did so, he ran into the brown-cowled figure. Jose felt something, a cold in his gut, and backed away. He saw the man was holding a knife out in front of him; the blade was dark red. Jose looked down at his midriff. Blood oozed from an angry puncture wound.

The man started to advance. Jose stepped back further as he did so, clutching a hand to his stomach. He stopped when he could feel the heat of the furnace prickling on his back. Still the man kept coming.

'I have money,' Jose stammered, 'I can give you money ... things ... whatever you –'

The man shoved him hard. Jose, far too weak to offer any sort of meaningful resistance, toppled backwards into the furnace, his body collapsing sideways as he fell into an orange and yellow world of unimaginable, searing agony. Every nerve end was simultaneously stimulated beyond comprehension. He smelt his hair burn and felt his skin tighten, the stinging, blinding pain firing off a seemingly infinite volley of wildly arcing neural signals across his brain.

Mustering a huge, last-gasp effort, he managed to haul himself around. His hands located the narrow stone hearth at the front of the furnace, and grasping it, he found the strength from some deep primal reserve to pull himself forward. His head was out, and then he pulled his chest out of the flames. Another effort – one more pull – and ...

He felt a pressure on the top of his head, pushing it down hard onto the floor. Jose couldn't move any further, and his hands grasped for whatever was holding him in place. He touched a leg, then the sandal-clad foot that was standing on his crown, and scrabbled weakly at it in an attempt to dislodge it. But he had no more reserves left.

Jose was held there by the man. Immobile. Helpless. His legs, still wedged deep within the scorching pyre of wood, began to contract of their own accord, the muscles and ligaments reacting to the intense temperature. The stench of burning flesh reached his nostrils as the skin on his lower limbs began to lose its integrity. He heard the crackle of the fat underneath as it oozed out, cooking, spitting, under the searing heat.

The flames had spread further now, creeping and licking up his torso. Jose's shouts and screams had stopped, his brain shutting down in the face of the relentless, overwhelming trauma. He had ceased all attempts at movement. The killer stood back and listened for a moment.

Jose's limp, now rapidly blackening body was still breathing, if you could call it breathing. It was more a sort of horrendous rasping, a ragged and rattling low moan, slowly in, slowly out; a noise like the bellows of purgatory.

Perhaps Jose was still in there, somewhere. A minute later, even the purgatorial bellows ceased drawing air and just the crackling and popping of the flames remained.

The man turned and left the room.

Chapter 24

A loud knocking stirred Judas from his slumber. He groaned, squinted through his eyelids, then decided that opening them fully was too much of an effort. He buried his head underneath his pillow instead.

The rapping on the door came again, louder and more insistent.

Judas hurled the pillow across the room. 'All right, all right, I'm coming.'

He rubbed his eyes to help them acclimatise to the light, climbed out of bed, threw on a robe and padded over to the door, unbolting it with some annoyance.

'Jeb?'

Jebediah the Cripple shuffled past him, saying nothing, his wooden crutch creaking with every step. He sat down at the table and waited for Judas to join him.

'Come in, please,' Judas said, walking over and sitting opposite. He stifled a yawn as his unexpected guest began rooting around in the stained yellow bag he was wearing casually over one shoulder.

'So, what brings you here? And how do you even know where I live?'

'I keep telling you, Judas, I may not live within the city walls, but I know everything that goes on in Jerusalem.' Jeb produced a crumpled piece of cloth from the bag and began to unwrap it. 'Unfortunately,' he added, as he extracted something small and black from the bundle and popped it into his mouth.

'Unfortunately?'

Jebediah nodded as he chewed and crunched. 'It's bad news, I'm afraid.'

'What is?' It was too early in the morning for this.

'Have you had breakfast?' Jeb asked, pushing the cloth forward on the table. Judas noted its contents and grimaced.

'No. And neither have you. I don't count cindered cockroaches as real food.'

'They're fried locusts, actually. I got them from a street stall.'

'After it had burned down presumably? Stop changing the subject, anyway. You don't normally bother with things like subtlety. What's the bad news? Tell me.'

Jebediah popped another locust into his mouth. 'There was another killing last night,' he said, between crunches. 'Killings, actually. The Romans are all over the Rose Mount bathhouse just now. There were four people all murdered together up there. One was a chap called Jonas, who worked there, but the others . . . ' He swallowed the remains of the insect in his mouth and stared directly into Judas's eyes. 'One was Gideon's father, Jose. He was burned to death, apparently. Pushed into the furnace.'

Judas stared at Jeb in horror. 'Jose?'

The beggar nodded. 'Another was Ugly Saul. He had his neck broken. A friend of yours too, wasn't he?'

'More my father's,' Judas mumbled. His head was spinning at the news. The knotted swirls on the table's wooden surface seemed to be dancing.

'Speaking of your father . . . '

Judas sat bolt upright and his eyes went wide.

146

'No, no, don't panic he's fine,' Jeb reassured him quickly. 'As far as I know, anyway. It's his brother.'

Judas felt a massive wave of relief engulf him. Followed swiftly by an equally massive wave of guilt. 'Uncle Daniel?'

Jeb nodded. 'He was boiled alive. Or boiled dead, really. In a super-heated plunge pool.' The beggar selected another locust from his seemingly endless supply, popped it into his mouth, and began to chew noisily.

The news was almost too much to take in. Three of them murdered all at once. This was an acceleration, a spree. A rampage even. This was bad. Beyond bad. Burned? Boiled? What manner of brutal psychopath would do that?

The sheer cruelty of this latest development began to sink in. Daniel, the man Judas had betrayed Jesus to save, had been murdered anyway. And in an even more awful manner than the Butcher had planned.

Boiled alive ... a hideous way to go.

And one which left a mixture of emotions boiling inside Judas. Fear, grief, and anger bubbled in an internal cauldron which threatened to spill over at any second.

Jebediah coughed into his hand.

'What?' Judas snapped. 'Oh I see, you want money now? Money, that's all that matters, isn't it?'

The beggar continued to cough. Judas drew a slow breath. What was he thinking, taking it out on the messenger? Jeb had come out here, first thing, straight away to tell Judas about this. Of course he'd want a donation.

Jebediah coughed once more, beating his chest a few times with a clenched fist. 'Locust,' he spluttered, 'went down the wrong way. That got it I think.'

'Ahh, I see. I'm sorry, I didn't mean to shout at you ... it's just that ...'

'I understand.'

'Wait a moment, I'll go and get you a couple of copper coins.'

'No. No need. Don't look so surprised. This is your uncle. It's family, Judas, family. I won't take money where that's concerned. But I would like to know why people around you keep dying.'

Judas shrugged. He'd desperately like to know the answer to that question too. 'I let a friend down. Badly,' was all he could manage.

'Right. I can understand that. Usually when someone lets me down, I go around beating their friends and family to death with my crutch.'

'I got him killed, Jeb. And now –'

'Someone's coming after you for revenge.'

'Yes.'

'It's a hell of a revenge. Why don't they just kill you?'

'I don't know. I think they believe I need to ... suffer.'

'You any idea who this maniac is?'

'None.'

Jebediah wrapped his locusts back up, then stood with the aid of his crutch. 'Yes you do. Or at least you think you do.'

'No, I don't.'

'Look, I told you I know everything that goes on in this city, and I do. The friend you got killed, well that's Jesus obviously.'

'No it's –'

'Don't bother lying, Judas. You got Jesus killed, he's back from the dead and people around you are dropping like flies. I can't see him being behind all this, though.'

'No?'

'You really think he is? You knew him far better than I did – I never even got to meet him – but it strikes me that settling scores isn't his thing. He's the messiah, so they say. He was a force for good, Judas, about as far removed from a psychopathic killer as you could get.'

'Who then?'

'Absolutely no idea.'

'But I thought you knew everything?'

'Everything but that. But you know who might be able to help? Perhaps give you some pointers.'

'Who?'

'Blind Mary.'

'The seer?'

'You know another blind woman called Mary?'

'No, but –'

'*She cannot see, yet she sees more than me.*'

'Yes – *She'll set me free, from all the doubts that be* – I know the rhyme. I just don't know if I believe everything people say about her.'

'You saw Jesus perform all sorts of miracles, Judas, is it really so hard to believe other people might have spiritual powers as well?'

'No. I guess not.'

'Besides, what have you got to lose?' Jebediah asked as he reached the front door.

'Wait,' Judas said, retreating to the back of the house, before emerging again to shake the crippled beggar's hand.

'What's this?' Jeb asked, looking at the two copper coins in his palm.

'Just take it. You're a good man. I appreciate you coming over, and your advice.'

'Thanks,' Jeb said, smiling. His teeth were black from the locusts and Judas was sure he could see legs protruding between the gaps.

Chapter 25

Sewing wasn't really Simon Iscariot's thing, he knew that, but while his typical effort at stitching up a hole might look somewhat crude, it didn't normally result in ripping an even bigger tear in the fabric.

He threw the robe onto the floor in disgust. He just couldn't seem to concentrate this morning.

He'd gone to bed early the previous evening, but had awoken abruptly, in the middle of the night, gripped by a strange, disturbing sense that something was wrong in the world. It was an uneasiness he'd been unable to shake even after he'd risen with the dawn.

Simon didn't like feelings he couldn't explain. And he didn't like sewing either. He reached down, picked up the discarded piece of clothing, and brushed the dirt off it. If only Judas had taken over Gideon's flock. They'd have enough wool to replace all of his tatty robes and there would be no need to do any sewing ever again.

He was about to resume his repair attempt when somebody knocked heavily on the front door. Three loud, insistent thumps.

'Hold on, I'm coming,' he said.

Chapter 26

Judas pushed on the door and stepped inside. The sensible course of action would have been to have gone straight to Ishmael's Rest. After all, that was his intended destination. He needed to see his father, to tell him the terrible news – if he hadn't already heard – and to make sure he was all right. But the diversion to Blind Mary's modest dwelling had proved too much of a temptation. It had only been a short way off the road and he needed answers. He'd probably be done in fifteen minutes or so anyway. His father could wait that much longer.

The room had a strange smell to it, one that Judas couldn't identify. It was sort of fruity, but fused with a weird decaying stench. As if someone had tried to mask the smell of a busy slaughterhouse with a thousand freshly peeled oranges and some lavender.

'Come in, sit down,' an old woman's rasping voice called out from somewhere in the shadows at the back of the room. Judas did as he was bid. There was a rustle and Blind Mary the seer came forward and sat down in the chair opposite.

Blind Mary defined the word hag. She was ugly to the point of being monstrous, with long dark curly hair that reminded Judas of dried, fire-blackened seaweed. A blindfold, made of some sort of crimson material, covered her eyes. Or rather the two empty sockets filled with intestinal worms from the bowels of Satan, if the stories were to be believed. She held out her hand and waited as Judas counted four copper pieces onto her palm.

'Who are you, and what do you want from me?' she asked.

'I am Judas Iscariot. And I –'

The hag raised one hand. 'I know you,' she said softly. 'You are Judas Iscariot.'

As far as miraculous acts went, divining someone's name after they'd already told you it didn't rank very highly. Still, despite his scepticism, Judas had no intention of leaving without hearing what the old woman had to say. Blind Mary had an impressive reputation and her prophecies were said to almost always come true. It was whispered that she had foretold both the birth of Jesus and the death of John the Baptist. By rights she should have been stoned to death years ago, but as Caiaphas was supposedly one of her more regular visitors, the Sanhedrin preferred to turn a blind eye to her activities. Appropriately enough.

'You are the fool who gave up the son of God,' Blind Mary said. The smell of death in the room seemed much stronger now. Judas shuddered involuntarily.

'You come to me seeking answers. People you know – people you love – are dying. You think you may be the cause, but you do not know for sure.'

Judas nodded, then realising that Blind Mary would be unable to see the gesture, he said, 'I do.'

'You are,' Blind Mary said.

'What?'

'You are the cause for what has happened so far. And what is yet to come.'

'Oh.' Judas felt his heart stop for a moment. The room seemed somehow darker and colder.

'You took payment for your act?'

Judas shuffled uneasily. For a woman with no eyes Blind Mary appeared to be doing a very good job of looking deep into his soul.

'Yes,' he said.

'Gold?'

'Silver.'

Even with the sash across her face Judas could see Blind Mary had raised her eyebrows.

'It was quite a lot of silver,' he said by way of explanation.

The seer nodded. 'The payment is cursed. For every piece of silver you took, someone you know will be murdered.' She coughed, the sound of drains being opened, and added, 'And you, Judas, will be the final victim. Your suffering, your terrible, terrible death – the very worst of all – will complete the circle.'

Judas looked at the face of Blind Mary and knew without doubt that she was telling the truth. This was just another of her many predictions that would come to pass. He had, on the whole and putting his recent act of betrayal aside for a moment, lived a good life. This turn of events hardly seemed fair. And his death was to be the worst? The murders of his friends had sounded quite gruesome enough as it was.

'Who is doing this to me?'

Blind Mary was silent for a long time. 'Your tormentor . . . ' she began before pausing once more. 'Is someone well known to you.'

It was his turn to be momentarily silent. 'I know them?'

The seer nodded.

'Who is it?' he asked.

'That I do not know.'

'Is there anything I can do to end this, then?'

Blind Mary coughed and cleared her throat. There was another long pause and then she said, 'Pay back the fee. Every last piece of the silver you took. Give it back to the person who gave it to you in the first place.'

Judas shook his head. 'I tried that, but the man who gave me the silver said no. And I spent some of it too. On woodworking tools for my uncle, and a horse I had to give back.'

'Then you will die in a more dreadful way than you can imagine. And that will not be the end of your torment, Judas Iscariot. You will spend eternity burning in the flames of hell while Satan uses your freshly flagellated skin to mop his horned brow.' Blind Mary slid back her chair. 'I am sorry I could not be of more service to you,' she said and stood up. Judas caught a whiff of her breath as she did so and recoiled. Like the room he was in, it reeked of death.

'Wait,' he said. 'There must be some way you can help me?'

'Well . . . ' Blind Mary hesitated.

'Yes?'

'There is one possibility.'

'Anything!'

'You could pass on the curse to me. I have lived a long, harrowing life and perhaps this will bring me the release I seek, open the gateway to the next realm.'

'You would be willing to do that for me?' Judas asked.

'I would.'

'And how would this work, in theory?'

'Give the silver to me.'

He blinked.

'Pardon?'

'Give what remains of the silver to me. It will free you from the curse.'

He really should have seen this coming.

'I'm sorry,' Judas said, standing. 'I may be the fool who handed over the son of God to the Romans for a handful of silver coins, to pay off a debt that didn't need clearing. I may be the fool whose friends are paying for my sins, and the fool who is fated to die the worst death of all, but I'm not that easily parted from my money, old hag.'

Blind Mary stared at him for a while, then said, 'Ah well, you can't blame a poor old woman for trying.'

'You were lying to me?'

'Yes.'

'The whole time?'

'Oh no,' the seer laughed. 'Everything I said was true, except the last part. Giving me the silver would have made a big difference to my life, Judas, but not to yours. You are going to die horrifically, and soon. As sure as after the sun has risen, the moon must fall. Nothing you or I can do will change that.'

Chapter 27

The walk from Blind Mary's hovel to his father's house was far too short. Between leaving one destination and arriving at the next, Judas had to try and think of the best way of telling his father that his brother and two of his oldest friends had been brutally murdered, and warn him that he was in grave danger too. It wasn't a conversation he was looking forward to. Blind Mary's words kept returning to him, making it even harder to marshal his thoughts. *You are going to die horrifically, and soon …*

Judas paused at a dusty crossroads and wiped his sweaty forehead. He could never atone for his betrayal of Jesus, he could never fully make it right; but he could do his personal best to minimise the number of people who died for his sins. Or at the very least make sure his father wasn't one of them.

He'd just have to report the news, say what he had to say and accept the inevitable consequences. Then, once he was sure his father understood the dangers and had found a safe place to go, he'd flee the city too. Head to somewhere where no one knew him, or could find him. Rome had a certain appeal. Or Egypt possibly. Going on the run wasn't ideal, but neither was hanging around waiting for death to come calling.

Maybe he'd take Baruch with him, and other old friends whose lives were now evidently in peril. Only ones he could trust, naturally enough. Perhaps he'd take Martha along too, if that was remotely possible. To say she'd need some serious persuading was a vast understatement, but he could at least try. She knew him, was precious to him, and that meant she was at risk. At least if they were together he could protect her. Or die attempting to do so.

Judas started walking again, faster and with a sense of purpose. He turned the corner, saw his father's house and stopped dead. Something was wrong. The door was ajar. At this time of morning, his father would be inside. The man always awoke early and did what needed to be done, before returning home to breakfast. He hated being disturbed during meals and always – always – closed the door, even on the very hottest of days. The sort of anti-social security-conscious act you'd expect from a man who used a giant boulder in place of a bolt.

Perhaps he had visitors? Judging from the sun's position it was just after nine in the morning so it was possible, if a little unlikely. Maybe someone had found out about Daniel and come to break the bad news. That would save Judas a job. Although ... a terrible thought flashed through his mind. What if his father's visitor had been of the unwelcome variety late last night? What if ... ?

No, please no.

Judas broke into a run, reaching the house in seconds. Right in the centre of the door was a smeared bloodstain. His stomach lurched and his vision began to swim. He pushed at the door, avoiding the rouged mark, and it swung open freely, revealing the stone head in the middle of the room. There were drops of blood on the sandy floor. He looked around for a body but saw nothing.

'Hello?' He shouted into the empty space. 'Father?'

There was no reply.

No, no, no, no. His heart was pounding.

He ran into the room at the rear, almost tripping over a broom in his haste. Still no sign of a body. A bubble of hope began to rise, but it was instantly punctured by the needles of fear stabbing inside him.

'Father!' he shouted. 'Father!' Still nothing. Perhaps the killer had come looking for Simon, hands still bloody from the earlier butchering, but had discovered he was out. Except his father never went out in the evenings or at night. Perhaps the killer had come calling this morning?

Shut up, shut up.

Still no sign of a body. The killer wouldn't hide it or move it, would he? So Simon couldn't be dead, had to be alive.

Judas felt sick as he moved around the house, looking for a corpse he knew he would eventually discover, all the while praying – to himself, not to God – that he wouldn't find anything.

Tears welled in his eyes and he blinked them roughly away.

'Father!' he screamed again, a primal cry of anguish.

He felt rather than heard the door close behind him. Spinning around he gasped as Simon Iscariot staggered forward into the room. He was panting heavily and covered in blood.

Chapter 28

'What in heaven's name is with all the shouting?' Simon asked as he pulled off his bloody robe and dumped it on a bench. 'I could hear you yelling all the way down the street.' He began rinsing the blood off his hands and arms with the same mucky water usually reserved for washing dishes.

'Why are you covered in blood?' Judas said, his voice almost hysterical. 'And breathing like that?'

'I'm covered in blood because Joseph's big pregnant cow got into difficulty calving this morning and suffered a ruptured birth canal. He needed my help to save her, but frankly any farmer worth his salt would have seen that was a lost cause. He should stick to growing onions.' Simon shook the last of the water from his hands, dried them on a dirty piece of cloth and pulled on the fresh robe that was lying nearby. Judas couldn't help but notice it had a large tear in it.

'Still I managed to save the calf, so that's good, and he's promised me half of the dead cow, which is even better seeing as I won't be getting any free lamb or mutton from you. Oh and I'm out of breath because I've just run down the road to find out

159

why my son was screaming for me at the top of his voice. What's wrong?'

The relief flooded out of Judas like someone had uncorked him. That was his cue then. He took a deep breath. 'You might want to sit down first,' he said.

Simon raised both eyebrows. He had a light peppering of blood on his face. Tiny droplets artfully transformed into crimson freckles.

'Why?' he asked.

'Just sit.'

'Tell me why first.'

'I've got something important to tell you. Some bad news. And I think you should be sitting down when I do.'

'I'd rather be standing if it's all the same to you. Just say whatever you've got to say but make it quick. I'm starving. I've not had breakfast yet. Bloody neighbours and their bloody cows.'

Judas cleared his throat. His mouth felt dry and his pulse quick. He spoke quickly, before he lost what little nerve he had. 'There was another murder last night,' he began. 'At the Rose Mount bathhouse.'

'Another one?'

'Yes.'

'Anyone we know? Elijah keeps sheep like Gideon did. It wasn't him was it? Imagine the size of the flock you'd have if you put both lots of those together.'

'Will you stop talking about sheep for five minutes? It wasn't Elijah. There were four victims this time. And you know three of them. Very well.'

Simon stared at his son. 'Three? Who?'

'Ugly Saul, Jose and . . . ' Judas couldn't bring himself to utter the last name. He stared into his father's eyes and saw the blood had drained from the old man's face. Even the red speckles looked paler.

'Go on,' Simon said, his voice a hoarse whisper.

'Daniel.'

A wave of different emotions and expressions flickered across Simon's face in quick succession, as if he was trying each one on for size. He eventually settled for confusion.

'My brother?'

Judas nodded.

Simon stared into space for what seemed like an eternity.

'I always said he'd meet a bad end. Always gambling, always getting into debt. It's no wonder someone decided to kill him. How did you hear about it before me anyway? Are you sure it's true?'

'Yes, I'm positive. I heard about it from Jeb.'

'Jeb? Who the bloody hell is Jeb?'

'Jebediah. He's a cripple. Spends his days begging in the lower city. He hears everything.'

Simon barked a mirthless laugh. 'You're hanging around with beggars now?' He shook his head. 'He misheard then, or just made it up. Cripples are not to be trusted. It's probably a scam to extort more money from you. How much did you pay for this *information*?'

Judas moved next to his father and put one arm around his shoulders.

'Nothing – he offered it freely. And he's trustworthy. He was positive it was Daniel,' he said softly. 'And Ugly, and Jose.'

'But how do you know? You don't. You only have the word of a beggar and that's worse than the word of a whore.'

'It's true.'

'I don't believe it. And you shouldn't either. Saul and Jose maybe, but I'll bet you Daniel is safe and sound somewhere,

161

playing dice and convincing himself that the next roll will be the one that wins him all his money back. But it won't be of course. That man was born with unlucky bones.'

Judas watched as his father walked over to a small wooden table at the side of the room, cleared some space on it, and laid out some bread, a small bottle of olive oil and some cheese.

'Do you want something to eat?' Simon asked as he tore off a rough chunk of flatbread and drizzled oil over it.

Denial was a common reaction to the news of an unexpected death. Judas had seen it first-hand on numerous occasions, but this was different. This was his father.

'There's more,' he said. His voice was barely a whisper.

Simon stopped what he was doing and looked over at his son. 'More what?'

'I know it was Daniel who died, and Saul and Jose. Because ...' His voice tailed off.

'Because what?'

'Because it's my fault they're dead.' The words came tumbling out in a rush.

'Your fault?' Simon's face was a mask. It was impossible for Judas to guess what he was thinking.

'I didn't kill them,' he said quickly. 'But someone who knows me did. I think.'

'The same person who killed Gideon?'

'Yes. And Ethan.'

'Ethan's dead too? How?'

'It doesn't matter.' Judas closed his eyes briefly, took a couple more measured breaths, and said, 'I think it was Jesus.'

Simon looked bemused. 'But he's dead isn't he?'

'Not any more.'

Simon's frown deepened. 'Not any more? Either he's dead or he isn't.'

'He isn't. He's been resurrected. And I think he's killing people to get revenge on me. For what I did.'

'Which is what exactly?'

Judas felt as if he was having an out-of-body experience as he spilled the whole sorry tale to his father. From his deal with Caiaphas to pay off Daniel's debt, and the betrayal at Gethsemane, to the crucifixion, the note, his dream, even what Blind Mary had said. The whole time he was speaking his father said nothing. He just stood there impassively, the forgotten piece of bread in one hand, and listened without uttering a word or asking a single question.

'And you're in danger too,' Judas finished. 'Serious danger. You need to go, leave now. Before he comes for you.'

'You're sure it's Jesus are you?'

'No, I'm not sure. But who else could it be?'

'How about that ex-gladiator you said my brother owed money to? If you ask me, he sounds like a far more likely suspect.'

'It can't be him, why would he kill my friends and Daniel's too?'

'Because he likes killing.'

'It can't be him, I paid him off. I cleared Daniel's debt.'

'Did you?'

'Yes, I told you I did.'

'But did you? Maybe you forgot to drop the money off, or you think you've paid him but haven't. You don't have the best memory in the world.'

'I paid him.'

'If you say so.'

'I did and it's not him. At the moment it's looking like Jesus is the culprit. And I can't believe I'm saying that.'

'But I don't even know this Jesus,' Simon said. 'Never met him.' He looked down and noticed that some olive oil from the bread had dripped onto the bottom of his robe and blossomed into a small greasy flower. 'Why would he want to kill me?'

'I told you. For revenge. To get back at me. You need to leave, now. Go somewhere far away. Somewhere he'll never be able to find you.'

Simon laughed, bitterly.

'If it's your friend who's killing everyone, and he really is the son of God, I can't see running away will make much difference. If he can find his way back from the dead I'm pretty sure he'll be able to find me if he really wants to. Thanks for the warning, but I think I'll stay here. I've lived most of my life in this building. If I'm going to die I'd rather it was in this house and not in some cowshed on the outskirts of a dump like Beth-phage.'

Judas rolled his eyes. To him the phrase 'somewhere far away' meant another land, where they spoke another language. To his father it apparently meant a nearby village that, on a good day, he could see from his front window.

As much as he hated to admit it, though, the man did have one good point. On the way here running away had seemed like the only real option. But if it was Jesus who was after him and his friends and family, then it really didn't matter where he went; it would never be far enough.

And if that was the case, the truth was he'd have to stay in Jerusalem. Stay and face whatever was coming. He could warn his friends, warn anyone who might be in danger, and hopefully that would be enough to keep some of them alive. But if he wanted to end this quickly, and before anyone else died, there was only one possible solution. He had to find a way of persuading Caiaphas to take the silver back. It would be like trying to persuade Peter to forgive him, but what other choice did he have?

There was no time to waste.

'I've got to go,' he said.

Simon nodded. 'Well thanks for coming all this way to tell me. I suppose I'd better go to the bathhouse. Identify his body. Make sure it really is ... him.'

'You might want to change your clothes first, father. That robe's got grease down it now and a tear in the sleeve.'

Simon gazed down at the failed repair, then up at Judas.

'Do you think I don't know that?' he snapped. His face began to distort. 'You think it really matters if I go out like this, or dressed in my finest? It doesn't. It doesn't matter, Judas. Nothing matters. Not that you'd understand. My wife, the only woman I ever truly loved, died giving birth to you, and as much as I might try to pretend otherwise, her sacrifice was not worth it. Not even close. And now my brother is dead, two of my best friends are dead. And you ... you ...' he snarled the words, 'are responsible for it all.'

He glared at Judas with undisguised hatred, and then as swiftly as the rage had arrived, it departed. His face crumpled and his shoulders began to shake. His eyes took on a watery sheen.

'How did he die, Judas? Did they die together? Was it pain-less?'

'I don't know,' Judas said, unable to bear telling his father the truth. How could he tell him that yes, they'd died together but it had been far from painless. That Ugly's neck had been snapped, Jose had burned to death and Daniel ... he'd been boiled alive. His Uncle Daniel, the man who had been there for him in the times when his father hadn't, had died a dreadful, painful death.

The very thought of it brought Judas to the brink of tears. He blinked them away. If he spilled a single one he was in danger of unleashing a flood of grief that might never stop. He had to hold it together for his father's sake. There would be time to grieve properly when all this was over.

'You don't know?' Simon was staring at his son.

'Jeb didn't tell me.'

'Did you ask?'

'He didn't know. But they were all together ... at the end.'

Simon dropped the soggy lump of bread onto the tabletop, wiped his oily fingers on his robe, and walked slowly over to the door. 'Get out,' he said. 'Get out, Judas, and don't come back. I want nothing more to do with you.'

Judas blinked in surprise. 'Father ...'

'Not any more. You are no longer my son. I wash my hands of you for good. I never want to see you ever again, Judas. And I mean it. Now get out.'

Simon pulled the door open and gestured at the street outside with his free hand. There was a brief pause while the two men regarded each other unhappily, then Judas simply nodded. Nothing he could say would change his father's mind. He had expected this, known it was coming, but still the utter finality of the dismissal tore a gaping hole in his soul. His lips began to quiver uncontrollably, and the tears he'd fought off before came roaring back, threatening to drown him in a flood of misery. He had to leave, and he had to leave now.

He stepped through the door, waited until he heard it slam behind him one final time, listened as the large Egyptian head was dragged into place, and then began the long, lonely walk back to Jerusalem.

Chapter 29

Simon stared blankly at the closed wooden door in front of him. His face crumbled and collapsed like the wall of Jericho. Fresh tears began to roll freely down his cheeks.

Daniel was dead.

As were his two closest friends.

And Judas, his son, was responsible for the loss that was now ripping him apart inside.

It made no sense.

Maybe there had been a mistake. Perhaps Judas had got it all wrong. Perhaps–

The front door rattled in its frame causing Simon to jump.

Several further knocks came in quick succession, reigniting the fire in Simon's belly.

'Begone, Judas!' he bellowed, wiping away the tears. 'Get out of here. I told you to go.'

Another knock.

Simon rushed over to the door, shouting through it, 'I said I never want to see you again, and I mean it. You can't apologise for this, there's nothing you can do. You are dead to me. You hear me? Dead!'

Again, a knock.

Simon pounded back on the inside of the door with all his might. 'Go to hell!'

The door rattled back at him.

In a fury, Simon yanked the stone head away from the entrance. When he'd made enough clearance, he whipped the door open, stepped out and drew his hand back to strike his Godforsaken son hard across the face. He'd physically expel Judas from his life if the fool failed to understand his words of rejection.

Only Judas wasn't there. No one was there. Simon looked left and then right, as his rage slowly subsided. No one. Was somebody mocking him now? Children playing games?

'Don't mess with me,' he said out loud, to whoever might hear, to the sky, to the world. 'Not today.'

He turned, head down, and shuffled back inside. Bending to pick up the rope that encircled the stone block he heard a rushing sound from behind. He made to turn but there was no time. Barrelled across the room by the force of his unknown assailant's charge, Simon had a fraction of a second to brace himself for the impact. It wasn't enough.

He slammed into the ground with the full weight of the man on his back and the air whoomphed out of his lungs. Dazed, he tried to twist his head around, saw a hand clutching a rock and then felt it impact upon his skull. Darkness embraced him.

Chapter 30

'Seriously?' Jonathan's eyes were wide like serving plates. 'Boiled alive?'

'Yes,' Judas said. He had to crane his neck to look at his friend, who was tall enough when on the ground, let alone when up on horseback. 'And poor Jose was burned to death.'

'Nice.'

'So obviously I thought I'd better let you know about all this as quickly as I could.'

'Why? Because I'm next?'

'No. Well I don't know. I'm warning anyone who might be at risk. I've just been to see Aaron on his stall. Told him the same thing.'

'This is a very comforting development, I must say. What the hell have you got yourself mixed up in?'

'I know. If I could go back in time ...'

'But you can't.'

'No.'

'I was thinking ...'

'What?' Judas asked.

'It's nothing. We can maybe talk about it later, I've got to get going on this job,' Jon waved a scroll case at him. 'If this missive doesn't get delivered before midday, I'll have an arrow in my back anyway.'

'Quickly, before you go, have you seen Baruch? He wasn't at home.'

'Yeah, I had a drink with him and Aaron last night. Said he was going to go to that new brothel he's found, and spend the rest of the night taking this weird herb stuff and working his way through all the girls until his money ran out. Maybe he's still there.'

'Still there?'

'Yeah, doesn't seem likely I know. But it was late when he left, and he swore by these herbs, said they keep him as stiff as a cedar branch for hours. Look I've really got to go, Judas, but good luck finding him.' Jonathan spurred his horse into action and galloped off down the road leaving a cloud of sandy dust behind.

The brothel was about a fifteen-minute walk back west across the lower city, but Judas, head down and feet marching, reached the place of ill repute in ten. There was no time to lose, and warning his friends like this was at least keeping his mind off the fact that he'd just been disowned by his father. It made him feel a little better that he was taking some positive action, rather than just sitting back and waiting for the next lot of bad news to come rolling in.

The front door was closed and bolted, as he'd expected it would be this early in the day. Obviously Baruch wasn't in there now. He'd just have to try him at home, again. As Judas began trudging back the way he'd come he caught a glimpse of colour out of the corner of his eye. At the bottom of the alley that ran down the side of the brothel, he was sure he'd seen a red and yellow cloak flash across the way. That red and yellow cloak.

There was only one way to find out for sure. He walked down the alley, pulling up swiftly at the end and flattening himself against the wall. He peeked out, and sure enough, there it was. There he was. Malchus. Caiaphas's toad had donned a dirty-looking grey robe over his more colourful garb, but as the wind caught it, Judas caught another glimpse of his silly fluttering silk cloak underneath.

Malchus was deep in conversation with a large man in a dark blue robe. They'd stopped not far away on the corner, where another narrow ginnel, perpendicular to the one Judas had walked down, met the main thoroughfare.

Whatever they were talking about, the discussion was clearly becoming more animated. Malchus started waving his arm at the other man and pointing emphatically down the street. Something on the stocky thug's short sleeve caught Judas's attention as he did this. It looked like a red stain – a splatter of blood possibly? It was a fairly generous one if so.

And then the stain was gone, along with its owner. Malchus headed in one direction, the blue-robed fellow in the other.

This was the second time that Judas had seen Caiaphas's right-hand man here. He was definitely up to something. Although given the sinister connotations of that red stain perhaps Judas was better off not knowing exactly what.

He sighed. Knowledge was power. Whatever was afoot, if it was something shady, knowledge of it might give him some leverage over Malchus. And that in turn could potentially help in dealing with the thug's master. Judas turned his attention to working out where Malchus had emerged from. The ginnel came to a dead end at the back of the brothel, so he must have come out of the rear exit of the building.

He sneaked up to the brothel's back door and tried pushing on it. It was locked, unsurprisingly. He examined the windows on the back wall of the building. They were six feet off the ground and chiselled so they narrowed in. He'd never fit through.

Judas returned to the entrance, got down on the ground, and tried to peer under the crack between the wood and the floor. It was very slight and he could see nothing. Standing, he pressed his ear to the door and listened carefully.

He heard what sounded like footsteps, quite near. Then he heard a cough and someone clearing their throat. Finally he heard a loud click.

The door swung open swiftly, struck him hard and sent him sprawling on the dusty ground. It took a couple of seconds to register what had happened. And to focus on the figure gazing down at him in some surprise.

'Judas? What are you doing here?' Baruch asked. 'The place is closed.'

'I was looking for you, funnily enough.'

'And here I am.' Baruch offered his hand and Judas pulled himself up.

'What are you still doing here at this time of the morning anyway?'

'I've been whoring all night. I must have passed out after the last one though as I woke up just now on the floor.' Baruch rolled his head from side to side to ease the crick in his neck.

'Did you see Malchus at all while you were in there?'

'Who?'

'Malchus. The high priest's lackey.'

'Don't know him. Anyway, I didn't see no one at all, but I heard Caleb, the owner, letting a couple of men out the back door a few minutes ago. I think that's what woke me. I had to wait until they'd gone so I could leave. They don't like over-nighters here. Even accidental ones.'

'Did they say anything?'

'Caleb said something like they better be back soon. And that he wasn't going to do it for them.'

'Do what?'

'No idea. Then I think I heard Caleb going upstairs.'

'Good,' Judas said, dusting himself down. 'I've got some important stuff to tell you, but first I need to have a look in there, before anyone comes back.' He edged up to the door and peered inside. There wasn't a soul around.

'You can't go in there. Caleb will kill you if he comes back down and finds you poking around. What are you looking for anyway?'

'I'm not really sure.'

'Won't that make finding it a bit hard?'

'Shh.' Judas put a finger to his lips and listened intently. There was definitely no one about. 'You stay here, I'll be quieter on my own. Watch the door. If you see anyone coming, stall them. I won't be long.'

'Stall them how?'

'I'm sure you'll think of something.'

Judas stepped into the back hallway. He recognised the large black patch, like a burn mark, on the wall of the corridor directly ahead of him. The doorway he'd seen Malchus hovering at during his previous visit to the whorehouse was right there. He sidled over and peeked around the edge of the red curtain which was hung across it to serve as a door. The room beyond was largely empty.

Entering, he glanced over the few items of furniture it contained. There was a mattress in the corner, stained with suspicious watery brown blooms that were neither water, nor blood.

A lamp sat atop a rickety table. Next to it was a bowl of fruit that was past its best. The lamp was still lit, even though there was now plenty of sunlight leaking in through the shuttered windows. And that was it – there was nothing else here. Whatever Malchus had been doing, he'd left no trace of it. Unless he was responsible for one or more of the watery blooms on the mattress.

As Judas turned to leave, something about the rug on the other side of the room caught his attention. There was a black line visible under one corner of it. He walked over and pulled the already skew-whiff carpet away from the wall, revealing a piece of wood covering a hole cut into the floor.

He dug his fingers into the small C-shaped indentation that had been carved into the trapdoor and yanked it upwards, revealing a crudely worked stone staircase heading down into darkness. The underside of the wooden square was padded with layer upon layer of thick cloth.

Judas picked up the lit lamp from the table, crouched over the opening, and gazed down. The stairs were steep, sloping sharply away into total darkness. What the hell was down there? He held still, listening hard for any discernible noise, but the dark was as quiet as it was inky black.

He stood, put one foot forward on the first step, and paused. Anything could be lurking at the bottom of the stairs. But whatever awaited him, he didn't have much choice other than to find out – knowledge was power, he reminded himself. And Judas was sick of feeling powerless.

Gingerly, he began to descend the steps. The flickering light source he carried made it seem as if his very shadow was trembling.

Chapter 31

The underground chamber was roughly hewn from the rock, vaguely square-shaped with the walls running to around fifteen or twenty feet in length. The low burning lamp cast a sallow light across the contents of the room. Against one wall was a bench stocked with an array of metal objects; short knives, longer, wickedly curved blades, manacles, a scattering of six-inch nails, and a multi-stranded whip dotted with barbs.

There were also small and strangely fashioned devices Judas couldn't even begin to identify. These bore little metal loops that looked like finger holes and sharp strategically placed spikes. Ropes hung on the wall behind, and a trident was propped up against it, the three sharp prongs of which wore a coat of red. Dark, relatively fresh-looking blood pooled in small slicks on the bench.

But worse still, worse than all this, was the sight which turned Judas's stomach. A pale, naked woman was chained to the adjacent wall by her limbs, spread-eagled with such tension that her bones seemed to be straining in their sockets. Only her head was limp, lolling to one side and largely obscured by her blood-matted hair. Long streaked cuts ran along her arms and puncture marks were clustered around her pubic region and inner thighs, entwining their bloody trails down her legs to the floor. Most of her fingernails had been torn out, with just a couple of half-shattered fragments remaining. Her breasts were unnaturally swollen, laid thick with fierce red welts and marks.

It was too much to take in. This was what Malchus had been doing? Judas felt an impulse to heave and had to look away from the poor wretch. As he stared at the floor, attempting to compose himself, something glinting near the wall caught his attention.

He walked over to the object and picked it up. It was a blood-stained ring of solid gold with a flat top and some sort of seal. Judas held it next to the lamp and studied the insignia closely. He ceased breathing momentarily as he recognised the emblem it bore. He'd seen this ring before, on the very hand that had crashed down onto the table and refused to take back his silver pieces at the temple. This little torture chamber wasn't Malchus's secret fetish. It was Caiaphas's . . .

He felt a rush of excitement at the revelation. This ring could be the answer to his prayers; his way out of this whole sorry mess. He looked up at the girl's mutilated body and shuddered. How could a high priest of the Sanhedrin do something like this? And if he had murdered this girl could he be responsible for other killings? Like . . . no, surely not. Caiaphas was evidently a sick bastard, but he couldn't be *the* murderer. He'd practically pushed Judas into betraying Jesus in the first place. He'd rewarded him for the act and was pleased with how well it had all gone. It made no sense to be seeking revenge for something he'd sanctioned himself.

Judas picked up a knife off the bench – one of the clean, seemingly unused ones – and carved a small section of cloth from the edge of his sleeve, before carefully wrapping the gold band in it. This was so much more than he'd expected to find. He could use the ring as a weapon against Caiaphas, to force the fat priest to take back the silver and thus end his curse.

Judas made his way quietly up the stairs, replaced the wooden cover, and hauled the rug over it once more. Checking the back hallway for signs of life – none, thankfully – he tiptoed to the back door and out, closing it softly behind him. Baruch was sitting cross-legged on the ground and picking at a callous on his hand. He looked up when he saw Judas approaching.

'Any luck?' he asked.

'You could say that. But then, it's about time my luck changed.'

'That's the best thing about visiting brothels. You always get lucky.'

'Come on, let's go. I've something I need to tell you but we can talk about it on the way to your place.'

'My place?'

'Yes. Your place. I need you to look after something for me, if you don't mind.'

'So how many does that make now? In total?' Baruch asked, as he stirred the broth which was simmering away in a pot.

'Six,' Judas replied, dusting off a cushion and sitting on it. His friend's small home was devoid of chairs.

Baruch whistled. 'Six people you know, all dead.'

'Well five, plus Jonas from the bathhouse. Although I knew him well enough to nod to in passing. I knew them all to some degree, I guess. Just like she said.'

'Just like who said?'

Judas thought quickly. 'I said, "much life shed."'

He really didn't want to get into the whole prophecy thing with Baruch.

'Anyway,' he continued, 'you'd better be careful. This maniac might try to come to your door at some point.'

Baruch snorted. 'Let him,' he said, as he ladled some of the broth into a bowl. He stirred it around a few times, grabbed a half-eaten flatbread and carried the food over, sitting down on a threadbare cushion next to his friend. 'You sure you don't want some?'

'Go on then.'

Baruch ripped a large hunk of bread from the loaf and passed it to Judas, putting the bowl down on the floor between them.

'So this whole thing doesn't worry you?' Judas said, as he dipped some bread in the bean and lentil soup, and ate it. 'Not even a bit?'

'Nope. Let him try his luck. I'll sort the lunatic out for you. I promise you, whoever he is he won't be poking my eye out, or boiling me up like a fish for supper.'

'I'm sure my uncle Daniel tried to avoid his fate, Baruch.'

'Maybe. But not hard enough.' Baruch ploughed a large chunk of bread through the soup, before chewing and swallowing it in practically one motion. 'Sorry, I don't mean to speak ill of the dead, but that wouldn't have happened to me. No way. If this fool comes here, I'll be ready.'

'Good for you, I guess.'

'I sleep with a knife under my pillow, you know.' Baruch made a stabbing and slicing motion with his extended forefinger. 'I'll gut *him* like a fish.'

Judas nodded.

'See how he likes the tables turned,' Baruch added, returning to wolf down more broth.

'I'm glad you're so confident. I wish I could share in that sentiment.'

Baruch shrugged, belched, and then smiled. If there was one trait of his friend's that Judas truly envied, it was his ability to never let anything bother him. Of course half the time, that was probably because those troublesome things called thoughts didn't bother him.

'You said you want me to keep something for you?'

Judas nodded, pulled out the small cloth bundle and placed it on the floor.

'What is it?'

'It belongs to the high priest Caiaphas.'

'Does it?' Baruch reached for the bundle. 'Can I have a look?'

Judas grabbed his friend's hand just before it touched the cloth. 'Let me unwrap it. We need to be careful with it.'

'Why?'

'Because it's got some marks on it that I don't want to rub off,' Judas explained as he revealed the ring.

'Are those little rubies?'

'Yes.'

'It looks like they've been bleeding,' Baruch observed, pointing at the thin red trails that had dried on the gold.

'Actually, that is blood.'

Baruch's hand recoiled from the object. 'A ring that bleeds?'

Nothing much ever bothered Baruch, except ridiculous, superstitious nonsense.

'No, the blood isn't from the gems. It's from a person.'

'Oh. Right. 'Course.'

'Aren't you interested in knowing whose blood it is?'

'Yeah. That was my next question.'

'Listen. This needs to stay a secret. An absolute secret. I'm trusting you with this, Baruch. Putting my life in your hands.'

His friend nodded his understanding, an earnest look in his eyes. If there was one person on this Earth who Judas trusted, it was Baruch. What he lacked in wit, he made up for with his fierce, stubborn loyalty.

'The blood is from one of the girls at the brothel. Caiaphas killed her. I think.'

'Really? Which girl?'

'I don't know. But look, you can't tell anyone. Not a soul. Unless I don't come back, that is.'

'Caiaphas killed a girl at the brothel?'

'Yes.'

'He doesn't look the type. Wait, what do you mean if you don't come back? Where are you going?'

'I'm going to see Caiaphas. Confront him. He can get me out of this mess I'm in – he can make things right. He doesn't want to, but I think I can force him to. With this ring and what I know.'

Baruch was silent in thought.

'Don't worry about the details,' Judas continued. 'All you need to know is I can make Caiaphas help me, by threatening to tell all about this prostitute. I'm going to go find him now. If I don't return from this meeting before sunset, take the ring to the authorities.'

'The Romans?'

'No. The other members of the Sanhedrin council, up at the temple. That will damage Caiaphas the most. Tell them the ring belongs to Caiaphas and that you found it in a hidden room underneath the brothel, next to a murdered girl.'

'Will they believe me?'

'I don't know. Maybe, maybe not, but it will cause trouble and that's the point. Anyway, I don't think it will come to that. I hope not, for my sake.'

180

Baruch frowned.

'I'll be back before sunset, I'm sure,' Judas said. 'Don't worry. Just keep that ring safe. Hide it away. And don't tell anyone about it, or any of this business. No one must know, no one at all. Unless I don't return.'

'You have my word,' Baruch said, carefully wrapping the golden band back up in its small parcel.

Chapter 32

A tingle of anticipation coursed through her naked body, as he pushed her down onto the floor, gently but firmly, and straddled her. His rough, searching lips met hers with urgency, and the taste of salty sweat.

This was exactly what she needed right now. This would help her to forget, if only for a short while.

She shifted her body, and opened her legs a little wider.

News of the murder had hit Atarah hard. All her life she had feared her father's gambling habit would lead to his death, but she had never expected his demise to be quite so gruesome. He was dumped into a boiling hot plunge pool, according to the Roman soldier who had delivered the devastating news as she and her husband were eating breakfast. No one knew who'd done it, or why. Just that Daniel had been killed in a steam room, along with two of his friends and the man who worked the furnace. There was no clue, no motive, but Atarah had her suspicions that dice had been involved somehow.

She had never been close to him. The gambling and the

willing women he'd spent time with behind her poor, unsuspecting mother's back had driven a wedge between father and daughter, but still she felt his passing keenly.

'Are you going to take me by force?' she whispered, placing a palm on her husband's deeply tanned chest.

'I am,' Dotan said.

He ran his hands – still coarse with dried mud from the fields he'd been working only minutes ago – up Atarah's slender arms, and pinned them to the floor. He leaned forward and kissed her again. She returned his passion and bit down softly on his lower lip as she felt his desire grow against the soft white flesh of her stomach.

Dotan shifted his weight off her and rolled Atarah over. 'I mean to take you from behind.'

'Yes,' she said, closing her eyes, her head resting on the floor, back arched. She spread her knees slightly further apart, ready for her husband, and gasped as she felt his heat inside her. A brief, blissful shudder ran through her body.

He began to move slowly in and out, but she knew he was only teasing her. Dotan was a big man and he was only partially entering her, not filling her fully as he usually did. He was going to make her beg for his whole length.

'Put it all in, husband,' she said, moaning aloud, longing for his full thrust.

He moaned in turn, echoing her excitement, and then he gasped. His manhood twitched with the sheer pleasure of making her wait.

'Please, I want all of you, now.'

He stopped dead.

'Let me feel the whole thing,' she demanded.

He withdrew.

'Dotan,' she said, hearing him take a couple of steps backwards.

'The game has gone far enough. Stop messing around and fuck me!'

Atarah opened her eyes and looked back over her shoulder to see what he was doing. Why had Dotan put a cowled robe on? And why had he picked up a log from the firewood pile?

Wait – he was slimmer than Dotan. Who the hell … She panicked and started to scramble to her feet, but the stranger was fast and pinned her back down again. Her face, pushed sideways to the floor, contorted in horror as she took in the scene behind her on the opposite side of the room.

Her husband was sprawled on the ground. His eyes were rolled back in his head and blood seeped from a red wire-thin line carved around his neck.

'Dotan!' Atarah let out a desperate sob. When her husband had partially entered her, twitched, then withdrew, he hadn't been teasing her – this madman had been throttling the life out of him while she begged for more. Her mouth, agape with realisation, was stuffed full with her robe by the attacker. She was still on her knees, in the same position as before, her rear end exposed and vulnerable.

The log was forced within, and Atarah shrieked with pain, clawing frantically at the man, but her flailing limbs were like twigs breezing in the wind to his strength.

She cried out some manner of plea, a half-gagged choking noise, as tears of both loss and pain welled in her eyes and spilled down her cheeks.

The man reached down underneath her and something cold touched the rounded flesh of Atarah's abdomen. A fierce pain came as he drew his hand swiftly across, from one side to the other. She reached down instinctively with her hand and felt the wet chasm that had been opened up in her belly. Her innards began to ooze out, spilling warm through her fingers, as her

184

body was rocked in piercing waves by the wood being jolted in and out.

And yet, the worst moment of this abominable assault was still to come. The finale that would be more traumatic than all of this. A sound that was more painful than being violated and left to expire, slumped in her own viscera, next to her murdered husband. Two sounds, in fact. The footsteps of the man walking towards the back room. Preceded by the noise of a woken, crying baby.

Chapter 33

'Not you again,' Martha said as she opened the door. Clearly the hostility she felt towards Judas hadn't abated, but at least she wasn't attacking him. 'Lazarus doesn't want to see you again.'

'I didn't come to see your brother,' Judas said. 'Not this time.'

'Who then?'

'I came to see you. May I come in?'

'No,' she said, and hefted the door shut.

'Martha!' Judas shouted through the solid timber. 'This is important. It's life and death. Please, just five minutes of your time.'

The door opened a crack. Martha's face appeared, framed by the woodwork.

'Talk,' she said.

'I think you're in danger. I came to warn you.'

'Danger?'

'Can I come in?'

'Warn me about what?'

'Let me in and I'll tell you. When I've finished if you never want to see me again I'll understand. I'll respect your wishes.'

'You'll never bother me or my family again?'

'I promise.'

She hesitated for a few long seconds before opening the door. Judas stepped inside. The air was cool and scented.

'My brother's outside. We'll go through to the atrium.'

Lazarus's house was large and tastefully decorated, with plush carpets and rugs throughout, the walls adorned with finely painted murals and rich silks. The family had money and had always been affluent as far as Judas knew. Lazarus had never done a proper day's work in his life and Judas admired him for that. If he had his way he'd never work either. Although once he returned the silver to Caiaphas he'd have to start looking for ways of earning a living again. Either that or starve.

They reached the atrium. The roof of the room was open to the elements so the sun could spill in to nurture the numerous saplings and plants in their clay pots.

'Start talking,' Martha said.

'You know I betrayed Jesus,' he looked down as he spoke. There was a large silver and blue woven rug beneath his feet.

'Yes.'

'I sold him out to the Sanhedrin. For money. Thirty pieces of silver.'

He could feel her frowning at him but knew he wasn't worthy of attempting to meet her gaze. To Martha, thirty pieces of silver was probably the price of a nice vase.

'I needed the money,' he continued. 'Not for me, for my uncle. He was in debt and the person he owed would have killed him, chopped him up into tiny pieces. The high priest paid me to lead the Sanhedrin to Jesus. I didn't believe they'd go through with arresting him. Or if they did I thought Jesus would escape. Just another miracle. At the meal we had that night, he said he knew someone was going to betray him. I

187

think he even knew that someone was me. He could have stopped events from happening. Could have left and gone somewhere safe, but he didn't. It was like he knew what was coming and had chosen to face it. Does that make any sense?' He looked up, snatching a glance, and their eyes met. She shook her head.

'I went to Golgotha, Martha. Saw him crucified. Even when he was on the cross I still believed he'd be rescued somehow –'

'But he wasn't,' Martha said.

'No, he wasn't. I watched him die and then I watched God claim him. I always knew he was special, knew he was God's own son, but until that moment I don't think I really, truly understood it all. I was one of Jesus's chosen. A member of his flock, an apostle. He was my teacher. My friend. He trusted me and I betrayed his trust. I got him killed.'

'What is it you want, Judas? Forgiveness? If so you're asking the wrong person.'

'No, I don't want forgiveness. I can't ever have forgiveness anyway.'

'Then I don't understand why you've come. At the door you said I was in danger?'

'You are, or you might be.' He paused for a moment. 'Did you hear about the murders at the bathhouse?'

'No.'

'Three people were killed. No, four actually. I knew them all. One was my uncle.'

'I'm sorry. But I don't see –'

'There were two other murders before those. Two more people I knew.'

As he looked up her eyes locked onto his. He had her full attention now.

'So far six people I know have died. Been murdered. And it's not a coincidence. After the first two, I received a note. From the killer.'

Martha gasped and put her hand up to her mouth.

'What did it say?'

'*I know what you did.*'

'What does that mean?'

'It means someone knows I betrayed Jesus after our final meal together.'

'And you think they're out for revenge? For what you did?'

'Yes. I do. It has to be really.'

'Do you know who?'

'No. Well, possibly.'

'Who?'

'When Peter came to see you, what did he say?'

'You think it's Peter?'

'No. What did Peter say to you?'

'He told us you'd betrayed Jesus, that you were the reason he was crucified.'

'And what else?'

'He told us Jesus was back from the dead.'

'Exactly. The man I betrayed, the son of God, is back from the dead.'

'I don't ... oh.' The colour drained from her face as she realised what he was suggesting. 'You've got to be joking.'

'I don't want it to be true! But what other explanation can there be? Hardly anyone knew I was responsible for the betrayal. Only a dozen of us were even at that meal.'

'But Jesus wasn't like that! He would sooner spill his own blood than accidentally harm one of God's chosen.'

'I know, I know.'

'How can you even think such a thing?'

'I didn't want to believe it. I didn't believe it. But then I spoke to Lazarus and he told me how he gets these rages. Death changed him Martha. You know better than I do just how much. What if it changed Jesus too?'

'Jesus was – is – the son of God. He didn't kill those people. Why would he?'

'I don't know,' Judas said. 'I don't know anything, any more.'

But he did realise Martha had a point. And Jeb had expressed similar sentiments. Jesus had dedicated his life to helping the unfortunate and healing the sick. The thought that he might have returned with bloodlust – killing people instead of curing them – made no sense.

'Who else could it be, Judas? Who else knows what you did and would be prepared to kill over it?'

'I don't know,' he mumbled. 'No one.'

A little light flickered on in his brain. There was something else that made no sense. The note: *I know what you did.* Why would Jesus, back from the dead, write a note like that? Of course he knew what Judas had done. He'd been there. He knew what Judas had done, just as Judas knew it.

Jesus wasn't a killer. The note wasn't the sort of thing Jesus would write. It couldn't be him. It just couldn't.

And yet ...

It seemed a bit too much of a coincidence that the killings had begun around the time of the resurrection.

'Think, Judas. Who?'

'I don't know, I just don't know,' he said. 'The one thing I do know is all the people I care about are dying and –'

Martha's hand flew up to her mouth again.

'You know Lazarus. And Mary,' she whispered through her fingers.

'But not well ...'

190

'As well as you know me! Thank you for the warning, but we're not your friends. We've hardly had anything to do with you.' She began hustling him towards the door.

'Martha . . . you and me . . . '

'There is no you and me. There never was.'

'But the kiss, the walk. Holding hands.'

'I don't know what you mean.'

'You can't pretend you didn't feel something.'

'I didn't. I was just being friendly. But we're not friends. We never were.'

'You know that's not –'

'The killer probably doesn't know you're here. If you leave now he need never know. Go on, hurry.'

'I'll go, but promise me something first.'

'What? Quick!'

'You'll stay safe. Tonight, lock yourself in and don't answer the door to anyone. I'll fix this problem and then I'll come find you, I promise.'

'No, don't come and find me. Stay away from us. As far away as you can. This isn't our problem. You did this.'

'I know.'

'Can't you just end it?'

'I might be able to. I think I know how to remove the curse. If I can just return –'

'No, I mean end it. Kill yourself.'

He stared at the woman he had once dreamed of marrying, standing there, terrified, suggesting he take his own life.

'I'll come back as soon as I can,' he promised.

'Please don't,' Martha said as she hurried him out of the room.

Chapter 34

Simon's head spun like he'd supped three skins of wine the previous night. It ached dreadfully, as did his midriff, which felt like a small imp had been dancing inside his ribcage. His ankles and wrists hurt too, bound tightly together as they were. To make things worse he was also gagged, to the point where it cut into his lips, and some form of material was right in his face, making breathing a somewhat laboured effort.

As his eyes adjusted to the dim light, he realised he was inside … something dark. Coarse and dark. It was a sack. He was tied up in a sack. He began to panic, his immediate sense of fear and desperation augmented by the claustrophobic nature of his predicament.

He frantically tried to move his hands, but the bonds were so secure, it was useless. His feet were the same. He bucked his body up and down a few times, but there was no loosening of any of his ties. He tried a different tack and attempted to inch forward within his prison of tightly woven goat's hair. The floor felt rough, with strands of something – was that hay? – beneath him. He got a little way, wriggling like a worm, but then the rope attached to his feet went taut. As well as binding his ankles together it was tied to something.

Simon tried to shout for help, but all that came out of his mouth were some muffled noises, that probably sounded even more muffled to the outside world thanks to the sack. He strained his lungs to make as much racket as he could, and then strained his ears to listen for any kind of response. All he heard was silence.

Fragments of the last conversation he'd had floated back through his mind; the words of his son, Judas. *'You're in danger . . . Serious danger . . . You need to go now . . . Go somewhere far away . . . Before he comes for you . . . '*

Evidently, it was too late.

Chapter 35

In one corner there was a solid bronze life-size statue of a loin-cloth-clad man frozen in the act of throwing a spear, its detailing intricate. The opposite corner was dominated by an ivory horn on a stand, a huge thing that must have been worth a small fortune by itself.

Judas had heard that the head of the Sanhedrin's villa was a study in opulence, but you had to actually see it to understand just how truly extravagant it was. The white vaulted ceiling of the capacious room he stood in sheltered all manner of riches, from exquisite tapestries on the walls, to marble tables topped with ornate vases, gem-studded goblets and probably priceless ornaments. None of which seemed to be particularly fitting for a man of religion, but then, Caiaphas wasn't really a man of religion. He was a man of power. The sort of man who had a policy of deliberately not noticing anyone entering a room to remind them of their insignificance.

'So here you are,' Caiaphas boomed unexpectedly, his voice cutting through the still air with such volume it almost made Judas jump. The high priest pushed himself upright on the deeply padded room-length red couch he'd been reclining on while reading. The pair of guards who had escorted Judas through the villa lowered their heads in deference.

'I assume you bring me news from the so-called apostles?' Caiaphas reached over to a small table next to him, and picked up a slice of fruited loaf, crammed with apricots and dates, and topped lavishly with butter.

'No,' Judas said.

'No?' Caiaphas raised an eyebrow as he bit into the slice, and chewed noisily.

'No.' He wished he could have seen Caiaphas up at the temple. This was a far more intimidating environment than the high priest's small office up on the Mount. But still, he had to show no fear.

'But you have delivered my message to them have you not?'

'No.'

'And why not?'

'I have an entirely different message for you. Where's your shadow today?'

'What is the meaning of this nonsense?' Caiaphas practically erupted with the words, flecks of spittle and fruit loaf sailing through the air.

'Malchus, where is he?'

'Malchus is none of your business.'

'Out is he? Cleaning something up is he?'

Caiaphas placed the fruited slice back down on the table, and eyed Judas warily. 'Guards, wait at the door.' The men departed, leaving the two alone in the room. 'What are you talking about?'

'I think you know. Should I mention the brothel?'

'You can mention it if you like,' Caiaphas cracked a thin smile. 'I expect you're an expert on those sort of places. No?'

'I've been to one or two. One in particular springs to mind.'

195

'Well. This is all very interesting. But I think that's probably enough of my time wasted for one day.' Caiaphas pointed at the door.

'One particular brothel I've been underneath,' Judas continued. 'And I've seen what's there. What someone has been doing.'

'Are you suggesting, Judas Iscariot, that I visit common whorehouses?'

'I never said it was common – but yes, it is in the lower city, you're right. Strange that you should guess . . .'

'Judas, you have fifteen seconds to leave, or I'll have you thrown in my dungeon. Piece by bloody piece.'

'I wouldn't do that. A friend of mine knows that I'm here, and if I don't return, he'll set a series of events in motion that you really don't want to happen.'

'What are you blithering on about, Iscariot?'

'I see you've lost that ring you were wearing the last time I saw you. Careless. I wonder where it could be?'

The priest glanced down at his bare hand. 'I haven't lost it. I'm just not wearing it. It's in my bedroom.'

'Are we going to play this game all day?'

'I have no idea what you're driving at. If you've got something to say to me, just say it.'

'I found your ring in the basement of the brothel with the dead prostitute you tortured with Malchus, and I'll have it delivered to the Sanhedrin council, with the full story of where it was found, and in what circumstances, unless you co-operate.'

Caiaphas let out an abrupt burst of laughter. 'And you expect they'll believe your ridiculous tale? No, Judas. They won't.'

'Maybe not. But there's a chance they will.'

'Your delusional ranting will make you seem exactly as you are. Insane.'

'And what about your wife? What would she think if I told her what you get up to?'

'She thinks what I tell her to think.'

'Her father wouldn't be too happy though, would he? Annas may not be high priest any more, but he still wields power in this city.'

'And what do you know of the political machinations of Jerusalem, Iscariot?' Caiaphas snorted derisively.

'At the very least, it will put doubts in the minds of your family and the Sanhedrin. Do you want that sort of attention?'

The high priest was silent.

'Caiaphas, are you really willing to risk this mess being aired?'

'You're a fool, Judas. You don't know what fire you're playing with.'

'Look, I don't want much. I don't want your massed riches,' Judas gestured around the room, 'or a hefty chunk from your vast coffers. In fact, the very opposite.'

'What?'

'I'll return the ring, and forget about this whole episode, if you just take back the money you gave me. Take the silver you paid me for betraying Jesus. That's all. Surely it's not that much to ask?'

Caiaphas stood and took a few steps to stand right in front of Judas, fixing him with a stare. 'Bring this trinket you claim is mine and I will take the silver back from you. Now leave.'

'I just need to get the ring and the money from where it's being kept safe. Won't take me too long, I'll have it for you tomorrow.'

Caiaphas leaned in even closer, his pupils burning with intensity. 'Just be warned. You're playing a dangerous game, Judas. Very dangerous.' He turned on his heel and said, 'Get out.'

Judas departed the room, the guards escorting him out to the courtyard where the sun was starting to dip lower in the sky. He walked across the yard towards the exit gate, down a path marked out by unlit torches that sat atop shoulder-height iron holders.

So far, so good. Now all he had to do was make the money back up to thirty silver – he was eight short of that mark, if his memory served him correctly – and deposit it all back into Caiaphas's grubby little perverted hands. Which was going to be a lot easier said than done.

Normally, when his finances were stretched, he'd ask his father for a loan. But Simon wouldn't have anywhere near that sort of money to hand, and besides, there was no chance of him even listening to Judas now, given what had happened. His uncle would probably have handed over the eight silver without even asking what it was for – assuming he was on a winning streak, of course – but he was dead. So that left his friends.

Baruch was the most obvious person to ask, but sadly also the least likely person to be in a position to help. The vast majority of his meagre wages went on whores, wine and potions. Aaron would probably have some spare cash, he always had a reasonable float on his market stall, but it was doubtful he'd be able to part with that much. He needed it to run his business and things were tight. Plus Judas was in no position to pay it back with any immediacy. Then there was Jonathan, but he was just as broke as Judas. Messengers didn't earn much, especially around here.

He could maybe try to get a piece of silver from each of them, but the very thought of effectively begging made him feel worthless. Besides, that could take ages, with time against him and the killer possibly about to strike again.

There was, of course, another potential option: Martha. Her family had lots of money and the chunk of silver he needed would be relatively small change to them. But he couldn't ignore the obvious. Warning her that she and her family were in danger and then returning to ask for payment to remove that danger smacked of it all being a scam. Even though it wasn't, she was never going to go for that. Unless ... unless she didn't know about it.

If he just borrowed it, got into the house somehow and helped himself, she'd be none the wiser. When, or if, the theft was discovered they'd have no reason to suspect Judas. Even if they didn't have any silver just lying around, he could always take a valuable item or two and sell it on. He'd find some way to pay them back in time, naturally.

So, Martha's house it was then. Although first, he had to run a couple of errands; a quick visit to Baruch to keep him appraised of the situation, and then back home to pick up a suitably stealthy garment for tonight's clandestine mission.

Chapter 36

Was that movement he heard? Simon listened intently. He'd been here for hours upon hours. Even in the sack he could tell it had grown dark, and must be the middle of the night now. His wrists were raw from working back and forth, in a vain attempt to loosen the ropes which lashed them together. His jaw was sore from chewing on the gag that silenced him, in an effort to split it. He could taste blood in his mouth and knew all he'd succeeded in doing was splitting the side of his lips.

He continued to strain his ears, trying to pick out any sound.

A door creaked. Someone was here. Unless it was the wind. Although the wind probably wouldn't make increasingly loud footsteps coming in his direction. Simon cried out, muffled shouts for help, but the sound of the footfalls remained regular, a methodical plodding towards him. There was no speeding up or rushing to his rescue as he'd allowed himself to imagine, and any fleeting glimmer of hope was snuffed out totally as the footsteps stopped, right in front of his head.

Simon closed his eyes tightly, in anticipation of a crushing blow to his skull, or a – the movement started again. His captor stepped over him, then Simon felt the cord on his feet tugging. The other end of the rope was being untied from whatever solid object it was anchored to.

Without warning, he was yanked by his feet and dragged across the floor by a powerful set of arms. Then his captor stopped just as quickly and he heard the creak of the door again. Simon could feel the cool night air begin to circulate inside his claustrophobic woven prison. He cried out for help as loud as he could. Several times.

But help didn't come. Although another cracking blow to the head did.

Chapter 37

Judas pulled the hood up over his head as far as it would go. He didn't want anyone recognising him. Not that anyone was likely to even pass by here at this time of night, but it didn't hurt to be sure. Pressing his body against the wall, he shuffled silently along until he reached the midway point and looked up. The moonlight showed he was at the right spot. There, directly above him, was a crumbling section of stonework. He remembered seeing it when he'd been with Lazarus in the courtyard. It had caught his eye because the rest of the building was so pristinely maintained.

The wall was lower here than elsewhere and seemed his best chance of breaking in. Unfortunately it was still much higher than he'd expected it to be. Maybe three times his height.

Judas swore under his breath. Now what?

He looked around but could see nothing. Partly because at that moment the moon had chosen to vanish behind some clouds, making it stupidly dark, and partly because there was just nothing to see. This section of wall was his only real option. He'd have to try and climb it, somehow.

Judas stretched up, dug his fingers into the sandy mortar between the stone blocks, and prepared to heave himself upwards. His muscles tensed, his fingers took the strain, and then just as he was about to begin the climb he let go and stepped away from the wall.

This was crazy.

What was he doing? Breaking into Lazarus's home in the dead of night so he could steal something to sell. It was all just so wrong. This wasn't him. He wasn't a thief.

He'd taken the money from the Sanhedrin to pay off his uncle's gambling debt. To save Daniel's life. The act of treachery had been deplorable, but at least it had come from a good place. But this ... this was theft, pure and simple.

Yes, Lazarus and his family would likely not miss whatever trinket he took, but was that really a justification for burglary?

Judas shook his head.

No, that wasn't the justification.

The justification was saving lives. He needed the money to pay back Caiaphas to end the killings. He'd betrayed Jesus to save one life, and now he was robbing Lazarus, robbing Martha, to save countless others. Two wrongs to try and make things right. Well, as right as they could ever be. He could never bring back Gideon, Daniel, or the others who had died as a result of his actions, but he could prevent future deaths.

Breaking into Lazarus's home and stealing an item of value was wrong, but it was also his only option. He had to do this, and he had to do it now, before his remaining courage evaporated away.

Judas blanked his mind, dug his fingers into the sandy mortar once more, and pulled himself upwards. His feet pedalled against the wall until they eventually found something to rest on. He was about one tefah, a palm's width, off the ground. He freed one hand, reached up, found another grip and pulled himself upwards once more. Tefah by tefah he crawled his way up the wall.

Several times during the ascent his feet struggled for purchase, and he came close to falling, before managing to locate a foothold and avert disaster. The many hours he'd spent climbing towering trees as a boy didn't seem quite so wasted.

Finally, Judas reached the crumbling top section and grunting with exertion he swung his body over, hanging there for a moment, readying himself, before letting go.

His feet hit the ground and he bent his knees to absorb the impact, only just managing to stay upright and avoid tumbling into the thorny bush he'd nearly landed in. He made his way over to where he recalled the door being, feeling around until his fingers detected the change from stone to wood. Placing both palms on the door he pushed hard. Absolutely nothing happened. It was locked. Well of course it was locked. He'd warned Martha to stay safe so she was hardly going to leave the back door open. So what was his next move? He'd scaled a wall for no discernible reason. He might as well just have stayed outside the equally bolted front entrance.

Then he remembered there was a window on this wall, lower than the ones at the front. It would likely be shuttered and closed, but easier to break than this solid oak slab.

He fumbled his way along the surface, located the window and pushed on it. To his surprise and delight the shutters swung open. He grabbed onto the ledge, then pulled himself up and in, dropping silently onto the floor inside. Now he just had to find some money.

He made his way along the corridor, walking silently on the scarlet- and gold-carpeted runs. Lazarus's home was really a collection of a dozen or so different-sized rooms that had been added over time. His grandfather had spawned a large family and had gradually extended the house, bolting on more and more accommodation for his children, their spouses, offspring and, by all accounts, anyone who happened to be in the area and in need of somewhere to stay for the night. These days it was home to just Lazarus and his sisters, and a number of the rooms were either empty, or being used for storage. It was one of these storage rooms that Judas was after. Surely he'd find something of value there.

The lighting in the house was intermittent. There were lamps spaced evenly along the looping corridor, but most of them had already died out, or been extinguished. Lazarus had left a few burning though, presumably to keep the darkness at bay. If the night reminded him of the blackness of death, the void beyond he'd previously spoken of, his phobia was now Judas's gain.

The first lit lamp was positioned almost directly outside of a room with an open curtain pulled up and across the lintel.

Judas inched forward and peeked through the doorway. The light spilling in from behind him cast a grey twilight-like pallor around the room. He could just about make out twin beds, and two long shapes lying on them, underneath blankets. Lazarus's sisters, Mary and Martha. Adrenaline fizzed through his veins. There was a nervous deliciousness in being here, within touching distance of Martha as she slept. He'd give anything to be lying next to her, stroking her hair, feeling the warmth of her body against his. He dismissed the thought abruptly. It was never going to happen and he couldn't afford to be caught spying on the sisters. He had a job to do. With one final longing glance into the bedroom, he quietly walked past the open doorway and made his way to the next.

There was a flickering lamp outside this one as well. It

looked to be burning more fiercely than the first, the flame dancing wildly, yet its light seemed to illuminate a smaller area. No, that wasn't quite right. As Judas edged nearer he could see the light appeared to die just inside the doorway of the room opposite. As if the inky blackness it contained was darker and more resistant somehow.

This had to be Lazarus's room.

He crept forward tentatively. The air seemed cooler around him. Or perhaps it was his skin, chilled at the sight of the looming shroud of darkness. Reaching the entrance, Judas peered in around the edge of the curtained doorway.

He could see nothing. The room was too dark to make out anything at all. He stared into the pitch-black for several minutes, forcing his eyes to become accustomed to the total absence of light until the rough outline of a wooden bed eventually emerged from the gloom. A shape lay motionless on top. Lazarus himself, presumably. Judas shuddered and moved on, grateful for the dancing light that washed the walls of the corridor around him.

The third room he came to was evidently unused. There were a few rolled up rugs propped against the wall, and some basic items of furniture, including a broken table and some chairs. The fourth room contained a pair of beds, with plump white pillows, and blankets pulled tightly over the mattresses. The fifth room was different from all the others in that it had a closed wooden door. Solid internal doors were something of a rarity in Jerusalem. A luxury usually only found in the likes of palaces, temples or the homes of carpenters with high aspirations and too much free time on their hands.

Judas tried the handle. It was locked. He peered through the keyhole but could see nothing. This was, in all likelihood, the very storeroom he'd been looking for. Beyond the wooden barrier he would no doubt discover a wealth of riches. Everything he'd been hoping for, and then some. He just needed the key, and unfortunately he had a pretty good idea of where he'd find it.

He made his way back to Lazarus's bed chamber. If anything it looked even darker inside than before. There was no way he'd be able to find a key in there. He'd have to fumble about trying to locate it, and his chances of doing that successfully were slim-to-none. He looked up at the lamp balanced on top of an iron stand and made a decision. Lifting it carefully off he got down on his knees and crawled forward, holding the lamp in front of him. The flame nibbled away at the darkness as he moved slowly into the room, all of his senses on high alert.

He crept cautiously onwards, grateful for the lamp's inability to cast more than an anaemic glow, and made his way towards Lazarus's bed. His heart was thumping as he drew near, and he realised he'd stopped breathing some time ago. He sucked in a quiet breath and waited, frozen, to calm and compose himself a bit more. There, on a chair next to the bed and alongside a cup of water and a belt, were the keys, threaded onto a solid iron ring. This was going to be easier than he'd hoped.

He placed the lamp on the floor, careful not to make a sound, and shuffled forward towards the chair. As he inched nearer to the low wooden bed, Judas could see Lazarus quite clearly. He was lying flat on his back, arms folded across his chest as if dead. Judas stared at him, fascinated. Most people he knew snored so loudly when asleep it was like sharing a room with a herd of pigs. His father in particular did an impressive impersonation of a sow being asphyxiated. Lazarus, on the other hand, made no sound at all. Even his breathing was quiet. Too quiet. If it wasn't for the minimal rise and fall of the man's chest, the barely perceptible movement of the blanket over the body, Judas would have sworn he was looking at a corpse. His gaze moved up the woollen covering to Lazarus's face.

The man's eyes were wide open.

For a second Judas had to fight hard to avoid bolting from the room there and then, but even as he struggled with his inner terror he could tell something wasn't quite right. Lazarus's eyes might have been open but they were alabaster white and unseeing. He was still very much asleep.

Unnerved, but determined, Judas moved forward again, his heart still pumping rapidly, and reached out a shaking hand. His fingers grasped the keys and bunched them together. All the time his eyes remained fixed on Lazarus's staring face. When the keys were secured – there were eight of them in total – Judas reached out his other hand and slowly lifted up the metal ring.

Lazarus stirred. Only slightly, but it was enough to cause Judas's heart to start thudding again. Those blind white eyes continued to stare upwards, unblinking. But Judas had the keys now, and all he needed to do was make his getaway.

He pulled the metal object towards him and hugged it close to his chest, holding the keys tightly to avoid making any kind of noise, and then shuffled backwards on his knees, away from the still sleeping figure.

He had, against all odds, succeeded in the first part of his mission. The hard part. All that remained was to locate the right key and open the storeroom door. That shouldn't be too difficult.

He shuffled backwards some more and felt his foot make contact with something small and solid.

The lamp.

He turned, eyes wide, in time to see the light source tip over and hit the floor with a thunk. The noise sounded a hundred times louder in the dead silence of the room. Judas's head whipped round and he stared at Lazarus, momentarily paralysed by fear. For a second he thought his luck had held, that just for once things were going his way, but then as the light behind him flickered and died in the pooling oil, Lazarus blinked twice and life began to return to his eyes.

There was no time and no other option available. Judas had to move now and move fast. The room was in total darkness, but he could see light outside the doorway. He span and crawled forwards, still clutching the keys, and headed for the opening. The split-second he was clear he jumped to his feet and ran for the storeroom door, hoping he'd been fast and quiet enough not to have been heard or seen.

He pelted down the carpeted runs, past the unused room and the spare bedroom, until he reached the storeroom door. He looked down at the keys and selected the most likely one, jamming it into the lock. It went in halfway and stopped. He pulled it out and tried another. This one went in nearly all the way but refused to turn. He cursed under his breath and reached for a third. As he did the ring slipped in his moist hands and the two used keys jangled together. The noise almost made Judas retch. He jammed the third key in and tried it. No luck.

He thought he heard a sound. A creaking from down the corridor.

The fourth key was too chunky to go in the hole at all. Did any of these blasted things fit any of the locks in this house? How many doors even had locks here? Three, four at most? From what he could remember there wasn't even a lock on the front door.

As he stood there, sweating, a long-forgotten memory bubbled to the surface. He recalled his father telling him, when he was just a boy, that if you were looking for a good apple in a barrel of rotten ones, it was always going to be the very last one you bit into. He grabbed at the eighth key on the ring and pushed it into the lock more in desperation than expectation.

Lazarus's voice boomed out, causing Judas to jump and the key to fall from the hole. 'Who's there?'

His fingers felt like they were all thumbs, moist wet shaking thumbs at that, as he tried the last key again. It slid into the lock, the notches aligning, and Judas turned it. His father had been right. It was always the last one.

He cast a glance back in the direction of Lazarus's bedroom in time to see a dark shape lumbering towards him.

'You – stop!' Lazarus shouted.

Judas grabbed at the door handle, but his hand slipped off it. He grasped it successfully with a second attempt, but couldn't help checking to see where Lazarus was as he pulled the door open. His pursuer was close now, and armed with what looked like a chair leg. Judas threw himself through the opening, just as Lazarus hurled the makeshift club in his direction. The wood thudded against the door as he slammed it shut behind him. He went to turn the key. Except there was no key. It was still in the lock on the other side of the door. The side with Lazarus on.

He heard the sound of someone moving up against the wood, followed by a clunking noise. Lazarus had done what Judas couldn't. He'd turned the key and locked the door.

'I've got him now,' Lazarus said. 'Martha!'

Judas's eyes darted around the small, wanly lit space. So much for a room filled with lavish treasures. There were shelves holding boxes, cloths, rags and buckets, along with a selection of brooms and mops propped up against the wall. There was some crockery as well, but not much else. And no other exit, aside from one narrow window set high up through which some moonlight shone, but that was inaccessible and not nearly big enough to fit through anyway.

He was completely trapped.

Chapter 38

'Martha!' Lazarus shouted down the corridor again. 'Mary!'

Judas could hear footsteps padding softly down the carpet. 'What is it?' Mary's voice asked.

'I've got the bastard trapped in the cleaning storeroom,' Lazarus said. 'He's locked inside.'

'Who is?' another female voice asked. Martha's.

'A thief, that's who. He'll rue the day he broke into my house.'

'A thief?' Mary sounded terrified.

'Are you sure it's a thief?' Martha said. 'Remember what Judas told me? There's a murderer on the loose.'

Lazarus barked out a laugh. 'This fool is hiding in a store-room, Martha. He's a coward, not a killer. A sneaky bloody thief, that's all.'

'We should get help.'

'Help? I've faced the darkness of death alone. I can handle one gutless robber!' Lazarus bellowed. 'Mary, go to the cellar, now. Fetch my sword.'

'Yes, brother.'

Judas heard footsteps receding. This was not good. A furious Lazarus armed with a chair leg was one thing, but a furious Lazarus armed with a sword was an entirely different proposition. He looked around the storeroom for some kind of object he could use to defend himself. A broom handle might be somewhat useful in the hands of an experienced swordsman, but Judas was nothing of the sort. He could try to throw a cloth over Lazarus's head and escape while the man was unable to see. But he'd only get one shot at that and the odds of success were poor at best.

He heard footsteps outside. Mary returning, and far too quickly for his liking. He just had to hope she'd failed to find the weapon, or had decided against fetching such a dangerous object for her clearly unstable sibling.

'Quick, give it to me,' Lazarus said, destroying that hope. 'And pull that lamp stand over, closer to the door.'

The stand scraped over the floor as it was moved, the light levels in the storeroom increasing as more illumination spilled through from under and around the door frame.

Judas yanked boxes off the shelves and began to rummage through them, desperately looking for something, anything, he could use to defend himself.

'Stay back,' Lazarus said, and there was a rattling sound as he grasped the keys in the lock. Time was running out. And then, at the bottom of one box, Judas found something wrapped in a thick blanket. He unfolded part of the covering, nodded to himself, and snatched it up, rewrapping it as he did so. There might still be a chance yet.

The lock clunked and the door swung inwards, banging against the wall. Light flooded the small storeroom as Lazarus stepped in, gripping his sword tightly.

Judas, attempting to blend into the shadows at the side of

the door, snatched up a broom which was propped against the wall and swung it wildly at the invading figure. Lazarus didn't duck, didn't even flinch. He simply turned and parried the blow, his sword snapping the wooden handle in two. Then, face contorted with fury, he swung the sword around and stabbed the point forwards, driving it directly into Judas's ribcage. The thrust caused Judas to stagger backwards. Memories of the final moments of his dream about Jesus came flooding back as he clattered into the shelves behind him and slid to the floor.

He couldn't breathe and his chest felt like it was on fire.

Chapter 39

'No . . .' Martha could barely gasp the word out. 'What have you done? You've killed him!'

Her brother stared at the lifeless hooded body in front of him, a puzzled expression flitting across his face. He raised his sword and then cried out in surprise as Judas sprang into motion, slamming the sharp end of the shortened broom handle into his left leg. Lazarus shrieked in pain and fell to one side, allowing Judas just enough room to scramble to his feet and jump through the gap, past Martha and out into the corridor.

Mary screamed as Judas darted in front of her. Grateful for the fact that his hood had somehow managed to stay up through all the turmoil, he began to run back the way he'd come. He dashed along the hallway, heading for the open window, before skidding to an abrupt halt after just half-a-dozen strides. What was he doing, going back to the window? There was no point him trying to get out that way. He'd still have to climb over the wall and Lazarus would surely catch him. There was a much better, more obvious solution in the other direction. He turned and pelted back down the corridor, towards the two terrified sisters who scattered as he drew near. He passed the open storeroom door just as Lazarus appeared, sword in hand and red-faced with rage.

Judas turned right, next to the dimly lit mural of the Mount of Olives which, if his memory served him correctly, marked the passageway to the front door. This corridor's lamps were all unlit. He ran as fast as he could in the near-darkness, keeping in a straight line, until he spotted hints of moonlight drawn around the frame of the oaken door ahead. Easing up his speed, he reached the exit, scrabbled for the topmost bolt and threw it back. He glanced behind to see if Lazarus had followed and saw the man limping into the corridor at the far end, a lamp in one hand, sword in the other.

'Get back here!' Lazarus roared.

Judas turned his attention back to the door. There were four bolts in total. Three more to go. He slid the second one open swiftly and dexterously.

He had to jiggle the third back and forth when it jammed partway, and during those precious seconds he could hear Lazarus's uneven footfalls getting louder, the lamplight becoming brighter on the door.

The third bolt went back.

He fumbled with the final one. He could hear breathing close behind him.

The fourth bolt slid free. He grabbed the door and pulled it open. As the solid oak slab swung back, it met Lazarus's sword, cutting its vicious arc short. The blade embedded firmly in its edge. A second or so sooner and it would have embedded firmly in Judas's collarbone.

Grateful for the door's timely intervention, Judas slipped through the opening and ran out into the night, still struggling to breathe and with a burning pain in his chest.

'I'll find you, thief, mark my words,' Lazarus shouted behind him. 'I'll find you, and I'll kill you. Do you hear me?'

Chapter 40

Jebediah looked down at his foot. All his life it had been a small, misshapen lump attached to a withered leg, but not any longer. He stared up at Jesus, and then back at the transformed appendage, unable to believe what he was seeing. He wiggled his long, perfectly formed toes, then twisted his foot from side to side, watching the ankle pivot. A broad smile formed on his face.

'Thank you,' he said, staring into the serene blue eyes of the messiah.

'Stand,' Jesus commanded.

Jeb grabbed hold of his crutch and began to pull himself up.

'You don't need that,' Jesus said. 'Not any more.' He took the wooden support from Jebediah and placed it against the wall.

Jeb stood unaided and looked down at his new leg as it bore his weight for the first time. The coolness of the sandy ground sent delicious shivers through the sole of his miraculous new foot.

'Now run,' Jesus said. 'Run free. Run far.'

Jeb took off, hurtling down alleyways and wide thorough-fares, revelling in his newfound ability. All around people stared, laughed and cheered him on. A man pulled a handcart into his path. Without thinking, Jeb hurdled over it, landing safely on the other side. Grinning, he continued to sprint along the streets, pushing himself to go faster, fire in his belly, wind in his ears, the ground beneath him being devoured at a giddy pace.

No longer would he be forced to beg for coppers and scraps. Now he could work for a living, earn his keep, and the respect of those around him. He could finally think about–

The crippled youth awoke with a jolt. Something had disturbed his sleep, and snuffed out the dream. He rolled over and peered around, but could see nothing in the near-total blackness. Waiting for his eyes to become accustomed to the dark, Jebediah listened intently. All was silent, aside from the deep rhythmic breathing of his father asleep a few feet away.

He lay back down on his mattress on the floor, closed his eyes and was just drifting back off when a sharp noise across the room snapped him once again into wakefulness. Probably just an animal in search of food scraps. He sighed, pulled back the blankets and felt around for his crutch, being careful not to wake his father. The man had a fierce temper and Jeb still had the month-old belt imprints on his back to prove it. He hauled himself up onto his good foot using the crutch. His withered left leg, ending in a misshapen child-sized foot, following uselessly as always.

Jebediah's eyesight was more attuned to the darkness now, and the moon peeking from behind the clouds provided just enough illumination to see part of the room around him. He made his way over to the corner and searched for the source of the noise. There was nothing there. Whatever had made the sound was long gone. He was about to return to bed when something small caught his eye. He crouched to get a better look – it was a piece of rock. Smooth, almost pebble-like. He picked it up, placed it on the small table and turned around.

Even in the semi-darkness he could see the unmistakable shape of his father sitting bolt upright on his mattress. This was not good. Jebediah had been very careful not to make a sound.

'Sorry,' he whispered. 'I thought I heard a noise.'

The older man said nothing.

Jebediah began to move back towards his bedding. His father's silence was unnerving; it was never a good sign. Jeb apologised again, but still no reply came.

As he reached his destination, Jebediah cast a sideways glance in the older man's direction just in time to see his head move. Despite the gloom of the night he could tell that his father was now looking upwards, towards the ceiling. Jeb followed his gaze, but it was too dark to make out whatever the man was staring at. He just hoped it wasn't a rat. It was too late at night to be trying to catch breakfast.

'What is it?' he whispered. 'What can you –'

His father's head nodded, and fell forward. And kept falling. It hit the floor with a dull thud and tumbled over a few times before coming to rest. For several heartbeats Jeb stared in shock at the head. He couldn't make out its features in the darkness, but he knew with certainty it was staring back at him.

His father was a tough man, but Jebediah had never appreciated just how tough until now. Even with his head detached from his body the old bastard still appeared to be breathing.

Although, as he listened, Jeb realised the sound seemed to be coming from directly behind him ...

A searing pain tore through his bad leg. He stumbled forward, tripped over something in front of him and felt the world give way. Jeb grabbed at the crutch for support but it slid away, causing him to twist as he fell. He struck the ground solidly and took a blow in the face from the wooden prop. It bounced upwards and clouted him a second time for good measure before falling to the floor.

He swore and hunted around in the darkness for it. His hand brushed against something wet and sticky. He felt around again and this time his hand encircled a stubby and unexpected object. He pulled it towards him and peered at the item responsible for tripping him over. It was his own foot.

He hurled it away in fear, found the crutch and tried to pull himself upwards, but just as he did so something sliced into his good leg. He howled in pain as whatever had penetrated the knee was levered back and forth with considerable fury and strength. Cartilage, tendon and ligaments were torn through with seeming ease. Jebediah clung to the wooden support as tightly as possible until the lower part of his limb finally came away. Genuinely no longer having a leg to stand on, he toppled forward and struck the ground hard for a second time.

Confused, panicking and in agony, Jebediah rolled onto his front and began to inch forward, pulling himself towards the door using just his fingertips. The exit was a matter of feet away. If he could only get to it ...

The blinding pain came again, this time in his left wrist. He scrabbled forward, sending his detached hand skittering across the floor. It came to rest as it hit the door, lying palm up, the fingers curled inwards like a dead spider.

Jeb had switched to survival mode now. He had been a cripple with only one good leg all his life. Now he had no legs and one hand, but he was still alive. Unlike his father. All he could do was keep going and try to make it to the exit. He was nearly there. Nearly ...

The attacker grabbed hold of Jebediah's stumps and dragged him all the way back across to the other side of the room. He tried to resist by digging the fingers of his one remaining hand into the ground, but his efforts were beyond futile.

The man let go of him. Determined not to give up, Jeb began the slow crawl forward, attempting to reach the door again, inch by cruel inch, his life force ebbing away with every movement. Out of the corner of his eye, he could see the attacker was now doing something to his father's headless body. Hacking at the dead flesh.

Then the killer moved towards him. Reaching Jebediah in three strides, he flipped the defenceless cripple over onto his back. With one powerful hand, the man forced his mouth open and stuffed something inside it. Jeb felt a large slick-skinned orb on his tongue. It was quickly joined by another fleshy sphere.

He tried to spit the objects out, but the man jabbed the handle of his weapon into Jebediah's open maw, ramming them down hard. One slipped away to the side, but the other jammed in his gullet, bulging as it did so, blocking his airway. A sliver of rough, hairy skin lodged next to it in his throat.

Jebediah the Cripple gagged, not just because he could no longer breathe, but also because he knew exactly what he was choking to death on.

Chapter 41

Elbows jostled Judas as he made his way through the crowds who were up and out early this Wednesday morning, doubtless in search of a bargain or two. He clutched the cloth-covered circular item in his arms, hugging it close to his body. The pain in his chest from the previous night had abated to a degree, but he still winced every time someone carelessly bumped into him.

He'd arrived at a small market on the north-west side of the city. It wasn't somewhere he frequented often, which meant there was less chance of anyone recognising him. He might struggle to find a buyer for his stolen loot here, given its value, but the streets elsewhere were patrolled far more regularly, especially at festival time, and the last thing he needed was to run into curious Romans while trying to sell his haul. He'd have to find someone here, and exchange his goods for the bare minimum he needed. He had double-checked his remaining funds before he'd come out and eight silver pieces would give him thirty again.

Scurrying along a row of open-fronted shops, he stopped as he heard the noise of metal-on-metal and peered into the smithy. This looked as good a place as any to try and unload his pilfered cargo. Judas stepped in and felt a wave of heat rush over him. The forge was at the far end of the room, the wall around it thick with black grime. The smith stood to one side at the anvil, hammering away at a sword blade, raining heavy blows down one after another. A tall and surprisingly wiry fellow, what he lacked in strength, he evidently made up for in vigour. The smith ceased his flurry of activity, and as the glow of the metal began to die, turned the blade over, examining it critically.

'Can I help you?' he asked, glancing up at Judas.

'Well, actually I'm hoping I can help you. I've got something you might be interested in.' Judas lifted the cloth-covered object up onto a nearby table.

'I sell things. I don't buy them.'

'You might want to take a look at this. At the price I'm selling, it's an absolute bargain.'

'Go on then, show me. If you must.'

Judas pulled the cloth away, revealing a silver plate with a vicious looking indentation in the centre.

'What is it?'

'It's a serving plate,' Judas said. 'A solid silver serving plate.'

The smith set down the half-finished blade and walked over for a closer look. 'What's with the dent?'

'Someone stabbed it with a sword.'

'A sword? You're lucky it didn't go all the way through.'

'I certainly am,' Judas said, touching his sore chest. He was also lucky the plate had been wrapped up in that thick blanket when Lazarus stabbed it with his sword. Otherwise the clang of metal-on-metal would surely have given the game away.

'Mind if I pick it up?'

'Go ahead.'

The smith held the plate up to the light and turned it around, closely examining the ornate carvings of imposing-looking buildings which were engraved around the outside. Then he put the edge of the plate in his mouth and clamped his teeth down on it gently. Finally, he made a grunting noise. It was unclear whether that was a positive or negative sound.

'It is silver, isn't it?' Judas asked.

'It might be. Where did you get this from?' The smith put the object back down on the table.

'I didn't get it from anywhere. It's mine.'

'I mean where did you buy it?'

'I didn't,' Judas replied.

'You didn't?'

'No. It's been in my family a long time. Like way back, in the distant past. My great grandmother's mother's, I think.'

'Hmm. Really.'

'Yes, really.'

The smith stared at Judas and furrowed his brow. 'Have we met before?'

'No. I don't think so.'

'Only I never forget a face. Unless I'm paid to do so. And yours is familiar.'

'Well I've never been in here before.'

'Perhaps we've met somewhere else then?'

'Umm,' Judas mumbled. He couldn't remember having ever encountered the smith before, but there was always the off chance. The man was staring at him and it was beginning to make him feel uneasy. Maybe this wasn't such a great idea. He was about to make his excuses and leave, when the smith grabbed the plate and hastily stowed it away under the table somewhere.

'Hey!' Judas lurched for his swiped goods, several seconds too late.

'Would you be interested in a sword, sir?' the smith said, in a louder voice than he'd previously been talking with.

'What?'

'This finely honed edge for instance,' the smith said, returning to the blade he'd been working on previously, 'will make an excellent weapon for your protection.'

'I don't want to buy anything –'

'Protection from *your enemy*,' the smith continued, nodding his head towards Judas as if he'd developed some sort of weird tic. Was he trying to tell him something? He heard a jangling sound behind him and turned around to see a Roman centurion standing there. The glow of the smith's forge reflecting off the soldier's finely polished steel breastplate managed to create the alarming impression he was on fire. The crimson cloak, draped over his shoulders and across his chest, did nothing to dispel the illusion.

'You're right, you don't want to buy anything from this idiot, he's useless,' the centurion said, shoving Judas out of the way. 'I've had it with you, Jethro. Titus Antonius's blade flew off its hilt as he swung it a couple of weeks ago. And last night Marcus Cornelius had his shield break in two when it was hit by a rioter's rock. It split right down the middle and just fell apart. The next rock hit him in the face. Downright shoddy bloody workmanship.'

'Calm down, Longinus. I can see you're angry, but –'

'Angry? Marcus's nose is spread across his face. He's a damn good soldier, one of my best. I can't afford to lose good men.'

'Of course I'll replace the weapon and shield, free of charge, and make sure –'

'You'll do nothing of the sort,' Longinus interrupted him once more. 'We're never using your sub-standard equipment again.'

'I'm sorry that's the way you feel.'

225

'And we want a full refund on the entire last batch you made for us.'

'A refund? Things can happen on the battlefield, you know, shock of impacts, wear and tear ...' Jethro the smith's words trailed off as Longinus put his hand on the hilt of his sword and withdrew it, just an inch, from its scabbard.

'Yes, fine, of course, sir,' Jethro said. 'But I haven't got that sort of money to hand. Can I at least have a bit of time to get hold of it?'

'You've got until sundown tomorrow to deliver it up to the barracks. If I don't get it before then, I'll be back, with some friends.'

Jethro nodded. Judas watched the centurion turn and then pause.

'I know you, don't I?' he growled at Judas.

'I wouldn't have thought so. I don't normally –'

'Yes, I've seen you before.'

Judas returned the man's scrutinising gaze and realised with a sinking feeling that he recognised him too. The last time he'd seen him was at Golgotha, his red cloak in disarray, his eyes wide with wonder. He'd only spoken a handful of words, but what he'd said in that moment was burned deep into Judas's psyche.

Surely he was the son of God.

They'd shared a moment that neither of them would ever forget, and now here they were reunited in a blacksmith's near the site of the crucifixion; the centurion, and the rotten apostle who gave up his master. Longinus continued to stare at him. Judas felt a bead of sweat drip from his eyebrow, convinced that guilt must be written all over his face. The guilt of what – the betrayal, or his thieving – he wasn't sure; all he knew was his throat was tightening and a queasiness was spreading through his gut.

'He's just got one of those faces,' the smith said, cutting through the dreadful silence. 'I thought I recognised him too.'

The centurion broke his stare, glanced at Jethro and said, 'You're probably right. All you bloody Jews look alike to me.'

He swept his red cloak imperiously back over one shoulder and strode towards the door, ducking as he went through it to avoid catching the plume of his helmet on the low frame.

Judas allowed himself to breathe again. That had been close. He looked back at the smith who was still staring at the door.

'Thanks,' he whispered.

'I know you stole it. Did you take it from them?' Jethro said, switching his gaze back to Judas.

'From who? The Romans?'

'Yes, the engravings on the plate are all Roman-style architecture. Did you swipe it from them?'

Judas wasn't entirely sure what to say, but apparently his silence was answer enough for the smith.

'I knew it,' Jethro said. 'That's what I was thinking when you made it obvious the plate wasn't yours. That's why I hid it when I spotted Longinus at the door.'

'Yes, thanks for that. I'm not the best liar in the world.'

'Lies or no lies, any enemy of the Romans is a friend of mine.' Jethro spat on the floor. 'Filthy money-grabbing invaders. Shoddy workmanship my eye! The moron. I weaken their weapons on purpose when I forge them.'

'Ah, I see. That seems to have landed you in a spot of trouble, though.'

'Yes. I might have got rather carried away this time.'

'Seems that way. Still, it appears fate is smiling on you. The solution to your money crisis is right here. Well, right there. Wherever my plate is. I want far less for it than it's worth.'

'How much?'

'Just eight silver. It's got to be worth a lot more than that.'

'Deal,' Jethro said swiftly.

'Silver staters, mind, not denarii.'

'I wouldn't insult you with Roman coins. I'll just get the money.'

Jethro headed off into the back of the workshop. The plate was probably worth three times what he was asking, if not more, but the precise value wasn't the point. In fact Judas didn't want to make any profit out of this episode. He wanted things evened out in no uncertain terms – he would have exactly thirty silver, and he would give it all back.

The smith emerged and counted the coins out of his burn-scarred hands into Judas's cupped palm.

'Eight,' the smith finished.

'Thank you. You don't know what good you've done here today.'

'You neither, my friend.'

Judas left the smithy, depositing the money into his pouch as he did so. It now held a whole, round, thirty pieces of silver. As he made his way up to the Temple Mount, something flickered within him. Hope, an almost forgotten emotion to Judas of late, once again dared to light a candle in the dark, bleak chambers of his heart.

Chapter 42

Simon blinked, trying to focus, his head groggy. He was, mercifully, no longer trussed up in a sack. He tried to move – less mercifully, he was still trussed up. And in the dark. He lifted his head up off the ground. There was something sticky on his cheek, which meant he had to peel his face away from the floor. He realised it was probably blood. A wave of nausea swept over him, and he took a few measured breaths to steady himself.

He appeared to be in a small, windowless room. He was lying on the floor, his legs up in the air, and his feet tied to something. His arms remained tightly bound behind his back, underneath him, and he was still gagged. Above, there was a slight crack in the ceiling, through which a little light crept; it was daytime now.

He tried to shift his feet, but they were attached to something big and very solid. With his eyes becoming more accustomed to the near-darkness, he could vaguely make out that it seemed to be some manner of large round pot. A weighty iron one by the feel of it. He could also see what appeared to be the outline of a door in front of him and to the left, as well as what looked like silhouettes of bags dotted around the room. There was a distinct smell of food. He was clearly in a storeroom of some sort.

Equally clearly, he had to find a way out of here somehow. Or he was going to die.

Chapter 43

As a pilgrim, you were supposed to climb the Temple Mount steps slowly, giving pause for reflection on life's long step-by-step journey as you went. Judas didn't have the time for all that though. Desperate to conclude the reversal of his deal with Caiaphas, he pelted up the steps, barging past folks, excusing and apologising all the way.

Such was his haste as he bounded up the stairs, he failed to notice an inky black raven on the wall above, its dark eyes following every step of his ascent.

Judas made it up onto the Mount, across the outer court, and into the inner temple complex in record time, pausing only long enough to tell the merchant who waved a necklace fashioned entirely from fish bones in his face to go choke on them.

Once more, he trod the chequered floor of the women's hall, looking for Malchus. He didn't seem to be anywhere in sight, but Judas now knew where the door to Caiaphas's office was, so made his way through to the court of Israel, and knocked loudly. Several times. It eventually opened and a temple guard peered out from behind a spear.

'Go away before I run you through,' he said.

'Charming,' Judas replied. 'But actually I need to see Caiaphas. Tell him Judas Iscariot is here. I'm expected.'

The soldier looked doubtful, but disappeared momentarily.

'I'm afraid you'll have to wait,' he said when he returned to the doorway. 'The high priest is attending an important meeting with the Romans. He'll be finished later this afternoon.'

'Can't you pull him out of the meeting?'

'No,' the guard said, and slammed the door shut.

It was a long and disappointing walk home. By the time Judas trudged through his front door he was in no mood for anything much, except rest. He had a few hours to while away now, and quite frankly a brief stint of recuperation seemed like a sound idea. He was exhausted. The adrenaline which had powered his morning mission to offload the silver plate had ebbed.

He collapsed into a chair, leaned his head back and allowed himself to rest his eyes. Just for a minute. Sleep crept up on him immediately, but didn't fully claim him. Instead it toyed with his consciousness. He drifted in and out, unable to move, but still aware of the world around him. He heard a clatter outside; a stone? There was laughter, young voices. The sound of children playing. His eyes opened languidly, struggling to focus.

And then he saw it.

Judas sat bolt upright in the chair. His hands involuntarily balled into fists as he stared at the letters smeared in blood low down on the wall. It had been so long since he'd received the note – it seemed like an eternity – that he'd almost forgotten about the killer's message. And now the madman had been into his house once again and left him another. Two simple words traced in blood, the edges of the letters coagulated to define them more boldly, as if they needed any further impact: 'She's dead.'

Who was dead? All the victims had been male thus far, so it had to be some woman he didn't yet know about. Who? Blind Mary? Surely she wouldn't allow herself to be killed without – wait – no . . . oh no . . .

Judas was already out the door and twenty paces down the street before his thoughts caught up with his feet. Not her. Please, not her . . .

Chapter 44

Simon had come up with an escape plan. Well, escape plan was a bit of an overstatement. He had an idea, at least. A fairly stupid idea, probably, but it was about the only possibility available to him.

He'd been ruminating at some length on what he could attempt to do about his predicament. Trying to keep his mind occupied and generally not focusing on the other less pleasant thoughts which had been flitting through his consciousness in this small, dark room. A room which seemed to be getting smaller and darker by the minute.

He was trying not to think about Judas, and how his son was responsible for this mess he was in. He was trying not to think about his son's wild imagination and ranting that his captor could be a man returned from the dead. He was trying not to think about his almost certain impending vengeful demise. But perhaps most of all, he was trying not to think about why he had been tied up with a cooking pot.

Simon's plan, such as it was, revolved around his feet. While they were attached to the pot, they weren't bound with rope like his arms. Instead, each foot was slotted through some sort of small metal loop, which in turn was attached to the cauldron. There was space enough to jiggle his ankles about a little, but certainly not enough to slip his feet out. However, using the full force of his legs, he could rock the pot slightly. With enough effort, he might be able to keep it rocking, gaining momentum gradually, and hopefully tip it over. Whatever was pinning his feet to the cauldron might just come free, then he could see about trying to stand up, and getting over to the door.

Maybe he'd still need to free his arms, too, but he'd cross that bridge when he came to it. Of course, this was all a long shot. An extremely long shot. In fact, it was akin to attempting to hit a centurion on the head with a stone from three hundred paces. And he knew how difficult that was from experience.

But the only alternative was to lie here and await the return of his captor, in order to find out what he was going to do to him. It wasn't much of an alternative.

Simon composed himself, as much as he could given the situation, and pushed with all the strength in his legs on the top of the weighty pot, moving it backward very slightly. He let it fall forward, then pushed again, even harder.

Chapter 45

'Judas!'

His legs were giving out and his lungs heaving; he needed to stop and rest, but couldn't. Had ... to ... keep ... going ... it might not be too late ...

'Judas!!'

He was vaguely aware of footsteps and then a figure in his periphery. A hand reached out and grabbed his arm, pulling him to a stop. He fought to shake it off, but the grip was too strong. He looked round and saw Baruch.

'I was calling you,' his friend said, releasing his hold. 'Where are you off to in such a hurry?'

Aaron ambled up alongside them. 'I've never seen you move so fast,' he said. 'Jonathan would be impressed. You could be a foot messenger.'

'She might still ... be alive,' Judas panted. 'Can't be ... dead.'

'Who? What are you talking about?' Aaron asked.

'There's a message,' Judas said, getting his breath back. 'On my wall. In blood. From the killer.'

Baruch pulled a sour face. 'I thought you'd found a way to put a stop to that?'

'I have. I just haven't had the chance to do it yet.'

'What did it say?' Aaron interrupted. 'This message?'

'It said "She's dead."' He was wasting time.

'She's dead? Who's dead?'

'I don't know. Martha I think. I don't have time for this, I need to get going.'

'Martha who?' Aaron looked confused.

'Lazarus's sister,' Baruch explained. 'The one with the nice ... everything. I hope she isn't dead, that would be – hey, wait. Stop.' He reached out and pulled Judas back.

'Get off me, I've got to go to her house. See for myself.' Tears welled in his eyes. Since all this started Judas had managed to build a wall around his grief, focus on the here and now. But it was getting harder and harder. As Blind Mary had said, people he cared about were dying and he was finding it increasingly difficult to hold things together.

'Are you crying?' Baruch asked.

'Of course he isn't,' Aaron said. 'He's just got sweat in his eyes from running. Haven't you?'

Judas didn't trust himself to reply.

'Anyway,' Aaron continued, 'I wouldn't worry about Martha, she's fine. Or she was ten minutes ago. I saw her at the market, with her sister. The plain girl.'

'Mary,' Baruch said. 'She's like a younger Martha you'd stand a chance with. If it was dark enough you could pretend she –'

'You're sure?' Judas cut in.

'Positive. She was buying fruit from that miserable git three stalls down.'

'You didn't know who Martha was a minute ago,' Baruch pointed out.

'Actually, I just didn't know which Martha Judas was talking about.'

'You know more than one?'

'I know loads.'

'You're absolutely positive it was her?'

'Yes, Judas. She was with Mary. And she was fine. I mean, I didn't talk to her or anything –'

'Like she'd ever talk to you anyway,' Baruch guffawed. 'She probably hurries right past your stall. She probably has a plan of the market so she can avoid your part of it entirely.'

'Says the oaf who has to pay women to sleep with him. I'm a married, family man, remember? Anyway, like I say, I didn't speak to her, but she looked fine. Definitely not dead, anyway.'

'So ... who?'

'Who what?'

'The message on my wall said "She's dead." If it's not Martha, then who is it?'

'It was written in blood?' Baruch said. He looked thoughtful, which was unusual.

'Yes, on the wall.'

'Was it dry?'

'I ... don't know. I went in, had a brief nap, just shut my eyes for a minute, really, and when I opened them I saw it.'

'So it wasn't there before you nodded off?'

'I don't know. I didn't see it. But I was tired so ...'

'So was it dry? Or still damp?'

'I don't know, Baruch, I didn't stop to check.'

'What Baruch is trying to ascertain,' Aaron said, 'is if the message was fresh. How long ago it was written. We need to know if the maniac left it before he went off to kill the person in question, or after.'

238

'It was written in blood, so it's safe to assume it was after, Aaron.'

'Not necessarily, we don't know whose blood it is.'

'If it was still damp,' Baruch said, 'it would be bright red. If it was dry, it would be a mucky brown. The colour of the blood changes with time, you see.'

Judas and Aaron turned to look at each other, then back at their friend.

'It's common knowledge,' Baruch said with a smug smile.

'Let's go back to your place and have a proper look, Judas. Martha is fine, for now. We'll look at this message and then decide what to do.'

'If you still want to go and check on Martha we'll come with you,' Baruch added.

'What other women do you know? Only if it's not Martha, or Mary for that matter, then it's probably someone else.'

'There's no one else. Just Martha.'

'Could be someone's mother. Gideon's father died after all.'

'Hmm. I suppose.'

'Let's just go and look at the message.' Aaron began to walk back in the direction of Judas's home. 'We can talk on the way.'

'Shouldn't you be on your stall?'

'No, Seth said he'd look after it for me while I helped Baruch with his new flock.'

'His new what?'

'Ah,' Aaron said, and lapsed into silence.

'My father got them for me,' Baruch said. 'After Jose died they didn't really have a home, so ... I'm sorry, Judas, I know you were interested.'

'I wasn't. I'm not. And I wouldn't have thought you were either.'

'Well, you know. Time for a change maybe. And I like mutton. And wool.'

Judas picked up the pace. It was good to know that Martha was safe, but this still felt like he was wasting valuable time. Time that could be better spent checking on her well-being for himself.

'Bloody Hades, Judas, wait up,' Baruch said.

They reached the house and Judas all but ran inside. The blood on the wall was brownish in colour.

'*She's dead*,' Baruch read out loud. He knelt down and touched the message with his finger, adding, 'It's dry. I reckon it was done yesterday.'

'It certainly doesn't look very fresh,' Aaron concurred. 'You sure you can't think of anyone else it might refer to, Judas? That Mary woman you used to know?'

'Martha's sister?' Baruch asked.

'No, the one who used to be a prostitute.'

'Massive Mary? With the cavernous –'

'No, shut up, Baruch.'

'Mary Magdalene?'

'Yes, her.'

'I don't think so.' It was a possibility, but somehow Judas doubted it. Whoever this madman was, he seemed to be going after his older friends and acquaintances only, leaving Jesus's inner circle untouched.

'I'm going to go,' he said. 'Check up on Martha myself.'

'Then we'll come with you,' Baruch said.

'There's no need.'

'There's every need. What if this maniac does come for her? You won't be any match for a killer. You'll need me to tackle him.' Baruch flexed his arms. 'And Aaron, of course.'

'What about your sheep?' Aaron asked.

'They'll be fine. They've got food. And my father will be back before too long, anyway.'

Judas nodded, grateful for the offer. He needed to go back to the temple to see Caiaphas later on, so Aaron and Baruch could continue to keep watch on Martha while he was gone. They only had to keep her safe for a little while anyway, just long enough for him to hand back the silver. By the time evening fell it would hopefully all be over.

'If you're both sure, I'd appreciate it,' he said.

'Will Mary be there, do you think?' Baruch asked as they left the house together.

Chapter 46

He pushed with his feet on the top of the cauldron once more, for what seemed like the hundredth time. Simon had already made several aborted runs at trying to build backwards and forwards momentum with the pot, but this one was going far more promisingly than the others.

Once again, backwards it went, then forwards it came ... the thick iron container was starting to wobble to the left slightly. He pushed harder, then harder still, with all the might that remained in his body. His energy levels were dropping close to empty, but his mental fortitude drove him onwards, encouraged by the pot pitching slightly more to the side.

Veins emboldened themselves against Simon's skin, droplets of perspiration trickling along the taut blue ridges, as he put a near back-breaking level of effort into the next couple of thrusts with his legs. The pot tilted, and toppled over sideways.

There was a snapping sound. For the briefest of moments Simon thought the bonds on his feet had broken as the cauldron hit the ground, just as he'd hoped they would. Then pain shot up his leg and he realised the noise had come from his left ankle, which had got caught and twisted sharply underneath the rim as it had smacked into the floor.

His mouth emitted some sort of low noise, somewhere between shock and anguish, muffled by his gag so it sounded even weirder in the darkness of the room. Then he could feel nothing – the sharp pain was gone as quickly as it came. He felt strangely ... calm. Maybe his leg wasn't so bad, after all? He tentatively tried to shift the limb. The room spun and a sensation not unlike an iron spike being driven into the heel of his foot sent his head lolling sideways. Simon drifted as the black drapes of unconsciousness fell in front of his eyes once more ...

Chapter 47

'This is totally pointless,' Aaron said. 'We're too far away. If someone came to the door now I'm not sure we'd be able to tell if it was Lazarus or one of his sisters. We need to get closer somehow.'

'We could move the bush?' Baruch said, rustling the foliage of the large Rubus sanctus they were gathered behind. 'Uproot it and move it nearer.'

'We could do, but I suspect a large bush suddenly appearing outside their front door might arouse a little suspicion. And it's not like all of us even fit comfortably behind it.'

'You all right, Judas?' Baruch asked.

Judas looked across at his friend and shrugged. 'Not really.'

'Of course he's not all right,' Aaron said. 'People he knows are being killed. How could anyone be all right with that going on?'

'I suppose.'

'It's not just that,' Judas said.

'What then?'

'It's hard to explain.'

'Try.'

Judas rubbed his forehead with his palm. 'It's just . . . I don't know. Look at us, hiding behind a bush, waiting for a killer to strike. It's crazy. Ridiculous. This time last week my life meant something, it had purpose. I was an apostle. I followed the true messiah, the son of God. And he was truly amazing.'

'Still is,' Baruch said. 'From what I hear.'

'What do you mean?'

'They say he's back from the dead.'

'Who says that?'

'Lots of people. Down at the market, they were saying he rolled away the stone outside his own tomb and just walked out.'

Judas was stunned. He hadn't realised the resurrection was quite such common knowledge already. But then, he had been rather preoccupied, wrapped in his own fearful world, to notice much of anything outside the horror that had become his life.

'My friend Jeremiah heard Jesus was dressed all in white, and glowing,' Baruch continued. 'Not a single mark on his funeral clothes. Still had the wounds from the nails through his hands and feet though.'

White and glowing. That was exactly how Jesus had appeared to Judas in his dream. A cold sensation spread from the base of his spine. There was no way Jesus could be the killer. No way. But still . . .

'Tell me to mind my own business, if you like,' Aaron began, tentatively. 'Only when we were up on that rocky outcrop the other day, you said you let a friend down and he was executed by the Romans. That was Jesus, wasn't it?'

'Shh,' Baruch hissed. 'We said we wouldn't mention it.'

'I know we did. But it seems crazy not to. Judas lets down a "friend" who gets executed. And then we hear Jesus has been

245

crucified. People Judas knows start being murdered and then we hear Jesus is alive again. It's all a bit of a big coincidence, don't you think? I mean I don't know this Jesus, but he's got to be the number one suspect hasn't he? It *was* Jesus you let down wasn't it?' This last question was directed at Judas.

'You don't have to answer, if you don't want to,' Baruch said.

Judas looked from one friend to the next, uncertain what to say. There was no way he could lie to them. They were out here with him, watching over Martha's house, even though they knew their lives were in just as much danger.

'It was Jesus I let down,' he admitted.

'I knew it!' Aaron said.

'Except I didn't let him down. It's my fault he died. I handed him over to the Sanhedrin.'

'You did what?' Aaron raised his eyebrows.

'Why?' Baruch asked.

'It's a long story.'

'Well it's not like we're busy doing anything important right now,' Aaron said. 'We've got time to hear it.'

So here he was again, faced with having to confess all. His father and Martha both knew the truth but this was different. For some reason he felt more embarrassed, more ashamed having to recount the story to his friends. If he told them how he'd betrayed Jesus it was hard to say how they'd react. Loyalty was important to both of them. Yet, they deserved to know the truth, didn't they?

Judas realised his finger was tracing around the outside of the moon-shaped birthmark on his neck. A nervous habit his father had failed to scold out of him as a child.

'My uncle Daniel got into trouble,' he began, forcing his hand back down to his side. 'His life was in danger and he needed a lot of money, quickly. It was a life and death situation. The high priest offered me silver to betray Jesus. I didn't have to do much, just identify him with a kiss. They did the rest.'

'A kiss?' Baruch looked surprised.

'I didn't think anything bad would happen to Jesus. I can see what you're thinking Aaron, but seriously, I didn't. I've seen Jesus do all sorts of wonderful and amazing things in my time with him. Escaping from the Sanhedrin, or the Romans even, should have been easy for him.'

'Well he outsmarted death, they say.'

'Exactly. So I thought he'd be all right. I'd get the silver and save Daniel. Jesus would escape and everything would be fine. I thought Jesus might even forgive me, if he knew why I'd done it.'

'But it didn't work out like that.'

'No. It didn't. They crucified him the very next morning.'

'I heard his death set off that storm,' Baruch said.

'And caused that huge crack in the temple,' Aaron added.

'It did. It did both of those things. I was there. It was ...' Words eluded him. 'But if you knew all this, why haven't you mentioned it before?'

'Because we thought you didn't want to talk about it. Jonathan said if you wanted to discuss Jesus you would, but in your own time.'

'Do you think Jesus is behind the killings?' Baruch asked.

'No,' Judas replied. 'I mean I did at the start. For a little while. But he's not like that. I just can't see it being him.'

'He wouldn't be very happy with you, though, would he?'

This conversation was getting uncomfortably close to the one he'd had with Martha.

'Why did Daniel need the money?' Aaron said.

'He owed it. A gambling debt. This ex-gladiator said he'd kill

Daniel if he didn't pay up, and then deliver his body parts to my uncle's wife and daughter, and to my father. That's why I had to do what I did.'

'This ex-gladiator wasn't called the Butcher by any chance, was he?' Baruch asked.

'Yes. You've heard of him?'

'Everyone has. He chops people up for fun. And your uncle Daniel owed him money? Not a good move.'

'No. It wasn't.'

Baruch lifted his white headdress to scratch an itch in the middle of his crown, before pulling it back down, and making sure it was on straight. 'Maybe he killed your uncle. And all those other people. That makes sense.'

'No, we paid him off.'

'You're sure?'

Now this conversation was echoing the last one he'd had with his father.

'Look, I don't know who the killer is, but I'm pretty sure it's not Jesus, and I'm even more certain it's not the Butcher. Daniel was boiled alive, not chopped up. And don't forget, Gideon and Ethan were the first two to die. If my uncle was the real target why kill them before him? And besides, you're forgetting about the note.'

'The note, it said, "I know what you did." And Jesus knows what you did.'

'Can we stop talking about this now, please? I don't know who the killer is, but it's not Jesus.' Judas wished he could be as certain of that as he sounded. It didn't make any sense for the messiah to send him a note like that, or go on a killing spree for that matter, but then nothing about this entire situation made any sense.

Aaron opened his mouth to speak, but thought better of it.

'If you don't want to talk about it, we won't,' Baruch said. 'We're just trying to help.'

'But if you do need someone to talk to, or run ideas by, we're always here.' Aaron patted Judas lightly on the shoulder.

'Of course we are. He knows that,' Baruch said.

'Thanks. Both of you. I really appreciate that.'

'No need to mention it,' Aaron said.

'Anyway, I need a piss.' Baruch began fiddling with his robe.

'Not here,' Aaron squealed.

'Why not? I'm behind a bush.'

'And so are we!'

'And?'

'And I really don't want to be crouching on wet sand with the smell of your urine in my nostrils for the next few hours or so. You'll have to hold it in. Or find somewhere else to go.'

'Shhh,' Judas hissed. 'There's someone coming.'

A lone hooded figure had appeared heading east along the road, walking towards Lazarus's residence. As he neared the house, Judas noticed that he was carrying something slender in one hand. It was hard to tell exactly what it was from this distance, but as he raised his fist to knock on the door, the shape of the object became clear.

'Shit,' Judas said. 'It's him. He's got a knife.'

Before the others could react, or stop him, Judas was up and running, sprinting towards the house.

The door was opening now. Just a small gap but getting wider.

'Shut the door,' he shouted. 'The door!'

The figure turned its head towards the sound of the commotion.

Judas could see Martha framed in the gap now, but it didn't matter, he was there and ready to give his life to protect her.

'Grraaaaagggghhhh,' Baruch bellowed as he hurtled past Judas and launched himself at the killer, knocking him clear off his feet. Judas hesitated briefly and then also threw himself on top of the felled assailant, alongside Baruch who now had both hands around the man's neck and was throttling the life out of him.

'What are you doing?' Martha practically shrieked from the doorway. 'Stop, stop, you're killing him.'

'We've got you now,' Judas said as he yanked the hood back to reveal the murderer's identity at last. His heart stopped beating as he gazed down in surprise.

A familiar face, turning bluer with every choking moment, stared back at him.

It was Thomas.

Chapter 48

The slap to Baruch's head wasn't hard, but it was enough to get his attention. He stopped choking the prone apostle, and seeing Judas's shocked expression, released his grip completely, just as Martha struck him again. With considerably more force this time.

'Gephh-ack-ophhh,' Thomas spluttered, drawing some gasping breaths back into his lungs. It was a struggle as he still had the combined weight of Baruch and Judas pinning him down.

'What on Earth do you think you are doing?' Martha said.

Judas had absolutely no idea. Thomas obviously wasn't the killer.

'Get off him!'

Judas shifted off Thomas and stood up quickly, motioning Baruch to do the same.

'What's going on?' Aaron said, arriving suspiciously late. 'Is this not the killer then?'

'Where have you been?' Baruch asked.

'I was keeping watch, making sure he didn't have any accomplices. It didn't need three of us to take him down.'

'It didn't need any of you to take him down,' Martha snapped. 'Judas, help him up.'

Judas offered a hand, but Thomas brushed it aside, got himself into a crouching position then stood up shakily. There were clear red handprints around his neck and the points where Baruch had been pressing down with his thumbs were almost purple.

'Are you all right, Thomas?' Martha asked. She bent down to pick up the object that Judas had thought was a knife and which had been dropped during the struggle. It was a long quill carefully fashioned from a sturdy reed. Several pieces of parchment lay scattered nearby and she retrieved those also.

'I'm fine, Martha,' Thomas said, his voice wavering between gruff troughs and squeaky peaks. He cleared his throat a few times to try and regain proper control of his vocal cords.

'I'm really sorry, Thomas,' Judas said. 'I didn't know it was you. With the hood up you looked suspicious and I thought that was a knife.'

'A knife? It's a quill.'

'Yes, I know that now. But it looked like a knife from where we were and I panicked. I thought you'd come to kill Martha.'

'Kill Martha? Have you gone mad? How long have you known me?'

'I said I didn't know it was you. Some lunatic has been murdering people I know and they left a message. I thought it meant she was in danger . . .' he trailed off.

'We've been watching out for you,' Baruch said to Martha. 'Looking over you. Like angels.'

She gave him a withering look. 'You've been spying on me? All three of you?'

'For your own good,' Aaron chipped in. 'Judas was seriously worried about you.'

'Look, I don't know what you're all playing at, but I want you gone. Thomas, I'm truly sorry, go inside, I'll be right with you. Lazarus is out back. Here, take these, and thank you.' She gave the still clearly shocked apostle the quill and parchment pieces, and steered him in the direction of the open door.

Thomas reached the entrance and turned slowly. His neck was still red, and the first bloom of a bruise appeared to be manifesting on one cheek. 'What is going on with you, Judas?' he asked. 'We used to be friends, all of us. Brothers. First you betray Jesus, then you attack me ...'

'I didn't mean to hurt you, Thomas, I thought Martha was in danger. I was trying to protect her.'

'Peter was right about you. They all were.'

'I'm sorry.'

'I don't doubt it,' Thomas said, and went inside.

'Judas, a word. Away from your friends.' Martha walked a short distance from the front of the building and he followed.

'I was only trying to keep you safe –' he began, but she cut him short.

'I don't know who you think you are, or where you get off scaring me with talk of murderers and then attacking someone outside my house, but this has to stop. I don't want you watching out for me. You or your creepy cohorts. I don't want you anywhere near me.'

'I just wanted to protect you.'

'Well don't. It's not your job to protect me. I have my brother and he will keep me out of harm's way. Not you.'

'But ...'

'A thief broke into our home last night and attacked Lazarus. My brother was injured but he still chased him away, then he gathered us together and watched over us all night. I have never felt so safe. You bring danger to our door, if anything, and I won't have that. Goodbye, Judas. Forever.'

253

She turned sharply, walked into the house and slammed the door behind her.

Baruch and Aaron watched as Judas trudged back to them.

'You all right?' Baruch asked. 'I take it she's not very happy with us?'

'No, she isn't.'

'I still think he could be guilty. I mean, why wear a hood in this heat?'

'He probably didn't want to be recognised.'

'Suspicious if you ask me. We should have searched him properly. He could still have a knife.'

Judas put his head in his hands and inhaled deeply. Martha was the second person in as many days to tell him she wanted nothing more to do with him. It was becoming a habit. He looked up at the sun. Then back down at Baruch.

'I need to go and see Caiaphas.'

'What do you want us to do?'

'Go get the ring, then meet me somewhere.'

'What ring's that?' Aaron asked.

'It's another long story,' Judas said, 'which I haven't got the time to tell now. I'll fill you in later.'

'Right, I'll get the ring,' Baruch said. 'Then do you want me to come along and see Caiaphas with you?'

'No, it won't be safe.'

'Who wants safe? I enjoyed that fight, even if the coward didn't exactly fight back.'

'Just fetch the ring and meet me somewhere.'

'At the temple?'

'Yes. No. Somewhere in the outer complex.'

'How about next to Akim the one-eyed money changer's stall? Near the Shushan Gate.'

'I have absolutely no idea who that is, but the Shushan Gate is as good a place as any.' Judas turned to Aaron. 'Do you want to stay here and keep an eye on things?'

'I could do, but ...' Aaron scratched his head, 'well it is getting on a bit, really, and I should probably be getting home. Make sure my wife is all right. I'll come round to yours after supper though, to hear this long story, and how things went.'

'Fine, I'll see you then. Hopefully with some good news.'

'I'm just going back to the bush for something,' Baruch said, adjusting his robe.

'Just make sure you're waiting for me with the all-important item. Don't be late.'

'I won't. I'll be waiting for you, next to Akim.'

'Next to Akim.'

'You know what he looks like?'

'I told you, I've no idea who he is.'

'Well, he's got one eye and tends to—'

'It's all right,' Judas said. 'I'll just look for you near the Shushan Gate. I know what you look like.'

Twenty minutes later, Judas was outside Caiaphas's office. He gave three knocks in quick succession and stepped back. The door opened and the same temple guard from this morning peered out from behind the same spear.

'I'm back,' Judas said. 'Has Caiaphas finished his meeting now? Is he in?'

'Yes. Follow me.'

The guard led him down the narrow corridor, his ring-mail vest clinking as he walked. As they reached the door of Caiaphas's chamber, the guard put out a hand and stopped him. 'Wait a moment,' he said.

Judas heard raised voices from beyond. He was sure he could hear the high priest's thundering tones and a shouted 'What!'

Then everything went quiet as the guard knocked. 'Enter,' Caiaphas's voice boomed.

The guard opened the door and poked his head in. 'Judas Iscariot is here.'

'Bring him,' came the reply.

The now familiar overpowering smell of cedar wood assaulted Judas's nostrils as he was ushered into the office. Caiaphas sat behind his desk, clad in a strikingly deep dark blue robe with a golden tunic over it. He was evidently fresh back from his session with the Romans. Malchus stood next to him, looking a little red in the face and flustered. Judas would have loved to have known what they'd been arguing about. They were both just staring at him now, so he figured he better get on with it.

'I have the money,' he said, producing the pouch containing the thirty pieces of silver.

As he approached the desk, he wondered if there needed to be some sort of ceremony. Some form of due process as he handed it over. Blind Mary certainly hadn't mentioned any formalities in her prophesying, but it seemed wrong not to confirm the act in some way. Make it official.

'I hand this back to the temple chest, the coffers even,' Judas said. 'From whence it came.'

He held it out across the desk for Caiaphas to take. Only the high priest didn't take it. He just looked at Judas and tilted his head slightly, before emitting a dark and disturbing chuckle.

'Judas, Judas. You didn't really think I'd let you push me around, did you? You didn't actually believe you could force me to take the silver back?'

Judas wasn't sure how to respond. Inwardly, he lurched through a series of negative emotions, before his resolve finally hardened around hate.

'You know what will happen if you don't,' he warned, his voice low.

'You pathetic excuse for a man. No one tells me what to do. No one.'

'Except the Roman Emperor, of course. And perhaps your father-in-law. So that would be Tiberius, Annas, oh and me, on this occasion. If you have any sense.'

'Insolent little rat, aren't you? This matter is ended. I won't take your tainted money back. Ever.'

'Fine. Then I'll make sure that the ring goes—'

'This ring you speak of, you will give it to me. Now.'

'I don't have it with me now. You think I'm stupid? It's close to hand, though.'

'Close?'

'Well, not that close – a safe distance, but near enough. I'll arrange for it to be delivered within the hour, when you take the silver back.'

'No. There's a new deal now,' Caiaphas said. 'You return the ring to me and I'll give you something you might want back.'

'Something I might want?'

'Yes. I hasten to add, it won't be your dignity. Since you accepted those thirty silver pieces, that will never be retrieved.' A venomous smile darted across the priest's lips, as he leaned in towards Judas. 'It's something very close to your heart.'

'I've had enough of this. Either take the money back, or –'

'No.' The single word was delivered with an ominous weight. 'Listen, and listen carefully. Do you ever want to see your father again?'

Chapter 49

'My ... father?' Judas stammered.

'Yes,' Caiaphas said. 'The very man who sowed your rotten seed.'

'What have you done with him?'

'Nothing. Yet. Malchus – a very resourceful man, as you know – has arranged for him to be held, shall we say, somewhere close. A safe distance, but near enough.'

'If you've touched a hair on his head ...' Judas said. The guard grabbed him from behind before he had a chance to move.

'You'll what? Doesn't feel so good now the tables are turned, does it, Judas? I've always been one step ahead of you. And now, this is the price you pay for clashing swords with me.'

'Please, don't hurt him.'

'He won't come to any harm. As long as you return the ring. Within the hour. But not here, bring it to me at my villa. I'm sure you remember the way.'

'But –'

'Guard, escort him out.' Caiaphas waved his hand dismissively.

Judas allowed himself to be marched off, still limply clutching the small leather pouch and its heavy silver burden.

Outside, back among the noise and the ever-milling crowd, he stood silent, still but for the jostling from those flowing around him. He had seemed so close, just minutes ago. Now his plans, his hopes, had been crushed. It almost felt like this latest cruel twist had pushed him past the point of anguish. Over the edge of despair and beyond, into some realm where everything terrible around him meant nothing. He was left merely with a sense of – not positivity, certainly not that – but a new clarity, of sorts. A calm in the eye of the storm. Judas knew exactly what he had to do. He had enough time, just, but he needed to have a word with Baruch first.

Weaving through the throng, he made his way over to the Shushan Gate. Baruch was there, waiting for him, as planned.

'Listen, I haven't got much time,' he began.

'Why?'

'Caiaphas is threatening me – my father – and I need to check –'

'Simon?'

'Yes, yes, I need to check on him. Make sure he's safe.'

'That bastard.'

'I know. But I only have an hour. I need to take the ring to the high priest at his villa, meet me there. If I'm not there and the hour is nearing, then take the ring to the high priest yourself. I will be back, but just in case, make sure you deliver it to Caiaphas. My father's life could depend on it.'

'Caiaphas now? Not the Sanhedrin council?'

'No. Give it to Caiaphas, and only to him. He's expecting it. I've got to go – but head to the villa and take the ring straight to him if I'm late.' Judas began to turn. 'You understand?'

Baruch nodded and Judas left, hurrying towards the hamlet

of Ishmael's Rest. It wasn't long before the familiar sight of his father's house came into view. As he approached he could see the front door was very slightly ajar. Not a good sign. He reached the entrance and pushed on the door gently; it swung open most of the way, until it hit a solid object. The stone head, presumably. He stepped inside and looked down. Yes, it was the head.

The table his father had been preparing food on had been knocked over, the cheese and bread scattered, the bottle of olive oil cracked, its greasy contents pooled on the floor. Clear signs of a struggle.

'Father,' Judas called out, tentatively. 'Father?'

There was, unsurprisingly, no reply. He stepped over the spilled oil and quickly checked the rest of the house, just to make sure. No one was home. Judas even went out back and peered into the barn. There was no sign of his father anywhere and no chance of him just being next door, helping a neighbour this time. Caiaphas had indeed abducted him, as he'd said.

There was no choice now. It might be the only real bargaining piece he had, but he couldn't see his father suffer. He'd inflicted quite enough grief on the poor man already. The ring had to be returned to the high priest. And he couldn't hang around. Within the hour ... Judas turned and hurried off, leaving the door to the empty house still wide open.

Half-running much of the way, he headed towards Caiaphas's villa, nestled in the upper city which, as the name suggested, rose haughtily above the rest of Jerusalem. Unlike the chaotic lower city, with its ginnels and alleyways, slopes and steps snaking here and there, this part of town was laid out in an orderly grid, after the fashion of a Roman city. Vast plazas, palaces and mansions squared off against each other, interspersed by constructions such as Herod's theatre, a huge open-air auditorium. Music performances, and dramas of Greek and Roman origin were acted out on its central stage, around which a horseshoe of stone benches rose up, one above the next, providing a reasonable view wherever you happened to be sitting.

The upper city was home to the wealthy, and the wealthier, with Caiaphas falling into the latter category. The high priest's residence was a sprawling building, with two wings extending to the sides, and one behind. The frontage was inlaid with marble, and semi-circular columns jutted out at regular intervals along its length. Up above, the roof was tiled with bright red slates, all except for a central dome. That too was white marble, cut with long, thin windows to let the light through into the entrance hall below.

In front of the building was an expansive courtyard, with gardens off to the sides dotted with groves of trees, ponds and covered walkways. Several fountains, identical tall and thin white stone pyramids, bubbled among the greenery.

Baruch was already at the villa, waiting dutifully just outside the gate to the priest's residence, when Judas arrived. An expression of concern spread across his face when he saw his friend.

'What the hell's going on?' Baruch asked.

'Later . . .' Judas paused to catch his breath. 'I need to do this now. Give me the ring.'

Baruch handed over the cloth-wrapped item. 'Want me to come with you?' he asked.

'No, it's fine, I doubt they'd let anyone in with me. You've hung around long enough, go get something to eat and come over to my place later. I'll explain everything then. There's no time now.'

Judas turned and opened the front gate. Traversing the

courtyard he approached the entrance to the villa, where he was met by two guards who spoke to him briefly, and then ushered him through a large external door plated with bronze and carved with intricate swirls.

Once inside, he was led along a corridor towards the rear of the building, and into a smaller room that served as Caiaphas's office when he was away from the temple. A large writing desk, fashioned from polished oak, dominated the room. The portly priest was alone, surveying the garden outside the back of the villa through a square window with thick wooden shutters either side.

A minute of silence passed before Caiaphas finally turned to face him.

'Judas, you look rather pale. I do fear for your health.'

'I have your ring, now release my father.'

'Let me see this ring you insist is mine. Give it to me.'

'It is yours. It has your insignia on it.'

'Just give it to me.'

'And then you'll let him go?'

'Of course. The ring,' Caiaphas said, as he took a step towards Judas and held out his hand.

Judas fumbled for the object in his pouch, unwrapped it, and placed the gem-studded gold band in the priest's waiting palm. Caiaphas made a show of examining it closely.

'I don't quite know what to make of this,' he said eventually. 'It seems to be covered in some manner of red gunk.'

'That's blood, and nothing to do with me. Now, will you please release my father?'

'Blood,' Caiaphas said, his eyes widening in mock surprise. 'Well that won't do. It's not good enough,' he continued, as he walked round behind his desk, placed the ring in a drawer and locked it with a small gold key.

'What do you mean, not good enough?'

'You could have at least had it cleaned before you brought it to me.'

'What?'

'And polished, for that matter. Wouldn't have cost the Earth and I know you have plenty of silver to spare.'

'I kept my end of the deal,' Judas said. 'Are you going to keep yours?'

'I was going to. But now, with this blood-covered offering, you've distressed me. I'm afraid the deal's off.'

'No. Please, release him. What's he ever done to you?'

'It's not what he's done. It's what you've done. Judas the greedy. Judas the meddler. And now, Judas the fool. I told you that you were playing a dangerous game, did I not? And you played it so pitifully badly. Walking straight into the lion's den with his treasure and expecting not to get bitten.'

Judas closed his eyes and stood silently for a few moments.

'My, you've turned even more pasty and wan, if that was possible,' Caiaphas said.

Judas dropped down to his knees. 'Please, I beg you ...'

'Throw this beggar out into the street, where he belongs.'

The guard grabbed Judas and pulled him up.

'But my father! What will happen to him?' Judas cried out, as he was bundled unceremoniously towards the exit.

'That is for me to know,' Caiaphas said, 'and for you to have nightmares about.'

Chapter 50

Clack. Clack. Clack. The old woman peered down at the collection of different coloured beads on the surface in front of her. Her hand hovered over a red bead, uncertain, and then moved to a yellow one, still undecided. Then she swiftly plucked a green one from the shiny multi-coloured mass, and with surprisingly nimble fingers for a woman of seventy, threaded the bead onto a cord held aloft in her left hand. It dropped down to join the others clustered in a growing line on the end of the string. Clack.

Another woman, olive-skinned and of middling age, sat on a bench that ran along the west wall of the room and stared at the floor.

Clack. Clack. Clack.

'Are you going to sit there, in silence, all night?' the old lady asked.

The younger woman, her eyes glazed over, said nothing as she continued her staring battle with the ground.

Clack. Clack. Clack.

'Do you have to do that now?' Abigail Iscariot snapped, finally breaking her silence.

'So you haven't forgotten how to talk then,' Leah said.

'Mother, I'm really not in the mood. How can you sit there, making that damn thing, as if nothing has happened?'

'It's better to be doing something, in my experience. We all have our different ways of coping with grief.'

'Coping? How can I possibly cope? My husband and daughter are both dead!'

Abigail buried her face in her hands and began to sob. Leah carefully set down the half-finished necklace and made her way over to sit next to her daughter on the bench. She put an arm around Abigail's shoulder and squeezed gently.

'I know,' Leah said. 'I'm hurting too. I feel Atarah's loss like a weight which is crushing my heart.'

Abigail sniffed. 'Of course, you don't care about Daniel.'

'I can't just pretend I liked him. I wouldn't wish the awful way he was killed on anybody. But your husband hated me. He wanted me gone.'

'He didn't.'

'You know very well he did. If I'd have died, Daniel wouldn't have mourned me either. He'd have been raising a wineskin, cheering his good fortune.'

'That's not true. He was a good man at heart.'

'A good man? He even lied to you on the night he was murdered, remember?' Leah continued, in a mock male voice, *'I've got to mend that table for Philip.* And was he mending that table for Philip? No. He was with Jose and that freak Saul up at the bathhouse, probably planning a whoring trip afterwards.'

'Mother, please! Don't you think I have enough to deal with, without you fouling Daniel's name even in death? If you can't say anything good about him, then just don't say anything at all.'

'Sorry, Abi. Maybe I should adopt your vow of silence.'

Abigail glared at her.

'Maybe we should talk about something else entirely,' Leah continued. 'Do you feel up to packing yet?'

'I'm not leaving.'

'But it might not be safe here. Daniel and Atarah have both been murdered, who's to say that –'

'I wouldn't care if I was dead.'

'Don't say that, Abi.'

'I can't think about leaving at the moment. I can't think about anything.' Fresh tears rolled down Abigail's cheeks.

'There's nothing to keep us here. Is there?'

Abigail shook her head. 'I can't believe Simon hasn't been over to see us.'

'Pfff,' Leah snorted. 'The other Iscariot brother is just as useless an excuse for a man.'

'Maybe we should go and see him.'

'At least that would get you out and about. Perhaps we could pack now and go to see Simon on our way out of Jerusalem?'

'I told you, I'm not . . .' Abigail trailed off as a brown-robed hooded figure came padding softly through from the adjacent room.

'Who the hell are you?' she said, standing.

'And how did you get in here?' Leah added, rising to join her daughter.

The man said nothing, but continued to walk towards them with a menacingly purposeful air. There was blood on his clothes.

Abigail bolted for the front door, and her mother went the other way. The man sprinted to intercept the younger, faster woman, and practically leapt at her with his final stride, swinging his fist as he did so. The savage hook caught Abigail bang on the jaw. She fell against the wall, and then onto the floor in a groaning heap.

Something whistled over her attacker's head, and he looked up at the wall above. A chisel had embedded in it. He turned around to see Leah rummaging through a toolbox on the other side of the room, and charged towards her. The old woman panicked, grabbed a handful of long nails and hurled them in his direction. The man put his arm up to shield his face from the flying pieces of metal, pausing just long enough for Leah to find the item she'd been searching for. She pulled the hammer out of the toolbox and ran at the intruder swinging it with all her might.

He dived under the arc of the hammer and tackled the woman around the thighs, pulling her to the ground. Managing to keep hold of the tool, Leah desperately tried to hit the man with it again, but he caught her hand in his, wrested the hammer from her grasp, and then heaved her up. Leah kicked out at his legs, but she may as well have been kicking at the wall for all the reaction she got.

He dumped her down in the chair where five minutes ago she'd been fashioning her necklace, and in a swift motion scooped something up from the floor. Squashing the old woman's relatively frail body up against the back of the seat, he flattened her hand down on the arm of the chair with a loosely balled fist. In the middle of which he held the object he'd just grabbed off the floor. With one heavy blow he walloped the top of the six-inch nail with the hammer, forcing the sharp metal spike straight through Leah's hand. The bones crunched as it parted them, and the old woman shrieked with pain. He hit the nail once more, driving it deep into the wood below and sending a jolting sensation up her arm.

In a fluid movement, the man sprung up, grabbed the back of the chair, and dragged the whimpering Leah backwards into the next room, where her wails were less likely to carry through

267

the walls to the outside world. He knelt on her remaining free arm, pressing it against the wood of the chair, and produced another nail. This time his strike walloped the spike clean through her hand, anchoring it to the armrest with one single overhead blow. She screamed again, but the sound was curtailed by a vicious slap across the face which was so hard it left her semi-stunned, ears ringing.

The man reached up to touch the cold metal of the hook he'd spotted as he'd walked through the house. It hung down at just about the right height and was attached to a rope tied around a beam above. He pulled it – the rope seemed sturdy enough, even though it would only normally be used for hanging lighter animal carcasses.

He dragged a stool over and placed it underneath the hook, then disappeared back into the front room, returning shortly with the semi-conscious, still murmuring form of Abigail over his shoulder. Leah's world came into stronger focus as she heard her daughter's groans.

The intruder stepped up onto the stool, Abigail still slumped head-first over his shoulder, drew out a knife with his free hand and plunged it into her upper back, twisting it afterwards. The younger woman yelped with shock.

'No,' Leah cried out, 'please, stop, please!'

The attacker showed no sign of having heard her. He withdrew the blade, dropped it, and then grabbed hold of the hook, grunting with effort as he levered it into the wound he'd just created. Abigail became conscious of what was going on just as the man released her. She swung backwards, suspended on the rope, and several vertebrae cracked as the cruelly curved metal hook took purchase and lodged fast.

Abigail wailed with pain and scrabbled to grab the hook. She could just about touch the top with her fingertips, but with her full weight bearing down on it there was no way she could pull it out, even if she had the stomach to.

The man noticed Leah bent over with the chair on her back waddling towards the front room in a bid for escape. He leapt down and grabbed the old woman as she reached the doorway. Yanking her towards him, he pushed her over so she fell flat on her back in the chair, unable to move like an overturned tortoise. The intruder then pushed Leah across the floor with his foot and she barrelled into the stool, knocking it out of the way. Her face was now directly underneath her daughter's feet. The man picked up the knife again.

'What are you doing?' Leah babbled the words hysterically.

Above her, Abigail had managed to reach up and grab the rope, pulling herself up a bit to take some of the pressure off the hook in her back. The man slashed at her robes, pulling them off, along with her undergarments, leaving her hanging there naked.

'Help!' Abigail screamed. The man slashed out with the blade across her right thigh, drawing a bright red line.

'Someone, help!' Leah echoed, and again the intruder struck, cutting a deeper gash, this time in Abigail's left leg. The naked woman sobbed as blood began to run down her thighs.

The man stood and watched the thicker trails as they snaked down her left limb, apparently admiring his handiwork. The dark red liquid reached Abigail's foot and began to drip off her heel slowly, spot by spot, onto Leah's forehead.

'You ... bastard!' Leah spat the words, moving her head to the side so the splatter drops landed in her hair instead.

The cowled figure lashed out with the blade again, this time at Abigail's flank, drawing a spray of blood.

'Help someone, help me!' Abigail shrieked. The intruder responded this time by standing up on the fallen chair that Leah was nailed to, pulling his arm back and unleashing it in a semi-circular slashing motion. The blade cut brutally across Abigail's neck and she gurgled as a wide crimson smile opened up on her throat. A red flood started to pour down onto her bosom. Abigail's arms went limp and fell away from the rope they'd been clutching. Her full weight sagged down on the hook once more.

'No!' Leah screamed. 'No, no –'

The old woman's shouting was abruptly muffled as the man leapt down and stuffed the sleeve of her daughter's robe into her mouth.

The attacker turned his attention back to Abigail, slashing her torso twice, three times, four, five, six, seven times, criss-crossing lines multiplying as the man worked himself up into a frenzy, applying stroke after stroke of scarlet horror to the flesh canvas.

The blood began to flow freely down Abigail's twisting body, and where there had at first been a trickle dripping from her feet, it now ran thicker. Such was the increased pace of the bleeding, whichever way she twisted her head, Leah was unable to keep out of the way of the claret waterfall. She could only screw her eyes up tightly as thick gobs of the stuff splattered over her face.

The hooded maniac was now stabbing with the blade, burying it deep into Abigail's listless body. As his rabid thrusting moved down to her leg, he pierced the major artery in her thigh and blood erupted from the gash. The man dropped his knife, moved round and bent over Leah's prostrate form. He pulled the cloth out of her mouth and forced her jaws open. Blood was now pouring down off Abigail, and the man held Leah's open mouth directly under the most copiously gushing stream.

Unable to spit, Leah was forced to gulp her daughter's blood down. She swallowed and swallowed, the metallic taste pungent in the back of her throat, the liquid heavy in her stomach as she was compelled to continue guzzling it down. She retched, then retched again, stomach acid spewing back up her gullet to mix with the blood in a hot acrid soup.

Still the man held her there, flat on the ground. The blood and regurgitated fluid clogged her windpipe. Her throat spasmed continuously, her gag reflex agonisingly overpowered by the thick liquid which now sluiced down into her lungs. Her breathing started to slow and only light burbling and gargling noises came from her plugged throat. Then the shallow rise and fall of her chest ceased, and the only noise that remained was the slowing spatter of blood which continued to rain down on Leah's contorted face.

Chapter 51

Simon took another deep breath. He had been mentally preparing himself for a number of minutes, and now it was time. He tried to move his leg, very slightly, and once again attempt to fully ascertain the extent of the damage down there. A flash of fire shot up inside his shin bone and he moaned a low wail of pain. His ankle seemed to have swollen up so much it was now wedged tightly inside the metal loop that secured it to the toppled cauldron. He was barely able to move it at all. It seemed there was nothing he could do now. Nothing. Alone, and in the dark, he began to quietly sob.

Chapter 52

Judas had failed. His plan to coerce Caiaphas into accepting the silver had backfired spectacularly. He'd handed over the one piece of evidence linking the Sanhedrin high priest to the underground chamber in the brothel – evidence that frankly wasn't all that compelling to begin with – and in return had received a future filled with desolation and death. It wasn't much of a trade.

Caiaphas still had his father captive somewhere, for reasons Judas couldn't bear to think about, and he still had the silver which meant, presumably, the killings would continue. Martha wanted nothing to do with him, and Thomas, the last apostle not to totally despise him, now totally despised him. It was hard to see how things could get any worse.

Judas finished scrubbing the bloody message off the wall in his home, took a long draught from a freshly filled wineskin, and then sat down and tried to eat some more of his dinner. He took another couple of bites of the cucumber, which was stuffed with chicken and spiced with cinnamon, and attempted to figure out what his next move would be. He could take the silver to the

273

temple and place it in one of the trumpet-shaped collection pots there. That would be returning it, in a fashion, but Blind Mary had said he needed to return the payment to the person who had given it to him; so surely it had to be accepted directly by Caiaphas to stop the killings? Caiaphas, after all, seemed to be the key to everything.

Maybe he could offer the high priest a monetary bribe – an additional thirty pieces of silver on top of the original amount. The fat fool clearly enjoyed the trappings of wealth, so maybe he'd consider such a proposition.

Judas massaged his temples with his fingertips. What was he thinking? Caiaphas had access to riches way beyond his imagining; a fortune so large that sixty pieces of silver would be swallowed up in the treasury like a grain of sand in the Negev desert. He'd laugh at such a paltry offer. And besides how would Judas get hold of another thirty coins, anyway?

Footsteps outside alerted him to the fact he had company. 'Come in,' he shouted over the sound of knocking.

Baruch did as he was told. 'How did it go then?' he asked as he crossed the room.

'Not well,' Judas said. He waited for his friend to sit, before outlining everything that had happened since they'd parted.

'We'll have to snatch Caiaphas,' Baruch said, after Judas had finished his sorry tale. 'It's our only choice. We'll grab him from his home ...'

'From his well-guarded fortress of a home ...'

'Or from the temple, and lock him up somewhere, until he tells us where Simon is and agrees to take back the money.'

'And how exactly would we make him agree to that?'

'We could torture him.'

'Torture him? That would make us no better than him, Baruch. And we are better than him.'

'It's what they call a means to an end I think.'

'We can't do that.'

'We can. I can. Unless you have any better ideas?'

'No, I don't have any ideas really.'

'Then it's agreed, we'll grab the priest, lock him up and torture him if necessary, until he agrees to do what we say.'

'Baruch, it's a nice idea, but it's wrong on too many levels. Besides, he's the high priest. He's well protected and people will notice if he goes missing. The entire temple guard, and probably some Roman soldiers too, they'll mount a search for him. It's not like he's some beggar off the streets.'

Baruch lowered the wineskin he'd just raised to his lips. 'Oh yes,' he said, wiping his rouged mouth with a dirty sleeve. 'I meant to say. You know Jebediah the Cripple?'

'Jeb? Yes, what about him?'

'He's dead.'

'Dead?'

'Last night. Murdered, along with his father.'

Judas felt the room spin.

'I heard some Romans talking about another killing after I left you at the temple,' Baruch continued. 'They said it was brutal and probably done by the same madman who went crazy at the baths, so I listened in. They were talking about their commander ordering more guards out on watch, because of all the murders, then they laughed about the size of the dead guy's leg. Don't think there are many Jebediahs who live out near En-rogel and have a shrivelled leg.'

'Why didn't you say something sooner?'

'When? You were telling me your news and I forgot. Sorry.'

More killings. How many did that make in total? Gideon, Ethan, Daniel, Jose, Ugly Saul, Jonas who worked at the bathhouse, and now Jeb and his father. That was eight. Twenty-two killings still to come, if Blind Mary was right. He felt sick, almost sick enough to physically vomit up the stuffed cucumber and wine he'd consumed. He closed his eyes and took several copious lungfuls of air to try and steady himself, and stop the room from lurching quite so violently.

As he opened his eyes again, the front door exploded inwards, followed immediately by Aaron. His face was ashen and he was breathing heavily.

'There's been more murders,' he gasped.

'I know, Baruch told me. Jebediah the Cripple and his father. Last night.'

'Heaven help us,' Aaron said, as he sat down and stared at Judas. His eyes were wide and frightened. 'I didn't know about them.'

'But I thought you ... who then?'

'I was just leaving home to come over when my neighbour stopped me. He told me a local family had been murdered. The man was decapitated and the woman ...' Aaron tailed off, unable to repeat the atrocity that had been shared so deliciously with him.

'Martha?' Judas sat upright, his body rigid.

Aaron shook his head. 'Not her. Your cousin.'

'Atarah?' Baruch said, speaking for the first time since Aaron had arrived so dramatically. 'Damn. She was nice.'

Judas feared his head might split open, such was the pressure crashing against his temples. 'Atarah ... and Dotan. Both dead?' That made ten victims – and the first woman to die. That was who the blood-scrawled message on his wall must have referred to.

Aaron cleared his throat nervously. 'Not just them.'

'No ...' Judas whispered, the inferred horror too dreadful to even contemplate.

Aaron nodded and looked away.

The motion of the room ceased, stilled as this latest revelation began to sink in. Who would be next then? His father, if he wasn't already dead? His three closest friends?

'I can't stay here,' Aaron blurted. 'In Jerusalem I mean. I can't just sit around waiting for my turn, Judas. I can't risk my family's lives. I'm sorry. We've got to leave. Go somewhere safe.'

'You can't,' Baruch said. 'We've got to stick together. The high priest is holding Judas's father prisoner. We need to abduct the fat bastard and rescue Simon. All of us. Working as a team.'

'That's why you were talking about Caiaphas earlier? He has your father? Is he behind the killings?'

'No, I don't think so. But he's the reason for them. Indirectly at least.'

'Bloody hell, Judas.'

'I'll bet he has a dungeon under his villa,' Baruch said.

'He does,' Judas nodded. 'He threatened to have me thrown in there when I first went up to his place.'

'Right, well I'll bet that's where he's holding Simon. We should go rescue him now. The three of us, or four of us if we can get hold of Jonathan. Under the cover of darkness.'

'Where *is* Jonathan? Anyone seen him lately?' Aaron asked.

Baruch and Judas both shook their heads.

'This isn't good,' Aaron said, rocking back and forth. 'What if something has happened to him? And his wife. He's so looking forward to finally becoming a father for the first time.'

'You want some wine?' Baruch proffered the skin. Aaron took it with shaking hands, draining it gratefully.

'We don't know he's dead,' Judas said. 'He might just be keeping a low profile, or he might have had to deliver a message somewhere remote. Or he might have decided to just leave town like you're planning on doing. The pair of them could have packed a few things and ridden off into the sunset.'

'Without saying goodbye?' Baruch said. 'I can't see Jonathan ever doing that.'

'Can't see me doing what?' Jonathan asked from the doorway. He was dressed in a pale yellow robe with a short white cloak draped around his shoulders. For a moment or two, the three friends just stared at the new arrival, but then Baruch stood and embraced the messenger heartily.

'Get off me, you fool,' Jonathan said, smiling. He extricated himself from Baruch's grip and dropped his bag on the floor. It clanged as he did so. Something metallic inside.

'You're all right,' Aaron said. 'You're all right.' The relief on his face was palpable.

'Of course I'm all right. What are you lot all doing here anyway? Why wasn't I invited?'

'We've been trying to get hold of you,' Aaron said. 'We thought you were dead.'

'I've been busy,' Jonathan replied. 'Something important to do.' He sat and then edged his way slightly over to the left as Baruch joined him.

'Busy doing what?' Aaron demanded. 'And why are you here, now?'

'I had to go and see someone about a job, and then drop off a message a few houses along on my way home. I saw the light of the fire in the window and thought Judas was here. Anyway, you haven't answered my question, and I asked first. What's going on here? A meeting?'

'People are still dying,' Judas said. 'That madman is still after people I know.'

'It could be Jesus,' Baruch said.

'It isn't,' Judas insisted.

'But it was him you let down?' Jonathan asked.

'There's more to the story than that,' Aaron said. 'But the big news is Judas's father has been abducted.'

'Abducted?'

'By the high priest,' Baruch said.

'What?'

The friends took it in turns to apprise Jonathan of the situation. By the time they had finished, even his tanned face showed signs of being drained of colour.

'So what are you going to do?' Jonathan's question was directed at Judas but it was Baruch who answered.

'We should break into Caiaphas's villa. Take him by surprise. Judas and I could hide in Aaron's cart, and you two could pull us right through the gates, up to the door and –'

'I don't have my cart with me, as you're well aware,' Aaron interrupted. 'And besides, I told you I'm not breaking into any villas. I'm not staying around to help. I just came to find out what was going on and deliver my news.'

'You're sure Simon is being held captive by the high priest?'

Judas nodded in reply to Jonathan's question.

'Right, well I'm with Baruch then. We should try and get him back. I owe Simon. Don't forget he saved my life when I was younger.'

'It's too risky, just too risky,' Aaron said, his voice rising in pitch as the words tumbled out one on top of another. 'Your wife's about to have a child, Jonathan.'

'I'm well aware of that,' the messenger snapped back. 'I'm the one who has to put up with the reduced sleeping space, snoring and constant complaining. But it's not as if we're going after the killer are we? We'll break into the villa, locate Simon, and bring him back here.'

'You make it sound easy!'

'Well it won't be easy, but it might not be as impossible as you're imagining either.'

'How so?'

'Because in my bag,' Jonathan nodded at the discarded leather holdall, 'is a message for Caiaphas. I'm supposed to deliver it tomorrow morning, to the temple, but there's nothing to stop me delivering it tonight, to his villa.'

'What does it say?' Baruch asked.

'It doesn't matter what it says at the moment. It's what it'll say when I deliver it.'

'I don't understand.' Baruch looked confused.

'All will be revealed shortly. Judas, could you pass me my bag please?'

Judas did as was requested. Jonathan reached inside and pulled out a scroll. His action caused whatever metallic objects were in the holdall to clatter against each other.

'This,' he said, showing them the scroll, 'is a message to the high priest from Pontius Pilate's office. It's nothing exciting, probably just some figures about fruit –'

'Fruit?'

'The Romans are always sending messages about fruit. And cheese, and meat. Anyway, I don't actually know what this particular scroll is about, but I do know that it's not urgent – which is why it doesn't have to be delivered until tomorrow – and it has a Roman elite wax seal on it.'

'I still don't understand.'

'I do,' Judas said. 'If you can prise the seal off, we can attach it to another message and deliver it to Caiaphas. Pretend the Romans want my father for questioning, and ask them to release him into your custody. That's brilliant.'

'It is rather. Although that wasn't exactly the plan I had in mind.'

'Oh?'

'If Caiaphas has your father, it's unlikely he'll have told anyone else about it. Least of all the Romans. My plan is to send him a message containing something that will get him away from his villa, preferably with as many of his guards and lackeys as possible. Then you, Baruch and Aaron, can sneak in, and try to find your father.'

'It still sounds very risky to me,' Aaron said. 'And besides, how are you going to get the seal off that message? It'll break.'

Jonathan laughed. 'I do it all the time.'

'Do you?'

'In my line of work it pays to know what you're delivering. If it looks like it might be bad news I take a sneaky peek and then take action accordingly. You know, give it to a guard to deliver and then get the hell out of there. That sort of thing. All you need is a knife and a fire. And, funnily enough, I have several knives in my bag and I believe you have a fire I can use ...'

'But what would we say?' Aaron asked. 'In the message. What would make Caiaphas rush off with all his men?'

'I know,' Judas said quietly.

Chapter 53

Jonathan's mouth felt dry and his face numb. He had removed seals from scrolls before, that was true. But only twice in his long career, and he'd never, ever interfered with a message.

He guided his horse down the wide street that led up to Caiaphas's villa. The gate to the front courtyard was lit up by two large, hanging ornamental iron lamps either side of it. They burned fiercely against the night.

This was a risk, Aaron was right. A crazy gamble, even, considering his wife was six months pregnant and he would lose both of his hands, if not his life, should the deception be uncovered. But Simon had saved his life all those years ago when, as a child, the horse Jonathan had been riding had collapsed – one leg just snapping under it like a rotten tree branch mid-gallop – and pitched him to the ground.

He'd barely had enough time to register what had happened, when the stricken animal rolled onto its side, trapping him. His short life had begun flashing in front of his eyes as he struggled under the beast's heavy burden, feeling the very essence being squeezed out of him with every equine shudder, then Simon had come out of nowhere, and pulled Jonathan free like a modern-day Samson. Jonathan had never forgotten that moment, and now many years later he finally had a chance to repay the debt.

He had another reason for volunteering, too. He hadn't told his friends yet, but he'd be away from Jerusalem – well away – the day after tomorrow. He was off to be a messenger in Rome courtesy of a friend of his father's connections. The money was better and he was ready for a change of scenery. The fact that some lunatic was bumping off people that Judas knew had also helped to hasten his decision. He had no intention of allowing either his wife or unborn child to come to any harm. He'd have to get used to dealing with more Romans, of course. That was the downside of the move, but he could live with that.

The villa loomed up ahead of him now, its white marble illuminated by torches affixed at regular intervals along the wall. He let go of the horse's reins with his left hand, wiped his sweaty palm on his robe, and then did the same with his right hand. He was taking a risk, yes, but it was nothing compared to the challenge facing Judas, Baruch and Aaron, who were following some distance behind on foot.

Jonathan reached the gate to the compound and dismounted. He opened it, then led his horse through the entrance and across the courtyard. The path towards the villa was marked out by more torches flickering in five-foot-tall iron holders. Two guards stationed at the front door watched him closely as he made his way towards them.

'Halt,' one guard said, pointing a spear menacingly in Jonathan's direction as he drew near.

'I have an urgent message for the high priest Caiaphas,' he said. 'From Pontius Pilate.'

'Show me,' the sentry demanded.

Jonathan reached into his bag and fished out the scroll, being careful not to touch the wax seal in case he dislodged it. He angled it towards the guard.

'Right, go through,' the man said, stepping back and opening the large, bronze plated door to the villa. The second guard took the reins of Jonathan's horse and guided it to one side, while the messenger walked on through. Jonathan's heart was pounding in his ears, but he kept his face impassive. That had been the easy part.

Chapter 54

Malchus entered the small, dimly lit chamber. It was late but Caiaphas was still awake, as he had said he would be. Clad in a white silken robe, the high priest was kneeling at the far end of the room, deep in prayer. Malchus stood and waited for him to finish. He knew better than to consider interruption as an option.

Unlike the rest of Caiaphas's ostentatious villa, this compact space was free of the trappings of affluence. In that sense, it was the most unique area in the entire building, despite being the most plain. Just a scattering of plush cushions lined the walls, one of which Caiaphas was currently kneeling on.

The high priest's robe rustled as he stood up and turned to face Malchus.

'A productive prayer?' Malchus said, more out of politeness than anything.

'I am guided, as always. It's a shame the same can't be said about you.'

Malchus shifted uncomfortably. 'Apologies, once more, for this morning. But I don't see what else I could've done. I got there very early, before dawn, and Iscariot's father was already gone.'

'Well, you should have got there earlier.'

'Someone else clearly beat us to it.'

'I've had enough of your tiresome excuses, Malchus. Luckily, your bungling didn't cost us. Judas gave back the ring as planned.'

'Did he?'

'You sound surprised.'

'What did he say when you told him we don't have his father?'

'I didn't tell him.'

'You didn't?'

'No.'

'Well what did you say to him then?'

'I simply told him that I wouldn't release his precious parent.'

'Why?'

'It seemed crueller that way, and Judas should suffer,' Caiaphas said. 'You know how I enjoy my torment.'

'Is it not dangerous to continue this bluff? To anger him further, just for the sake of fun?'

'Fun, Malchus? Torment isn't just about mere pleasure, it is also my duty. The weak and the gutless, the fearful and the worthless, they will soon enough find that eternal anguish and torture awaits them in the next life. Experiencing it in this life may awaken them to that fact; may reform and reshape them. Save them. Everything is perspective, Malchus, and when you look deep enough into pain, you'll find there is pleasure. When you look deep enough into torment, you'll find there is redemption.'

'I understand,' Malchus said, although his lowered gaze betrayed the fact that he clearly didn't.

'Besides, Judas is no threat. The man had little, and now we have the ring back, he has nothing. I assume everything went well at the brothel?'

'Yes, I cleared out and cleaned the cellar completely.'

'And the keeper of the whores?'

'Caleb has been dealt with, as you asked.'

'Good.'

A tentative knock came at the door. Caiaphas waved Malchus in the direction of the sound and watched as his servant had a brief discussion with a thickset guard through a gap in the doorway.

'Well?' he said when Malchus returned.

'There's a messenger to see you.'

'At this time of night?'

'He has a scroll bearing the Roman elite seal. Says it's urgent.'

Caiaphas sighed. 'It had better be or there will be one less messenger doing the rounds come the morning.'

Chapter 55

'Do you think this is going to work?' Aaron asked for the third time since leaving Judas's home.

'It had better,' Judas replied. They were hiding, along with Baruch, in an alleyway which led down the side of a mansion, just off the main street. Crouching against the wall's thick lime-stone blocks, they had a clear view of the high priest's villa ahead.

'But what if it doesn't? What if Jonathan gets captured?'

'That won't happen. Jonathan's smart. He can talk his way out of anything. Remember when we were children and he stole those oranges? He managed to not only persuade the stall holder to let him go, but he got to keep the fruit.'

'But what if he can't talk his way out of trouble this time?'

'Then we'll have to rescue him as well as Simon,' Baruch said. He spat out a large glob of something that vanished into the darkness.

'We don't even know your father is being held here,' Aaron said. 'This is crazy.'

'We don't have a choice. I don't have a choice. You can leave if you want, but I've got to go through with this. I've got to at least try to save him. It's my fault he's in this situation.'

'And this rescue is my idea,' Baruch said. 'So I'm going in there too.'

'I'll help, of course I will,' Aaron said. 'I'm just saying it's risky, that's all.'

'Shh,' Judas said, pointing towards the villa, 'someone's coming out.'

A figure emerged from the front door. One of the guards at the entrance departed, and returned leading a horse.

'That's Jonathan, isn't it?' Judas asked.

'I think so,' Aaron said.

The figure mounted the horse, and rode up through the courtyard, towards them.

'Yes. That's him.'

Jonathan trotted past their hiding place without acknowledging them. He went a little further up the street, before doubling back around and coming up the alleyway from the other end. The three friends walked a short way down to meet the messenger, who pulled his horse up next to them. He had a small lamp clutched in one hand to light his way.

'They fell for it,' Jonathan said. 'At least I think they did. As I was leaving the high priest was calling for some guards and horses. I don't know how many he'll be taking with him, but that'll definitely be a few less swords to worry about. Whatever you wrote in that message certainly did the trick. Caiaphas nearly exploded when he read it.'

'What did you write anyway?' Aaron asked.

'It doesn't matter,' Judas said. 'How long do you think we've got before they're ready to leave?'

'No idea,' Jonathan answered. 'Caiaphas looked in a hurry. I don't think I've ever seen him move so fast. Ten minutes, maybe five. As long as it takes for them to get the horses ready.'

'Good, thanks. We'd better get ready then.'

'How will you get in?' Jonathan asked.

'I don't know yet. I'm hoping an opportunity will present itself.'

'Well, good luck. I'm going to head straight home but I'll stop by your place tomorrow morning and see you. And hopefully Simon. Give him my regards.'

'I will. Thanks, Jonathan.'

The messenger nodded goodbye, dug his heels gently into the side of the horse, and cantered off into the night.

'What now?' Aaron asked.

'We get back to the top of the alley, we watch, and we wait.'

They weren't kept waiting for long. Barely a couple of minutes had passed since Jonathan's departure when the villa's doors opened, spilling yellow light into the night and devouring the darkness all around it.

Silhouetted figures criss-crossed in front of the doorway, and more men came from the side of the compound, leading horses.

'They're mounting up,' Baruch whispered.

'We'd better move further back,' Judas said. 'We can't risk being spotted.'

The trio retreated a short distance, hiding in an archway, heads peeking out so they could still see the street. A short while later, the noise of clattering hooves reached them, growing louder and louder. It was a sizeable entourage – there were too many riders flashing past to count the exact number – which was definitely a good sign.

'Did you see Caiaphas?' Aaron asked when they were alone once more.

'I think so,' Judas said. 'And I'm pretty sure Malchus was with him too.'

'We should get going,' Baruch said. He stepped out of the archway and scurried off towards the main street. The pair of them followed him up to the villa, slipped through the gate and into the courtyard. Their luck was in – there was no one about, and the front door had been left unattended.

Baruch, still hurrying out in front, reached the building and dived off to the right, flattening himself behind one of the semi-circular pillars that jutted out from the wall. Judas and Aaron caught up with him swiftly.

'What did you see?' Aaron asked him.

'Nothing.'

'Well, what are you doing then?'

'Hiding.'

'Great. Can you stop hiding and help us figure out a way to get inside?'

'Try the door.'

'I think it's likely to be locked, Baruch.'

'Try it anyway, you never know.'

Aaron rolled his eyes at the suggestion, but crossed the short distance from the pillar to the entrance and pushed on the carved bronze slab. There was a click and the door swung inwards. Yellow light spilled forth, as it had earlier. Aaron pulled the door back towards him to reduce the illumination.

'See, told you,' Baruch said.

'Why's it unlocked?' Aaron asked. 'Doesn't that seem suspicious to you? It could be a trap. Maybe they didn't believe Jonathan's message. Maybe they just rode out to fool us into thinking they'd fallen for it, but they're really just circling around.'

'I doubt it,' Judas said. He pushed the door in a little way further and peered into the brightness. 'Caiaphas wouldn't have gone with them if that was the case, he'd have stayed in and just waited for us.'

'But why is the door unlocked?' Aaron persisted.

'He's the high priest,' Baruch said. 'Who would be stupid enough to try to break into his villa?'

'He has a point,' Judas said. 'I'm sure there are usually a couple of guards posted here. There certainly was the last time I visited. And that alone would be enough to deter most unwanted visitors.'

'But they aren't here now. Doesn't that strike you as odd?' Aaron looked around nervously, as if expecting an ambush at any moment.

'No,' Judas said. 'Caiaphas was in a hurry, he probably wanted to take as much manpower with him as he could. It's late. It's likely some of his servants and guards would have been asleep. He wouldn't have wanted to hang about until they got suited up and ready, so he just took whoever was available. Which, luckily for us, included the door guards.'

'I suppose.' Aaron sounded uncertain.

'Are we going to stand around here all night or are we going to get in there and rescue your father?' Baruch pushed the door open wider and without waiting for a response, stepped inside.

'Maybe I should wait here?' Aaron said. 'That way I can warn you if I hear anyone coming.'

'Just do what you think's best,' Judas replied.

'I think waiting outside might be best. Keeping watch for you two.'

'Fine, but remember there's a maniac on the loose murdering my friends. If he's followed us here . . . '

'All right, maybe I'll come inside. With three of us the search should be over quicker anyway.'

'Good. Come on then, let's go.'

Judas stepped into the light, followed by Aaron. Baruch was nowhere to be seen. Near the door were several rows of shelves filled with oil lamps, some of which were already lit; the source of the illumination they'd seen from outside. Judas and Aaron collected a lamp each and looked around.

The layout of the villa was simple. They were standing in a vast, domed entrance hall with a floor made up of large, square, perfectly trimmed flagstones of alternating eggshell blue and terracotta colour. Pillars carved with swirls and twisting patterns reached up to the roof, and three corridors led off to the north, east and west wings. There were several large lamp stands positioned along each corridor, providing a degree of light. To the right, a ten-foot-wide staircase swept up to the first floor in a gentle curve.

'Where's Baruch?' Aaron whispered.

'No idea. Could be anywhere.'

'I knew this was a bad idea.'

'There he is, there.' Judas pointed up ahead at Baruch who was just exiting one of the rooms positioned around the central hallway. He had a glowing lamp in one hand.

'What are you doing?' Aaron hissed at him.

'Looking for Judas's father,' Baruch replied. His booming voice echoed all around, bouncing off the domed ceiling.

'Shhh!' Aaron hissed, his eyes wide.

'What?' Baruch's voice boomed again.

'Shut up!' Aaron whispered as loud as he dared, 'Shut up will you?'

'Why?'

'In Gabriel's name stop shouting at the top of your damn voice.'

'We need to be quiet, Baruch,' Judas said, his voice low. 'We don't want to draw any attention to ourselves.'

'I thought all the guards had left?' Baruch lowered his voice to match Judas's volume.

'Some did, but I doubt if that was all of them. Others might be asleep, or around somewhere. And there are bound to be some servants still awake. We have to be very careful.'

'Right . . .'

'Did you find anything?' Judas asked.

'No. Not in there. Just food,' Baruch said as he padded over to join the other two. 'Oh and there was this silver goblet, studded with these green gems –'

'You didn't steal anything, did you?'

'No.'

'There's lots of expensive stuff here, but let me make this very clear. Don't take anything – do not take anything – from this man.'

'Stealing from the high priest would be insanity,' Aaron added.

'I know,' Baruch said. 'I haven't taken anything, and I won't take anything.'

'Good.'

'Should we split up?' Baruch asked.

'Why don't you go exploring?' Aaron said. 'Me and Judas can search elsewhere.'

'If you like,' Baruch said, and before Judas could speak he darted off to the right and began tugging on the handle of a locked door.

'Do you have any idea where this dungeon could be?' Aaron asked.

Judas shrugged. 'None. It's somewhere underneath us, obviously, but the villa is huge. It could be anywhere.'

'You've been here before though, right?'

'Yes, but only twice. Caiaphas mentioned the dungeon, but didn't give away any clues as to where it is.'

'What about down there?' Aaron pointed down the long corridor to the left, towards the west wing.

'It's as good a guess as any.'

They began to make their way along the corridor, passing several waist-high jade vases and a three-foot-tall model of a cedar tree fashioned entirely from silver, which stood atop a marble plinth. Elaborate frescoes were painted on the walls, and a striking mosaic of flowers burst with colour across one large portion of the left-hand side. They passed occasional doors and tried the handles as they did so. Somewhere in the distance they heard a dull thudding sound. They both halted and listened intently for a moment.

'Probably Baruch,' Judas said.

'What is he doing?'

'Trying to get into a locked room I'd imagine.'

'He's going to get us caught.'

'He might. We should hurry.'

Up ahead the corridor ended in a solid wall. There was a bare stone arch on the right with steps leading downwards. A faded sign next to the arch read 'Dungeon'.

'Well that was easier than I expected,' Judas said.

'We should be careful,' Aaron said. 'It's quite possible there will be guards down there.'

'You're right. Do you want to get Baruch and meet me back here?'

'We might as well check it out ourselves, now we're here.'

'All right,' Judas said, placing his lamp on the floor. 'I'll have a stealthy scout first, without any light, just in case. I'll be back up in a minute, just wait here.'

Judas edged his way down the stairs, back flat against the wall, and descended cautiously into the darkness . . .

Chapter 56

It was pitch black in the room now. The hint of light which had filtered through the crack in the roof had been swallowed by nightfall, and Simon's thoughts were darkening by equal measure.

He'd been here for . . . how long now? Too long. If he moved his ankle even slightly, immense pain burned through his leg, which was why he'd been lying prone on the floor, attempting to stay motionless, for some time now. He was in a living hell in which monotonous seconds of nothingness oozed past glacially, punctuated only by occasional spikes of agony.

What was that? Simon listened hard, the terrible boredom momentarily shattered. Either he was imagining things, or he'd heard a noise close by . . .

Chapter 57

Judas reached the bottom of the stairs. He could see nothing. The dungeon was in total darkness, and deathly quiet. He made his way back up towards the light, and the waiting Aaron.

'There aren't any guards about,' he said. 'In fact no one at all from what I can tell. It's so dark down there you can't see anything. Let's take a look with the lamps.'

Judas descended once again, holding his flickering oil lamp out in front of him as he led the way. Aaron followed closely behind. When they reached the final step Judas thrust the lamp up and out. It illuminated the space around them. Caiaphas's grand dungeon was little more than a large, practically empty stone room. There were a few broken statues against the walls, a couple of cracked wine barrels and a mound of rusty spear tips and arrow heads. There were manacles attached to the walls but they too were rusted, and didn't look as if they'd been used in years.

'This is his dungeon?' Aaron said.

'It can't be. Can it? Look, though. There were cells here,

originally.' Judas pointed at the floor. The lamp showed roughly hewn stone lines. 'The walls have been taken out.'

'So maybe Caiaphas has had a new dungeon built elsewhere?'

'Why?'

'I don't know. Perhaps he needed a bigger one. Larger, sturdier.'

'Is this it?' Baruch's voice from behind made them both jump. As he came closer the light from his lamp pooled with the yellow slick from the other two, revealing more of the room.

'We don't know,' Judas admitted. 'It's possible there's another dungeon somewhere.'

Baruch shook his head. 'Not inside there isn't. There's another set of stairs at the back of the villa. I found a small courtyard back there. But they go up to the floor above. Oh, there is an underground chamber carved down in the east wing –'

'What's that?'

'The cistern.'

'Ahh.'

'It's full of water,' Baruch added.

'Really?'

'Yes. Other than that, I just found a load of rooms. Some with doors, some without, some locked, most open. Storerooms, a kitchen, rooms filled with the most rubbish ornaments ...'

'Yes, we get the idea. You didn't see anyone about?'

'No. But I haven't tried upstairs.'

'I think we can rule upstairs out when it comes to the location of a dungeon. We must have missed something.'

'What exactly did Caiaphas say to you about his dungeon?' Aaron asked.

Judas tried to recall the exact phrasing. 'He said, I had ten seconds to leave, or he'd throw me in the dungeon. Piece by bloody piece.'

'You don't think he was bluffing? About having a working dungeon I mean?'

'I ... don't know.'

'He's the high priest,' Baruch pointed out. 'He could have multiple prisoners locked up in dungeons all over the city. There might be one under the temple. Maybe that's what he meant. If your father's not down here, he could be there.'

'He could be behind any of the locked doors,' Aaron said. 'Or chained up in the stables.'

'He could be in a whorehouse cellar. Like the one we found.' Baruch shrugged.

'You found a cellar in a whorehouse?' Aaron asked.

'We did. Well, Judas did,' Baruch said. 'With a dead wh –'

'We're wasting time here,' Judas interrupted. 'We need to look elsewhere; he's got to be here somewhere.'

Aaron took Judas's arm. 'He's not here. And if he is here, we'll never find him. We need to think about leaving.'

'No,' Judas said. 'I'm not leaving without my father.'

'Caiaphas could be back soon. And your father isn't here,' Aaron said. 'You need to accept that.'

Judas nodded slowly as an idea formed within his mind. 'You might be right. He may not be here, but I know something that is. Baruch, go back and check any doors you missed. Aaron, go with him and keep an eye out.'

'What are you going to do?'

'I'm going to get my bargaining piece back.'

Chapter 58

Judas headed in the direction of the north wing of the villa, towards the office where he had last seen Caiaphas. As he drew near he spotted something on the floor just in front of him. The scroll Jonathan had delivered a short while before had been discarded. At least it looked like the same scroll. He picked it up and opened it, just to be sure.

As he moved his lamp nearer, the light fell across the words he'd written earlier, the ones which had caused the high priest to leave with such urgency.

'Joseph,' the message began. 'The man they call Christ has been captured near the temple. I can confirm it is indeed him, and that he is alive. He's all yours, if you want him, but you will need to collect him tonight. Bring some men with you. Pontius.'

Judas had no idea if Caiaphas and Pontius Pilate were on first name terms or not, but he'd hoped the very suggestion that Jesus had somehow cheated death would be enough to grab the priest's attention, and it had clearly worked. He folded the scroll and tucked it inside his robe.

There were three doors between Judas and his destination.

He tried each handle as he passed. The first opened and revealed a room with a short flight of steps leading down into the deepest, widest bath Judas had ever seen. The entire floor was a mosaic, patterned with closely locked geometric shapes and swirls.

The next chamber was some form of reception room. Several tables with granite tops and dark wooden legs bore an array of fruit-filled bowls, jugs and goblets. Low wooden couches, padded with plush red material, were arranged in a circle around the tables.

The third door was locked. Judas listened, his ear pressed up against the wood, but could hear nothing.

At last he reached his destination, Caiaphas's office. He listened outside and tried the handle. The door opened, the lamplight illuminating the room, which was pitch dark inside as the shutters were now closed and locked. Judas made his way over to the desk and tugged on the drawer he had seen Caiaphas deposit the ring into earlier. It was also locked. Well of course it was. He had watched the high priest secure it with a small golden key.

If he was going to get the ring he'd need to find some way of breaking the drawer open. There were numerous objects and ornaments scattered around the room, but nothing that looked up to the task. He needed something relatively thin ... like the spear tips he'd seen discarded in the disused dungeon. Yes, maybe one of those would be strong enough to lever open the drawer or snap the lock. The key Caiaphas had used was a delicate-looking thing – hopefully the lock itself would be equally puny.

He left the room and made his way swiftly back to the dungeon. The villa was still deserted. Inside the stone room he quickly searched the pile of spear and arrow tips, and found one that seemed sturdy enough. As he returned to the office he could see Aaron and Baruch trying the last of the doors up ahead. Back inside, he placed his lamp on the floor, and inserted the spear tip into the gap between the top of the desk drawer and the desk itself, before yanking down with some considerable force. Nothing happened. The wood resisted his advances. Damnation.

A thought occurred. Maybe pulling downwards wasn't the right approach. He wiggled the spear into position just above the lock, stood back and kicked upwards, hard. The drawer shuddered but didn't budge. He repeated the action, and did so once more. This time there was a slight splintering noise. Encouraged, he kicked it one further time with all his might. The drawer made a cracking sound and sprang open.

'Yes,' Judas hissed to himself, a little louder than he had intended.

He grabbed the spear tip and threw it across the desktop. Now he just had to hope that Caiaphas hadn't removed the ring.

'You,' a voice said from the doorway. Judas looked up to see a man in a tunic of black interlocking scales, with gold trim and a scarlet cloak. He was holding up a lamp in one hand and clutching a sword. 'What do you think you're doing in here? This is Caiaphas's private office.'

Judas thought quickly. 'I know, he asked me to get something for him. From his desk.'

An expression of uncertainty flickered across the guard's face. Then he looked down and saw the bent spearhead.

'By breaking into it?'

'Yes. He locked the key inside the drawer. It was the only way I could open it for him.'

'I don't think so. You're coming with me.' The guard thrust his sword towards Judas. There seemed to be little choice but to cooperate, but he wasn't about to leave empty handed. He pulled open the broken drawer and grabbed the ring that was sitting atop a pile of papers.

'What are you –'

The guard's words were cut short as Baruch struck him from behind with what appeared to be a small golden bust of Augustus Caesar. He crumpled to the ground, dropping his sword. The lamp clattered onto the floor alongside it, began flickering wildly, and went out.

'We need to leave,' Baruch said. 'Now. There's a couple of guards near the entrance. It must be time for the new watch.'

'Where's Aaron?'

'Outside already. We ditched our lamps as soon as we heard noises and he ran off. Come on, hurry.'

Judas didn't need telling twice. He slipped the ring on his finger, hoping the blood was too dry to rub off easily, and leaving his lamp on the floor, followed Baruch out the door, pulling it closed behind him. They made their way back down towards the main entrance hall. As Baruch had said, there were two guards standing by the lamp shelves some distance in front of them. Another sentry hailed the pair from the stairs and they acknowledged him with a wave. There would soon be three guards between them and freedom. Judas and Baruch slipped into a doorway without saying a word and looked at each other in the semi-darkness. Baruch tried the door handle. Locked.

'Is there another way out?' Judas whispered.

'Probably,' Baruch said. 'But I haven't found it.'

Judas tried to gauge the distance to the main door. It was probably seventy or so feet, maybe a bit further. They might be able to make it if they ran now, but the guards had spears, swords and extensive training. It was likely he and Baruch would be cut down before they were even halfway to the exit, element of surprise or not.

The third guard reached the first two and collected a lamp from the shelves. Judas cursed under his breath. They were running out of time as well as options. It was possible they could make their way back to the office, and smash open the window shutters to escape that way, but the villa was built with security in mind and the shutters would likely take quite a pounding. Even if he and Baruch could break them open, the racket that would make was bound to attract the guards. Given that, the odds of making it out of the grounds alive would be slim at best.

'I've got an idea,' Baruch said. Judas raised his eyebrows. A Baruch idea was rarely a good thing. 'Stay here. Whatever happens don't move until you see your chance.'

'My chance?'

'When you see it, run.'

'How will I know when –'

Baruch didn't answer, he just turned and scurried back the way they had come, to the office. Surely he wasn't going to try smashing open the window shutters to create an escape route? Or just as bad, make some sort of loud noise that would cause the guards to come running in this direction. Did Baruch think they'd just rush past Judas without noticing him? It was crazy. Judas wanted to shout after his friend, tell him to come back, but he was terrified of alerting the guards. He turned to watch them, praying they wouldn't spot Baruch. Fortunately two had their backs to him, and they were obscuring the view of the third.

Judas watched and waited for what seemed like forever. It was clear the guards weren't going anywhere any time soon, and Baruch seemed to have just vanished. He was debating going off in search of his friend, when another guard holding a lamp appeared in the corridor behind him. Judas pulled his head back in and pressed his body hard into the small door well. This was it, then. Guards in front, a lone guard behind, a locked door to the side. He was trapped. He could attempt to overpower the new arrival, but that would only serve to alert the others. This, and a thousand other thoughts were flashing through his mind when he realised there had been something odd about the new guard. The uniform he was wearing seemed, well, a little tight. And a little too long.

It was Baruch. Had to be. He was wearing the garb of the man he'd rendered unconscious back in the office. That was his plan then. To disguise himself and … and what? Walk out through the front door unchallenged? Taking Judas with him as a captured prisoner, perhaps? It was never going to work.

Baruch marched past Judas without a word or a glance in his direction. He didn't get much further before one of the soldiers noticed him and alerted the others. They turned to face the new arrival.

Judas had no idea what Baruch said to them, but whatever it was in no time at all he'd ingratiated himself and had the group smiling and laughing. One of the soldiers even slapped him on the back. At one point he gestured at his uniform, presumably a reference to how ill-fitting it was, and two of the guards pointed in the direction of a room. Baruch said something else, one of them shrugged and the group began moving away from the front door. Unbelievably, Baruch's crazy plan was working.

The group of guards took Baruch into the room they'd indicated. This was Judas's chance, as Baruch had promised, and he seized it without hesitation. He ran for the front door, yanked it open and hoped there wouldn't be two more guards stationed outside.

There were no guards. No sign of anyone, in fact. He glanced down momentarily at his prize – the ring still had trails of dried blood on it – then he heard a sound. A rustling noise. He looked up and could just make out a figure dodging between bushes in the garden over in the east side of the courtyard. Whoever it was, they were coming rapidly towards him. Judas froze, then thought about hiding – but he'd obviously already been seen, and . . .

'Judas,' the onrushing stranger hissed. 'It's me.'

A terrified-looking Aaron emerged into the torchlight.

'You gave me a hell of a start,' Judas said.

'Thank heavens you made it out. Are you all right? Where's Baruch?'

'He's inside. Pretending to be a guard.'

'Is he all right?'

'Last time I saw.'

'What are we going to do?'

'I guess what you were doing. We hide in the garden, and wait for Baruch.'

'Caiaphas must be due back soon.'

'I know. We've got to wait for Baruch though.'

'Of course. I was just saying, we need to hide well.'

The pair made their way back out into the garden, and further onwards in the direction of the exit gate. Finding a trellised walkway thick with climbing greenery to conceal themselves in, they watched the mansion and waited.

About half an hour or so later, the doors to the villa opened and two guards with spears came out. One was tall and athletic. The other was Baruch. They stood there in silence for several seconds, then Baruch said something. The real guard shook his head. Baruch said something else, and the guard shrugged, opened the door and stepped back inside.

Baruch dropped his spear and pelted up the path towards the courtyard gate. Seeing what was going on, Judas ran to meet him, followed by Aaron.

'We've got to go, now,' Baruch panted, pulling off his tunic and hurling it away as he ran. They followed him through the gate, and up the street, diving into the alleyway where they'd previously hidden just as a group of horses appeared up ahead. Caiaphas and his entourage were returning.

They flattened themselves against the wall, breathing heavily as the riders cantered past.

'Close one,' Baruch said as he glanced at Judas sideways.

'Too close.'

Chapter 59

The walk back involved taking as many shortcuts and back-streets as possible. Baruch had discarded the rest of his uniform and was strolling bare-chested as they made their way cautiously through the city. The dark of the night meant they had to move slowly, but that suited Judas. The last thing they wanted to do was draw attention to themselves, what with Baruch's state of semi-undress, Aaron's bush-torn sleeves, and the valuable cargo Judas carried.

'Baruch, that was amazing,' Judas whispered, as he stopped on a corner to lean out and look ahead.

'I know.'

'No patrols, let's go.' Judas gestured them to move. 'So what did you say to the guards?'

'Just that I was a new recruit, arrived that evening,' Baruch said. 'I told them that Caiaphas and everyone had ridden off before I'd had a chance to be properly introduced, and the uniform they'd given me didn't fit. They were a good bunch, showed me where the spare uniforms were kept, gave me a bit of a guided tour. Apparently they all hate door duty, nothing much really happens, so they were happy when I volunteered.'

'Amazing.'

'Yeah.'

'But we failed, didn't we?' Aaron pointed out. 'Your father wasn't there. Caiaphas still has him somewhere.'

'It wasn't a total failure,' Judas said. 'At least I've got the ring back, to bargain with again.'

Even as the words left his mouth he knew it wasn't going to be quite as simple as that. It was one thing finding the ring in the brothel and using it to blackmail the priest, but this time he'd broken into Caiaphas's villa and stolen the object, damaging the desk drawer in the process. It would be clear from the moment Caiaphas entered the room what had happened, and who was responsible.

Would the ring offer Judas any protection this time around, or would the high priest simply order his death and the death of his father, and trust that would be the end of the matter? It seemed quite likely. Which left Judas with a conundrum. He could try to meet up with the priest again, and repeat yesterday's bargaining with the aim of somehow securing a more favourable outcome this time, which seemed unlikely to say the least. Or he could find another way.

Maybe sending Jonathan with a message would be better. Arrange to trade the ring for his father, at some sort of crowded location. That seemed like a good idea. But he couldn't exactly ask Baruch or Aaron for help, they'd both risked too much tonight as it was, and Caiaphas would surely recognise Jonathan as the deliverer of last night's false missive and have him arrested immediately.

Judas's eyes closed involuntarily and he stumbled on the stony ground. He was shattered and in need of sleep. He didn't relish the idea of going home, or taking refuge in his father's deserted house. Those would be the first two places Caiaphas would look for him.

'You know what we should do,' Baruch said. 'Celebrate with a whore each.'

'I'm not sure we should be celebrating, Baruch,' Judas said. 'My father is still in danger, remember.'

'I'm going straight home,' Aaron said. 'Sarah and the children will be wondering where I am. They don't know about the killer, but they're going to be worried about me all the same.'

'Can I come with you?' Judas asked. 'I think it's risky to go back to my place now. With this ring. Caiaphas doesn't know where you live, so it'll be safe.'

Aaron pulled a face that suggested he'd just sucked on a particularly bitter lemon.

'You can't,' he said. 'Sorry, Judas. You're a friend, but someone is killing people you know and I can't risk my family's lives. Having you in my home is going to make things even more dangerous. I'm sorry.'

'It's all right, I understand.'

'You can come to mine,' Baruch said. He gave a big yawn. 'We'll have a sleep, get some breakfast and some lady pleasure in town, then take the ring to Caiaphas and use it to get your father back.'

'Thanks,' Judas said. 'But I don't think it'll be quite that simple.'

After a few more minutes they came to a crossroads. Aaron lived in a house some distance down the road to the left. 'All right, well this is me,' he said, and offered his hand.

Judas embraced him instead. 'Thanks.'

'For what?' Aaron asked.

'For tonight. I know you didn't want to come along.'

310

'It's not that I didn't want to, it's just –'

'I know.'

Aaron looked away. 'Whatever you decide to do, be careful Judas. I'll come to your place tomorrow after sunset, Baruch, find out what happened. I can do that much at least. If I see Jonathan I'll tell him where you're staying, Judas. He won't tell anyone, you know that.'

'Thanks again, and be careful, Aaron. The high priest hasn't seen your face, he doesn't know you're involved, but stay safe anyway.'

'I will. Good luck, Judas. I hope that ring does the trick and you can save Simon.'

Baruch and Judas watched Aaron disappear into the gloom of the night, and then resumed walking. It took another ten minutes to reach Baruch's modest dwelling, by which time Judas was exhausted. He ate the small portion of dried fruit and seeds offered by his friend, and then turned in for the slight remainder of the night. Although there was only a hard floor to use as a bed, Judas was asleep the moment he lay his head down.

Caiaphas surveyed the scene before him. A half-naked groaning man lay sprawled on the floor. A thin trail of blood ran from the prone guard's head, pooling in the cracks between the flags. A golden bust lay face down a few feet away. The polished oak desk bore a scuff mark across its surface, caused no doubt by the spearhead lying nearby. And there were fine splinters of wood scattered about. The priest circled the desk slowly, observing the mess. He noted the open drawer with its bent lock and looked up at Malchus.

'Iscariot,' he growled.

'Has he taken the ring?'

'He has.'

'So what now?'

'So now we wait. The fool obviously thinks he can use it to bargain with me for the life of his father. But of course he cannot.'

'Because we don't have his father.'

'Because we have no need to bargain with him. The unfortunate situation has been cleaned up, so it's just his word against mine now, and all he has is a ring with a little blood on it. Blood that could have come from anywhere.'

'So when he comes to you –'

'He will not have the chance. I want you to go and find him, Malchus. Have him arrested and give him to the Romans. I am sure they will appreciate the gift of one of that deceased rabble-rouser's cohorts. He has been an annoyance for too long. And this audacity,' he gestured around the room, 'cannot be allowed to go unpunished.'

'Very well.'

'And find the messenger who came here last night. He must have been a part of this act of rebellion.'

'Do you want him arrested as well?'

'No. Kill him. He is of no consequence.'

'Very well.'

'And just one more thing, Malchus.'

'What?'

'Will you stop doing that,' Caiaphas said, his voice raised with irritation.

Malchus moved his hand sheepishly away from his ear, where he'd been rubbing it.

'I've a good mind to chop the damn thing off myself,' the priest said as he exited the room.

Chapter 60

Jonathan turned to look at the squat houses he was cantering past. He had delivered his last message in these parts and was looking forward to starting a new life in Rome, and a new role as a father to Benjamin if it was a boy, or Adina if it was a girl. He and his wife had decided on the names when he had returned from his perilous adventure last night. He wondered how the mission had fared after he had completed his role. And whether Judas had succeeded in finding and freeing his father. So far this morning, he hadn't heard anything about trespassers being caught up at the villa, so he had to assume –

Thwack!

A forcefully thrown rock hit Jonathan smack on the side of the head. Bright lights sparked in front of his eyes and the world slowed to molasses as he pitched to one side, then he was falling, his limbs scrabbling at the air in a subconscious effort to save himself before he . . .

Hit the floor, with a crunch. His left shoulder took the brunt of the impact, but his head whipped down and received a second sharp blow from the unforgiving ground. His skull felt like it had been stuffed with wool, thick and heavy. The muffled sound of clattering hooves faded gradually in his ears.

Then he was moving. Was he? Or the world was. He wasn't sure which. Something was spinning though, and rapidly. Darkness cosseted him, briefly. Still he could feel the sensation of motion. And then ... floating. Was he dying ... ascending?

His eyes opened, the lids moving languidly over the teary film which blurred his vision. No, he wasn't dead. Jonathan blinked his eyes several times and his sight began to clear. Something was tightening around his foot up above him. A shake of his head, along with a few more blinks of his eyelids, and Jonathan began to focus on the scene in front of him.

An upside down man wearing a brown hooded robe was closing an upside down door, shutting the outside world away. As his mind started to get a grip on the situation, Jonathan realised that neither the man nor the world was upside down – he was. The blood was rushing to his head, which was suspended two feet above the ground. His arms were dangling loosely downwards and he could feel the cold touch of the earthen floor against his knuckles. A damp cloth had been stuffed into his mouth, a tightly tied thin cord holding it in place.

Although the windows were shuttered, the room wasn't in total darkness. What sounded like a fire popping and spitting close by provided a degree of flickering orange light.

The brown-robed man turned and started walking back towards him.

Jonathan pressed his hands palms-down on the floor and used the leverage this provided to crane his neck up, ignoring the pain in his shoulder caused by the fall from his horse. He could see that each of his feet had been bound tightly with separate lengths of rope. These, in turn, had been tied around metal loops attached to the ceiling. The loops were a few feet apart, so he was suspended in a Y-shape, his legs akimbo.

He looked back down to see the man's sandalled feet as he walked past, heading towards the back of the room. The bottom of his robe was splattered with blood.

Jonathan tried to yell for help, but the foul-tasting rag in his mouth muffled his cries. As he reached for the cloth with his hands to attempt to pull it free, he heard a flurry of movement behind him.

The robed man grabbed Jonathan's right arm, and after a brief struggle, his left, tying his hands together with cord. They were securely bound from the wrists to the fingers so they hung down beneath Jonathan's head, touching the floor as if clasped in prayer.

The man removed his helpless victim's one remaining sandal – the other had come off when he'd been dragged in here, Jonathan could see it over by the door – and then began stripping him naked.

All was quiet, save for the crackle of the fire. Two items were sheathed in its orangey flames and the man picked up one of them. It was a large pair of tongs, the circular ends of which glowed a demonic red.

Jonathan felt the instrument being moved down between his legs. After a few seconds the aroma of burning hair reached the messenger's nostrils. The heat gradually became more intense until he could feel the tongs within touching distance of his scrotum. The man cupped the grippers over one of the exposed testicles and pressed them together hard.

Jonathan let out a series of muffled shrieks and bucked his body violently, but the hooded figure simply stood on his bound and clasped hands, pressing them to the floor to limit his range of movement. The man further tightened his grip on the tongs.

A number of interminable seconds passed as the delicate orb burned and started to bubble gently inside its small circular oven. Jonathan grunted in agony.

His torturer dropped the tongs and moved behind him once more, stooping to retrieve the second instrument heated by the flames.

The smell of burning flesh thickened in the air as this new implement also found a home between Jonathan's spread legs. This time between his cheeks. Forced down into the fleshy valley, the blade of the tool seared the smooth darkened area. A triangular metal tooth found a nesting hole into which it sank, melting the inward folds of skin and knitting them together; slowly sealing the orifice shut.

And then it was re-opened, as the serrated edge moved backwards slowly, the jagged metal drawing blood. The saw was thrust forward and drawn back once more, cutting a stinging trail of inconceivably raw pain as it sliced through his sphincter.

The metal teeth rasped back and forth as the man got into more of a rhythm, carving down into the anal canal, millimetre-by-millimetre through muscle and connective tissue.

Jonathan's torso swayed and rocked with the increasing pace of the sawing. The man's sturdy foot on his victim's bound hands kept the body anchored solidly enough to give the instrument enough purchase to cleave deeper still. Droplets of claret sprayed back and forth with each motion of the blade, although most of the blood flowed downwards, internally.

The messenger's gagged shrieks were now uncomprehending, low sepulchral moans. He was dimly aware of something hitting his face and plopping down on the floor in front of him. His eyes blinked open to see what it was, but took several seconds to focus and recognise the bleary, bloody lump of curled flesh. It was half of his penis.

He should surely have passed out by now, given the outright horror being inflicted on him, except the blood that had rushed heavy to his head seemed to be keeping him conscious with some considerable insistence.

The movement and friction was in Jonathan's abdomen now, splitting layer upon layer of intestines as the blade continued to carve its way through his torso. His mind attempted to shut itself off from the ordeal, to distance itself in order to endure the unendurable. But he could still feel the sickening grind of the saw as it reverberated in his gut and spine.

Then the man stopped sawing and removed the bloody instrument. It took several hard pulls to free it from Jonathan's butchered body.

The attacker hurled the object across the room, where it clattered against the wall, and then placed a hand on either side of the gaping wound. He pushed down hard on the inside of Jonathan's thighs with a vicious turn of strength; once, twice, three times. A bone cracked somewhere and the red chasm widened, its depths revealing a blended mess of thick blood and sliced pinkish-purple tubing which spilled spots of dark faecal matter.

The hooded figure turned away from his gruesome handiwork, bent down and retrieved the tongs from the floor. He plucked a fist-sized hunk of flaming blackened wood from the fire, took a step back to the messenger, and dropped it into his yawning, mutilated mid-section. It sizzled atop the wet wreckage of his intestines for a moment or two, then began melting slowly downwards, towards the heart of his belly. Jonathan's eyelids flickered rapidly and his fingers twitched.

The man moved to pick up another item. He scooped a bucket into the firepit, half-filling it with blazing wood coals and burning hot embers and, holding it in both hands, returned to the messenger one final time . . .

Chapter 61

Simon blinked his eyes open. He must have fallen unconscious for a short while. The morning sun was glinting through the crack in the roof, once more giving the room a hint of illumination. Any respite from the stifling darkness, no matter how slight, was welcome.

There it was again – the noise he thought he might have imagined when he first heard it. That damn bird hopping about on the roof. It had been there all night, occasionally pecking and flapping its wings.

Wait – no, this was different. This sound was coming from inside the building. From another room. The hairs stood up on the back of Simon's neck. He strained to listen. It sounded like ... movement. Someone was definitely here. Was that a voice? His captor? Who had come to ...

He didn't want to think about that. Simon continued to listen, but everything seemed to have gone quiet.

Then he heard them. Heavy footsteps approaching the door. His pulse quickened. The footsteps halted right outside the entrance to the room. After a slight pause, a noise emanated from the door itself. It sounded like the person outside was scratching a fingernail down the wood. It would stop, and start again. The chilling scraping sound occurred repeatedly – over and over and over – with each scratch gouging a deepening sense of dread in Simon's mind.

Eventually, the noise ceased and the footsteps gradually receded. Although the sense of dread still remained.

Chapter 62

Judas awoke sometime before midday. Although he'd slept right through the remainder of the night and morning, he felt drained. His slumber had been haunted by dreams he couldn't quite remember, but fragments of images he could recollect left him feeling very uneasy. A massive boulder. A crucifix. A man in a shining white robe.

Baruch was still asleep and snoring loudly. Judas stood up and left his friend's house without waking him. Baruch would want to go whoring and that was the last thing on his mind. He had a far more important task to attend to.

Judas made his way to his home and after checking he hadn't attracted any unwanted followers, opened the front door and slipped inside. He changed his clothes, ate a brief breakfast of melon, followed by a few figs, and then retrieved the thirty silver pieces from their hiding place. He still had no idea how he was going to return them to Caiaphas, but he didn't want the coins being stolen or going missing in the meantime. He placed the pouch containing the pieces inside his robe, and was about to leave when he became aware of a shadowy presence behind him. Before he could turn an arm hooked around his shoulder and he felt a slim metal blade press gently into the soft skin of his throat.

'Good to find you at home,' Malchus said. 'We have a little business to attend to, you and I.'

Caiaphas's right-hand man guided Judas towards a chair in front of a table and indicated that he should sit.

Judas lowered himself unsteadily into the seat, his legs trembling. 'What do you want?' he asked. This was it; the end of the road. Malchus was here to kill him.

'I want to talk to you,' the stocky thug said, pulling the blade away as he did so. He sat down opposite Judas.

'That was quite a stunt you pulled last night,' Malchus continued. 'Ballsy. I wouldn't have thought you had it in you.' He stabbed the blade into the wooden tabletop. The handle rocked backwards and forwards several times.

'Where's Caiaphas?'

'Not here. It's just you and me I'm afraid.'

'What do you want?'

'You have the ring once more. And you're carrying it, I would guess. Give it to me and I'll make sure it gets into the right hands.'

'With pleasure. Once you've released my father.' Judas hoped he sounded braver than he felt.

'I would, but there's one small problem. We don't have him.'

'What?'

'Oh we meant to capture him. I went all the way out to Ishmael's Rest. But by the time I arrived, he was gone. Signs of a struggle. Someone else got there before us.'

Someone else? 'You're lying.'

'No, I'm not. Nothing to gain from it. We don't have your father.'

'But Caiaphas said –'

'He wanted the ring so he said what you needed to hear, to force you to give it up.'

'This is a trick.'

'It's no trick, Judas –'

'But, hang on ... even after I'd given him the ring back, Caiaphas still said he had my father.'

Malchus nodded. 'That's true. In case it's escaped your attention, the high priest doesn't like you. He's a cruel man, particularly to those who cross him. He just wanted you to suffer some more.'

'I don't ...' Judas began, then trailed off.

'Listen. My orders are to have you arrested and handed over to the Romans. I could do that, but if you give me the ring now, I'll let you go.'

'Why?'

'My motives are irrelevant. If you give me the ring, you can go. Free to find out who really has your father. If you don't give it to me, I'll have you arrested, take the ring and your father will stay where he is. Wherever that might be.'

'Why would you defy Caiaphas and let me go?'

Malchus laughed, an unhinged sound. 'I'm not defying him. Caiaphas said I should arrest you. But I haven't found you yet. Of course, if I find you after you leave here, then I will have you arrested. Or I might just kill you. Whichever's easiest.'

'He honestly doesn't have my father?'

'He doesn't. Give me the ring.' Malchus held out his hand. Judas hesitated for a second or two, then pulled the golden circlet out of its hiding place in his clean robe and dropped it into the soldier's cracked palm. Thick fingers closed around it.

'Thank you. You are free to go. Free to find your father. But I meant what I said. I won't be so merciful next time.'

Judas stood, his head spinning. He'd parted with his bargaining piece a second time, but it had proved to be worthless anyway. Someone still had his father captive, but if Malchus was to be believed it wasn't Caiaphas. What Malchus had said about the high priest rang strangely true. And Judas had seen for himself that his father wasn't a prisoner in Caiaphas's villa, surely the most obvious place to hold him.

If the priest didn't have his father, it didn't take much imagination to work out who did. But why would the murderer have taken Simon and not killed him outright like the others? Maybe he hadn't captured him. Maybe his father was dead.

He dismissed the idea the instant it entered his head. He couldn't afford to think like that.

Leaving his home he tried to think of what to do next, but he'd run out of ideas. The murderer was still out there somewhere, enacting his bloody revenge. His father was missing, and Caiaphas was seemingly in the clear.

Because he couldn't think what else to do, Judas took a long walk to Ishmael's Rest, trusting that maybe something – some next step to take – would occur to him along the way. Nothing did, and the small hope he'd carried of finding his father safe and well inside was crushed the moment he arrived. The house was empty as before.

He sat for some time on the crumbling wall that ringed the hamlet, looking out at the scenery. At one point a pack of wild dogs approached the settlement, and he eyed them warily. Normally, they'd feed at the rubbish-dumping grounds outside Jerusalem, but the bigger or braver ones sometimes ventured into habited areas, in search of juicier scraps. They barked at him briefly, before moving on.

Eventually, one of the locals spotted him, and came over with a few kind words, and some honeyed dates that entirely failed to sweeten his mood. Judas then took a meandering route back, out past Lazarus's home. There was no sign of anyone inside, as far as he could tell. And then, when the sun began to sink, marking the end of a sad and unproductive day, he made his way to Baruch's home. Baruch wasn't there, but Aaron was.

'Jonathan's missing,' the stall holder said by way of a greeting.

'What do you mean, missing?'

'I mean, gone. His wife came to see me. His horse came back around lunchtime, but there was no sign of him.'

'Maybe he tied it up loosely and it got free. He might just be walking back from somewhere?'

'You know that can't be true. Jonathan is the king of knots, anything he ties up stays tied up.'

'He's right,' Baruch said, entering the building through the back entrance. 'He tied me up once when we were kids. My father had to cut me free with a knife.'

'Exactly,' Aaron agreed. 'There's no way Jonathan would let his horse get away from him. Unless something bad happened.'

'Jonathan's resourceful and fast,' Judas said. 'I'm sure he'll be fine.'

'But you can't know that, can you?'

'Where did you vanish to this morning anyway?' Baruch asked.

'I went to get something from my house, and plan my next move,' Judas replied. 'Only Malchus found me there.'

'Damn. What happened?'

'I gave him the ring. I had to.'

'Are they going to free Simon?'

'No. It turns out they don't have him. Yesterday's raid was all for nothing.'

'What do you mean, they don't have him?' Aaron asked.

'Whoever has my father, it isn't Caiaphas.'

'Do you think it's the –'

'Probably.'

'I'm really sorry, Judas,' Aaron said. 'That's awful. But I've got to tell you this. Tomorrow morning I'm taking my wife and children far away from here. We've relatives in Bethlehem, so we'll go there for starters and then who knows where we'll end up.'

'You can't leave,' Baruch protested. 'Judas needs us.'

'No, Baruch,' Judas said. 'He should leave, and so should you. It's too dangerous for you both. There's nothing more you can do for me and who knows when that madman will strike again. You know you're at risk.'

'I'm going nowhere,' Baruch said. He reached inside his robe and withdrew a sharp knife. Both Judas and Aaron shrank back in alarm. 'If that son of a whore comes anywhere near me he'll get a lot more than he bargained for.'

'Bloody hell,' Judas said. 'Put it away, Baruch.'

'It's protection. I told you, I'm not going down without a fight.'

'We believe you,' Aaron said. 'And I pity that lunatic if he does try to mess with you. But anyway, I suppose I'd better be going. Get back to my wife and my children. We need to start gathering our things together.' He made to stand up.

'Not tonight,' Judas said, putting a firm hand on his friend's arm. 'It's dangerous out there. Wait until the morning and then go. It'll be much safer if we all stay here together tonight. Take it in turns to keep watch.'

Aaron hesitated, but it was clear Judas was right. If something had happened to Jonathan, one of them could be next. There would be safety in numbers, and he'd already planned for this eventuality anyway, packing his wife and children off to stay with her family as soon as he'd heard the news about Jonathan's horse. Sarah's father and her three brothers would make sure no harm came to them tonight, and one last evening with his oldest friends was the least he could do. Who knew when, or if, he'd ever see them again.

'Who wants to keep watch first?' Judas asked.

'I don't mind,' Baruch replied, twiddling the blade between his fingers. 'I'll get some wine first though. It's going to be a long night.'

Chapter 63

There was no hint of light from above him now. Night had fallen again. Another interminable day had dragged past, but the nights in Simon's own personal hellhole were far worse. He was enveloped in inky blackness, making his prison feel more complete and enclosed. More suffocating. He drifted in and out of sleep, or rather in and out of an uncomfortable slumber, his tiredness offset by nightmarish thoughts, sweats and the pain. Every time he shifted slightly in his drowsy half-sleep, the throbbing from his swollen ankle jolted him awake.

At times, Simon wasn't even sure of the difference between his nightmarish visions and reality. The maniac scratching on the door during the day – had that been real, or just some manner of phantom horror? He was starting to doubt everything, bound as he was in this black pit of racking trial and anguish, suffering second by cruel second.

And then, there was light. A flickering yellow glow danced around the outline of the door. Along with it came the noise of approaching footsteps. The light, stronger now, spilled underneath, illuminating the floor in a semi-circular patch. He heard a noise that sounded like something heavy being dragged across the ground just outside of the room. There was a brief pause and then the door opened.

A figure stepped in, bearing a lamp which burned Simon's dilated pupils like hellfire, forcing them reflexively shut. When he managed to re-open them, squinting into the light which had now been placed on the floor, he saw a hooded figure looming with his hands on the cauldron.

The man swiftly righted the toppled pot, yanking Simon's damaged leg back up in the air. The pain was unbearable. Simon bit down hard on his gag and a strangled-sounding shriek emerged from the back of his throat. The hooded fiend pushed Simon onto his side, reached down and cut through the rope which bound his wrists together. Simon's arms were now free, but all he could do was scream in agony as his bad leg was jerked and twisted around by his captor's actions.

Simon became aware that his left hand was being pinned to the floor. He could barely focus through the pain that was still surging through his system, but he saw now that the man was kneeling and had raised something above his head, holding it in both hands.

It was a cleaver.

Before he could react, the blade came down with a savage chop, slicing clean through Simon's left arm. Blood pulsed from the limb, which had been severed just below the elbow, and Simon, reacting automatically, grabbed the stump end with his good hand. Dark, warm liquid spilled around his fingers as his face froze with shock.

His attacker picked up the detached arm and hurled it away like a piece of rubbish. Then he stood and exited the room, his light casting demented wobbling shadows on the walls as he left. The door slammed behind him.

Simon screamed at his departing attacker, a primal howl akin to that of a badly wounded and desperate animal.

Blood continued to spill down his side and the arm he was clutching his amputated limb with. A few seconds passed before Simon noticed there was something heavy lying on his stomach. An object of some kind. He reached down with his remaining hand and discovered a notched wooden handle. He felt further along, until his fingers detected the coolness of metal underneath them. The attacker had left him with the cleaver.

Chapter 64

Judas forced his eyes open. His right temple was throbbing, the combination of a little too much wine and sleeping on a hard floor with a thin balled-up blanket for a pillow. He yawned and rolled his head from side to side, a feeble attempt to get the crick out of his neck, then he stretched and looked around. It took a second or two for his brain to make sense of what he was seeing, and for the terror to set in.

A cry of panic escaped his lips as he went from horizontal to vertical almost instantly, his heart pounding. The speed of the movement caused his feet, still clad in leather sandals, to slip in the viscous liquid pooled around him and he crashed back down again, landing on his hands and knees.

'No, no, no!' Judas scrambled back up and ran for the door, skidding as he did so and partly shoulder-charging the frame. He ignored the jarring pain, threw back the bolt and just ran. He pelted down the largely empty streets, not sure what he was doing; going for help, or just getting the hell out of there, but he knew he couldn't stay. People had been dying because of his actions for days now, but this was the first time he'd physically seen it with his own eyes.

Reaching a corner three streets away, he stopped and retched hard. Thick wine-coloured vomit burned the back of his throat as he threw up. The muscles in his stomach contracted violently with each involuntary heave. The few townsfolk who were about their early Friday morning business stared at him as they hurried on their way, oblivious to the horror he had witnessed.

Every time he blinked the gruesome scene imprinted indelibly on the back of his eyelids returned to taunt him. He tried to focus on breathing, but that just brought on another wave of nausea. He dry heaved and spat on the ground, the taste in his mouth acrid and vile.

He'd been tired, sure, but how on Earth had he managed to sleep through his two best friends getting slaughtered just a few feet away from him? It made no sense. The only possible explanation was that the killings had been executed in a quieter and more efficient manner than the carnage he'd awoken to had suggested. He closed his eyes and studied the scene which was engraved in his mind.

Aaron had been lying on his back with an angry gash across his windpipe and multiple stab wounds over his body. The murderer must have snuck up behind him, put one hand over the merchant's mouth and slit his throat with a knife at the same time, catching him unawares while he was supposed to be keeping watch. It was even possible Aaron had fallen asleep. Early mornings on the market, two late nights, a skin-full of wine ... it was certainly feasible. Maybe the other stab wounds had been added later, once both friends were dead, the murderer wanting to further mutilate the bodies. Or make sure he'd done the job properly.

Baruch's corpse had been behind Aaron's. He was lying face

down and partially obscured. It was hard to tell how he'd died. Stabbed in the back while he slept seemed the most probable guess. A cowardly way to kill such a brave and loyal person.

The vomit on the ground was already beginning to dry around the edges now, soaking into the sand and frying in the early heat of the day. Judas felt light-headed as he straightened up and tried to summon the courage he was going to need for his next move.

He had to go back. He knew that, accepted it. He couldn't just leave their bodies like that, but there was another reason for his decision. It had only been a fleeting glimpse initially. Something that hadn't registered to begin with, but the more he closed his eyes, the clearer the image became. The stab wounds on Aaron's body weren't as random or frenzied as Judas had first thought. Quite the opposite in fact. They were deliberately and carefully carved. Letters, forming words.

The killer had left him another message.

Judas began to retrace his steps slowly, torn between the need to find out what had been written on Aaron, and the desire to never see that dreadful scene ever again. But as much as he wanted to turn and run, to leave and never go back, he kept walking. His two oldest friends had died in Baruch's home – while he slept – and he was responsible for it.

He owed them.

As he drew nearer Judas noticed traces of his bloody foot-prints in the sand. Faint at first, but becoming redder and more defined. He averted his eyes from them and just concentrated on walking. One foot in front of the other. Until he was back inside the house.

He was right, there was a message written on Aaron's body. Large tefah-sized letters, deep and bloody, etched into the merchant's chest and stomach. It seemed an odd thing to have written, short and cryptic, and Judas would certainly puzzle over it in due course.

But right now that wasn't his priority.

When he walked back into the room, the scene was exactly as he'd pictured it in his mind. Exactly how he'd left it. With one major exception.

When he'd fled the building there had been two dead bodies on the floor. Now there was only the one.

Baruch's had vanished.

Chapter 65

There was a considerable pool of blood on the floor. The faint light of the dawn sun filtering through the gap in the roof was reflected in the dark oily slick of Simon's life-force which had drained out onto the ground.

After the madman had departed, Simon had managed to reach out, grab a nearby sack of grain, and pull it towards him. He'd then sat himself up using his arms – his arm, rather – and leaned back against the sack, while he kept pressure on his bleeding stump with his remaining hand as best he could. But the battle was clearly a losing one.

He didn't know how much longer he would last, but he did know that his head was starting to feel light and that wasn't a good sign. Plus his shattered ankle had ballooned up even more, and the iron manacle which secured it to the cauldron was now cutting into it. Simon reached down and grasped the handle of the cleaver. By leaving the weapon his tormentor had seemingly given him two horrendous choices. The first was to sit here and bleed to death. And the second was to use the cleaver to … free himself.

The first option wasn't appealing. The second option, which involved hacking off both his feet, was also seriously lacking in the appeal stakes. That said, it would free him and then he'd be able to pull himself to the door, and hopefully out into the street to get some help. Although whether he'd be in any state that a physician would be able to save him was another matter.

Still, at least he wouldn't have to worry about his painful ankle any more. That would be one way of dealing with it. Simon's face contorted into a grim smile in the darkened room.

His hand moved back to stem the continued bleeding from his severed arm. If he was going to do it, he would have to do it now. One thing was for sure, and that was the longer he waited, the less substantial his already small chances of survival would be. All this prevarication could be costing him dearly.

Simon grabbed hold of the cleaver and lined it up with his mangled left foot. He raised the weapon, keeping it in a straight line, drew a long, slow breath, and braced himself.

The cleaver came down, thudding onto the floor as his hand released its grip and he dropped it. Simon's head bowed in despair and his shoulders began to shake. He couldn't do it.

III

REVELATION

Chapter 66

Judas struggled with the flood of thoughts and questions that was swamping his mind. Baruch's body had disappeared. Did that mean the killer was still around? Had he taken it in the ten minutes Judas had been gone? Surely that was a ridiculous thing to do. Why the hell would he come back for the body?

Why would he ... wait – his thoughts crystallised on a single point of clarity. He hadn't actually seen any of Baruch's wounds. Aaron had been lying in front of him, obscuring his corpse. But what if it wasn't a corpse? What if Baruch hadn't been stabbed at all? What if he'd just been playing dead? And he had murdered Aaron.

What if Baruch was the killer?

Now that he thought about it, his friend had been strangely calm when Judas had first told him about the killings. Not worried at all. He'd also said some slightly odd things. Judas recalled one phrase in particular, when he'd suggested to Baruch that his uncle Daniel must have struggled to avoid being killed. Baruch had replied, 'Not hard enough.' It had seemed harsh at the time, but what if it hadn't been harsh, but rather literal?

What if Baruch had first-hand knowledge of just how hard, or otherwise, Daniel had struggled?

Then there was Gilead. He'd been like a second uncle to Judas during his childhood. It seemed strange that Baruch's father had managed to avoid the grisly fate that had befallen his contemporaries. Unless his son was the one choosing the victims.

There was certainly no denying Baruch had a violent streak. Thomas could attest to that. It was interesting that even after everyone else had accepted that the apostle he'd battered wasn't the killer, Baruch continued to cast aspersions – a possible attempt at misdirection? Everyone thought Baruch was stupid, but he could be oddly bright at times. Disguising himself as a guard so they could escape Caiaphas's villa was an incident that sprang immediately to mind.

And then there was the knife last night. Baruch had claimed he had it for protection, but was that really the truth? It was clear Aaron had been killed with a similar-sized blade.

But what could possibly have driven Baruch to do all this? Judas knew his friend had felt betrayed when he left to follow Jesus. That had created a distance between them which was evident upon his return, but they'd never discussed it. Maybe Baruch was killing people to get back at Judas for betraying both him and Jesus. Or maybe he was just killing everybody that Judas knew until he was the only friend left.

The idea was preposterous. Although it was in his head now, and the more he tried to dismiss it, the more likely it seemed. But why would Baruch fake his own death here, now? There was no obvious reason. However, there was one clue he had yet to examine.

Judas approached Aaron's mutilated body. The blood leaking out of the gashes had run together, making the letters cut into his torso hard to distinguish. He bent, used his sleeve to wipe away the surface layer, and then stood back. The two words were clearer now. 'Dan's' carved on his chest, and 'Den' on his stomach. Dan's Den. He realised what it meant immediately. Or at least what it was referring to. His uncle Daniel had a secret second home, one he used for gambling and seeing women other than his wife. It had been there that Judas had lost his virginity to his cousin Atarah, Daniel's daughter. How she'd known about the place, Judas wasn't sure. He'd never asked. But she'd called it her father's den. And he'd only ever told one other person of its existence.

Baruch.

The final puzzle piece fell into place with a click.

Baruch.

The name circled inside his head, suddenly the harshest sounding two syllables he'd ever heard in his life. It was no longer the name of a steadfastly loyal friend, but a killer, a murderer, a slaughterer. A betrayer.

Judas steadied himself against the wall in the face of this sickening revelation. He tried to focus, to think more clearly.

Why would Baruch want him to go to Daniel's den? There had to be a reason, and if Judas wanted to find out, he would have no choice but to follow the macabre directions. Perhaps his crazed, rejected friend would be waiting for him there. But to what end? Lying in wait to kill him? That didn't make any sense – he could have killed him along with Aaron, as he slept.

Judas picked up the thin blanket he'd used as a pillow, shook it out, and was about to lay it over the murdered merchant's corpse when he noticed something he'd missed earlier.

A slash on Aaron's stomach next to the carved letters had a faint mark on the end of it, like some kind of symbol, partially obscured by blood. He wiped it with his already stained sleeve and it became more visible. It was a sideways V, which crowned the slashed line to form an arrow. It struck Judas that the message might not make sense because it wasn't finished. Was this pointing to ...

Before he even had a chance to finish the thought, Judas had rolled his dead friend over onto his side. There, carved into his back, was a third word: 'Simon'.

Judas relinquished his grip on Aaron's body and it slumped over onto its front, the hidden word fully visible now. What did it mean? Baruch had his father at the den? A torrent of emotions flowed through Judas; recrimination and rage, followed by fear and panic, before a final realisation gripped him. Maybe it wasn't too late to save his father.

Chapter 67

It was dark inside Daniel's second home. A burnt smell hung in the air, tinged with an unpleasant metallic edge. The windows of the house were shuttered, and the light from the open door cast only a faint illumination which barely troubled the darkness. Judas yanked the shutters of the nearest window open, then moved to the next set of shutters and flung those back too. He spun around as the fresh light spilled into the room, revealing the largely empty space.

Empty but for a few items of furniture, a table and a couple of chairs pushed up against the opposite wall, and a body which was suspended by its feet from the ceiling.

Judas dashed over to the naked corpse. He knew instantly it wasn't his father. The physique belonged to a much younger man. A much younger, horribly mutilated man, whose torso had been split asunder partway, his charred-black abdomen cleaved down the middle past the navel. He looked down at the corpse's face. It was mottled, blood splattered and contorted in frozen agony. The pain that he must have gone through was unimaginable. Judas staggered backwards and shook his head, as if that would somehow dissolve the vision. It was one thing for Baruch to have stabbed Aaron to death, but how could he have done something as indescribably awful as this to Jonathan?

But it wasn't his father. His father! The thought jolted Judas back into motion and he rushed through the curtain-covered doorway into the room beyond, which was also in near-darkness. He wasted no time in whipping open the shutters on several windows, whirling as he did so to scan the area. There was some bedding in the corner, a blackened saw and some other tools on a bench, another table with some rope on it, and a stout wooden chest jammed up against a door at the far end of the room.

The door had something written on it. Something scratched into the wood and stained with blood. Two crudely daubed words read: 'Our Father.'

Judas took a few swift strides over, placed a foot on the heavy chest and shoved it out of the way. Blood had seeped out under the door. He yanked it open and cried out in anguish as the ravaged figure of his father slumped out, onto the floor.

Simon's left arm had been amputated at the elbow and both his feet were missing, hacked off at the ankles in a ragged and haphazard fashion. Judas knelt down in the slick of blood that was pooled around his father and cradled him gently, one hand supporting his head. Simon moaned, a low guttural noise coming from deep within.

'Did that bastard Baruch do this?' Judas asked, his voice cracking. 'Did he do it? Was it him?'

Chapter 68

The dying man stared up at his son, his eyes pale and unseeing. His lips moved but no sound came from them. He was trying to say something, but making the words audible required more effort than he was able to summon from the last dregs of his ebbing existence.

'Was it Baruch?' Judas spoke softly. 'Baruch?'

Simon coughed and repeated what he'd said before. This time a whisper escaped his lips. 'I forgive you,' he said. His head lolled to the side and his breathing began to slow. The gasps went from every second to every few seconds, until they were so far apart that Judas was sure each new breath would be the final one. And then, with a deep shuddering inhalation, it was.

Utterly bereft, Judas stared at the lifeless body for some time, unable to move. He wanted to shake it, bring his father back, do something, anything. But he knew it was too late. He was too late. Tears began to stream down his face, forming rivulets of stinging regret.

Judas lowered his father's bloody mutilated body to the floor and tried to blink away the tears. His eyes were blind with

345

them, his face wet. He could taste them in his mouth. He wiped his face with his hands and licked his lips. Instead of the salty taste he was expecting, his tongue detected a wholly different flavour. His father's blood.

He looked down and saw his hands were crimson. An unholy cry tore forth from his lungs, a noise of utter desolation. He stood and began to back away from the scene in front of him. Wiping his hands on his robe he stumbled against the wall and felt something soft touch the back of his head. He turned to see what it was, blinking hard to clear his vision and then blinking again to try and make sense of what his eyes were showing him.

It was a robe on a hook. Brown coloured, with scarlet stains. Next to it was a knife with a bone handle.

Judas stared at the items blankly. Some of the stains on the robe looked fresh. He touched the sleeve with shaking hands and then turned his attention to the blade, which was balanced across the top of two rusty embedded pegs. Was this the weapon Baruch had used to kill his victims?

Judas lifted the knife off the pegs. Holding the bone handle carefully, he placed the iron blade on the palm of his other hand and examined it. Something about it seemed very familiar. Where had he seen it before?

He closed his eyes and tried to remember.

From out of nowhere a vague recollection began to take shape. He concentrated on it, going over the details in his head.

After leaving the crucifixion he'd gone to the temple – to find Caiaphas – but why? To return the blood money? He wasn't sure, although he did recall when he had got there, he'd discovered the quake had cracked the building. People were milling around everywhere, panicking, shouting; a scene verging on chaos. He remembered that clearly now. Failing to find the fat priest, he had wandered in a daze around the streets of Jerusalem until eventually he'd come to the iron-smith.

He shivered involuntarily as he pictured himself going through the door. The smith had greeted him with a grunted hello. A disinterested welcome punctuated by the clanging of iron as the man rained down blows on his latest creation. With a jolt, Judas realised he knew the proprietor. It was Jethro. The tall, wiry Roman-hating smith. What was it he'd said when Judas had sold him the stolen plate? *I never forget a face. And yours is familiar.* No wonder. They had met previously, but the encounter had somehow been erased from Judas's memory. Until now.

His eyes still closed, Judas recalled browsing the smithy, looking for … for what exactly? An image obligingly formed in his mind. For a knife. He had wanted to kill himself. And had wanted a knife to do it with. He had found this one, and impressed with its perfectly weighted balance and exquisitely carved handle, had purchased it.

It had cost him one whole piece of silver.

The missing piece from the thirty. The coin he thought he'd carelessly lost.

How could he have forgotten all of this?

With his back pressed against the wall, Judas studied the knife carefully. The blade was much finer edged than when he'd first encountered it. He had a vague memory of sharpening it on his wheel, but couldn't quite place when.

After getting home he'd swapped his soiled black robe for a brown garment – the very one now covered in blood and hanging on the wall in front of him – and following a simple meal, had headed off into the countryside to find the ideal spot for his act of atonement. Somewhere his body wouldn't be discovered for a while.

Walking near the forest he'd spotted Gideon tending his flock up on the hill and that had given him the monstrous idea. He'd kidnapped the sheep and staked it to the ground. Knowing that Gideon would eventually realise the animal was missing and come looking for it, Judas had hidden in the woods and waited patiently until ...

Gideon! No, no, no, please, it couldn't be true ... Judas's legs buckled from underneath him at the memory and he slid to the floor, still clutching the knife.

Fresh tears welled in his eyes, but before he could begin to weep for his friend he was struck by a realisation. There was something not quite right about all this. A flaw in his flashback. He'd staked the sheep with a rope, made the trap for Gideon with a length of it too. But why did he have the rope with him in the first place? He remembered taking it from home now, but couldn't recall the reason. Had he decided to hang himself? End his life that way instead? His memory returned a blank.

He began turning the blade over and over in his hands. Light pouring in through the open window reflected off the metal, sending flashes of luminosity skittering up the walls and over the ceiling.

He'd gone to the forest with the intention of killing himself but had butchered Gideon instead.

The act was clear in his mind now, just not the motive.

He spun the blade faster and faster. Watching as the light danced up the walls, seeming to become brighter with every rotation. The knife's razor sharp edge caught his thumb and sliced through the flesh but he didn't notice.

None of this made any sense. Why kill his friend and not himself?

Why take the rope?

There was fresh blood on the blade now. Not for the first time.

Incandescent light streamed from the metal as it whirled, flashing across the walls like lightning.

Why take the rope? Why kill Gideon?

The razor edge snicked his hand again. He felt it this time and looked down at the knife. A bolt of white reflected light lanced into his eyes, piercing through them, slamming him against the wall and blinding him with a sudden, terrifying clarity. He dropped the knife and heard it strike the floor a million miles away.

He remembered, now, finally.

He remembered everything.

Every last bloody detail.

Chapter 69

A maelstrom of memories had been unleashed in his mind, and Judas felt like he was floating.

He recalled sitting at home some days ago, with the knife in his hand, planning.

Sharpening its blade on the stone, repeatedly.

Listening to the sound of the wind whispering over its razor edge.

He had taken the dagger and the rope, and had gone out not to end his life – never to end his life – but to murder Gideon.

He had planned it all. And not just the shepherd's death.

He remembered leaving his father's home on the pretence of taking an evening stroll and following his good friend Ethan into the physician's, where he'd used tongs to ... he recoiled in revulsion at the memory.

He remembered writing the note to himself, *I know what you did*, wrapping it carefully with the eye he'd taken from Gideon and the tooth from Ethan, and placing it on the table. He'd been so afraid when he had discovered it just a short while after. So afraid of the threat, and then later, so afraid of the killer. The sick, depraved maniac that had been ... himself the whole time.

He'd killed Gideon and Ethan. The four men in the bathhouse, poor crippled Jeb, his own cousin Atarah, her husband and ... and their twin babies. He dry heaved at the thought of his actions. A boy and a girl, Zacharias and Elisheba, helpless at just six months old. He'd sliced them open like ripe fruit and just left them to die, screaming in agony.

He'd abducted his father, first hiding him in the barn until the cover of darkness came, then moving and imprisoning him here in his uncle's home, a building he'd adopted as a makeshift base. Somewhere that no one knew about, which was spacious and central enough for his needs. Unable to kill Simon outright, he'd chopped off the man's arm and given him a choice – bleed to death or hack off your own feet and try to make it out alive. Both options always leading to the same, inevitable outcome. He'd killed Jonathan just one room away from the door to his father's prison, and then etched that message into the woodwork.

And most recently, he'd stabbed Baruch in the back several times with his own knife when the fool dozed off in the middle of keeping watch for a murderer who was right there in the room with him. The commotion had woken Aaron and so Judas had stabbed him to death, delighting in the twin expressions of betrayal and terror on the merchant's face as he did so. Afterwards he'd carved the words into the coward's flesh as it turned clammy and cold, cackling as each letter was formed. He had been so involved in that task he'd somehow failed to notice that Baruch was still breathing. The oversight sparked a burst of emotion – anger? – but he knew the wounds he'd inflicted were deep and would prove fatal, regardless of wherever his trusting friend had managed to crawl off to.

351

He remembered doing it all, but still it made no sense.

Over the past week he had been overwhelmed with guilt and bludgeoned by despair. He had tried, not always successfully, to cope with the pain and biting loss, but it just kept coming, more and more of it being heaped upon him. The one thing that had kept him going – kept him sane – was the knowledge that the nameless maniac out there had to be stopped, one way or another. That had been his focus, but now that purpose had been stripped away. There was no nameless maniac. There was only himself.

The numbness that had enveloped him like a blanket since these terrible memories had been unlocked now began smothering him with its embrace, making it harder to breathe. His father was dead. His friends were dead. And unlike Jesus, they were never coming back.

He closed his eyes and was instantly assailed by wave after wave of the most horrific images. People he knew begging for their lives, before being killed in the worst ways imaginable. By him.

It was all too much to bear.

He felt a lurching sensation deep inside, as if he was about to keel over into some internal, unending, abyss of misery; then the touch of cold metal brought him back to the world.

His eyes flicked open. He'd picked up the knife again, without even realising. He was turning it over and over once more. Why was this instrument of death back in his grasp?

The worst thing was that somehow the weapon felt ... natural, at home in his hand. Like he'd been born holding it.

But how could he be the killer? He'd agonised, endured such a weighing burden of guilt over betraying Jesus, an act he'd undertaken purely to save his uncle's life. A life he had then snuffed out so callously in the steam room. It made no sense.

How could he be responsible for one of those terrible deeds, let alone all of them?

A different voice answered in his head. *You did it, Judas, and you enjoyed it. You kept it a secret because you didn't want the killing to stop.*

Another voice, deeper than the oceans, added, *And we haven't finished yet. There is still more work to be done. Not God's work. Our work.*

Judas didn't understand what was happening. Why did he suddenly have these voices in his head?

You're quite, quite mad, another voice answered.

Oh I wouldn't say that, a child's voice protested. *A little mad perhaps?*

Judas's mind was filled with a babbling cacophony. There were people talking and laughing, weeping, dogs barking and what sounded like donkeys braying somewhere. He pressed his palms tightly to his temples, feeling the coolness of the bone handle against the side of his head, and tried to blot out the noise, but to no avail. The chatter was relentless.

'Who are you?' Judas shouted, his words echoing around the still room. 'What are you doing in my head?'

A gruff man's voice whispered a reply. *You know*, it said. *You know us.*

'I don't know you! Who are you?'

You know us.

'I don't!'

Oh but Judas you do.

We are Legion, the voices answered in unison. *For we are many.*

Fear gripped Judas, its crushing talons tightening around his chest. Legion was the entity of demons that had possessed a man in the country of the Gadarenes. Jesus had cast out the fiends into a herd of nearby pigs.

Yes, you know us. You remember us.

But it couldn't be. The pigs had hurled themselves into the sea and drowned. Legion had perished.

That thought was greeted by a howl of derisive laughter.

'How did you survive? What are you doing inside my head?'

Enough talking, an old woman's voice snapped. *More killing.*

'There's no one left to kill!' Judas bellowed. 'You've murdered everyone I care about.'

Not quite everyone . . .

'Who? No!' Judas shook his head violently. 'No, not Martha, you're not killing her, you're never killing her!'

The harlot, the woman's voice hissed.

Diseased whore, the gruff voice barked. *Hiding behind the unliving one!*

'The unliving one?'

He who was brought back, several voices said in unison.

'Lazarus . . .'

Couldn't touch the whore, the child's voice said, full of sorrow, *she had to be alone, was never alone.*

'Lazarus stopped you?'

Brought back by his hand, his power, the deep voice boomed, *the unliving one cannot be harmed by our kind.*

Could not risk giving ourselves away to him . . .

He could have undone everything . . .

She needed to be alone, why wasn't she alone, it would have been so sweet to taste her death, the child's voice whined.

She could prove useful yet, the deep voice said.

'What do you mean, useful?' Judas demanded.

It matters not. For it is time.

'It's time for all this to stop.'

This isn't the end, the gruff voice laughed. *It's the beginning.*

The beginning, the beginning, the other voices chanted.

'The beginning?'

We should start with the doubter, the twin.

'The beginning of what?'

Didymus, Didymus, the voices screamed in excitement.

'Didymus? Thomas?'

Yes, yes. Thomas, the doubter.

'No you can't. He's –'

The first, the gruff voice interrupted.

'The first? What do you mean the first?'

You know, you've always known.

'I don't –'

The realisation hit Judas hard.

Eighteen dead so far. Twelve more killings to come.

The demons in his head.

They were going to start killing apostles.

'I can't let you do this. I won't let you do this. I won't do this!'

You don't have a choice, dagger-man. We need you. With us now.

'You didn't need me for all the other killings – why these?'

Apostles, Judas.

'I don't –'

You must identify them for us, friend.

Now he understood.

Identify them for us.

All of them.

Each and every one.

With a betrayer's kiss.

Chapter 70

The knock on his office door caused Caiaphas to start and curse loudly. He'd specifically asked not to be interrupted this morning.

'What is it?' the priest boomed.

He heard the door open and someone enter, but didn't look up from his scrolls. The sound of a man clearing his throat, as boldly as he dared, drifted across the room. Caiaphas glanced away from his work. The unwanted visitor was a broad shouldered fellow with a tan which suggested he spent a great deal of time outside.

'I bring a message for Joseph Caiaphas,' the man said.

'Well get on with it, then.'

'Annas requests your presence at his house.'

'Annas?'

'Annas,' the messenger confirmed.

This sounded ominous. His father-in-law hardly ever wished to see him these days, and when he did, it was rarely pleasant. Annas took every opportunity to remind Caiaphas that he had also held the title of high priest of the Sanhedrin, and he had done the job better. Indeed, such was his continued influence in Jerusalem that some folks still referred to him by the title, as if Annas had never left the office. Caiaphas hated that. It was over fifteen years since Annas had been ousted from the position, for Heaven's sake.

'What does he want me for?' Caiaphas asked, standing.

'I don't have that information. I was simply told to inform you that he needs to see you now.'

'Right now?'

'Yes.'

Caiaphas had taken half a step away from his chair when an object flew in through the window. It struck the wall hard and exploded, a cluster of small shiny projectiles shooting off in every direction. He ducked hastily behind his desk, while the messenger jumped back, flattening himself against the door.

When the discordant jangling had subsided, only a single sound remained. Caiaphas could hear a gentle rolling noise coming from the top of his desk. He cautiously raised his head. A solitary silver coin was trundling along, wobbling in a semicircle. It hit a scroll and fell flat on its side. All was silent. Across the floor, he could see silver staters everywhere. There must have been twenty of them, at least, maybe more.

'I'm not sure what's going on here,' the messenger piped up, 'but I am sure it wouldn't be a good idea to keep Annas waiting.'

Chapter 71

Thomas had the strangest feeling that someone was following him. He stopped, turned, and slowly surveyed his surroundings, attempting to identify the source of this peculiar sensation.

Dull-eyed and trudging slowly forward, Judas tried to resist the bidding of the demons inside him. Thomas was a good man, like all the apostles, but more than that, he was Judas's closest remaining friend. It wouldn't be a worthy or noble death. It would be brutal and savage. And necessary. The demons cackled with glee. Judas tried to block out the laughter by focusing his mind on all the things he still cared about. God for one. He tried to ask for salvation, but the interference in his mind cut the attempt at prayer brutally short. The rope over his shoulder felt heavy. The bone-handled knife in his hand strangely light.

Out of the corner of his eye, Thomas saw someone walking towards him. A cloaked figure. There was something odd about the man's gait, and although his hands were hidden in the sleeves of his long robe, Thomas could tell he was holding an object in one of them.

'Dear Lord,' Judas whispered, forcing the words out between gritted teeth.

Go fuck yourself, a demonic voice interjected, that of a petulant child.

Judas could feel he was losing the battle for control. He was nearly there. So very close now.

The stranger was almost upon him. Thomas found himself recoiling as the figure drew near.

'Dear Lord,' Judas said, louder this time. He shrugged and the coil of rope slipped from his shoulder. He grabbed hold of one loose end, gripping it tightly.

Thomas recognised the man and reluctantly went to greet him. As he did so the person raised the item in his hand. It glinted in the sunlight, and for the first time the apostle saw it clearly.

In a swift movement Judas hurled the rope upwards and over the branch. A raven, perched above, watched his throw keenly before spreading its inky wings and taking flight. Judas caught the end of the rope as it fell back to earth and plunged the knife vertically through the sinewy fibres, deep into the trunk of the tree. The demons, sensing betrayal, roared through his body. Judas's arms became heavy, his legs like lead. His vision blurred so badly he could barely focus on the rope as he struggled to tie a solid knot.

'Alms for a poor old beggar?' The disfigured man rasped the words out, shaking the battered metal cup at Thomas with his one good hand. The two copper coins within rattled against the sides noisily.

'Of course,' Thomas said, fishing in his money pouch. He dropped a single coin into the beggar's receptacle.

The noose was around his neck now. He just had to hope the blade held fast. His head was pounding, his vision almost completely gone. 'Dear Lord,' Judas whispered. 'Dear father ... forgive me.'

'Bless you,' the beggar said.

'No, bless you,' Thomas replied. He watched as the old man limped off back in the direction he'd come.

Judas stepped up onto a log he'd balanced upright, on its end, using his very last ounce of being. A sentence whispered through his mind, the seer Mary's voice, echoing back from nowhere ...

After the sun has risen, the moon must fall ...

After the son has risen ...

Judas kicked away the log from beneath his feet, and he plunged downwards, the noose tightening fast, biting deep into the crescent moon-shaped birthmark on his neck. He began pedalling in mid-air, and the rope slipped down slightly, but then went taut. The knife was holding. His body began rocking violently from side to side, causing the blade to quiver, but it was embedded too deeply.

Even though he could barely feel anything now, some part of Judas was still aware of the demons, struggling, trying desperately to escape. His stomach began to cramp. The last of the air in his lungs was burning as if it had caught alight in his chest.

As he thrashed and bucked about on the end of the rope, a serene thought floated through his mind.

Not.

Much.

Longer.

Lights began to dance about him, like fireflies. His eyes had rolled so far back in his head that he couldn't see anything else, but he could see them. They were beautiful. His body jerked and jolted even more violently in the noose and Judas, somewhere very far away now, knew the moment had come.

As the death throes took hold, the engorged stomach of the body he'd once inhabited exploded. An unholy force tore outwards, howling through the air and showering the ground with blood and intestines. Entrails slopped forth as his lifeless corpse shuddered one final, dreadful time, then Judas Iscariot's blind eyes closed forever and a fierce white radiance burned away everything around him.

Chapter 72

'Be seated,' Annas said.

Caiaphas pulled up a chair at the large rectangular table. It was fashioned from some manner of dark wood he wasn't even familiar with, and polished with such vigour that it gleamed as much as the silver strips which were inlaid around its outer edge. The rest of the room was sparsely decorated, the only other feature of note being the thick marble pillars which ringed the table, running from floor to ceiling. Annas's personal palace was understated and, quite frankly, Caiaphas found it a bit dull, lacking in curiosities and antiquities; indeed, in personality.

'When I was a younger man,' Annas began, his voice pouring out into the air like a measure of velvety wine, 'I made some unwise judgements.'

'So I recall,' Caiaphas said.

'And it seems you are determined to follow in my ill-placed footsteps?'

'I'm not sure what you mean.'

Annas shook his head, his grey locks brushing over his shoulders. 'I think you know exactly what I mean.'

'Are you talking about Jesus?'

'No. Although losing the body of that rabble-rouser was rather careless.'

'That wasn't actually my fault. I requested guards to be placed on the tomb immediately, on the Friday, but an administrative error –'

Annas held up his hand, halting Caiaphas in mid-sentence. 'This is not what I wish to speak about.'

'What then?'

'So blunt, Joseph, as ever. You always were a blunt instrument.'

'An instrument? I have held the office of high priest for fifteen years. That takes quick wits, guts, and inner strength.'

'It takes lapping at the Roman's feet, Joseph, an act you have admittedly undertaken with a quick and strong tongue.'

'I have had to rule, Annas – to rule! Perhaps you've forgotten what that's really like.'

'You are forgetting yourself, priest,' Annas said, his smooth-toned voice running cold.

'My apologies,' Caiaphas said, diverting his eyes from Annas's stare.

'Never forget, I put you into office, Joseph. Without me, you would be nothing. Just another face among the clustered council members with their petty duties and squabbles.'

Caiaphas made eye contact again, but said nothing. Instead he gave the very slightest of nods.

'But now,' Annas continued, 'it seems you are becoming a liability.'

'Surely you can't –'

'Silence, Joseph. You have lasted, I will grant you that. Your enthusiasm for the Emperor has carried you a long way. But I fear your time is now drawing to an end. And I think Rome would agree with me.'

'What? Why?'

'There is someone here who will enlighten you.'

'Who?'

Annas motioned to a guard at the far end of the room, who quickly departed. Caiaphas watched the large arched entrance he'd disappeared through without blinking. The guard returned, followed by a burly man in a red and yellow striped cloak.

'Malchus?' Caiaphas said, unable to stop his beady eyes widening in surprise.

'I believe, Joseph, that you have developed a liking for torturing young prostitutes,' Annas said.

Caiaphas paused for just a moment. 'Utter nonsense,' he said smoothly. 'I don't know where you've heard such scandalous lies, but I'm sure Malchus here will put you straight.'

Malchus simply stood there, saying nothing.

'Perhaps if you expended your – shall we say, energies – more in the bedroom at home,' Annas said, 'rather than playing with whores, my daughter would have a son, or at least some manner of offspring, to show for her marriage.'

'I . . .' Caiaphas began, but then fell silent.

'And I am told you actually killed one of these prostitutes a few days ago?'

'Malchus,' Caiaphas said, shifting uncomfortably. 'Has your position, the life I've given you, meant nothing to you? Will you not speak up and defend me from these outrageous accusations?' A hint of desperation was creeping into his voice.

Still Malchus said nothing.

'I doubt he will,' Annas said, 'given that it was dear Malchus who told me about this.'

'You did what?' Caiaphas glared at Malchus with an intensity that threatened to outdo the sun's rays which were streaming through the window and playing on his brightly coloured cloak. 'Why? Why would you say such a thing?'

'I couldn't go on this way any longer.' Malchus spoke quietly.

'You couldn't go on living well, eating well, drinking well, on my money, taking whichever girls you pleased . . .'

'Watching you torture that woman, hearing her scream over and over. Just hurting her more and enjoying every second. And then snuffing out her life. It sickened me, made me realise –'

'Guilt finally got the better of you, Malchus? It was him, he killed her,' Caiaphas said, pointing an accusing finger at his bodyguard and servant.

'Now we all know that isn't true,' Annas said.

Caiaphas jabbed his finger towards Malchus. 'It's my word against his. Who are you going to believe?'

'There is another party involved, actually,' Annas replied. 'A man Malchus has been kind enough to introduce me to. His name is Caleb.'

'Who?'

'The owner of the brothel where you indulged yourself in these insalubrious activities.'

'I couldn't do it,' Malchus said. 'I couldn't kill Caleb. Or anyone for that matter. I'm a changed man – ever since I was touched by him.'

'This isn't about that bloody ear of yours again, is it? That was some manner of illusion or trick, you imbecile,' Caiaphas hissed.

'It was no illusion. I felt the pain, then I felt his touch, his power, flowing right into me. I've tried to deny it, I've fought against believing, Lord help me, but no longer. Don't you see? It was a miracle!'

Caiaphas turned to Annas. 'Have you heard this blasphemy?'

'I don't care what you think any more,' Malchus said, the volume of his voice growing as he spoke. 'I realise now that his way is the truth. That I can't be a part of your terrible schemes any longer. I must seek redemption before it's too late, and the first step on that path is what I've done today. Stopping you before you do any more harm. I don't know if I'll ever be able to atone for my sins, but I have to try.'

'Insanity,' Caiaphas said, shaking his head. 'And blasphemy.'

Annas nodded. 'He will be dealt with.'

'I welcome my penance,' Malchus said.

'But you must also be dealt with,' Annas said. 'You clearly aren't fit to be high priest.'

Caiaphas turned a shade paler. 'It's all lies. Malchus and this Caleb fellow clearly concocted this whole nonsense. Where is the evidence?'

'I have this,' Annas said. He reached into a pocket and pulled out Caiaphas's ring of office.

'That's not evidence,' Caiaphas roared. 'That blood could be anyone's. More treachery.'

'You must have exceptional eyesight to see blood on this ring from there, Joseph.'

'I –'

'Perhaps you could explain how you knew there was blood on it?'

Caiaphas's mouth opened, but no words were forthcoming. The game was up.

'I didn't think so,' Annas continued. 'And when Pilate finds out about this, I think we can safely say the Romans will take a dim view of the whole affair. Of course, they do not have to hear of this matter.'

'They don't?'

'Not if you do as I say. My son Jonathan is to succeed you. He is not quite old enough, not ready for office just yet. But it will only be a short matter of time before he is. Until then, you must continue as the head of the Sanhedrin. I cannot have the possibility of an outsider gaining control of the council. Although needless to say, Joseph, all of this torturing nonsense will stop henceforth.'

'And what will happen to me when Jonathan becomes high priest?' Caiaphas mumbled, his head bowed, eyes fixed on the surface of the table.

'I have a place in mind out near Galilee, a perfect spot you will retire to. Alone. It's a modest farm. There you may get as grubby as you please. And you can look after a flock of an entirely different and more appropriate kind. Animals, just like yourself.'

Caiaphas continued to stare down at the tabletop. From beneath the pristinely polished wooden surface, a broken, powerless man gazed numbly back at him.

Epilogue

The old woman shuffled out of the shadows towards Matthew. She wore a crimson blindfold over her eyes, yet she walked with an apparent awareness that made him wonder if she really was blind. There were many things he doubted about this crone, but the fact remained that she was one of the few people who could shed light on what had happened to Judas following the betrayal.

The seer navigated herself unfailingly to the table, pulled out a chair and sat, then indicated for Matthew to do the same.

'I'm trying to make sense of what happened to Judas, and was hoping you could share anything you know with me,' Matthew said as he inched his stool a bit closer to the table. 'I was told that you met with him, before he ... before all that unfortunate business.'

The old woman was silent.

'And I have been told that your visions hold much weighty importance,' Matthew added, hoping he didn't sound pompous or insincere.

'I see many things,' Blind Mary eventually said.

'What do you see?'

'I see I have yet to be paid for the knowledge you seek.'

'Oh. My apologies.' Matthew fumbled for some coins and counted them into her outstretched palm.

'Who are you, and what do you want from me?' the seer asked.

'I am Matthew, an apostle of Jesus, our saviour. And I want to know –'

The woman raised one hand. 'I know you,' she said softly. 'You are Matthew, an apostle of Jesus.'

'I just told you that.'

'And much more,' she said, her cracked, brown-stained teeth appearing in some semblance of a smile.

'Right. Fine. Then tell me about Judas.' Matthew pulled out a parchment and writing materials, placing them on the table.

'What do you wish to know about him?'

'I never saw Judas again after the last supper we had with Jesus. There are stories that he was responsible for the murders of his loved ones after the crucifixion, and I hear they even found the bodies of two more friends just the other day, in a house in the lower city. One mutilated, the other curled up in a back room, clutching a knife as if planning to attack whoever had done this to him.'

'Baruch,' the old woman said. 'Brave and foolish to the last.' There was a tinge of sadness in her voice.

'Are the stories all true? Some say that's the reason Judas killed himself, and it wasn't just the guilt of betraying our master.'

'Did you not know Judas?'

'I used to think so, but obviously not. If he could betray the son of God, then maybe he was wicked enough to –'

'Judas was not a wicked man,' Blind Mary interrupted. 'He was a cursed man.'

'So Judas wasn't a killer?' Matthew asked as he began to jot words down on the parchment in front of him.

'No. Judas did not kill anyone himself.'

'But you say he was cursed?'

'In trying to do a good deed he made a very bad choice. He accepted thirty silver coins to give away his master. And from that moment, he was cursed, doomed. When he came to me, I could sense there was evil present – a great evil – but it wasn't him; it was around him, about him.'

'What was "it"?'

'Judas also demanded to know who, or indeed what, tormented him. At the time, the only message that came to me was that it was someone he knew well.'

'Let me guess – himself?'

Mary nodded. 'A couple of days ago I felt something – its touch again. A hideous, babbling, many-tongued presence from the unending depths. I think it was departing, and I think this evil had travelled with Judas. Within him.'

Matthew had stopped writing and was shaking his head. 'This is what you told my friend this morning, isn't it?'

'Your friend?'

'John, a fellow apostle. The one who told me about you. He said that he thinks, now what were his exact words ...' Matthew paused. 'I believe it was Satan entered into Judas.'

Blind Mary nodded, but said nothing.

'Judas was a man, that's all,' Matthew continued. 'I don't know about many-tongued beasts or other such notions. But I do know Judas was fallible and foolish. He got what he deserved, it's as simple as that. Just as Jesus promised at our final meal.'

'Think what you will. I judge no one.'

'I'm not judging. I'm just trying to record the facts. Speaking of which, do you know when Judas died?'

'They found his body yesterday, I believe.'

'Yes,' Matthew said. 'But he was a mess. He could have been

there for a while. Do you have any idea when he hanged himself?'

'Judas died when he betrayed Jesus.'

'I see what you mean, but when did he actually hang himself? On what day?'

Blind Mary sat in silence, again.

'Any idea whether it was yesterday? Or two days ago?' Matthew prompted. 'Three?'

'He died the moment he betrayed Jesus.'

'Fine,' Matthew sighed, as he began to scribble more words down. 'I'll just put he went off and did it. Sometimes I wonder why I bother. It's not like anyone will ever read this anyway, is it?'

Blind Mary felt the touch of the future, like an icy cold hand on her shoulder, sending a shiver down her back.

'I'm not so sure,' she replied.

The Bible Knows What He Did Last Supper

Passages quoted from the Catholic Public Domain Version of the Bible, a new translation of the Latin Vulgate, using the Douay Rheims as a guide (www.sacredbible.org).

John 13:1

'Before the feast day of the Passover, Jesus knew that the hour was approaching when he would pass from this world to the Father ...'

13:21-22

'... [Jesus] was troubled in spirit. And he bore witness by saying: "Amen, amen, I say to you, that one among you shall betray me." 'Therefore, the disciples looked around at one another, uncertain about whom he spoke.'

13:26-27

'... when he had dipped the bread, he gave it to Judas Iscariot, son of Simon.

'And after the morsel, Satan entered into him ...'

Luke 22:3

'Then Satan entered into Judas, who was surnamed Iscariot, one of the twelve.'

Matthew 26:24

'"But woe to that man by whom the Son of man will be betrayed. It would be better for that man if he had not been born."'

27:3-5

'Then Judas, who betrayed him, seeing that [Jesus] had been condemned, regretting his conduct, brought back the thirty pieces of silver to the leaders of the priests and the elders, saying, "I have sinned in betraying just blood." But they said to him: "What is that to us? See to it yourself."

'And throwing down the pieces of silver in the temple, he departed. And going out, he hanged himself ...'

Love mash-up fiction?

Lose yourself to temptation as the classics collide with the contemporary in our latest fantastic mash-ups from Piatkus . . .

JANE EYROTICA

'Holding my gaze, he removed a curtain tie from one of the bedsteads. I was confused when he uttered huskily, "Put your hands out in front of you." I obeyed.'

Jane Eyre has lived a sheltered, callous life. Orphaned at a young age and despised by her remaining family, she is shipped off to Lowood School and can only dream of tenderness and affection. Upon accepting a governess position at Thornfield Hall, a world of passion, desire and sex explodes before her naive eyes in the form of the brooding, dashing master of the house: Mr Rochester.

After playful attempts to evade Mr Rochester's advances, Jane finds herself succumbing to his savage, brutal lust and losing herself in the intense heat of her yearning. Jane believes that beneath Mr Rochester's dark, handsome, and sometimes brutal exterior there must be a heart, and she is desperate to find love in his hungry caresses. But then, she discovers something in the attic . . . and her world is turned upside down for ever.

Sex collides with corsets in a burst of erotic ecstasy and dark secrets, and one of literature's finest novels will never be read the same again.

978-0-7499-5942-5

FIFTY SHADES OF DORIAN GRAY

Night after night she awoke in a feverish sweat, her hips writhing on their own accord, the bed sheet balled in a coil and clenched between her legs. It was so . . . real. Like he'd really been there.

First published to sensational scandal amidst accusations that the novel was hedonist, unclean and depicted distorted views of morality, *The Picture of Dorian Gray* was a hit back in the day. In 1890, the *Daily Chronicle* wrote that Wilde's novel 'will taint every young mind that comes in contact with it.' Well, Victorian critics, gird your loins and prepare to meet Audrey Ember's *Fifty Shades of Dorian Gray*: hotter, lewder, sexier, steamier and more morally corrupt than Oscar Wilde's original story!

Rediscover this celebrated novel as it traces the moral degeneration of a beautiful young Londoner seduced by art and beauty into a cruel and reckless pursuer of pleasure. Meet artist Rosemary Hall and follow her inevitable downfall brought by her lust for the famous Dorian Gray – a tale both familiar and new in this brilliant erotic mash-up of one of the world's most beloved novels.

With a mix of old fashioned Victorian debauchery and erotic 21st-century lust, this cleverly sexed-up classic will leave you wanting more!

978-0-7499-5943-2

THE GREAT GATSBY UNBOUND

Nick Carraway, a young virgin from Minnesota, moves to
New York in the summer of 1922 to find love. He rents a house in
the West Egg district of Long Island, a wealthy but unfashionable
area populated by the 'new rich', a group prone to garish,
extravagant parties full of wild, erotic activities.

And Nick's next-door neighbour is the worst of them all:
a mysterious man named Jay Gatsby who throws open the doors of
his gigantic Gothic mansion every Saturday night to house the most
opulent, seductive sexual encounters. But who is Jay Gatsby? And
what will happen when Nick steps into his raunchy, wild mansion?
Is the American dream all it's cracked up to be? Or have the treasured
ideals of happiness and individualism disintegrated into the mere
pursuit of wealth . . . just like the erotic, kinky extortion of love?

978-0-3494-0046-4